THE GOOD LION

The Good Lion

Len Doherty

1889 books

Copyright © The Estate of Len Doherty

Sincerest thanks to Len's surviving family for their support in bringing this work back into print.

Likewise I am extremely grateful to the estate of Gerard Dillon for permission to re-use and re-work his original artwork for the cover.

Thanks also to artist, Karen Reihill, an authority on Gerard Dillon, for her support and encouragement.

Also thanks to Jack Windle for his support and contribution to the project of bringing this book back to life.

First published in 1958.

All rights reserved.

The moral rights of the authors have been asserted.

Cover Artwork © 1889 Books, closely based on the Dillon original.

www.1889books.co.uk
ISBN: 978-1-915045-15-7

The Foreword (by Clancy Sigal that almost was)

Jack Windle shared the publisher's enthusiasm for the idea of re-introducing people to *The Good Lion* (Jack was fornerly Honorary Research Fellow at Sheffield University, his PhD title being W*orking-class writing – Class, Culture and Colonialism: Working-Class Writing in the Twentieth Century*).

Jack had been in correspondence with the American writer Clancy Sigal. Clancy knew Len Doherty (and moved in similar literary circles – see Introduction – knowing Doris Lessing amongst others) and regarded him as a great influence over his work. He also retained a fondness for Sheffield from his time in England "a long time ago, before the Internet, Pret a Manger, decimalisation, armed police and decent pub hours." In correspondence, he asked Jack: "You can answer a question for me: Just before arriving in England I'd been working in Hollywood where things were slick and sleek and up to date. Once I plunged into northern England I felt incredibly comfortable in all that dirty smoke and dirty macs and ancient club secs, shabby and toothless and people walking around (and dressed) as if it was still 1935. Instead of being repelled by all the dirt and smell and brilliant English lack of hygiene (remember the old plumbing), why was I so happy there?"

Clancy had promised to do a foreword for us. He had good intentions, but was focused on getting his memoir published and dealing with his health issues. Clancy sadly died in 2017. He sent Jack this draft from his memoir (published posthumously) *The London Lover: My Weekend that Lasted Thirty Years:*

> Another bus ride up to Thurcroft to show Len Doherty the manuscript where at a table in the Miners Clu' I nervously watch him flip the newborn pages and lick his thumb to read every single fucking word, studying, judging. He lays the last typed page atop the pile, and has the power to stop my writing career then and there. He sighs, "It will be the making of thee." The implied insult is, I'm using him and his village to advance myself.
>
> The next morning he takes me to the bus, unpins the hammer-and-sickle badge from his coat that a delegation of Russian Don Basin miners had gifted their Yorkshire

counterparts and fastens it to my sweater, followed by a swift punch on the arm as I board the coach. His last words to me are: "Guttersnipes of the world, unite!"

Postscript: Len, with lung ailments and reeling from exhaustion, at last finds work outside the mine – a blow to his self-pride – as a writer for the local rag, the Sheffield Star, which evolves into full time reporting. Returning from an assignment in Vietnam, he passes through the Munich transfer point during the '72 Olympics when masked Arabs toss a grenade among the passengers on his airport bus. Len lunges at the grenade to kick it away from children, saving their lives, but it explodes killing a husband and wife and leaving Len with painful neck and spine wounds from which he never quite recovers. Weighed down by guilt, and feeling responsible for the married couple's death, he commits suicide.

Today nobody knows his name. The Thurcroft library doesn't carry his novels, The Man Beneath, A Miner's Sons and The Good Lion, and the village's web site fails to mention him. When I inquire of his London publisher the gentleman can't recall him except, "Oh, you mean that drunken miner?"

I owe him a life, too.

2023 marks forty years since Len's death, and sixty-five years since the publication of *The Good Lion*, so it seemed a fitting time to re-release it.

Introduction

Len Doherty

The Good Lion is a remarkable piece of writing. What is even more remarkable is that neither it nor its author received their deserved recognition, and that the book is no longer read. To understand why that should be, we need to know a little about the complex man that Len Doherty was.

Walter Leonard Doherty was born at 192 North Woodside Road in Glasgow on the 22nd July 1930, to John and Beatrice Doherty. North Woodside was a densely populated area. In the neighbourhood were ironworks and a mineral water factory. His father was an electrical goods storeman. He left school at the age of 14 and moved to Hertfordshire and then to London with his family. At seventeen he became a miner at Nunnery Colliery in Sheffield as a Bevin boy. (He was apparently given the nickname "Downhill Doherty," according to recollections on a Sheffield History website, presumably due to his early inexperience in keeping the seam's face level.) He was married at twenty-one to Doreen Coles. They lived at St Withold Avenue, Thurcroft, where he continued to work as a miner.

He fitted the writing of his first three novels between shifts at the coalface, in a house with four young children. He wrote in three thousand word bursts, apparently sometimes going without sleep. It was at Thurcroft that he met Frank Watters, the Yorkshire Coalfield organiser of the Communist Party who is thinly disguised as Frank Wells in his first novel, *A Miner's Sons,* 1955. Also influential on the younger Doherty was Arnold Kettle, a lecturer in English Literature at Leeds and with the Workers' Educational Association, and a member of the Yorkshire District Committee of the Communist Party. *A Miner's Sons* is dedicated to Kettle, and presumably Mainwaring in the book is modelled on him. Another influence on Doherty was Jim Bradley the local union president who had hoped that Doherty would succeed him. *The Man Beneath*, 1957, is dedicated to Bradley.

Doherty's writing pre-dated that of Sillitoe, Waterhouse, Barstow and Storey and yet he never received the "angry young men" hype that they did. *The Good Lion* is a far more accomplished piece of writing than *Saturday Night and Sunday Morning*, a better study of coming-of-age masculinity and emotional conflict than *This Sporting Life*, and yet it has been forgotten.

It could be argued that it was Doherty who picked up the baton from DH Lawrence and in some ways Henry Green; though no one could ever accuse Doherty of any of the pretence or condescension of Green.

If *The Good Lion* had been written by an American at the same time, I have no doubt it would be held up as one of the "Great American Novels." Instead it has faded into obscurity. Why? I believe there are several explanations.

Firstly, Doherty was not the sort of person the literati could tame and patronize. He was not a product of the grammar schools, that the middle classes could pat on the head and say — look what we've given to these working class boys through our magnanimity — a classic attempt to disarm and neuter the class argument — subsume it and pigeon-hole it as a cultural phenomenon, market it and give it a name that demeans: "angry young men" (bless 'em it'll pass once they grow up). Doherty was not an "angry young man" — he wanted social change.

This is not to say he did not rub shoulders with London literary figures. In his memoir, Frank Watters talks of the time after Len's falling out with the Communist Party: "Len at this time was under the influence of other Communist writers, like the now famous Doris Lessing. Len was enjoying the social snobbery of his regular weekends in London with the literary elite." Doherty's works had some success in left-wing intellectual circles — in Clancy Sigal's *Weekend in Dinlock*, the character based on Doherty makes frequent, wild, drunken trips to meet his new London friends. But he never really fitted in in the capital, and it seems he found he no longer really fitted in back home either, though he continued to live in Thurcroft.

Was it because he could not be tamed that he was ignored, that he was a communist and a miner and not a product of a grammar school and university education? His gifts were not bestowed upon him by the establishment. He wrote nothing of interest to the literati — setting his novels in mining communities in filthy, disgusting, South Yorkshire: so where could there possibly be any merit in his work?

It was around the time of the publication of *The Good Lion* that Doherty was persuaded by Bill Linacre, the editor of *The Sheffield Star*, to enter into journalism. At *The Star* he wrote the lead column "the Vulcan." For most of his working life at the paper he was under the pioneering editorship (from 1968-1978) of Colin Brannigan. Brannigan was the driving force behind Len's visits to Belfast, Vietnam and the Middle East. Unheard of work for a regional newspaper today.

He was clearly a troubled soul and a complex character. In his autobiography, Byron Rogers, a contemporary at *The Star*, tells stories of his reputation for drinking and violence, once tearing piping from the urinal in the toilets and emerging in the lounge bar with the green, dripping copper wound around his neck like a Dark Age tork: "Woke up quite a few bastards that!" Rogers describes the many Lens he knew: the showy Len, the sensitive, the over-emotional, the fatherly, the tense, the kind, the bullying, the vulnerable: "Under all this was a sadness. I was 23 with no past except childhood. Len at 35 had nothing but past, many pasts, each of which had closed behind him, each time with bitterness." David Nobbs, also a contemporary on the newspaper refers to booze-filled evenings such as one where he was egged on by ring-leader Doherty to pose as a representative of Hughie Green and conduct fake auditions for *Opportunity Knocks* in the upstairs bar of The Lord Nelson.

He won the title of Provincial Journalist of the Year for 1968 and unusually for a regional paper was given foreign assignments. He was at the peak of his journalistic career. He reported from Vietnam and the Middle East. This work and "sideline activities" sadly prevented him writing any further novels. The dust cover for *The Good Lion* says his fourth novel "is nearing completion." And Rogers refers to a historical novel set in Roman Britain he was working on. It is not known what happened to these manuscripts. Is it too much to hope that they still exist in a drawer somewhere?

His first two books were published by Lawrence Wishart, the Communist Party publishers, so one supposes whatever their literary merit they were never going to be adopted by the establishment.

The Good Lion was first published by Mcgibbon and Kee, after Doherty's falling out with the Communist Party following the Red Army crushing of the Hungarian uprising in 1956.

It was on the 10th of February 1970 returning from Israel that Doherty's fate took a further twist — he was on a transit bus at Munich airport with El-Al passengers when a grenade was rolled into the bus by terrorists. He described it in his own words: "There were other people farther up the bus and a few stood around the sides inside. As the bus was about to leave there was a scuffling just beside the entrance of the transit lounge. I could see airport police struggling with two men.

"There was a loud explosion and I shouted for everybody to get on the floor because I knew from being in Vietnam what it was.

"It was sheer panic on the bus. Then there was shouting. I took a look around the door and saw somebody throwing a pistol at the bus. Then there was the sound of feet running towards the bus and a hand came round the door and a bomb rolled in.

"I tried to kick the bomb out but I could not reach it. I shouted to everybody, grabbed the girl and pulled her out of the door.

"Outside, firing was still going on and the airport police were shooting at a man running away. I carried the girl away from the action until my legs gave way. We were both covered in blood and the girl was badly hurt in the chest."

It is believed that these events further injured Doherty psychologically as well as physically. It is said he blamed himself for people's injuries in his failed attempt to kick the grenade away. His marriage broke up and he was in and out of hospitals, and made several suicide attempts. He was admitted to hospital on the 9th of July 1983 having taken an overdose. Rogers continues the story, on the 21st of July: "Finally, about to return to work, he visited the paper which all this time had kept his job open for him and found the office full of people he no longer knew, and, what was worse, who didn't know him." The following day on his 53rd birthday he was found hanging in his garage at his home in Hurlfield, Sheffield.

The Good Lion is a semi-autobiographical account of the author's first stay in Sheffield. It is the most accomplished of his works — by this time Doherty had learnt the art of storytelling and plotting, as well as characterization, the setting of atmosphere and his ability to transport the reader to another world. His first novel, *A Miner's Sons*, has merit. It is strong on character depiction, Doherty showing his superb ability in putting into words what makes men behave and act as they do: there can be few better writers about masculinity than Doherty. And that is not meant in a macho sense, although that does feature, but he also studies their vulnerabilities, their sensitivities, relationships, and struggles for self-definition that are just as relevant in the 21st century, if not more so, when what it means to be a man is so often questioned. In the 1950s the male role was defined by having to fit into the straitjacket of work as breadwinner and by the aftermath of the war. Now it is more fluid and harder to define but the same questions remain. Each of his novels was an improvement on the last. *A Miner's Sons* suffers somewhat from the lack of a strong plot and story line, and is a little heavy on the polemics. In the same way that *The Ragged-Trousered Philanthropists* slows down a little too much at times, *A Miner's Sons* requires concentration as Doherty sets out to use the novel form to explain something very important to him and possibly inspire and convert. That will be of interest to many people but it does mean the novel in itself is relegated. *The Man Beneath*, is much more rounded as a novel and a really good read as a result. It has a strong story and plot and, in addition, suspense, which is largely missing from the debut novel. From the first chapter there is no question that you want to get to the end to find out what happens to the main character. As the title suggests, the novel explores the character of a seemingly enigmatic man, and does so superbly through flashbacks and recollections of a man trapped underground: "beneath" in more than one sense.

The Good Lion opens in the late 40s. It tells the story of three years in the life of Walter Morris, starting as a seventeen-year-old arriving in Sheffield for the first time to carve out a new life for himself. His plan is to become a miner, which has the added advantage of avoiding National Service. The 'good lion' represents Walt's initial outlook on life: basically self-centred, looking out for himself only – the lion that kills a deer not being a 'bad lion.' The story sees him struggling for a meaning in his life and moving away from this initial framework.

Saturday Night and Sunday Morning is more sensational perhaps, but the plot is less tightly written: things happen for no apparent reason, and there are strange shifts of point of view. As Sillitoe admits in the preface to the 1979 edition, it was a first novel, "with all its liberties and limitations." The fact it was made into a film perhaps explains its enduring popularity. By contrast, in *The Good Lion*, everything is part of the whole, building the voyage of self-discovery that Walt is on and it explores the psychology of the lead character, where there is a gap in Sillitoe's exploration of Seaton.

In June 1956 (with his work-in-progress clearly in mind) he wrote in the Communist Party of Great Britain weekly *World News* about of his aims – his desire to write something that could hold its own against contemporary works. "Our writing must be essentially an expression of the people – not of any single individual alone – and through the medium of working-class people it must endeavour to express something of all men. It must become as wide in its scope and yet as deep and as sincere, as significant to everyone, as was the great literature of the past. To quote Alick West again: 'We must write so that they can recognise in our writing their own lives and see more clearly the meaning of their lives.' "

The novel has a wonderful ending fitting with what George Moore wrote of endings in a "minor key," which show "a skilful use of anti-climax" and a "sensation of inextiguishable grief, the calm of resignation, the mute yearning for what life has not for giving. In such pauses all great stories end."

Like Arthur Seaton, Walt is a young man full of tension, whose growing up includes much drinking, womanising and fighting. Perhaps as a book about contemporary society its appeal was limited, but now, when Walt would be in his nineties, if still alive, it has matured like a good wine: the reader reflecting on the lives of their parents or grandparents and finding plenty of interest other than just a well-crafted plot and the problems, opportunities and mentality of a post-war teenager.

Sheffield is never actually named – it is simply "the city" and the locations are all fictional, though very believable. It is a time of bomb damage: "chopped timbers hanging awry and the pale grey of solitary walls against which staircases leaned leading nowhere," a time of rationing, smoky dance halls where bands play waltzes, jazz or "bop," of suede shoes, fights between gangs, fear over the cold war and atom bombs. It is a time when someone could commute to London from a new house built onto a village consisting of a pub, a post office and a cluster of farm labourers' cottages with no running water and lit by oil lamps; cottages, no doubt now demolished or yuppified and surrounded by modern estates and Waitroses.

His writing is at times quite lyrical. His love and respect for the people and places he writes about shines through. This beautiful passage, for example, on the way to see his dying father: "a few snowflakes fluttered in their faces and settled on their coats. Hoar frost covered the paths through the grounds and had turned each separate blade of grass into a brittle silver spike, naked branches into pale cold arms. Grey clouds rose out of the earth only fifty yards away on every side, pressing down over the hospital in plumed and whorled ripe heaviness." Or is there a better description anywhere of the effect of four pints: "a whirling fluffiness was spreading through his head, like cotton-wool wisps in a fairground candy-floss machine which spin round and round as they slowly gather into a light pink mass; and many normal thoughts and feelings were being smothered like encumbrant weaklings leaving him aware of himself in a fine new way. He felt reckless, confident and invincible." And anyone who knows Sheffield will understand this description of the post-war city: "The city was ugly and knew it, and tried to cover its knowledge with a touchy self-sufficiency, but it was this ugliness, brusque gruffness and lack of sophistication which made him like both the place and the people…"

Doherty writes well about fighting and brings to life the old-style gang culture; his description of the boxing match is particularly well done. Doherty was an amateur boxer in his youth, so writes from first-hand experience. All the tension of the fight comes through. The writing is tight and restrained, perfectly paced, and Doherty avoids any descent into cliché or predictability.

As in all his work he conveys beautifully the sense of honour, courage, humour, loyalty and community amongst miners. I first drafted this introduction as the last large scale deep coalmine at Kellingley closed. It puts an extra angle on this novel: that these things will now be studied as "history."

Minor characters are superbly drawn: the tenderness of the depiction of Walt's landlady, who becomes a sort of surrogate mother figure to the young Walt (and whom he grows to respect, if not love) the big, brash Bryan, and his room-mate Bill. The humour and tragedy of the little scene with Brenda's parents is particularly memorable, so much is packed into it.

In same *World News* article Doherty wrote about the difficulties working class writers faced in portraying their characters, and it reveals much about his success in bringing them to life:

"Working people in general don't wear their hearts on their sleeves, and lack the time to be introspective about their lives. A working man cannot be shown as acting, feeling and talking in the way that a middle-class character might. They are often laconic about the things that matter most to them. The emotion and conflict that the writer seek are very deep down and must be dug for – often they are felt only in a vague and confused way, and the writer must search for ways of expressing them. People whose vocabulary is limited cannot give the shapes to their subtler feelings that a writer might wish, but these feelings are none the less present. So if a sixteen-stone coal miner or steel-roller cannot be portrayed as a soul-searching type, the writer must search for other ways to show how he feels, or must create characters typical of the ordinary collier or steel-roller and yet different in special ways."

The complex character that was Len Doherty, as referred to by Byron Rogers, was clearly a troubled man even before Munich. However, the extent to which *The Good Lion* is autobiographical will perhaps (thankfully) remain obscure. Doherty was probably likeable, loathsome, infuriating and endearing all on one. There are interesting themes in the book, of relationships with parents, and in particular the notion of "the sins of the father." Little is known about Doherty's upbringing other than the hints by Rogers, but it is perhaps not too speculative to wonder how difficult relationships affected him as a person and are therefore reflected in his work.

There is just one short section of the novel where Walt meets his mother:

> 'I know what the life did to you,' he told her.
>
> 'You're very like him,' she answered, after looking at his face for a long time. 'Be careful of yourself.'
>
> When she had said good night and gone, he thought miserably of how unhappy he must have made her. But this —this was the very core of the sudden, tensing blind antagonism that often overpowered him—this smothered rage that set him against his own mother. What evil essence had imbued his father's seed?

Walt continues to wrestle with this idea, and to try to shake it off. How inevitable is it that he will end up like his father? He says at one point, as if accepting the inevitability: 'I'm not like your sort, either. I can't help it. You can't help where you come from and what's put into you.' Walt's brother, Charles, believes it is only by forgiving the father that you can overcome it, but Walt characteristically chooses his own way.

It is very much a coming of age novel. One of the most touching bits of the book is where his landlady concedes: 'Tha'rt no man yet—no sense yet. Happen tha'll make one…' In the end he does.

— Steven Kay, 1889 books, 2023

Notes on text

The footnotes are a 2023 addition. No other changes have been made to the 1958 edition, including language that would not be acceptable today.

The Good Lion

*To my wife, Doreen,
with gratitude
and love*

Part One

The Rhine was red with human blood,
The Danube roll'd a purple tide
On the Euphrates Satan stood,
And over Asia strech'd his pride.

From Islington to Marylebone
Jerusalem, William Blake

Regardant

I

Long, long ago, the moon was an omen of magic, the stars merely holes pricked in the floor of heaven, fire was the ultimate deterrent, and a few huts were bunched around a ford in a huge valley. Some men there knew the secrets of metal; they worked in bronze and iron. The ford joined two narrow tracks coming from east and west of the high surrounding hills at a clear, wide and shallow river, entering by a gap in the north to flow through the valley and curve around the edge of marshy flatlands. From the river, woods stretched out to climb the hills in dark profusion, crowding the horizon on three sides like green crests on an army's battle helmets.

By Chaucer's time there was a village at the ford; some of the pilgrims to Canterbury carried knives which had been made there. It took several hundred years for the village to become a town, the slow growth matched by the gradual thinning of the woods as trees were cut to make charcoal for smelters, planks for builders, and props and beams for the ore-miners. It was when the ironmasters came, building in stone to last, bringing knowledge of new uses for coal and steam, that real growth began. Rapidly and haphazardly the town spread out around the river and across the valley, heedless of appearance in the need to house landless thousands coming to dig ore and coal and make steel. On the flatlands squatted down the first foundries and steel-works, pouring out heavy smoke over the valley by day and making the river glow by night. The railway came, following the old dirt tracks to the ford where a new iron bridge spanned the river.

On the hillside sprouted wooden headgears, replacing the vanishing trees, then as ore and coal seams gave out the headgears also vanished, replaced by a few steel-and-concrete structures which were larger and more austerely imposing. The railway brought ore and coal to feed the furnaces from the other side of the hills. To the glory of God was raised a cathedral. And since the masters were hard-headed men who never gambled, a monument was erected to the outlived god of metal-workers, Vulcan. With two such patrons the city thrived, bursting unto fresh growth as more steel was needed, its buildings clambering on the tall hillsides like fledglings crowding a nest. The valley was filled by row upon row of houses with steelworks flanking then, and factories hulking in their lines. The older districts were mainly homes of the poor.

In the first world war the city turned out steel for thousands of weapons and tanks which went to plough in the mud of Europe and remain after victory. A new monument was erected to men who had also gone in thousands and remained with the rusting steel. The older houses were now so deteriorated that they were becoming an embarrassment, and a slum-clearance project was begun; then no one needed steel any more. Half choked by poverty, the city could not afford all the new houses it needed, so the slums remained, and those living there, while deserving some sympathy, were also looked on with some distaste. True lovers of the city, however, could claim that its steelworks were among the country's largest; its old town hall, new city hall, university, college, museum and public libraries were among the finest.

The housing problem was eased slightly by the next world war. Not only did it destroy much more steel than the first, its improved techniques also destroyed many of the older houses along with their occupants. A fresh addition to the war memorial made it impressive enough to rival Vulcan, though not the cathedral; the cathedral, after all, had been on the city's side both times, and everyone knows that Vulcan is no fighter nowadays.

Having survived wars, enemy bombing and a slump, the city—in a different world from the kind it had known—continued the business of making more steel and growing. Like aged, monsters stubbornly surviving in a new era, the slums thickened their dirty hides while the steelworks crawled on to the last flatland and the council houses conquered the ancient hills. Soon there was talk of yet another world war, but since cities could now be obliterated in a minute and it was a mere matter of time before every country knew the secret, few people liked to think of it. The knowledge was difficult enough to live with.

By the spring of 1948 when young Walt Morris first came looking for a home in the city, it held over half a million people and covered the valley and the hillsides in concrete, brick and slate. Over it drifted a perpetual pall of smoke from the flatlands; refuse wallowed in scum where the river crawled sluggishly past factories, and little houses ringed the horizon where had once tossed the green crests.

II

The train was running late as it neared the city. It had begun its journey well, shooting out of the London station in a proud and powerful hurry, but before long its speed had grown erratic. It slowed down, and for long miles crawled along like a brown centipede forcing its tired length over muddy ground, while neat farms with level fields already rich in promise, small tidy villages and white, glass-fronted factories presented themselves to its windows and dwindled away. The engine gathered breath for a sustained rush through a heavier land smothered in misting rain with low towns squatting under their own clouds, and then, winded, it crawled and grunted its way once more towards the sunlight, with merging railway lines, huge black-girdered sheds, tanks, towers and massive boilers flowing slowly past on either side. Its speed only increased when it reached a broken country of roughly ridged hills and moors with the sun shining timidly over a dappled variety of blacks, browns and greens. The city was a few miles in front.

The burly man had tried several times to begin a conversation, with currently popular jokes about how the trains didn't seem to know they were nationalized now and weren't trying any harder than they'd ever done. Walt's polite smile but vague grunts had defeated each attempt; he seemed unable to realize that there was someone in the warm carriage with him.

In London, as soon as the carriage doors slammed raggedly and the whistle screeched, Walt had told himself: This is it—your new beginning! He had looked joyfully at the burly man for an unguarded moment, then remembering his new dignity had settled back on the twined moquette, raising his book, and resolved to be calm and patient. Usually he could ignore everything with a book in his hand, but this journey was so important, his mind having drawn the analogy between this and the real, the living journey which would begin when this was ended, that Walt's patience had given up its old hopeless struggle before an hour had passed. After that he had changed seats and then changed back, stood out in the corridor several times, read a few pages of his book, and glanced at the *Daily Telegraph* and *Reader's Digest* which his companion offered, without knowing what he had read. He now sat looking out of the window, at one moment scowling impatiently and at the next stretching his features in excitement or interest as he twisted to watch some passing scene. Body, features and eyes never rested, not even when, determined at least to appear relaxed, he pressed back against the cushioning with his legs rigidly crossed and his torso crushed into a posture of ease.

The burly man smiled, his eyes twinkling at Walt under bushy grey brows.

'Don't like travelling by train, lad, do you?' He was grey-haired and square-faced, solid and comfortable in a tweed suit and smoking a drooping pipe with solid and comfortable satisfaction. On his knees lay an open briefcase and on the rack above a tweed overcoat and grey hat.

'It's too slow.' Walt turned to the window again and the burly man remarked that he wasn't so keen on it himself. As a cloud of smoke wrapped itself around the carriage, Walt could see the reflection of him settling back with the pipe and taking a few papers from the case. He thought wistfully that if the other disliked it he made a competent job of lumping it. He admired such placid patience and its air of inner strength, and had already determined to cultivate it; yet here he was in the locked carriage of the moving train, feeling that it wasn't so much things he wanted to do as the knowledge that he couldn't do them if he wanted to which was making him uneasy and restless, and bored with a book he should have enjoyed. He sighed loudly and the burly man smiled again, his lowered eyes slipping sideways to study him.

Long arms and legs made his fairly tall body look slender. His blue, carefully pressed suit was shiny at the creases and elbows, its neatness incongruous because Walt had pulled off his tie in the first half-hour and his white shirt was carelessly open at the collar. A small chin and lean jaw widened to broad cheekbones under large dark eyes, thick black brows and short black hair. At the moment, with his face pressed to the window glass as he stared out, the mouth looked sensuous, the upper lip delicately edged and the lower slightly pouted. Animated, his features looked youthfully attractive and you felt the huge vitality in the too slender shell, but, when he was still, there was a suggestion of sulkiness. This quick changeability made him resemble some overgrown schoolboy whose features still lack the shape and confidence of maturity, and the burly man reflected that he was probably a bad-tempered young rogue with an eye for the girls. His grubby raincoat was bundled on the rack beside two suitcases which were secured by leather belts, without which one case would have burst at the lock, the other at the hinges.

'Won't be long now,' the burly man remarked as Walt's head, with disconcerting suddenness, jerked round to find him watching. All his movements were swift and sudden, like those of an animal whose life depends on instinct.

'Good,' Walt said, looking out of the window again. As the wheels clattered and clicked under his feet, stumbling over points, he was thinking: Come on, train; come on, come on—and his body was tensed forward like a jockey urging on his horse. He thought of that first colliery he had seen, frail and tiny under an overbearing black slag-heap which, as he twisted to look back, had seemed to sprawl away endlessly, smoking in places like smouldering hills. He was looking out for another one and thinking that he liked this noble and austere country in spite of its bleakness. It was more suited to his new life than the easy, gentle beauty of the South. The difference was like that between a man and a woman.

He felt like this because he also felt that he was rushing away from what was normal; away from the comfortable trap of routine living, touched as it was with the rot of ease and weakness; and towards risk and change, a hard life which had to mean strength.

He had it all worked out. Problems were things you could only solve by direct simplicity and determination which were characteristics of the strong, and strength came from living and working as only the strong could. So the journey was important. How many could say that at seventeen they were spitting Destiny right in the eye and going off to shape their own ends? He was vaguely aware that he might, perhaps, be carrying a little of the old with him into this new life, but even that would soon be discarded. So, in the stuffy carriage, with smoke slowly drifting to the window where factories and small stations jerked past and the sun was shining, glinting and throwing scudding shadows over the moors beyond, Walt could look at the other seat and feel glad of being Walt Morris, life-shaper, and not a dull business-man with a dull life behind and a duller retirement to come.

The burly man looked up at this moment and Walt immediately reached for his book.

'Any good?'

'This? Yes. It's Hemingway—short stories.'

'Oh aye...' The burly man sucked hard on his pipe, which bubbled but released no more smoke. As he reached for his lighter he said:

'Never read him. Like a good detective meself.'

Walt nodded politely, though he considered anyone who preferred detective stories to Hemingway a lost soul who should be pitied rather than condemned. One of his cases was full of books, some bought second-hand and some left behind by his brothers; all of them would have been classed as 'good' or 'serious' by most critics, although no one had guided Walt's taste since he left school and he bought or kept only those books which he could read and enjoy often. The fact that he did not fully understand some of them had never spoiled his enjoyment. Even when he was a schoolboy his mother had scolded him countless times for burying his nose in a book and ruining his eyes.

'Reading in bed with a torch under the blankets,' she would say. 'Reading at every meal, reading on your way home from school... Anything could happen to any of us and you'd never know...' In spite of the truth of her observation, her conclusion had been false.

In a fresh cloud of bitter grey smoke the burly man glanced up at Walt's luggage and asked was he coming up for a holiday or for good?

'For good,' Walt answered, closing his book as he added proudly: 'As a miner.'

'A miner? Oh…' The burly man looked critically at him. '…New to it, I suppose? Aye—had some Londoners in t' pit during t' war. Bevin boys, you know. A tough job is pit work.' He sounded unimpressed with Walt's chances as, broadening vowels and clipping consonants, he went on to admit grudgingly that, of course, it did keep you of the Army, didn't it?—conceding the common sense in that.

'I'm making a career of it,' Walt replied indignantly. The Army! Being called up meant you were one of a bunch in the same boat; not alone and independent as he would be. 'I'm going to be a mining engineer! And I'm not a Londoner, anyway.'

The other leaned over to pat Walt's knee, beaming encouragement.

'Good for you, old son. You'll have some study to do—some hard going at front of you, eh? But it's something to see a young 'un with a bit of ambition these days. No go in most on 'em. None at all.' He leaned back again, shaking his large grey head. 'This Welfare State stuff—it'll ruin this country, lad, you watch. There aren't enough like yourself. Life's too damned easy for young 'uns as it is—everything put on their plates—and they haven't really started yet.'

He went on at length about how the Labour Government and its Socialism would have the country on its back in another three years, and Walt nodded without listening. He had forgiven the doubtful tone of a minute ago, though this bugle call of ambition had aroused memories of his parents. It was nice to pretend, while the condemnatory voice rumbled on, that he might really become a mining engineer.

'Thought you weren't London, though,' the other said at last. 'Belong up north, don't you? Scotland?'

When Walt nodded he looked shrewdly pleased; a detective with a theory proved correct.

'Knew it. Not much accent, mind, but I could tell. You roll your r's.'

With a quick impudent grin Walt said that wearing a kilt made you do that, and the other frowned and then slapped his knee as he laughed delightedly, shaking his head.

'By, you belong up north all right, lad. You belong up north.'

Which wasn't true, Walt thought, because he didn't, feel that he belonged anywhere. He had been moved about too often and from too early an age to have roots; no one place, no special house rose in his mind as a symbol of home. Home was somewhere in front, not behind, and London had been only the latest stop, scene of the final stage of family disintegration with himself the last seceding member. *They* were on their own now; together, but on their own. And he wished them lots of luck but didn't want to share it.

Where I'm going, he thought—that could be home. He would become a miner, strong, stern and hard-working. Some day he would have a wife—an extremely pretty one, he could see her now—and they'd have children to whom he'd be kind and protective... Perhaps... Or years of lonely study in shirt-sleeves, chin in hand and books propped open on a table in front of him. He could see that too; you got tired, but kept going, chin stuck out and eyes lowered to the books. Transformed by some miracle into a mining engineer, off he would go to Brazil, Peru, Africa; the whole world. Like the films... Or a writer? He'd always liked the thought of that, especially with William having been one. A deeply serious one, of course, like those he most admired, brilliant in conversation instead of seldom knowing what to say, and bravely honest with the pen instead of loathing the idea of writing even a letter. A playwright or novelist, and films being made of your work... An actor? No. They had listened to his Mark Antony and the mob speech—his favourite at that—and turned him down for the school performance in his last year when he was fourteen. A writer would be better; you only needed paper and pen to start...

The carriage was dim as low hummocks of scorched ground hemmed the windows, and the train was crawling with ropes of thick white smoke looped along its length.

'Last haul up to the station.' The burly man rose and reached up, grunting, for his coat and hat. As Walt fetched down his suitcases the other went on: 'Every place you go now will be up a hill or down, lad. Built on hills she is. Like what's-its-name...'

'Rome,' Walt said, tugging at his raincoat, which flopped down over his head as the burly man said: 'Aye, Rome. There she is.'

He threw the coat on to the seat and looked out. A segment of the city lay below, and first you saw the background: two great black gasometers at one side like drums for a giant timpanist, and three even larger brick-kilns on the other like mighty brown hour-glasses. Then you saw the towering, tapering chimneys, with smoke pouring out in oily rolls over the dirty little houses, crammed in tight rows in grey streets, long black factories among them on whose black roofs were stencilled names which were famous all over the world. People moving in the streets looked overborne, as did the houses, by the giants surrounding and among them, and by the tram-cars and petrol buses which clanged, hooted, rumbled and rocked as they kept pace with the train. There came a high-walled market place, with the crowds swarming and breaking among the square or oblong groups of canvas-roofed stalls, then the view changed and the burly man said: 'That's one o' the spots where old Jerry had a bash.'

Under the smoking sky the drab silhouette was broken up by gutted ruins like gaps in a line of infantry when a rolling barrage lifts. He saw the brown and green of grass-tufted rubble, the rich blackness of charred timbers hanging awry and the pale grey of solitary walls against which staircases leaned leading nowhere. In places there was only the flattened, blasted ground, naked except for rubbish strewn like sores or scars over its brown length.

' 'Course we never got it as bad as London, say, or Coventry... There was an undertone of independent pride. '...but we took our fair share o' t' knocks.'

Walt stared out and back as the train lunged into a tunnel and high, streaming stone walls cut off the view.

'But—it's not all like that, is it?'

The burly man chuckled and assured him, as they put on their coats, that it wasn't all like this. He lived in a fairly nice part himself and there were the housing estates, of course, all around the city centre and grand and clean. Up on the hills they were.

'Slum clearances, you know. But what city hasn't got its slums, eh? We can stand some competition, one road and another.'

Walt said he was going to live on the Clifton estate. He was glad that it was not to those cramped houses and streets, so like the place where he had been born, that he was going 'Mainby Road,' he said.

'Mainby's a nice part—there's some hard, characters live up that way, mind you. I'll show you your bus.'

In the station he led the way down the platform, with one of Walt's battered cases in his hand looking odd against the tweed overcoat. For a moment Walt was suddenly timid, as he stood by the engine which was belching out steam, and watched the mass of people flowing away, all of them obviously sure of where they were going and sure it was worth going to. Then, as he hurried after the burly man, his timidity was forgotten in the excitement of looking at the people and hearing the bubbles of exciting dialect boiling up out of their talk. He pushed past arm-linked groups and ecstatically kissing couples, past women screaming their pleasure at reunion and men thumping each other to show their affection, and by the time he squeezed through the turnstiles he was smiling. Outside the huge arched entrance he caught up with the burly man. They dashed past the taxi ranks and across a great square with a traffic island in its centre around which swirled motor buses and cars, hooting and honking at the scurrying people.

'That's yours,' the other shouted, and ran towards a bus which was poised at a stop, its engine throbbing. He bundled Walt aboard and shoved the case after him just as the bus began moving.

'Ask for the Luxor picture house,' he called, and Walt waved to him, staggering on the platform as the bus jerked into the stream of traffic. He wished he knew the man's address so that he could visit him some time.

Later he realized that his progress wouldn't have impressed the burly man, anyway.

He tried to see something of the city from a downstairs window but the glass was obscured by mist, and a drizzle of rain outside made his glimpses brief ones. The large shop windows and bustling raincoated people, the traffic and occasional hawker's barrow or sheltering newspaper-seller made him think it much like any other. The people in the bus had the usual bored and vacant look too, and the only difference was the clipped and abrupt harshness of their speech. The bus climbed for a long time up through row upon seemingly endless row of little houses, with groups of small shops nestling among them, and by the time it reached the Luxor cinema the rain had almost stopped.

When he found Mainby Road he halted at the corner to rest his arms, with an occasional raindrop still patting his head and steam writhing over the pavements around him. A rich heavy scent was coming from the hedges and the grass and shrubs in the gardens, but the road, though far more pleasant than those he had seen from the train, had little character. The houses were all alike, with scabrous gravelled walls and close-curtained windows, each pair separated from the rest and defended by privet hedges which were all clipped to approximately the same height. There was no one around. It was quiet; a dull and life-less street like one glimpsed listlessly from a quick train, the chimneys smoking thinly and the raindrops making shimmering rings in the puddles.

He was afraid again as he stood looking. It didn't seem friendly, this colourless street. Nor the regimented estates, nor the people in the bus, nor the whole self-engrossed, work-grimed city in which he would have to live.

What city's not like that? he thought, and shrugged without knowing it before he picked up his cases and walked on to No. 13. As he went up the path he noticed a bespectacled little face peeping through a gap between the lace curtains of the house next door, but as he looked the face jerked away and the curtains twitched into place.

He had already formed his own picture of his new landlady: since she was a widow and old, she would be a frail little thing with white hair, and he would have to shout to her, probably. As the door opened he faced a brawny-armed woman as tall as himself and much broader, stout and shapeless in a green overall which hung to her thick ankles. Her head was too small for her big body and the incongruous effect of this was increased by the way her white hair was drawn tightly back in a thin bun on her thick red neck.

'Mrs. Stevens you want?' The voice was unsuited to the massive, sagging chest; it was high, off-pitch and harsh. In a face like that of a walnut figurine, with the wrinkles of nearly seventy years scored from her shiny high forehead to her heavy jaw, her small eyes looked like set opals.

'Yes... My name's Morris and I—'

'You've found us, then. Good. Thought you'd got lost.'

As he lowered a case she turned away, and he offered his hand too late. He was standing looking at it and beginning to blush when she called from inside: 'Come along in, then.'

There was no hallway, the stairs facing the front door and the room to his right. He put down the cases and went into the room, with a gawkish feeling warning him that this was a time when he was likely to do everything wrong and blush at each mistake; acutely conscious of every move and every word.

'In here; that's right.' She was waiting before a large old-fashioned kitchen fireplace with a large old-fashioned easy chair on either side. Walt thought that everything in the crammed room looked old-fashioned until he saw the youth sitting by the table in a high-backed knobby-legged chair. He was small and plump with a round friendly face and wide smile. His brown hair was brushed to one side but had a tendency to spring forward and flop over his eyes when he moved his head so that he was constantly half raising a smooth, plump arm and a hand as small and neat as a girl's ready to push it back. Mrs. Stevens introduced him as Bill Spenser and asked Walt his first name.

'Walt.' He stood by the table, unbuttoning his coat and wondering how you moved about in here. Apart from the easy chairs and oak table, there was a long sofa with wooden legs and back, a huge glass-fronted cabinet full of plate and ornaments, four straight-backed chairs and several statuettes. On the wall behind Bill hung 'A Stag at Bay.'

'Walter Morris, Bill.'

'Pleased to meet you, Walter,' Bill said, bouncing out of the chair and pushing out a hand.

'Walt,' he said firmly, stiffly jerking Bill's soft hand a few times. 'Like yours is Bill.'

'Okay, Walt. Pleased to know you, anyway. His smile widened, and Walt, whose two front teeth had been knocked out when he was sixteen and replaced by screwed-in false ones, envied the neatness and whiteness of Bill's.

'Sit down, then, Walter,' the old lady said. 'Bill can take your cases up while I mash tea.

He shrugged off his raincoat and sat in the nearest easy chair, which sighed and took him lower than he had expected. The old lady went into the kitchen while he was struggling up from this enfolded depth and Bill went to the stairs. There was something faulty in the way he walked which, although not a pronounced limp, jarred on Walt's acute sense of physical correctness. He looked around him, at the two paintings, the pictures of wedding groups and the embroidered mottoes on the walls, and sighed. He leaned back, but a sensation of helplessness as his body sank deeper and deeper brought him upright again.

Bet she's got an aspidistra somewhere, he thought. At least it was clean. Glass and metal and linoleum all shone; the chair covers were bright and the steel grate sparkled back the fire's ruddy reflection. On top of the cabinet was an interesting statue of a nude bronze female with pointed breasts, extravagantly posturing beside a rearing bronze horse. He liked that one better than the china Alsatian who crouched on the old radio, or the little Dutch boy holding his girl's hand on the window-sill.

Over strong sweet tea and thick slices of fruit cake they chatted about his journey. He began to relax and feel he was performing with fair dignity after all until the old lady leaned forward and said it was time they sorted things out. Walt felt defensive, bogged down with a teacup in his hands and his knees almost as high as his chin, as she towered over him with her big mottled hands set firmly on her green-tented knees. He noticed Bill smiling as he leaned back in his own chair and lit a cigarette.

'You'll be goin' to t' Labour Exchange in t' morning?' she began. He assured her he would, put the cup and saucer down and fumbled in his pockets, turning out ration books, identity card and thin wallet before he found the proper forms.

'I'll be starting work Wednesday, I expect,' he said, feeling obliged to prove his good intentions. She picked up the ration books but ignored the other forms.

'Had a Londoner here once afore,' she mused, with a mildness which made him wary. 'Bevin boy. Didn't stick it long.'

He told her he wasn't a Londoner, wondering what everyone had against them, anyway.

'I thought that were your home?' In her gnarled face, as she leaned in, her green eyes became even smaller as they grew shrewder. Her nose was a little blob with a wart under the left nostril.

'I haven't got a home. Not really. I was in lodgings.'

She asked if his folks were dead and he shook his head. 'They've got a little flat.' He said no more because it wasn't her business and had been left behind. She studied him, but he stayed silent, returning her look, until she asked abruptly why he had come to this city.

'It's a hard place to live in and work in unless you're the kind as can fit in.'

'I can fit in.' Her questions were arousing his defiance. He had not left home to look for this.

'That's all right, then. An' you're going to be a pitman. That's hard work...' She leaned back on the chair and looked at her hands. 'My man were a pitman and he wouldn't let none on our three go down. They're all in good jobs now. Real good jobs...' She looked at him again with a small smile. 'But it reckons to run in families. It takes a fair man to be a good collier. You're nobbut a young lad yet, are you?'

He felt awkward and embarrassed under her look and Bill's look, and did not know if she were being kind or superior, for it was hard to interpret any expression on that graven face. So he simply shrugged and smiled politely and saw immediately that she had taken this for disdain.

'Think tha'rt man enough for a tough job like yon?' Her voice had gone harsh again. Full of exasperation at his own self-conscious stiffness, he mumbled that this was the only way he'd find out.

'Ah well, we shall see, shan't we? So you've growed up lonely, eh?'

'Not all that lonely!' He looked over at Bill, who winked and grinned with the cigarette cocked upward in his mouth. 'I can take pretty good care of myself, I guess.'

He began to blush fiercely as he saw the wrinkles spreading, curling and tightening over her face while she smiled, her few teeth showing like discoloured stalagmites in the entrance of a red cave.

'Happen you can. Stick it here and we'll find out, lad, eh?' Then with the wrinkles hurrying back to their usual set, she went on briskly: 'We've nowt fancy here, Walter, but you'll get good snap and be treated fair if you behave. I like young chaps to keep respectable hours and work regular and behave theirsens, and this'll be a home for you as long as we all get on all right.'

Then she told Bill to show Walt their room.

'You two's in t' one and me in t' other,' she told Walt, and Bill, as he stood up, said:

'Well, we couldn't all be in the same, could we? You snore too loud for a start.'

'Don't thee get cocky 'cause there's an audience,' she snapped, whirling round on him. 'If you don't like me snoring you know what to do.' Then she stumped off into the kitchen as Bill winked slyly at Walt again and led him upstairs.

'It's best to always go for her dignity,' he whispered over his shoulder. 'Gets her all confused—only I always lose when she starts. She can shout you down. Guess I'm scared of her.'

He was still smiling, however, when he opened the bedroom door. 'Our cell.' There were two single beds with a small table between them, two chairs and two sets of drawers, one with a mirror on top.

'Where's the aspidistra?' Walt asked as he lifted the cases on to the nearest bed and began unpacking. Bill said in the kitchen, and after a moment asked how he had known. Then they both laughed and Bill slapped Walt's shoulder.

'She's really all right, you know. A tough old dragon—but she grows on you.' He told Walt where to put his clothes and then sprawled on his own bed, talking about the old lady and himself. He had been here for two years; had been a student at the city college, and was now working as a laboratory assistant in a steelworks. His mother, a widow, kept a small shop in Leeds with Bill's younger sister to help her. Bill talked quickly and smiled all the time as though everything he said were amusing or as though he half expected Walt to think so. He was twenty.

'You're seventeen, aren't you?' he asked.

'I'll soon be eighteen.'

'I thought you looked older downstairs.' When Walt looked up at this, Bill said quickly: 'Not now, mind you. Only—when you were standing up to her.' As Walt continued unpacking, he said: 'You weren't scared of her, were you?'

'Why should I be?' He was glad that Bill, at least, hadn't realized how nervous he was.

'Oh no—you shouldn't be...'

As Walt opened the other case, Bill jumped up with a delighted shout and knelt on Walt's bed to look at the books.

'Put 'em in your bottom drawer. Fancy—all books! We can swop, can't we?' As he passed each one to Walt he read the names aloud: 'Let's see: Faulkner, Steinbeck, Hemingway—you like the Yanks, eh?'

'It's the way they write,' Walt said, kneeling by the drawer and putting the books in carefully. 'You feel they're tough about life. They've got guts —they're not sloppy. I can't always make Faulkner out, mind you...'

'They say that's only a cover-up for sentimentality. Just a trick of hiding it...'

'It isn't!' Walt looked fiercely over his shoulder, as furious as though he himself had been accused. 'That's the kind of stuff intellectuals chuck about, I bet. Because they can't write.' Had he been asked to define an intellectual he would have frowned and said vaguely that everybody knew what one was like. He did not know how he had learned to associate this word with high-browed effeminacy and general uselessness, but that was what it meant to him and seemed to have always meant. Bill frowned for a moment and then, with a shrug went on: 'Melville, good Lord! Graham Greene, Zola, Jack London and— ah-ah—*The Technique of Sex*, eh?'

Walt took it from him with lowered eyes and put it in the bottom of the drawer with several books on top to hide the title.

'And these others,' Bill went on, after a sly grin which Walt refused to acknowledge. 'What a mixture! Mine are non-fiction mostly, I'm afraid—modern science, philosophy, politics...'

'Politics!' Walt grunted. 'I'll stick to the Yanks.'

'We're dead lucky to be sharing a room, anyway,' Bill rejoiced as Walt closed the drawer and rose to sit on the edge of the bed. 'I'd expected somebody different. I mean...' He went on to explain, and seemed embarrassed as he did so, that there was nothing wrong with people who worked hard and drank beer and never read—he was all for them, in fact—only it was easier to live with someone more like yourself.

Walt said that he hardly ever drank and didn't smoke.

'No vices?'

'No.'

'Girls?'

'I haven't known many.'

Bill looked at his face critically.

'Funny—I sort of took you for a ladies' man.' At a fierce look from Walt, who had begun to blush, Bill added hurriedly: 'In the best sense of the word, mind. Don't pay any attention to me—I'm always saying the wrong damned things and getting people's backs up.' And he smiled, pushing his hair back anxiously until Walt smiled also.

'My brother's name was Bill,' Walt told him. 'Well, William, that is.'

'Was it?' After a moment the polite smile changed to a frown: 'William Morris? That's some handle, isn't it?'

Walt knew, from the tone and the earlier remark about politics, the real question Bill meant to ask. But he chose to answer:

'Yeah, I'll bet the kids at school tormented him plenty of times. My folks were like that, though. It was always William. William and Charles and Walter.'

'So that's what the "call-me-Walt" was about.'

'I suppose so.' Walt, he thought, was a better name, anyway; more suited to this new life. 'In London I lived in a house where I got called Wally.' He looked so indignant that Bill laughed and then apologized, patting Walt's knee as he warned him: 'You'll be Walter to the old lady, anyhow. You made it too much of a challenge for her to miss it.'

They were quiet. Now that the rain had stopped there was sunlight chequering the floor and turning Bill's face white as he glanced at Walt several times and looked down again. Walt waited for the question.

'Were your folks Socialists? Calling him that, I mean?'

'Yeah. Staunch Socialists.'

Bill frowned, drawing one leg under him.

'Why do you say it like that?'

'Like what?' he asked doggedly.

'As if you didn't like it.'

'I don't care.' Then he shrugged, finding cynicism harder to imitate than he had thought. In a spate of phrases he said: 'They were Socialists and William was a Socialist, and he wrote poetry and so I suppose he didn't mind.'

'Didn't mind. Has he changed now?'

'I don't know,' Walt said stiffly. 'He died when I was only about seven so I don't what he made of it all at the finish.

'Oh, I'm sorry.' But the withdrawn look in Bill's eyes showed his mental calculations and also the next question, which Bill didn't yet know he was going to ask.

'Yes. He got killed in Spain.'

'In Spain,' Bill repeated quietly. 'Gosh! In Spain...'

Walt stood up and dug his hands into his pockets, hunching his shoulders as Bill went on:

'Well, listen, Walt. I really *am* pleased to know you.'

'It was William that did it, not me,' he answered, his voice flat because it truly had nothing to do with him what his brother, whom he had scarcely known and could barely remember yet loved intensely, had done or had felt and died for. Bill looked at his face and said no more about it. He was obviously puzzled, but Walt did not care. Since his childhood there had always been a sadness imprisoned inside him like an underground spring which bubbles in a tiny cavern and cannot escape. Mention of William made a fissure in the rock so that the sadness did escape and for a while seeped and ran through every part of him.

Bill changed the subject by saying he had something to show him. He led Walt on to the landing and opened the door of the other bedroom, then nudged Walt and pointed. Beside the brass-railed, huge-knobbed head of the bed was a marble-topped table on which stood a white jug and basin, and just above that Walt saw a truncheon hanging from a nail. It was an old truncheon, two feet long, with a wooden grip and part of its leather covering worn away.

'See it?' Bill murmured. 'With that and her strong right arm she's ready to defend privacy, property and chastity any time of day or night. Nearly seventy years old, eh?'

Walt said he could admire that kind of guts, as Bill closed the door.

'Who doesn't?' Bill answered. 'She's a holy terror, and yet—you can't help respecting her.'

After a large dinner they went to the first show at the cinema. It was Bill's suggestion, and they had to go early because he was on night shift.

'Fancy a chemist having to work shifts, eh?' he said. So in a warm, comfortable seat in the dark hall, Walt sat beside Bill and watched a film version of the Battle of Britain, with anti-aircraft guns thudding, planes disintegrating before the camera, parachutes bobbing and clusters of bombs tumbling down to end in little white smoke-rings. Then, as often happened to him in a cinema, he was led to think of something else; something real. He recalled that view from the train of a shattered silhouette, imagining the impact of bombs on those crammed houses; the thunder and fire and panic as the walls toppled, and the staircases left desolate to point at the deadly sky. He moved uncomfortably in the seat as a film siren wailed in a rising and dropping dirge.

He could remember nights in Glasgow spent beside his mother and sisters in a crowded street shelter, his terror doubled because some of the adults were showing theirs. He remembered very well the throbbing broken drone and the hand-clenching as it grew louder; then the sudden *whump-whump-whump* of ack-ack, the ring and clatter of bouncing shrapnel and the deep *oof!* of a striking bomb, as though the streets and houses staggered from a blow to the belly. He had often trotted through littered streets, searching for shrapnel fragments and silk parachute cord, and skirting fences which guarded unexploded bombs or mines. Once he had watched a dog-fight by daylight between Hurricane and Heinkel and cheered madly with the others when the Heinkel planed down in a smoking, oblique white streak with no small parachute floating away.

'We took our fair share o' t' knocks,' the burly man had said, and Walt remembered the touch of pride. '...Never got it as bad as London, say, or Coventry...'

He emerged from this reverie in time to see the hero win a D.F.C. and a girl too; he could guess what the parts he had missed had been about. On the way home he asked if Bill ever sat dreaming in a cinema.

'I guess so,' Bill grinned. 'Not when it's a film like that, though.'

The daylight had not quite dissolved and the street lights were still pale as they walked along. Walt said he had too much imagination and that films like that made him think of the war.

'I was just a kid when it started,' he said. 'I mean—I grew up in it.'

'It makes you wonder what the next one's going to be like if they keep on,' Bill said. 'Doesn't it?'

'There won't be a next one.' In spite of newspapers which cried every day of the threat of war, the threat of Communism, the need to be ready, he refused even to think of it. 'I read a Yankee officer who said that if the Reds ever get the atom bomb and we have another war, then the one after will be fought with bows and arrows again. They won't push us that far.'

'It's if we push them...' Bill remarked, and hesitated.

'Why should we?' Walt asked, but Bill looked down at his feet and didn't answer.

'We won't go too far, any more than they will. Anyway'—he shrugged and said cheerfully—'it's us that's got the bomb if anything did start.' When he asked if Bill had done his national service training, Bill said:

'You didn't notice? Really?' He looked delighted. 'I've got a short leg—the left one. Only a little bit, but I failed the medical.'

Walt assured him he hadn't even guessed, but he was now aware again of the hesitant swing in Bill's walk. They were almost home when Bill said that he hoped Walt would do all right in the pit.

'Think you will?'

'I don't see why not,' Walt answered peevishly, at the same time drawing his shoulders higher and tensing his body. 'I don't know if I look fragile or something, but it happens I can run a fair half-mile, chin the bar umpteen times and put up a pretty good scrap against anything around my weight. I'm no sissy!'

'I didn't think you were. Don't get me wrong.' Bill seemed always ready to apologize for a statement before he heard the answer. He raised an anxious hand to his forelock, smiling with his face cocked up towards Walt as he assured him he didn't think him fragile at all. He just thought it must be a hard job and wouldn't fancy tackling it himself.

'It's all right, Bill,' Walt said as they reached the house. It'd just be nice if somebody encouraged me for a change.' After a moment, he added: 'Not that I'm bothered what people say. A man has to do what he thinks is right.' He would not look at Bill as he said this, because he realized that he had read it somewhere, and didn't yet know whether this was right or not.

'You're quite right about that,' Bill said as they entered the house. 'Quite right, Walt.'

At nine o'clock, when Bill had gone to work and Walt was yawning in front of the fire, the old lady began putting on a black coat which was as long and shapeless as her overall.

'I always go to t' Cross Keys for a glass at this time,' she told Walt.

Walt, with embarrassment suddenly mushrooming up in him as he remembered, took out his wallet and found the only three pound notes he had. He held them out to the old lady, who stared at him while she drew a black silk scarf from her pocket. He began blushing as he asked if this would do until he drew a wage.

'I expect it'll be a couple of weeks,' he said. She looked at the money and he glanced away, his cheeks burning and itching furiously. He hated to ask favours.

'Didn't say you had to pay in advance...'

Walt repeated stiffly that he would have no wages for two weeks.

'Aye. Everybody's got to work a week in hand. I know that better'n thee.'

The notes rustled as she took them from his sweating hand, folded two up and put them in a tin on the mantelpiece. It was a tea-caddy decorated with coronation pictures of the Royal family, and as she replaced the lid she told him, looking at him: 'I keep all me money in there. Never lost none yet.' Then she held the other note out to him.

'Take this for expenses.'

'I'll manage,' he said. 'I've got a few—' She pushed the money into his pocket.

'It might cost thee more'n than tha thinks over t' next two weeks. You'll be makin' money soon enough if you're any good.' She watched him lower his head, his eyes ashamed, as she put the scarf over her head and tied it under her chin.

'Weren't a prouder man walkin' than Abe Stevens,' she said quietly. 'But he could take the downs as well as the ups. When folks get too proud here they get called big-heads.'

'Thanks a lot,' he said. 'I'll pay you back in a couple of weeks.'

She answered over her shoulder on her way to the door:

'You're best to see if you last a couple o' weeks first, lad.' From under her scarf the white bun of hair protruded like the rump of a jacketed racehorse. 'Leave t' light on if you go to bed.'

Left alone he climbed the stairs to his bedroom. He sat on the edge of the bed, tired and with his head aching. All the impressions of the day were spinning around discordantly in his head each in its own orbit. He could not co-ordinate them yet. The room was cold and the windows shone black, and when he said aloud 'Well, this is your new home,' his voice did not cheer him.

He decided he liked Bill, though he seemed a bit too anxious to please all the time. He hoped Bill wouldn't prove too ardent over politics, because he had lived with that and seen it, and knew the difference between what these political types professed and how they actually lived. As for the old, lady—with her indiscriminate mixing of 'you' with 'thee' and 'tha'—she was a character, certainly, but she either distrusted strangers in general or simply disliked him.

Clasping his hands together, he leaned forward, body gently rocking as the sound of traffic and broken speech came from outside in recurrent whispers as though surf were washing on distant rock. He felt lonely and wondered if it were homesickness.

For where? he asked himself contemptuously. Don't get carried away.

A girl would be nice. A girl to lean against. A real girl worth having. Those few he had known since leaving school, he thought, had acted and kissed like kids playing house. His fantasies were always of older and much more sophisticated ones. He was a little afraid of such girls (they made you feel that you were the kid), but he wouldn't be, once a miner.

There was a small section of Walt's mind which had often spoiled his most pleasant moments by assuming a decidedly adult and critical pose. On nights when, lying in bed with eyes closed, he had seen himself crouching behind a dead horse on the hilltop with El Sordo and his band, chasing Moby Dick with Ahab on both sides of sea and land, standing behind a hedge at Poitiers with other men in leather jerkins and steel caps or shouting from a high poop as the Spanish galleons closed in; on nights like this when his intensity relaxed, that perverse voice would say in its hidden corner that most kids stopped doing this at fourteen. It was this voice which now demanded why he wanted to be a miner. He had never been near a coal-mine; a few scenes from *The Stars Look Down* were his only clues, and, in case he'd forgotten, half the cast of that film had been blown up, drowned or suffocated. Why was he doing this? And no 'man doing what's right' business either...

He didn't know why, at first. Then he remembered his mother saying at the station: 'You can always come back if you don't like it, can't you? You could get digs again near us.'

He did know why, and his body stopped rocking as he raised his head in the cold room. No more grinding out dreary hours in a dull office; no more drifting from one stifling job to another; no more boxing a few rounds in the nearest gym with the best opponent he could find, merely to feel that this was at least something he was good at. He would smother the memory of his father's voice from boyhood repeating many, many times that you needed to have brains and to use them, needed to have ambition and use that, and would know this for himself if he had either. There was also to be smothered the memory of his mother's advice during the past three years, constantly warning him that common people had no security and that he must have ambition, must get on in the world, must win a good position as Charles had done.

'You've got to make something of yourself, and never forget. Or you'll end up like your father...'

Yet both, when the old cycle reunited them one more time, were satisfied to see him a studying clerk, with his feet set only too firmly on that famous bottom rung from which they might have raised a step or two in a decade.

'Not me,' he told Bill's bed. 'I broke out.'

Had broken out by finally winning their permission to take up this job. It had been difficult and he could not go without their written consent, but he had been determined and he had succeeded, though only after a quarrel with his father which had grown so furious that his mother had begged both of them to stop it and had broken into tears when the older man, his temper flaring, had lifted his hand and Walt had said: 'Not now, you can't. Maybe with the others, but not me. Not now.'

'It's for your own good,' his father had said, with Walt watching the slowly lowered hand. 'I walked out at sixteen and was sorry afterwards. It was a long time before my father spoke to me again.'

'It isn't as if you'd been around very much to talk to me since I was a kid,' Walt said. 'And I am out—I got shoved out as soon as you came back. I'm just moving a bit farther away.'

To his surprise his father had quietly told him that since he was back they could talk to each other now. Walt had stared at him and then turned and walked out of the flat. Their reluctant consent had been finally won by his promise to study for a mining engineer's certificate. He had been prepared to promise anything, even this—when half-marks had been his highest in science and mathematics in school and he had passed exams only by top grades in such non-engineering subjects as English and history.

It served them right, he thought. Why should they try to control his life? A woman who had lost her family as each member reached adolescence, because she could not turn her back for good on a man who had repeatedly bullied, betrayed and deserted her; a man who from crippled ex-soldier had reached such peaks as, first, a full-time union official, later a small businessman, only to slither right back down each time because he lacked the strength of self-denial. A harsh judgment, this, on his elders. But no harsher, no different, he told himself, from that he was prepared to pass on himself.

His first victory had been won and now he was going to be a miner. He would belong to the country's most important industry—the first to be nationalized—on which every other depended. The miner was needed and would always be needed. He had security, and he also had strong hands and lived by old traditions, facing danger with resolution and bound to others who were bound to him. Because he lived with risk, those who lived with less risk admired him. His was the toughest, the hardest and most dangerous of jobs by all accounts, and Walt was scornful of half-way ambitions. If he had been born in a slum, he did not have to endure a dullard's life feeling grateful for any small rise in his station. No man of action had to stand that.

He felt like a miner already. He undressed quickly and cheerfully and climbed into bed, falling asleep within a few minutes. When he woke the house was quiet and the darkness heavy. A cat was mourning outside and he could hear a murmur of distant traffic. Someone yelled, the cat was silenced and a window slammed. Drowsily Walt was aware of a new sound which he felt through his whole body rather than heard: a faint but regular thudding like an amplified heart-beat. Some huge hammer, he thought, pounding steel in the city somewhere. He fell asleep still listening to this beat which never faltered or varied but steadily thudded through the whole night.

III

'I realize that you worry,' he wrote, 'but please don't. Things have changed and it isn't as bad or dangerous as people think. One more week of training and I'll start at my own pit. I'll be a proper miner then...'

After a few more reassuring lines he finished the letter, hoping his mother would be convinced. She got upset so easily, he thought; and he didn't want anyone to be upset or worried about him. His new life had to be free of such obligations to the past.

He sat back from the table. The electric light was burning and the windows were streaked by drizzling rain. In an easy chair by the fire the old lady had a piece of sacking spread over her knees and was pegging rags of bright cloth through it to make a rug, her head lowered as she worked. Bill was spending the week-end with his mother, so the house was quiet.

Two weeks had changed many of his notions, and becoming a miner was taking longer than he expected. His imagination had pictured him squatting before a wall of coal, in a dark vacuum as it were, and hacking at it with a flashing pick. He hadn't expected three weeks of training, nor had he dreamed of what the coal-face, the miles of underground roadways and the pit bottoms were really like. At a colliery outside the city, a group of soot-layered concrete buildings with two bony head-gears rearing up in their centre, he and a dozen others rode the shaft each morning in a steel cage which swayed terrifyingly as it plummeted through hissing and rattling darkness. They followed their instructors along hot and dusty roadways, finding feet and heads had become nuisances as they stumbled over pulley-wheels or bumped their helmets into sudden low roofs which sagged between arched supports. Walt still wondered how men found their way through those mazed dark miles where suddenly the roof came low or the sides narrowed in and where other black tunnel mouths opened up on either side with no indication of where they led. He still wondered how you worked hard in that stuffy heat where raising an arm meant sweat trickling down your chest and ribs. It was going to take longer than three weeks to become used to it all; to working in only thin cotton pants besides boots, helmet and cap lamp, to utter darkness in which the lamp thinly flashed, to the sensation of being completely enclosed and to the fact that only a little of your surroundings could be seen at a time. Look up at the roof and the floor was invisible; look down and the roof was in darkness. A man had to turn his head and cap lamp constantly as he worked or walked, and was never completely sure of what might be in front of him or behind.

When he had tried to explain this to Bill, Walt had said that it was a different world and you just had to get used to living in it. Bill had remarked that before nationalization there had been no such training schemes and Walt should be grateful. But that was just his way of getting them back to politics so Walt had ignored it.

He grinned to himself as he thought of what he had said in his letter and remembered all he had seen. Young haulage hands had darted among the tubs as they clipped long trains of them on to a moving wire rope; a stumble could pitch them under the steel wheels grinding over the rails. He had watched them fasten the runs to overhead ropes by long chains, and seen how fumbling might mean severed fingers when the chain jerked and fifty tons of coal rumbled forward. In dark engine-houses the drivers listened to bell signals sent from miles away, and he was told that lives depended on those coded signals being followed correctly as the ropes throbbed around spinning drums. He had even visited the coal-face, crawling down an avenue of props three feet high for two hundred yards, with a wall of glinting coal where colliers knelt on one side of him and loaded conveyor belt running on the other, the waste ground beyond it a mass of jumbled stones where the roof had caved in. He had a confused impression, recalling this, of men with bodies streaked where sweat had washed away black dust, hurriedly working in cramped darkness among props and heaps of coal. It wasn't quite the way he had written, he thought, but he was eager to learn all this and he had attended closely when the instructors taught them simple jobs and lectured them on mining theory.

He rose from the table and gathered his things tidily.

'Put t' light out if you've done,' the old lady said. 'Save bills if we can.'

When Walt had switched off the light he sat in the other easy chair, looking at the flames sparkling on the steel grate and throwing shadows around the over-furnished room. He had no money for the cinema and it was raining too hard for him to be able to stroll around the city as he had been doing most evenings. He liked to take a bus down to the busy centre, and there, with the massive buildings surrounding him and the traffic rumbling past, he would watch the people and listen to their talk. He often looked at young couples with their arms entwined or noisy groups of his own age and wished that he had friends; the books which had always seemed more important than the places where he lived, and the pastime of boxing which had been his one outlet, were not enough for him now.

He sat in the firelight thinking that he wanted to become a part of the city and of its thousands of hard-working people. This was where he meant to live; the home of his own choice and therefore as much his as it was theirs who had merely been born here. The bombed ruins in the city's centre were like battle scars to him, making its courage manifest. The city was ugly and knew it, and tried to cover its knowledge with a touchy self-sufficiency, but it was this ugliness, brusque gruffness and lack of sophistication which made him like both the place and the people...

'What's look o' misery for? Homesick?'

Walt looked up and found the old lady watching him with a slightly derisive smile.

'Of course not.'

'Homesick'll get thee nowhere.' She looked down at her fingers as they forced the steel peg through the tough sacking. 'Sorry for hissen never made a good collier yet.'

'I'm not,' he said. He was wary of her, because, although she fed him well and was civil, he felt that she was sterner towards him than to Bill. It was as though he were being continually and secretly judged by her.

After a moment she told him that she had been orphaned at fourteen with two young brothers to care for.

'Never had time to be sorry for mesen,' she finished. 'Better for it and all. I brought 'em up. And dead now, both o' them.'

'You're right,' he said. 'People ought to stick up for themselves and make their own lives.'

She glanced up without answering. When she did speak, it was of her husband, who had died ten years ago of silicosis.

'Coughed his life away,' she said. 'And never shed a tear o'er hissen.' With the peg gleaming as it darted through the sacking, and one side of her face touched by the orange glow, she told Walt about her three sons who had all done well for themselves and were now in different parts of the country. Good lads they had been, she said, and had fine homes now of their own. He listened respectfully, seeing her pride, but he felt that the sons deserved a little sympathy, since, with such a mother to judge them, they must have been terrified of not doing well.

'And what about t' pit, then?' she asked abruptly. 'Think you'll stick it?'

'Sure.'

'Tha'll find it a far cry from this when it comes to risin' at four and goin' to graft instead of trottin' after a teacher.'

'I can do it,' he said. 'Don't you worry.' When she was quiet after that, he felt the victory was his.

At precisely nine o'clock, as on every other night, she went to the local pub with Mrs. Watson, the next-door neighbour whom Walt had seen peeping at him on his first day. She was a bespectacled, bony-faced little woman who cocked her head like a magpie while probing for gossip, or repeating it with smooth, precise malice.

'Tell Watson nowt,' the old lady had warned him. 'She were vaccinated with a gramophone needle.' Two other old women, as stout and almost as formidable as their champion, usually went with them, and he could imagine a sudden tension, a prospect of subdual, filling the men in the Cross Keys when it was time for the Gorgon-eyed quartet to arrive.

He went to bed early and lay reading one of Bill's books on popular science. Bill was at home by the time the old lady went out on Sunday evening and he and Walt sat reading in the easy chairs. They were already friends and had discussed in the past fortnight most of the subjects which appeal to young men who read a great deal; their own ideas being favourite. In spite of their basic difference in attitudes they rarely argued, because Bill would smile when Walt grew heated, and say in his usual diffident way that most things were just a matter of opinion, anyway. But he was much more enthusiastic about politics, and that night he put down his newspaper and began indignantly haranguing Walt on how a Member of Parliament had been expelled from the Labour Party because, with forty others, he had sent a goodwill telegram to an Italian Socialist Party.

'But those Eyeties are pro-Communist, aren't they?' Walt grunted behind his book.

'So what? Why can't British Socialists wish other Socialists luck?'

He ignored the question; it was rhetorical, anyway. Bill knew as well as he did that the word 'Communism' was used as a synonym for the cause of every trouble in divided Europe; or in China, Greece, Malaya and all other countries torn by civil war or rebellion.

'Answer me,' Bill said. 'I'm serious. Will you?'

Walt lowered his book for a moment, irked by the idea of another one-sided argument. He pointed out that the Prime Minister had said that the fight was on, the country involved and that Communists would be barred from security positions.

'You can't go on saying stuff like that and have your own gang sending them goodwill messages, can you?' he asked reasonably. 'I mean, it makes him look a bit daft.'

Bill said that wasn't the point. Communists and Socialists were anti-capitalist whatever country they belonged to, and so was the Labour Party.

'Why should they be enemies?' he demanded, his hair already hanging over his eyebrow. He was prepared to force the issue for once.

'I've told you I'm not interested in politics,' Walt said, and raised his book again.

'But just answer me this, please. I want to know what you think.'

'I don't think anything!' He snapped the book's covers together. Politics bored him intensely because they were involved and pompous-phrased and because he knew that when all the long-winded talk was finished the same things would still be going on. He had rejected politics in the same way that another generation had rejected religion; they were part of his parents' standards, not his.

'Look,' he said, 'I've got nothing against them and don't care what they do in their own countries. But they aren't like *us*, you know. I mean, it's all right in those backward places where half of them can't read or write— they don't mind dictatorships and military rule—but...'

'Why, that's nonsense,' Bill exclaimed. 'You know nothing about them. That's propaganda straight from the papers, and the papers are against them.'

Still patient and reasonable, Walt answered that Bill could only know what he read also.

'The stuff you read is propaganda for them. So why should we argue?'

'I can't understand you,' Bill said. 'With a family like yours—yet you turn your nose up every time I mention politics. Walt—' with his eyes round and earnest in his round, earnest face, he leaned nearer—'don't you believe in Socialism? The thing in itself?'

'The thing in itself?' Walt repeated the words in a mockingly pompous way, holding up the book like a lay preacher brandishing his Bible before a street crowd. Then half seriously he said: 'What you mean would be great. No more slums and poor people—no drunkards—no more wars...' As Bill nodded approvingly, Walt tapped his head with the book and grinned. 'Wake up, Bill! Not in this kind of world with this kind of Socialists and this kind of people. It's a dream that all your political talkers will never see.'

'If you could see yourself...' Bill sat back, looking disgusted, while Walt grinned. 'A blasé ninety-years-old look in your face!'

'And if you could hear yourself, Comrade Spenser! Spouting that stuff from your books and pamphlets. This is about the fourth time you've started this and the first time you haven't dragged Joe Stalin or Bernard Shaw or Marx or somebody else in to talk for you!' Bill looked so surprised that Walt, beginning to enjoy himself, leaned forward in his turn and went on: 'You're a quoter. You do make some sense when you talk for yourself, but when it's politics you chuck out your own ideas and use theirs. You're not saying what you really think— don't know what you really think. You're talking lumps of somebody else. You couldn't argue without your quotations.'

'Who couldn't?' Bill demanded, nervously pushing his hair back, his fair skin flushed. Walt, grinning callously because he felt that Bill deserved teasing for being so intense yet so sensitive over rebuttal, and also because he meant to balk now every hope of further argument, tapped his knee and looked into his shining face as he said: 'You couldn't, Bill. I've heard some real quoters on about all this; Charles and his pals and my old man —my old man could go on for hours when he was drunk and in that mood—and they'd have talked rings round you. They made it sound like long-winded, big-worded tripe, and so do you. Have sense and drop it.'

'It's important to me,' Bill said with dignity as Walt sat back.

'No it isn't,' Walt said. 'You'd have done something about it. You'd be in the Labour Party or the Communist—though I don't know how much difference that makes. But at least you'd be banging a bigger drum with a lot of your own kind then.'

'That's just it, Walt,' Bill was immediately almost suppliant, stretching out his small hands, palm up towards him. 'You've lived with this—I haven't. I can't make up my mind exactly—'

'You're a talker and a quoter, that's why.' Walt suddenly picked up his book again, because he had grown unreasoningly angry at Bill. 'Shut up about it!'

'All right, then,' Bill said huffily, and picked up his newspaper. 'I just wanted your opinion.'

'The only bloke I know who was genuine and not a talker and quoter,' Walt said, holding the open book tightly with a page slowly tearing under a rigid thumb, 'got himself killed before he could tell me his opinion. So I don't have one. I just know it wasn't for *politics* he did it.'

Bill looked up again to argue, but he saw Walt's face and, after a moment, shrugged and resumed his reading. Walt rose from his chair a few minutes later and went to bed, to lie alone and listen to the incessant slow thud from far away.

On the following Friday he completed his training, filled in a test paper on simple arithmetic and mining theory and returned to his own colliery in the city. He was told to start work on Monday morning at half past five.

'You'll go pony-driving,' the labour officer said. 'Twenty days' training and then you're on your own.'

As soon as Walt had stamped into the living-room at home where Bill was curled up dozing in an easy chair, he began expostulating over the continued training.

'Twenty days,' he said indignantly. 'When am I going to be a miner?'

As Bill, who had gone to work at five that morning, blinked sleepily at him, Walt added fiercely that he didn't want any of that 'grateful' stuff either. So Bill smiled, with a finger to his closed lips, and shrugged at him. After a moment Walt muttered:

'At least I'll be getting up early now—so she won't be able to make cracks about that!' And he nodded towards the kitchen where the old lady was cooking dinner behind the closed door.

'Consolation already,' Bill said. 'This feud gets dead exciting at times, doesn't it?'

They went out together that evening.

'It's pretty early,' Walt said, as they stood in the street with the tall standard lamps burning white above them in the twilight and many people hurrying by. 'What shall we do?'

'Come on, we'll go to Atwell's. I've a friend there I want you to meet, anyway.'

As they walked towards the district where the biggest theatres and hotels and cinemas were, and where there were always crowds at night, Bill answered his questions about Atwell's.

'It's a sort of cafe, you know... People go and drink tea or coffee and natter. A whole crowd used to go from the university and college, but they seem to have dropped off lately. At one time you couldn't get a seat and they'd be at it all night—just talking and meeting each other.'

'Who's the friend?'

'A bloke called Andrew Mason. Lectures at the college.'

'Oh.' He was a little disappointed that it was a man, but went along cheerfully, looking at the couples lingering around doorways and shop windows and the young people laughing and, chattering as they passed in groups. From the open windows of dance halls came snatches of music and singing voices, and with the buildings around them bulked against a lowering dark sky, the traffic flashing and the people jostling at corners, he felt the excitement and gaiety of the coming night and wished he could have more share in it. Glancing round at Bill, who was walking with his head down and hands in his jacket pockets, Walt told himself that he had the wrong kind of companion.

'I'm glad I'm my age,' he said. 'By the time I'm twenty-one or so we'll have got over the war. There'll be plenty of everything again and we'll be able to have smashing times.'

Bill looked up as they turned a corner and they went on walking down a dark and quiet street behind a theatre which wore huge posters on its grey walls.

'If we live that long,' he said. 'If we get the chance...'

'Oh, for Pete's sake!' Walt pushed his hands into his pockets and scowled. 'Knock it off.'

'We could be in one before you know.' They came to a lighted doorway beside a long lace-curtained window and Bill stopped. He faced Walt and said: 'You can growl, but there could be a blow-up any time.'

'All right, if there is, there is!' He raised one shoulder impatiently. 'We can't stop it whatever we do and we'd just have to try to come out of it alive. There's more important things to think about than that.'

'Than war? Another war?' Bill stared up with his face wrinkled as though trying to perceive Walt's real thoughts; as though his words could not possibly be meant literally.

'Just you keep thinking about it, then—you'll go off your nut in this world. This the place?'

Bill nodded as his hand slowly rose to push back his forelock. He opened the door with a last look at Walt over his shoulder, and they entered a yellow-lit room where there was a monotonous secretive drone of quiet conversation. Most of the square tables were occupied and a group of girls with coats around their shoulders were sitting on stools at the long counter. Bill waved to someone in a far corner while Walt was still blinking in the sudden light, which was not actually very bright. The stout, dark-complexioned and black-eyed woman working behind glinting, steaming copper urns and glass-encased shelves laden with cakes and sandwiches poured two coffees for them.

'Chorus girls from the Empire,' Bill murmured as Walt glanced round at a shrill and ragged laugh. Their make-up looked orange in this light and their eyes blue-shadowed and peculiarly hollow. He felt that the one who was laughing had seen him turn, had studied him briefly and looked away while her head was still tilted back and her mouth was open.

Bill picked up the cups and led the way to the corner table with Walt following and still glancing round at the seated people he passed and at photographs of variety stars which decorated the blue walls.

'Hullo, Bill. We hoped you'd come.' At the table were three men and a girl, the oldest man standing up and smiling across the table at them. He was tall and thin with a fleshless and big-boned face, and eyes made huge by thick rimless spectacles. One patch of light brown hair still grew on the crown of his head and was plastered thinly over as much of his skull as was possible. Bill introduced him as Andrew Mason. As they shook hands, Walt staring fascinated at the cadaverous face and prominent, convex teeth, Mason said: 'Pleased to meet you so soon. I've heard of you, you know.' He wore a brown corduroy coat, grey trousers and a brown knitted tie with a soft white shirt. Bill introduced him to the others, then they sat down, Walt in front of the table with the girl on one side of him and one of the young men, a handsome, slight youth also wearing a corduroy coat, on the other, while Bill went around to sit opposite with

Mason. The stocky young man sitting at a corner between Mason and the girl was growing a beard, which was at present struggling through in fuzzy brown patches. The girl was small and dark-haired, her face softly tanned, which seemed to him curious for an English girl in early May. Her name was Elaine Stewart and she was very pretty. She wore a tweed coat and skirt and green sweater.

'The friend of Bill's I mentioned,' Mason was saying to the others. He smiled again to Walt. 'A coal-miner, I understand?'

As Walt nodded, knowing that Bill was quietly watching and beginning to wonder if there were a purpose behind his being brought here, the stocky youth asked him what he thought of nationalization.

'I mean,' he said, 'you're seeing it at first hand, aren't you?'

Walt said it was all right, glanced suspiciously at Bill and lifted his cup. He tasted the coffee and remembered he didn't like it.

'John is doing economics, you see,' Mason said. 'He's naturally interested.' They were watching Walt as though disappointed.

'You're at the university, then?' Walt looked at the bearded youth. Mason's voice, although his tone was pleasant, was high-pitched and, as though because his teeth were too big for his mouth, his speech was slurred at times in a slightly unctuous way. Walt disliked both high-pitched and unctuous voices in men or women and felt uncomfortable when he looked at the teacher. The bearded youth said that all three of them were students.

'You're lucky,' Walt said casually and pushed his cup and saucer away.

'Elaine.' Bill was first to speak after a moment. 'You're a keen novel-reader, aren't you? You should really talk to Walt—he knows his books.' Then he turned to Mason and said he wanted to talk to him. As Bill, Mason and the two young students leaned their heads together, Walt was left to look at the girl and smile uncertainly, thinking nervously that she was awfully attractive.

'What are your favourites?' she asked. 'I love to read, too.' Her voice was light and quick, yet each word was clearly enunciated. As he talked to her, half turned in his chair, he watched the light from the neon tube above them ripple over her black and glossy hair, sparkling when she moved her head. Her large dark eyes slanted upward a little at the corners, the long black lashes looking heavy, just as the wavy frame of her hair looked too thick and heavy for such tiny features. When she smiled he felt a slow heat in his neck and ears.

You'll have to get used to girls like this some time, he told himself severely, but he had to look away before the blush would fade. The familiar sense of his own awkwardness stiffened his neck and lips and he jerked his chair back a little from the table, sprawling and shoving his hands into his pockets with his chin down. She mentioned some lady novelists and he had to admit he had read none of them.

'Oh,' she said, 'I prefer women as writers. Haven't you read any at all?'

'I'd rather read men,' he answered, and as they looked at each other he thought her eyes changed expression and her lips twitched and wondered what was funny. After this admission he had to make further ones: he didn't know much about poetry, didn't know much about jazz and hadn't read reviews in the *New Statesman*.

'What magazines do you read?'

He said none actually, and no special newspapers either.

'Well, it's all the same old stuff, isn't it?' he added, and her eyebrows arched. He stuck his legs straight out and looked at the others, who were still huddled together. He frowned petulantly and muttered: 'Politics again, I bet!'

'Don't you like them?' She put an arm on the table and leaned towards him a little with her head on one side.

'Me?' Walt said. 'I've enough to live for without them.'

'That makes a change,' she smiled. He noticed the bearded youth glancing round for a moment and glancing again at Elaine before he turned back to Bill.

'He your boy-friend?' Walt asked quietly, nodding his head at him.

'John? Well—in a way. Why wouldn't you tell him about mining?'

'I didn't say I wouldn't! I don't want to talk about what he'd want to talk about, anyway.'

'Would you tell me about it, then?'

He nodded. The way she said 'tell me', with a smile and dark wide-eyed look, suggested a special intimacy and he began blushing again. He glanced at Bill to make sure he wasn't listening, then said casually that right now he was pony-driving.

'Is it really bad? Are the conditions awful? I mean—such a job...' Even her tiny shiver and frown of distaste were attractive and it occurred to him that each movement seemed a trifle too graceful and each word a little too carefully modulated to be completely spontaneous.'

'Well, of course,' he said gravely, 'you have to be up to it physically.' And went on talking with the air of a veteran about what he had seen at his training pit, while telling himself that if she could put it on so could he. He drew his chair close to the table while he talked and Elaine leaned back, one arm hanging over the spar behind her. As she did so, her breasts made twin points in the loose sweater with the green cloth sliding to the curve of her waist, and Walt, forgetting awkwardness and blush, felt his arms and legs grow tense as though he had climbed into a boxing ring. When the chorus girl's shrill laugh suddenly jarred on him his whole body jerked. He went on talking, his eyes lowering to her sweater repeatedly and hastily rising again to her face. When Andrew Mason spoke to him, Walt had one arm on the table and was leaning over just as the girl had recently been doing.

'But we're ignoring you Walt. How impolite.'

He assured Mason it was quite all right, but everyone Was sitting back in a way that made the conversation general, so Walt reluctantly looked at Bill, who had gone on talking:

'The point is that they can urge other Social Democrats to hold out against them all they like, but they just can't!' Walt sighed at the familiar tone and phrases, but the others were listening and Mason was nodding. 'Europe's divided between capitalism and Communism, and Social Democracy hasn't a hope. We can't go on living in the past and thinking purely island thoughts.'

'Quite true,' Mason agreed. 'That much I admit—'

'Hey,' Walt interrupted. 'Are you a Communist?'

'Well, no.' Mason smiled as he shook his head. 'Some of my ideas, I'm afraid, aren't compatible with the party line. Others don't suit the Labour Party,' he added flippantly and smiled wider.

'You have to decide where you stand,' Bill said hotly, the forelock bouncing.

'Calmly, Bill, calmly...' Mason soothed him, then said to Walt: 'I'm afraid Bill is the budding Communist here—highly promising material. The rest of us at present are more or less observers—sympathetic, mind you, but trying to make sense, if we can, of everything. Elaine's sister is another fire-eater who feels a little contemptuous of us now, I think.'

'Of course she doesn't,' Elaine protested.'

'Good—I have great respect for Judith and Don.'

Walt felt sorry for Bill. Mason had spoken in a kindly way to him, yet there had been a touch of admonitory condescension.

'Bill and this Judith look the best of your bunch to me,' he said briskly. 'If they believe in it there's more credit in doing something than in sitting around talking like a bunch of intellectuals.'

Bill grinned delightedly, the girl frowned and forgot to look cute, and the other three stared at one another.

'He uses the word quite indiscriminately,' Bill told them, with difficulty, since he could not stop grinning. 'He has a poor opinion of these intellectual types.'

Mason leaned over the table, blinking behind his spectacles to say that surely, from what Bill had said, he was something of an intellectual himself? He jerked back quickly at Walt's fierce outburst.

'I'm a man of action,' Walt said, when he had finished telling them that he was no sissy, then he glanced to see how the girl liked that, saw her staring, and sat back satisfied.

'Go on,' Bill murmured softly to Mason, and Walt looked sharply at him. 'I've been wanting to see this...'

'Very well,' Mason said, smiling again. The others lounged back in their seats, looking at Walt over the stained cups on the glass table-top. Voices still droned on all around them, but the chorus girls were leaving, the banging door cutting off the last harsh shriek of mirth. 'As a man of action, Walt, what is your plan for this world of ours? The Communist Party?'

'No,' he answered. 'I thought that was yours. I haven't any plan and I'm not interested in politics.'

'But...' Mason was leaning towards him again, thoughtfully scraping a long fingernail on the glass. 'Don't we all have to be interested in the future?'

'I guess so.' Bill was smiling as he lit a cigarette, obviously preparing to enjoy himself. Walt felt sure that this had been engineered, and also felt, resentfully, that an attempt was being made on his right to his own ideas. 'The future's going to come through, whether we're interested or not.'

Mason suggested, like a prosecutor forcing slow admissions by casual but adroit questions, that surely politics determined what kind of future it was going to be?

'Why does it have to be politics?' Walt asked, as mildly and casually as the questions were put, tilting back his chair gently but growing warily stiff in the legs and arms.

'For the good reason that politics affect everything and involve everyone—including yourself, Walt.'

'Not me,' he said.

'Even you.'

'No!'

'Careful, Andrew,' Bill grinned. 'Walt can get tough on this subject.'

'If what you've said is true...' Mason glanced at him and then smiled amicably at Walt. 'What he has to say is worth at least listening to. Why aren't you involved, then, Walt?'

He frowned. He had never examined the subject, and, when he tried to, found irritation prickling up with every thought. He had condemned Bill for quotations, yet it was easier to draw analogies or examples from the neatly expressed ideas in the library of his own mind.

'In a book of Graham Greene's,' he said slowly, while he mentally thumbed through one page after another in a frantic search for answers to the next probable arguments, 'there's a piece about a battle that's going on in some mist or smoke or something... Anyway, each soldier has his own little fight to sort out and he doesn't know how the big one's going on, and doesn't much care either as long as he keeps winning. That's natural. My personal scrap is enough for me right now.' He lowered the chair gently on to its front legs again, hoping they would be awed into silence, but Mason spread out his hands and said happily: 'There you are. You admit you're part of the battle—and if the battle is lost the soldier is lost.'

'I'm not a part the way you mean. Anyway, this battle goes on and on, and it will after I'm dead.'

Mason said with surprise that surely it was his as much as anyone's.

'How can you feel you're not responsible?'

Coming from a self-styled observer, he thought, this sounded too much like argument for its own sake. And Mason and the other youths sounded too much like those intellectuals he despised. Therefore Walt suddenly planted his elbows on the table, knocking over a cup which Elaine caught at the table's edge, and said brusquely: 'Now listen. This country's in a mess, right? Because of the war. So's the world, too—that's what you're binding about. But it was all decided and done before I was born or old enough to have any say—and I've no say now. Listen...' Without knowing why, he was saying defiantly: 'I was born in a slum!'

'That's a shame,' Mason said sympathetically, but seemed to have missed the defiance. 'Not a very easy place to grow up in, I imagine.'

'Never mind that.' He was half ashamed because he had spoken boastfully. 'I meant to say this: my old man got crippled in the first world war and my brother got killed in another. There was a war in China the time I was born, and there was a war in Spain, and then the last war, and there's all sorts of little wars going on now. But it was you—' his stabbing finger almost struck Mason's nose—'your generation that balled yourselves up. I didn't pick it and I'm not worrying about it any more than I have to. I've a life of my own I haven't worked out yet.'

All were quiet for a moment; Walt breathing a little heavily with his jawbones protruding, the girl looking at him, Bill thoughtfully trimming his cigarette and Mason smiling gently over pyramid-joined hands at Walt, his elbows also on the table. Walt was staring back as though at an enemy.

'A world you never made,' Mason said softly. 'It's an old cry, you know, Walt.'

'I couldn't give one damn less!'

'What happens to the world has to involve you, don't you see? Its standards, morals and values are yours too. If it's in a mess, then so are you. You and—'

'No!' Walt jerked back in the chair and slapped both hands on the table. 'I'm me, whatever the world is.' Out of the defiance and dislike, the anger goading him, came a remembered phrase that he happily welcomed as inspiration. To their surprise, he grinned suddenly, relaxed, and said, 'I'm a good lion,' and leaned back, lips pursed, turning his head airily to look at the couples and groups at the other tables. Most of them looked a bit snooty, he thought, though there was a group of his own age talking and nodding cheerfully across the room.

'Well, tell us,' Bill asked at last. 'What is a good lion?'

'You should know; it's in one of your magazines,' he answered, and leaned on the table again as he explained, his mind many phrases ahead of his words: 'It's a scientific world—I mean, we can split atoms and all sorts of things—so you need a scientific outlook.'

Mason removed his spectacles and squinted hard at him while polishing them on his handkerchief. Walt waited politely until he had them on again.

'Well, the scientist doesn't see life as intellectuals, and that kind do. He doesn't care about morals and standards or ordinary good and bad. He thinks functional value and survival value are what count. So, to the biologist, the lion that kills a deer and eats it isn't a bad lion; it's a good lion.'

'Just a minute!' Mason interrupted incredulously.

'Let me finish.' Walt waved a hand at him, his ideas joining and eagerly supporting one another like good soldiers. It was as though he had rehearsed this many times before. 'The lion is functioning properly. It doesn't give a damn what the others are .doing or who's king of the jungle; it's doing what's natural to it, what's right for it and what it wants to do. It's got functional value and survival value. So—' he raised both hands, palm up—'I'm going to have survival value and I'll do what's right for me and what I want to do. You please yourselves.'

He sat back smiling while Mason ruefully shook his head, its bald half gleaming.

'That's a childish argument, Walt.'

'Okay,' he agreed mildly. 'Knock it down.'

'Well, it's so— Look here, what if we all went about like that? The world would *be* a jungle—we'd go back to prehistory. And pity the poor deer in it!'

'The world *is* like that,' Walt protested indignantly. 'The deer are those who don't realize it. A different kind of jungle—it's a scientific one, like I said. You've been on about Europe —the Reds are trying to kick us out of Berlin. They want to grab Germany for themselves and be the bosses in Europe. They're being good lions. We're being good lions and won't let 'em. The world's running like that.'

He turned to Bill, who was watching with round, perplexed eyes.

'You were on about Churchill the other night, Bill, and reeling it off about his always changing. You couldn't understand how he could once turn bayonets out against the miners, then be a brave war-leader and then say silly things about Gestapos against the Labour Party. That's what you said.'

Bill nodded.

'He's a good lion,' Walt told him. 'He's consistent—fighting every time for what he believes in and attacking what threatens his cause. The miners were deer and Labour was deer...' He paused reflectively. 'I guess you couldn't call the Nazis deer, but, anyway, all the great men like him were really good lions. What's happened to the world's been a sort of side-effect of them doing what they wanted to do.'

'He can talk the hind leg off a donkey when he does start,' Bill muttered. He threw up his arms and asked Mason: 'Andrew, what is he? Anarchist, nihilist or what?'

'Egotist?' John added, glancing at Elaine before he looked at Walt.

'He's seventeen,' Mason said, smiling now at them all. He reached over and patted Walt's hand, which was immediately withdrawn. 'He was doing quite well for a while there, but— Tell me, Walt, are you classifying us as deer—or pariah dogs?'

'I don't think we'll have that one answered, if you don't mind,' Bill said, pushing his chair back as he stood up. 'Come on, Walt, let the deer and the lion amble off together.'

Walt was still sitting tensely, though appearing relaxed, smiling speculatively at John's beard, then looking up into his eyes.

'To be a lion,' he said, 'you have to be better at fighting than talking.'

'Are you?' John asked with interest.

'Yes. Are you?'

'Come on, Walt,' Bill said at his shoulder, pulling his coat. Walt stood up and looked down at Elaine. Her eyes were slowly moving, contemplating his hands, his chest and shoulders, then his face. As he grinned her eyes widened momentarily, then the heavy lids drooped and she smiled in return.

'Walt, you must come again,' Mason said heartily. 'I can't let you get away with that.'

'Maybe,' he said.

'Do come,' Elaine said, and leaned back to look up at him, her breasts protruding once more. 'And we'll talk about books, not biology or politics.' Knowing that she was being consciously provocative did not make her any less attractive. He felt she was the kind of girl who should be having fun with others like herself instead of sitting in this dull place, and wondered why she came here.

'I'll be seeing you,' he said, as they went to the door.

It was dark outside and the traffic passed the end of the street in a chequered flow of light with people suddenly jerking into sight against the bright background and vanishing again. Walt was trying to apply his theory to as many facets of his life as he could. He decided it was pretty good, especially as he had worked it out while he talked. You'd have to go along with your own kind of conscience, of course; to go against it would be against yourself—a bad lion.

'I'm just a genius, I suppose,' he said, cheerfully facetious as they walked along.

'Walt, you really live by fiction, you know. You said some trite things. Besides—'

'What?' They turned a corner, making their way by dark side-streets to the bus station.

'You'd be completely on your own. Nothing to believe in except Walt Morris.'

'It's good fiction, anyway,' he answered. 'I don't want any more politics.'

'Okay,' Bill said. 'Only I know some really good arguers you should meet.'

'Communists, I bet.'

As Bill began to say this made no difference Walt repeated sternly that he wanted no more of that stuff. Their footsteps clopped back at them as they walked past dark, silent warehouses and offices with shiny black windows.

'John nearly got a punch on the nose,' Walt remarked after a while. 'Egotist!'

'Ah, he's all right. He's nuts on Elaine, that's all. She's not serious, though.'

Walt asked how Bill had come to know them, and Bill explained that he had first gone to Atwell's with students from the college and become friendly with Mason and his group because they talked politics.

'She's good-looking, isn't she?' Walt remarked when Bill had finished.

'You're only interested in her, aren't you? She's broken a few hearts at the college. She's a bit of a flirt, but from what I've heard she's no free-and-easy type about her virtue. Her father's some kind of business-man, you know.'

'And her sister's a Socialist?' He stared round at Bill.

'Well, sure.' Bill shrugged and said: 'Judith and her father don't talk, so they say, but Elaine lives with her, anyway. He's in London.'

'Idle rich, eh?' Walt said enviously.

'Oh, I don't know. She has to go to university, but she does commercial classes at the college too, for some career she's after. She's a nice kid and she's bright. Likes people. She doesn't go to Atwell's very often, mind you.'

Walt was thinking, while Bill talked, that he was going to meet some more girls like that if he could. He was going to have some friends, too. But not the kind Bill had.

IV

For a moment the white light glistened over the pony's glossy, clay-splashed coat. Then Walt dropped his head again and strained harder as the pony scrambled on the slope with his belly sucked in, his back arched and hooves splashing and clopping. Walt's naked shoulders, bunched like the pony's powerful haunches, were set against a cold iron tub and his heavy boots slipped repeatedly on the wet ground. Bryan Foster was shoulder-heaving at the first tub and yelling: 'Go on then, Tommy lad! Dig 'em in, old love.'

The pony stopped struggling and rested, leaning against his chains and gathering his strength tight while the two youths helped him fight the weight of five empty tubs. Their lamps beamed in one another's faces as Walt stiffly turned his head and Bryan grunted to him: 'Knows he should only have three on at this steep, see?' Then the light flashed over the surrounding stone as he turned: 'They's two on us pushin', Tom. Come on then.'

The pony snorted violently, raising his leather-shielded head and making harness and side-chains rattle and jingle as he shook his whole black body.

'Now, Tom!'

Down went the hammer head and up sprang the jaunty, docked tail; the chain cracked tight and Tom's head rose again, ears erect, neck rigid and eyes glaring as the tubs eased upward. Bryan and Walt thrust out their legs and dug their heels into the slippery ground while their lamps patterned the darkness with white streaks. Both shouted encouragement as the sturdy pony bounded up and on to level ground with the tubs rolling after him one by one, and then Bryan yelled to Walt: 'Jump on, kid. Its downhill now and he'll stop for nowt.' He sprang between two tubs and Walt jumped on to the buffers of the last one. As he clung there, with the tub rattling and jolting, the rocky sides and arching steel supports flying past, his lamp's beam flickered about and the darkness leaped after it. Over the iron tubs could see Bryan's bulky figure, his grimy singlet and thick arms muddied, and he could see the sway and jerk of Tom's haunches and the bobbing of his bushy tail.

This is the life, he thought happily, though sweat had pasted his singlet to his skin and made the leather in the rim of his hard hat chafe his forehead. He could hear Bryan singing:

'Back to Sorre… hento…Or I-hi…muhustdie…'

The stone suddenly swept down and he had to crouch, clinging by his hands with his head bent and his lamp glaring on his doubled knees, looking at the ground rushing past close below. This was the kind of risky thrill you might get from careering down a long hill at night on a bicycle without lights or brakes. How did the pony manage to gallop, avoiding sleepers and other obstructions and ducking under low roof, when he was in darkness? Walt could not understand; yet the pony never hesitated or broke step once before the ground began rising again and he slowed down. He stopped without orders when they reached a branch line which curved off from the main rails into a low roadway. When Bryan had thrown over the point rail and Walt had unlinked the last two tubs, the pony moved again, pulling into the tunnel, but he halted when Bryan called:

'Whoa-back, Tom; let's have a minute.'

As Tom turned his masked head to look back and struck one hoof impatiently on the ground, Bryan said to Walt: 'He knows it's about snap-time and wants to get up there. But we'll have a minute first and let him get his wind.' He squatted on his heels, looking up at Walt, who stood by the pony's head and stroked his bristled nose.

'Gettin' the hang of it, Walt?'

'Have a heart,' he answered, smiling as he pushed back his helmet to ease the weight of the lamp from his chafed brow. He was still confused by the little roadways, all alike, which branched off from the main level.

'This is Joby's stall? Right?'

'Right,' Bryan nodded. 'You'll soon gaffer it, kid. You're doing fine.'

This seam—a shallow one and cold and wet—was being worked by old-fashioned methods. Pairs of colliers drove their stalls through the coal so that there was a maze of narrow tunnels with pillars of coal between them. The pony-drivers took in empty tubs for them to fill and brought the full ones out to the main haulage level, where other lads took over. There was another and much deeper seam where the coal was got by the modern method of long-faces on which many colliers worked; that seam was hot and dry.

'Don't you get tired, though, on this shift?' Bryan said. He had switched out his lamp for a moment. 'I were out while twelve last night.' He was two years older than Walt and of the same height, but more heavily built than the average full-grown man, with broad heavy shoulders, a bulging chest, thick waist, and rib-box a massive arc. Walt thought his square, heavy-jawed face more likeable than any fine-featured good looks. He was cheerfully friendly and frequently singing snatches of popular songs.

Walt said he felt tired too, though he had gone early to bed the previous night. That morning at half past four as he had struggled sleepily out of bed he had envied Bill, who grunted 'Good morning' and turned over. He and Bryan had been in the pit for four hours now, and although they had been working hard they had also talked a great deal. Bryan was full of questions about what the young ones wore in London and what the girls were like and what kind of night life there was.

'Hey?' he asked, as the pony impatiently stamped again. 'Ever go to one of them night clubs?' When Walt said he hadn't, he said:

'By, I would've done if I'd been you. Anyroad—' he rose slowly, switching on his lamp again and stretching his arms wide as he yawned —'let's get up there or Tom'll be leavin' us.'

This time they ran in front, bent over under the low roof with the pony chasing their flashing lamps and the three tubs drumming on the rails behind him. They ran into the stall where two colliers knelt shovelling, and stopped by a tub loaded with lumps of glittering coal. Tom came up the fifty yards in a panting gallop, straddle-legged and lathered, stopping when his nose touched the tub.

'It's about snap-time, you know, lads,' one of the colliers said as they put their shovels down. They turned the tubs empty tubs over and lowered the full ones to the bottom, then went back up to the stall where Tom was waiting, his nose twitching and his eyes glaring orange inside leather circles. Bryan and Walt took their snap-tins off their belts and sat on a wooden prop, the two colliers sitting opposite with water-bottles between their knees.

'And how does pit work suit thee, son?' one of the colliers asked. He was Joby: a squat man with thick arms and a huge paunch which glistened naked above the waistband of his trousers. His mate, Cyril, was a thin man with rounded shoulders. Both were over forty and both men's bodies were oily with sweat and dust, their teeth and eyes shining white in black faces. Walt said pit work was fine.

'And our Bryan's goin' filling, eh?' Joby went on. 'Think he'll make a collier, Cyril?'

Cyril grunted, his mouth full of bread. The pony came nosing among them, reaching out with large convex yellow teeth, and Walt, reminded of Andrew Mason, grinned as he held out a crust.

'Turn your light down,' Cyril told him, and Walt switched his lamp over to the small pilot-bulb as the others had done. In this dim ring of light they ate their sandwiches and drank cold water, with the pony moving his head constantly from one to the other of them and receiving his share of bread.

'That's the lot, Tom,' Bryan said at last, pushing his head away and holding up his empty snap-tin. 'Go on, shift up, now.' Tom sniffed on the ground for crumbs and then ambled off to stand near the tunnel-face of coal, with his head drooping and chains dragging on one side. Walt leaned against a cold steel prop, his body heavy now that he was still. He looked up at the black roof, then at the tub waiting to be filled before a heap of coal, and his eyes closed. He could hear the coal crackling and crunching and the grunt of a wooden prop set near to it as the roof weight settled. He could smell the oil on a boring machine, the dampness of roof and floor, and the sweat of the men and the pony. He felt very tired.

It's hard work is coaling,' Joby was saying. He pronounced it "coyling."

'I know,' Bryan answered airily.

'Tha'll wish tha were back drivin' again.'

'Gerraway!' Bryan sounded as amused as Joby did. 'Twenty quid a week for shifting a bit o' black stuff? Any mug can do that.'

Joby laughed.

'Tha's been readin' t' papers again,' he said, and his mate added sourly: 'Tha'll be lucky if tha gets twelve at this pit when tha'rt on full money!'

How did you get used to rising so early? Walt wondered, feeling the pony's nose damp against his shoulder.

'Come wi' us, Bryan. Well give thee some graft to go at.'

'Likely! Modern mining, me. Long-wall work in t' Beasley seam. This pillar-and-stall work's played out.'

'So's pit work! You want to get out altogether.' Walt opened his eyes in surprise at Cyril's bitterness. He saw the thin man ramming the cork angrily into his bottle as he said: 'You and that young 'un there—you want to get out afore you're tied down wi' a wife and kids and you're too old to get out.' He switched his lamp over to full power and Walt blinked. ' 'Cause if you don't, you'll end up no better than that poor bugger there!' He jerked an arm at the pony, who stared with blank, luminous eyes and nodded back as though recognizing a salute. Walt sat forward with an effort.

'Old Tom's happy enough,' Bryan said, sounding used to and a little scornful of such advice. 'Take Tom out o' t' pit and he'd be lost. Me dad's had it all his life, hasn't he?'

'You'd never a' been down if you'd been mine,' Cyril said.

'Tha'd've been all right tryin' to stop me,' Bryan answered, amused again, and Joby chuckled.

'You're a young rip, you are.' His bald head shone startlingly white as he removed his helmet and took from it a large piece of chewing tobacco. He broke off a piece and threw it to Bryan. 'Here... Your dad's got my sympathy wi' one near as big as hissen to gaffer. He were sayin' in t' Falcon as he'd gied o'er tryin'.'

'Thanks, Jobe,' Bryan said, biting off a piece and tucking the rest into a pocket. 'Me dad's all right. It's me mother that's allus on at me.'

As the four of them struggled up, crouching low, the colliers putting aside their tins and bottles, the pony stepped towards them, with his harness trailing. Walt tidied it and began leading him down the roadway with Bryan behind them. Joby and Cyril were kneeling down among the coal.

'Bryan,' Cyril called. They turned. They could not see the colliers for the tub, though the lamps shone on the coal.

'Hey-up?'

'I'll gie thee t' next best bit of advice as anybody can.'

'What's that?' Bryan asked, as Walt crouched listening, with the pony licking at the salt sweat on his shoulder.

'Watch your back, kid. Allus make sure your back's covered safe. You'd be surprised at t' young uns as forget that.'

'Fair enough, Cyril.'

'He's right,' Joby added. 'Let some other mug be first to finish—you be him as lives longest. Watch your back, eh?'

Walt remembered two colliers he had seen greeting each other that morning in the pit bottom. One had been on night shift, and as he entered the cage had called to his mate (as other men might say 'Look after yourself' when parting):

'Watch your back, old lad.' He realized the words had significance.

'I'll do that, Joby,' Bryan answered, without their gravity. Then they went on down the roadway, leaving behind them the scraping of shovels and thud of coal on iron.

For another two hours they were busy delivering empty tubs to colliers who cursed them, some good-naturedly and others fiercely, if they had been waiting. After that it was easier, and at last they sat down to rest at the junction of three roadways where the ground was dry and even dusty. The pony knelt down in the dust and lurched on to his side, rolling in grey clouds with his harness jingling, his head curved between his waving legs and his eyes glittering in the light of their lamps.

'Don't know why he does that,' Bryan said. 'But he loves it.' They began talking, switching their lamps low, with the black tunnel-mouths facing them and the pony struggling to his feet to stand gently rocking, his head hung down. Bryan said he liked to hear a chap talk properly without sounding stuck up, and he'd bet Walt was well educated.

Just ordinary,' Walt said. 'I didn't like school.'

'Me neither. I were a proper dunce.' He told Walt of a fight he had been in on Saturday night at a dance. 'Two sailors, they were. Dead big-headed till me an' Hughie sorted 'em out. We're allus havin' barneys at the Memo... You go dancing much?'

'I've never been to a proper one,' Walt admitted. Bryan glanced casually at his slender body and said he guessed Walt wasn't the kind that liked scrapping. It was the look, the knowledge that he was thin in spite of all his exercise in the past, that made Walt say: 'I've done a lot of boxing. Lightweight.'

'Honest? Hey!' Bryan immediately suggested that Walt team up with him some time; he fought for a few pounds in local clubs now and again.

'It's all right when you want a few quid. My mate's a bit of a pro. I'll take you to Thorpe's gym wi' me some time.'

'I only meant youth-club stuff,' Walt said. 'I've packed it in now.'

He had begun boxing at thirteen, after his father, in one of those morose moods which usually preceded his leaving home or the family leaving him, had remarked: 'Well, however badly you seem to be doing, you won't end up a navvy. I doubt if you'll have the build for that!'

But Walt had decided that there wouldn't be any more boxing now he was living differently.

'I'll take you to the gym some time, anyway,' Bryan repeated as they began the long walk back to the stables with the grey-coated pony trotting in front of them. They left Tom snuffling at his manger and being cleaned down by an ostler with a wisp of hay between his teeth. In the steel cage, as it hurtled up the shaft to the sunlight with a cargo of men, Walt found himself sad for the pony's sake: Bryan had told him that Tom had spent fourteen years in the pit. Then, as the cage slowed and rose through brightening twilight, he told himself angrily that this was merely the kind of trite, gushing feeling he had to learn to control. This was the kind of life where you had to accept such things—yet he still felt sorry for Tom and his two dozen companions in the brick stables below, swaying and rocking as they slept or waited in the thick smell of bran and hay and urine.

The one-thirty hooter blared as they were putting their lamps away, and was still blaring as they walked across the dirty pit yard with the headstocks towering over them, wheels spinning, and the 'afternoon' men passing on their way to the shaft-side. The first shift was over, Walt thought, walking in a group of tired black-faced men with the sunlight warming him. He must have changed a little now; now that he knew the value of the sunlight and of air free from stale dampness, of seeing the whole of his surroundings and being free to move where he chose. He could see the world properly, he thought; simply and directly. You felt almost noble when you knew you had earned a day's wages by your body's strength.

'Thank Christ that's over,' Bryan said. 'I hate Monday—soon be weekend now, kid.' And Walt guiltily lowered his head, telling himself that he would really have to stop it; he wasn't reading books now.

The pit-head baths were in a long, low building and had been built many years ago. The men's clothes were hung on hooks which were pulled up to the ceiling by ropes and the showers were in cubicles all around the sides. The young ones skylarked and shouted insults at each other while they bathed and dressed. Bryan had let Walt share his hook, and while they were towelling themselves he introduced him to some of the others.

'Walt comes off the Clifton estate same as me,' he said, and added to Walt: 'We'll be able to go home together, lad, won't we?'

'He's Bevin boy, ain't he?' one youth asked. 'A Cockney!' He was a fairly broad youth with thick hair and long side-burns. It was difficult to tell if the hairs on his upper lip were the forerunners of a moustache or if he hadn't yet started shaving. Bryan told him that Walt was all right, adding casually as he rubbed his blond curly hair that Walt had done a bit of boxing.

'What were you? Featherweight?' the youth asked, and Bryan said:

'Knock it off, Mike. You're allus there wi' t' new lads.'

Walt said nothing, but from moments at work, in youth clubs or those other places where young men meet and some must try others out, he recognized the tone of voice. When he and Bryan were travelling home together in the tram, with two youths called Tug and Joe who also lived on the Clifton, he was feeling disturbed about what Mike had said.

'Does he like to take the mickey out of blokes?' he asked them.

'Old Mike? He does at first, but he's all right when he gets used to you,' Bryan told him. 'Listen, don't you forget you're coming to Thorpe's gym some time, kid.'

That afternoon Walt slept on his bed for two hours and had to be wakened at tea-time by Bill, who was on night shift. Over tea he described Bryan and the others and told Bill about his job while the old lady sat by the fire glancing at him now and again.

'New friends, then?' Bill said.

'They're smashing. Only they all call you "kid". It's like being in a gangster picture.' Later, before Bill went to work, he remarked that Walt hadn't thought much of Mason and the others, had he?

Walt said he thought Elaine was nice.

'They're not so bad really, you know,' Bill said. 'I mean, you just got off on the wrong subject. Andrew can be very interesting to listen to.'

'I just want to make friends with my workmates,' Walt said. 'I like them better.'

He was eager to be liked by them, just as he was eager to make a good miner. It was both these things which caused him to clash with Mike Fletcher, who was not a particularly dislikeable person but did feel that Walt should understand he was a novice. Walt's eagerness to learn and to do well, and the speed with which, during the week, he became friendly with Bryan and other youths, annoyed Mike. He treated him with a contemptuous brusqueness; a pose which impressed Walt at first. Arrogance usually did impress him at first, because he felt that people who acted in a self-confidently superior way towards him must know they had cause; but faced by arrogance, his own pride always eventually rose. By Thursday his temper was at a pitch of strained compression, and he could not stop thinking, when alone, of the trifling remarks which Mike had made about him in the pit or baths. What he lacked was the final drive of fear, and that came on Thursday afternoon when he turned on Mike after a reference to 'barrow boys'.

'You've been down on me all week,' he said. 'What's up with you?'

'Me?' Mike was grinning. They were drying themselves among a naked group of youths beside the cubicles with clothes hanging overhead, men strolling past with towels around their waists and the sound of singing and shouting all around. 'Maybe it's the lah-de-dah way you talk. Gets up my back.'

'I don't. And don't let it kid you, either.'

'Well... tough guy, eh?' Mike reached out, still grinning, to tousle his hair, but Walt pushed the hand away. The others were watching, but no one spoke, and an excited trembling fluttered in Walt's legs and loins as he realized that they considered this something for him to handle alone. He dropped his towel as Fletcher moved closer, furious at the grin, knowing the other only meant to impress on him his superior size and weight by a little rough handling, grappling and throwing him to the ground perhaps, but furious also at the idea of that. His own father had been heavy-handed in his morose moods, and Walt had a dread of physical helplessness, a terror of being in the grip of a stronger man.

'Keep off,' he warned as the hand reached out again.

'What you shaking for, tough guy? What you scared of?'

His left hand cuffed the reaching arm aside and he moved so suddenly, from a passive crouch to instant action, that Mike Fletcher was still grinning and glancing sidewise to see if the others were watching when Walt's left foot smacked on the wet floor, his body turning and all his weight lunging behind the rigid left arm as his fist hit Fletcher's mouth.

Walt felt a jolt, a shock travelling with infinite satisfaction through his arm to his heart, as the bigger youth staggered back and threw out his hands.

'Hey-up!' someone yelled. Walt's right was a mere steadying tap on Fletcher's chest, then the viciously powerful straight left hit the same place as before and the youth bounced back, feet skidding and legs shooting up, to thud down, sprawling, on the tiled floor.

'Bloody good hit,' an excited voice shouted. Walt's arms were jerking as he looked down and said: 'I told you to keep off.'

'I'll keep off,' Fletcher said, touching his bleeding mouth, then pushing himself unsteadily to his feet. 'I'll bloody kill thee!'

He moved to rush on Walt, who crouched with his fists up, but Bryan Foster pushed two youths aside and jumped between them. Water was sparkling on his hair and dripping from his arms.

'No you don't,' he said. 'You've been at him all week. Mike. It's fair enough.'

'He hit me when I weren't ready,' Fletcher complained, and tried to dodge round a thick, long arm. 'I'll kill him.'

'Let him come,' Walt said. 'Let him try and kill me—I'm not scared.'

They bristled and stuck their faces forward like fighting Irish Reds being breasted by their handlers, but Bryan kept them apart with the calm authority of one too big to be defied.

'He were stickin' up for hissen, same as you'd've done,' Bryan told Mike. 'Now that's that.'

'He can bloody shift,' a youth said. 'Did you see him, Bry?'

So the fight was stopped. As they were going home, sitting on the top deck with cloth-capped men on every seat, Bryan told Walt that Fletcher would leave him alone now.

'There's nowt wrong wi' Mike that belt on' t' teeth wouldn't fix,' he said, 'for all his rattle.' Then he questioned Walt eagerly about where and how he had learned to fight like that. When Walt said it came natural, Bryan sighed.

'Wish I could land a straight left like that.' As he turned excitedly, Walt was crushed against the window by his bulk. 'I like a bloke that's quiet and then sticks up for hissen. Just come to t' gym and let Alec Thorpe have a look at you—he knows his stuff and he loves to see a lad as can go. It's a real posh gym, you know, and he gets some real toffs there, but—' he smiled, proud of his friend—'old Alec only charges such as us a dollar a week. Got some money has Alec.'

Walt agreed to go, since Bryan was so keen to show off either him or this Alec Thorpe. As they parted outside the Luxor picture house, Bryan said, pushing his cap back over the damp curls, that a chap needed pals who were the right sort.

'I've cottoned on to thee,' he said, as shoppers and workmen strolled past them and the traffic rumbled in the street. 'Any time you need a hand, just whistle, see? I'm straight out, me. I'm t' pod in our mob but I've no special pal, except old Hughie and he's... Well, anyroad, I like a kid like you. Okay?'

'Okay,' Walt answered, and they solemnly shook hands. Bryan looked well satisfied as they left each other. Next morning in the pit he said several times that he was a lad who stuck to his mates once he'd made them, and stuck by them too. They went to Thorpe's gym that afternoon.

It was not far from the pit; a low green building like a huge shed behind a three-storeyed ivy-covered house, standing at the end of a wide drive in its own grounds on the outskirts of the city. In a little dressing-room, Bryan told Walt to strip while he fetched Alec Thorpe.

'He'll be in t' gym,' he said. 'He's never away. He's got a share in their kid's business, but he don't seem to do anything—knows everybody in the boxing game, though.'

Walt was sitting in a pair of trunks which had been lying on the bench when Bryan came back. With him was a man in. a white polo-necked sweater and flannels. He was of medium height, and though his cropped hair was white it was hard to assess his age, for his cheeks were smooth and rosy, his grey eyes brightly clear. His boneless nose was a little flattened, but not ugly.

'Well, well, well...' He examined Walt, smiling at him. 'I half expected Jimmy Wilde to be sat here after what Bryan said. What are you—nine and a half?'

Walt said about that, and he stood up, feeling embarrassed as they scrutinized him like a proud merchant and a buyer. Thorpe muttered that he had good long arms and legs, then asked abruptly: 'Who's your favourite boxer, Walt?'

'Freddie Mills.'

'Why?'

'Well...' Walt shrugged after a moment. '...You know. He's got more guts than the rest put together. He keeps taking 'em on bigger than himself. Well, he's a *real* fighter!'

Thorpe nodded thoughtfully, then said he'd like to see Walt in action. When Bryan had changed and both youths had put on a pair of light boots, they went into the gym, where a few men were already exercising. It was well equipped with swing-ball, punch-balls, a rowing machine and parallel bars. There were climbing rungs on the walls, weight-lifting apparatus in one corner, and in the middle of the room a large boxing ring raised two feet above the floor.

'In you get.' Thorpe put light boxing gloves over their hands before they clambered into the ring, then he sat on the edge of the dais watching them.

It was strange to stand again in a corner. Strange but exciting, with a deeper, more intense yet indefinable feeling in it than pleasure. Away, he could not recall how it felt; this slow preliminary tensing compounded of pugnacity, a touch of fear, and mounting energy. Walt Morris he still was, self-conscious and nervous, yet knew that in a moment that person would be evicted while his body fought. He and Bryan approached each other, one slow and massive like the great whale who has only to smite once, the other slender and taut, a hammerhead viciously intent on striking where he can without being struck. But they began badly, feinting and dodging slowly and throwing soft punches which were easily caught on the gloves.

'Come on,' Alec Thorpe called. 'Where's this lightning speed? If you're scared of hurting each other you'd better come back out.'

The trouble was, Walt thought, that he wasn't afraid of Bryan. He was conscious of his limbs and of the punches he intended to throw.

'Mix it a bit,' Thorpe said briskly. 'Push him a bit, Bryan.'

Bryan nodded and closed in on Walt. He said good-naturedly: 'Don't let me down, kid,' and a hard cuff jerked back Walt's head and blurred his eyes. Bryan tapped him twice in the face as he retreated.

'All right?' he asked, and came in again when Walt nodded.

'Go easy, now,' Alec Thorpe warned him, but that was needless, because Walt had gone through the transition which he could not control in any way and which always startled even himself. He had begun fighting in the only way he could fight well; with desperate ferocity and the fear that losing would mean being struck down, powerless. As Bryan swung, he ducked and skipped away crouching. He could watch and admire the skill and speed of his body as the left hand repeatedly jabbed at Bryan's incoming face. His head was low, his shoulders indrawn yet relaxed, and his legs smoothly moved as he skipped away or skipped aside, swerving adroitly when he sensed the ropes near his back. Three times Bryan struck, and missed badly, with Walt driving in a body blow for each miss. Bryan had to chase him, and he began frowning as some of his swings made him lurch, body extended.

Walt watched the ribs which Bryan's right swings uncovered, watching the weaving gloves too and the set of Bryan's feet, but he kept his eyes low all the time and gave nothing away. Again and again his punches struck Bryan's ribs while the big arms flew past his head, but he lacked the strength to make him stagger. His breath was like a hissing explosion through his nose each time he lunged or punched. Bryan grew tired of these rushes which only left him open to stinging punches, so he began wheeling his body around in the centre, covering up stolidly as Walt circled him and worked off his fury on the brawny arms.

Then Walt feinted, lowering his guard, and Bryan tried a left hook, dropping his right glove at the same time to guard his ribs, exactly as Walt had intended. Walt's counter hit the right side of Bryan's jaw, and as the big youth flinched and dropped his head, he saw exposed the old-time mark: the point where ribs join breastbone. He was already striking, left foot slamming down on the canvas, his weight behind the arm in a straight line to the solar plexus, and he felt that sudden jolt once more as Bryan grunted and bent away in pain.

'Time,' Thorpe called. Walt had already sprung forward and seized Bryan's arms worriedly, but Bryan was grinning as he straightened up.

'That were a fair thump, lad,' he said, patting Walt's shoulder when he could breathe properly again.

'Not bad at all,' Thorpe said. 'Come out of it, now.'

Walt asked Bryan if he wanted another round to get his own back, but Bryan cheerfully rubbed a glove over his head and said he was satisfied.

'Showed him, didn't we?' He climbed through the ropes and walked over to the swing-ball which was suspended between floor and ceiling by two rubber cables.

Easing down was difficult for Walt once his body was charged for fighting. He wanted to be rid of all his energy in one great burst. After a moment he vaulted out of the ring, picked up a rope from the floor and began skipping, with Alec Thorpe watching him.

Thorpe remarked quietly that Bryan had been right, he was pretty fast.

'First I've done for a while,' Walt answered, the rope vigorously lapping on the floor.

'I tell any lad who's any good the same thing...' Thorpe folded his arms and leaned against the ropes behind him. If you're keen, make some money out of it.'

Walt said that it was only a hobby. He was surprised at how good it felt to have fought again and how happy it had made him with himself. He had thought this was over.

'Look, amateur's all very well,' Thorpe said. was one—that's how I got this.' He pressed his flattened nose. 'I like amateur boxing, but I'm putting your point of view. Look you're at the age for dancing and girls, etcetera. Next week, in this game, you could have a busted nose or cauliflower ear...'

'Bryan was talking about something like that—' he breathed evenly as the rope whirred around him and smacked under his feet— 'but I wouldn't make a pro.'

'Bryan fights four times a year or less in some dingy club and thinks he's a pro! I wasn't thinking of that. What do you get out of it, Walt?'

He slowed down, then stopped and let the rope fall. As he sat down beside Thorpe, he said: 'Just fun. How do you mean?'

'Everybody gets something out of it.' Thorpe lifted his hands and smiled. 'Pros do it for the coin and because it's what they're good at. Some amateurs say it's the challenge, and so on—but you're the tiger type. They're the best and the worst and they can go a long way or do themselves a lot of harm.'

Walt frowned at him. Beside one wall he saw a fat man who was standing at a machine with a jiggling broad strap around his belly. Walt grinned and Thorpe said: 'Don't you grin at him. His kind make me a lot more money than you young ruffians do.' He waved his arm, indicating other men who were heaving at weights or working the rowing machine; one worriedly tapping occasionally at a punch-ball above his head and ducking when it flew back. Bryan was rhythmically punching and swaying as the swing-ball flew round in fast circles. 'It's the fat ones who pay.'

'Go on, then,' Walt said. 'What's a tiger type, really?'

'You know yourself—you know what you are in a ring. Bryan wasn't the right kind of opponent—he's simply a scrapper, not a boxer—but I was watching, and I'm an old hand. You don't fight for sport.'

'I enjoy it,' Walt said indignantly.

'Oh, sure, sure. Thorpe stood up, one hand in his pocket as he faced Walt. 'You'll enjoy it ever so much and be a real sport until someone really hurts you—then you'll try to murder him or you'll crawl away. You can never tell until the first time it happens. If you didn't crawl, and if you trained hard—I'll tell you frankly—you could do well in your own weight.'

Walt shook his head.

'I don't want to be a pro.' He did not want to base his future on that violent change which took place in the ring; he felt that there was a threat of guilt hidden in that. 'But'—he looked up—'I'd like to use the gym. Can I?'

'Sure.' Thorpe patted his shoulder. 'Five bob a week to you. I'll give you some tips, too. You know, I've been running this gym for ten years—I know a bit about boxers and about young lads. Be as good a pal as you like with Bryan, but don't get into any silly scheme of fighting at his kind of place.'

As they were changing again in the dressing-room Walt assured Bryan that he liked Thorpe.

'He gets a bit snotty if he knows you've been boozing or smoking,' Bryan said. 'But he's good wi' young 'uns. Could've been a pro, you know. His wife and kid got killed a long time ago. Wouldn't you reckon he'd get married again?'

'He'd be a good bloke to have as your old man,' Walt answered. As they were going home, Bryan asked him to come dancing next evening. Walt only hesitated because he knew that Bill would be home that weekend and might want his company.

'You can meet the gang and that,' Bryan said. 'We'll have some fun. How about it, kid?'

Bill had his own friends, after all, Walt thought. He could hear Andrew Mason saying that surely he was something of an intellectual himself... Mason should have been in the ring.

'Okay, kid,' he said with a sudden wide grin. 'Tomorrow night—we'll go dancin'.' His voice and accent were exactly like Bryan's.

V

The breeze in his face was scented by open country. At the back door that afternoon the old lady had said to Mrs Watson: 'Straight from Blackpool, that air. You can't beat livin' up here.' People were wearing their week-end suits, and as Walt walked along he glanced at pretty girls strolling by in short coats and summer frocks. He also glanced down occasionally at his own polished shoes and sharp-creased trousers, fastidiously brushing at his coat, which he had carefully sponged to disguise its shine. He felt very smart; Bill's blue tie matched his white shirt, and Bill's cream glistened on his hair.

'Ah, those poor, poor girls,' Bill had sighed while Walt was examining himself in the mirror which showed your reflection like rain wavering down a window, and the old lady had said that if he kept trying to push waves into his hair he'd be seasick.

The disadvantage in being almost eighteen was having to act with dignity in public when you were alone, however much you felt like leaping about, therefore Walt strolled soberly around a corner and past a long queue of people outside the cinema. Bryan was waiting at the pavement edge, the traffic hooting, clanging and rumbling behind him. He wore a dull green tuxedo-cut sports coat, dark brown. slacks, a yellow shirt and thick-soled, two-toned shoes. As he saw Walt and waved, a wrist-watch flashed above his cuff.

'Come on, kid,' he yelled. 'Where you been?' Since Walt was forty yards away many people looked to see whom he meant, and Walt stopped abruptly as they stared at him.

'Come on, kid! Don't let's waste Saturday.' Bryan signalled for him to cross the street, and when both had run across, dodging the cars and buses, he slapped Walt's shoulder and said happily: 'Let's go.' He was very different from the half-naked or cloth-capped and soberly dressed workmate Walt was accustomed to. As they walked along, Bryan with one arm around Walt's shoulders, he talked about the Memorial Hall.

'We're going straight in, see? Most o' the lads'll be boozin' till gone ten, but I've had two birds lined up for a while now and you're just the one can help me get 'em.'

'Me?' Beside Bryan he felt shabby. He looked at the colourful clothes, the rosy square face and curly hair shining in the ruddy sunlight, and he said: 'I'm not very dressy, I guess. These are all I've got.'

Bryan squeezed his shoulder and assured him he looked swell, glanced round for a moment at two saucy-eyed passing girls and then continued planning as they weaved along.

'Just leave it all to me,' he said. 'You'll be okay.'

In a quiet street several blocks away from the main road stood the Memorial Hall, an austere, grey-walled building like a church with a date carved over the arched entrance, from which came the sound of dance music. At a table inside a burly man was seated with a coil of tickets in his hands, and as they paid their half-crowns Bryan said to him: 'Saturday again, Joe, eh?'

'Just you behave yourself tonight,' the doorman warned him. His beefy, battered face and bald head made Walt think of an old wrestler.

'Joe here were a pro one time,' Bryan told him, grinning as he added: 'Past it now, mind you...'

'Start owt in there tonight and you'll see if I'm past it. I can handle you lot, young Foster.'

'Sure!' Bryan led Walt to the swing doors. 'That's why you allus have a copper here after ten.'

The music blared as they entered the hall. A few girls were dancing on a floor large enough for fifty couples, with motes of french chalk stirred by their feet rising through daylight coming from high windows. On the stage a small band was playing a listless foxtrot, but among the other girls seated on wooden chairs along both sides, and among the youths gathered around the stage, the mood for dancing and gaiety seemed absent, as though it were awaiting the inspiration of semi-darkness, artificial light or more people. Some of the talking girls looked up as Walt and Bryan walked to the stage.

'You'd better meet this lot and let 'em see you're one of us,' Bryan said before they reached the group. Walt felt even more out of place as he saw that they were wearing either bright sports clothes like Bryan's or suits which had long draped coats with padded shoulders and wide-bottomed trousers hoisted high enough to display bright socks.

'Walt, this is Blackie,' Bryan said, as they faced a youth of similar height and build to Walt, with a thin sallow face and oily black hair. As he examined Walt, lazily it seemed, his jaw slowly ground on a piece of chewing gum.

'Another pitman, huh?' he drawled.

'He works wi' me. Better watch this kid, Blackie. He's lightning when he goes.'

Blackie looked at Walt again and drawled that he didn't say much, did he? Walt stared back at him, grinning bewilderedly as he tried to guess whether the blank stare and gum-chewing drawl were intended as menacing or as a joke. He thought Blackie looked and sounded silly.

'Do I look funny?' Blackie asked him, frowning.

'You do a bit,' Walt grinned, and then Bryan, with a pleased look of sly malice, said: 'It's like this, Walt. Blackie's mob don't work in t' pit like ours. And not Blackie's mob nor anybody else's tries owt wi' us, neither. Right, Blackie?' He thumped the other's shoulder as though affectionately, making him wince and almost stagger. The other youth smiled, thinly and warily, and Walt realized that all this had been not merely play-acting but some kind of deliberate exchange.

As they strolled away and sat down farther up the hall, Bryan casually explained that Blackie sometimes chose to try new-comers out, but that Walt would be all right now. Walt looked at the muttering youths around Blackie and demanded if this was a dance hall or some kind of private club.

'Well, its a tough place, kid—you got to have your own crowd. But we're the top dogs here, don't worry about that.'

'But that Blackie! Why the deadpan look and phoney drawl? Does he think he's a gangster or something?'

Bryan explained that people had once said that Blackie walked and looked like a famous cowboy of the films, and Blackie had never forgotten.

'I knew him at school,' he said, as Walt grinned. 'He's nothin'. Only they reckon he carries a little leather cosh, so watch him if he gets boozed up. He'll get filled in one of these days.'

Walt shrugged after a moment. Why should he worry about what kind of place they had come to? Bryan had accepted him as a friend and would make him one of a crowd; he could take whatever else came during the evening. When the music stopped, Bryan nudged him and nodded at two girls across the floor. The smaller one, a pretty brunette in brown skirt and grey sweater, was smiling to Bryan as he whispered: 'That's Marie and I've took her home a few times. They come drinkin' wi' us sometimes, see, only Marie won't go steady wi' me because of Brenda. And Brenda won't go steady wi' none on our lads.'

Walt had only glanced at the girls before lowering his head. He had seen that the other was a tall blonde.

'Brenda Carter they call her and she was courtin' a bit since, only they packed up. She's hard to get—but she's one o' t' best lookers round here. What about it?'

'What?' he asked, embarrassed now he was almost face to face, so to speak, with Bryan's project.

'Just for a few weeks, that's all,' Bryan urged him. 'I'll bet she's all right if you get her on your own, and I can't get off with Marie if you don't—well, I'm depending on you.'

'Well, I'll try,' he said without confidence. 'I'll dance with her, but if your other—'

'Ah, they know nowt about lasses. Walkin' in here at ten o'clock and thinkin' lasses'll come runnin' when they whistle. We'll put the charm on now, kid. Just put the charm on, that's all.'

With Bryan's arm around his shoulder and his low, conspiratorial voice urging him, he glanced up. The blonde was looking at him while her friend whispered, and he quickly looked down again. As pounding waltz music began, Bryan slipped a small packet into his hand.

'Here, you can have this one.'

'What is it?' It felt like a rubber ring when he squeezed it. He almost dropped it as Bryan said: 'Don't show everybody, you dope. Put it away. You might want it.'

A furious blush beat over Walt's lowered face as he hastily stuffed the packet in his top pocket. In spite of his book about sex, this was his first actual contact with any of its modern appurtenances.

'What did you give me that for?' he hissed, and Bryan answered that it was all right; he'd got two, and you never could tell... Then he said excitedly that the girls were dancing.

'Come on, Walt. Let's split 'em up.'

Walt kept his head lowered. The more he tried consciously to be calm, the hotter grew his face and neck. When Bryan asked if he could waltz, he nodded, but said:

'Let some more get up first.' He glanced up again as the two girls passed and found that Marie was still whispering and the blonde, Brenda, was watching him again. Her dove-grey skirt and blue sweater were tightly stretched over long, full hips and tautly prominent breasts. Walt told himself that she looked awfully proud of her figure, and felt sweat on his palms as he rubbed his hands together.

'Come on!' Bryan looked round at his darkly red face and glistening eyebrows and said suspiciously: 'You're not scared, Walt, are you?'

'Who, me? No!' He jumped up and strode over to tap Brenda's

shoulder. Then he politely asked if she would mind dancing with him. Both girls stared for a moment, and it was Marie who answered, as she turned to smile at the grinning Bryan: 'Gosh, no. Didn't come to dance wi' each other, did we, Bren?'

Then she and Bryan moved away, smiling at each other and beginning to talk.

At sixteen Walt had learned some basic steps in a youth club where everyone had been learning to dance, but as he began steering Brenda around the floor he had to concentrate hard on keeping time, and stared apprehensively over her shoulder as other couples loomed in front.

'First time you've been, isn't it?' she asked, looking at him. He nodded and she went on conversationally: 'You're awful polite for the Memo. We knew you was goin' to break us up. Old Marie's got a right pash on Bryan, and she wants to go him, only she wants me to make a four up and I keep tellin' her she should go wi' him on her own if she really likes him— shouldn't she? As he nodded and smiled vaguely, she repeated: 'Shouldn't she, though?'

'Yes.' He bumped into another couple, halted to apologize and found that they had moved on and that he had lost the step.

'Relax.' Brenda tugged him into the correct movement and smiled. 'Are you shy?'

'No.' His tongue felt huge and dry and he was afraid that to swallow would mean a noisy croak. His shirt was coldly clinging to his back and his embarrassment was growing more and more intense.

'Just take it easy,' she said gently, still smiling at him. He envied her the ease with which she smiled at him and at others while they danced. She asked him questions about where he lived and what he worked at and he answered, grinning nervously each time he realized how curt he sounded. Her eyes were a striking blue, her features bold and attractive, and her hair fell in a yellow curve to the blue collar. As they talked he held her stiffly away from him, acutely aware that each time they turned her breasts brushed against his top pocket which held the little rubber ring. He told her where he came from.

'I knew you was Scotch,' she said. 'You can tell how you say some words.'

'Rolling my r's?' He managed a dry-lipped grin. 'That's with wearing a kilt.'

'Oh, aye? I knew a Scotch lad once in t' R.A.F. He sent me a tartan pincushion and things...' He felt suddenly relieved. At least, he thought, he didn't have to be scared of her mind.

'...I reckon they're a lot nicer than this bunch here,' she was saying. 'I said to Marie you looked different as soon as you walked in.' As the music stopped he released her waist, but she kept a light hold on his left hand as she went on: 'I mean look at Bryan and t' rest on 'em. They're dead leery.'

'What?'

'You know—flashy, fly.' The music started and they began dancing again. 'They're all big-headed. I'm browned off wi' them. I'd sooner see a lad as didn't slouch or swagger about as if he was King Kong.'

He listened attentively to her criticism. When he mentioned later that he lived in lodgings, her eyes grew wide and the pupils seemed so pale for a moment, so lightly touched on the white, that he told himself you could almost see through them.

'Did your folk get killed in t' war?'

'Oh no!' He began explaining a little about himself and about his plans to shape out a fine life, and she listened, wide-eyed and serious. When the dance ended he walked with her to the edge of the floor and politely thanked her.

'Well—' For a moment she looked confused. Marie stared at him. 'You're welcome. Just started talking, really, hadn't we?'

As he returned to where Bryan was frowning and waiting, Walt would have swaggered a little had the girl not condemned swaggerers. Bryan demanded to know why he had gone over there with her: '...I thought you'd duffed me for a minute, kid.'

'Just putting on the charm,' Walt answered airily, then quickly swayed to take a heavy thump on the shoulder.

'Kid, we're in. You're about the fastest worker I've— Here! Have a fag.' He produced a packet of cheap Turkish cigarettes. Good cigarettes were scarce. 'Go on, take one—won't hurt if you don't inhale. Blimey, they're gabbing away ten to t' dozen o'er there. I knew I picked a right mate at last.'

Walt's first two cigarettes, at thirteen, had made him sick. He held this one gingerly, screwing up his nose at the smell and puffing out smoke as Bryan continued joyfully chattering.

'Hey, and don't forget you're nineteen—them two are. They can tell some lads aren't because they haven't been called up, but they can't tell wi' us bein' pitmen what age we are, see?'

'I don't look nineteen,' he protested. 'Sure you do. You say it and they'll believe it.'

He danced with Brenda several more times. She seemed mainly interested in his idea of planning out one's life, but she also answered some of his questions. She was a buffer in a factory, and told him it was a mucky job but the pay was good. When she casually mentioned her wage for that week he realized it was thirty shillings higher than his own.

'You wouldn't recognize Marie and me if you seen us comin' home,' she said.

In one corner Blackie was dancing with a small girl in a long skirt which gave her a dumpy appearance. He weaved on rubbery legs, spinning the girl around him and bending backward as she passed behind until his body was almost parallel to the floor. His friends were snapping their fingers and shouting encouragements, but Blackie's face was impassive, his jaws grinding, as he whirled the girl away and tugged her back with the impersonal artistry of a matador rehearsing passes with his cloak.

'Can you jive?' Brenda asked. He shook his head.

'You're not a bad dancer, anyway.' He was surprised until he saw that Bryan and some of the others were pushing their partners around the floor, doing one monotonous plodding step. They were also holding their partners much closer than he, with his consciousness of the arrogant buttresses between them, dared to hold Brenda. At half past eight they walked off the floor to find Bryan and Marie waiting for them with linked arms.

'What about the Castle, kids?' Bryan said.

'Huh?'

'The boozer, Walt, the boozer.'

Brenda nodded, but Walt, fingering the three half-crowns in his pocket, said: 'You three can go. I'll wait for you here.'

'Are you kidding?' Bryan asked. 'You girls get your coats.'

When the two girls left them Walt explained that he couldn't afford to go. Bryan pushed a ten-shilling note in his hand and told him to buy a round with that. As Walt tried to give the money back, he began pleading: 'Aw now, Walt—it's Saturday. Look, my old man's got one o' the best-paid jobs in t' pit. They let me keep most of my money, so I'm okay, see? You're doing me a favour, kid, honest. A few pints won't hurt us. Please...'

Walt said he would go, but he would pay Bryan back.

'Aw now, were mates, aren't we? For Pete's sake—it's Saturday, Walt —Saturday. Let's bang things up a bit.'

The breeze outside had grown stronger and cooler, and shadows were crawling out from walls and hedges. Bryan and Marie, their arms around each other's waists, hurried on in front with heads close together. Marie had a high whooping laugh which reminded Walt of the chorus girl in Atwell's, and now and then she threw back her head as the laugh tore across the evening quiet. Brenda asked why he hadn't wanted to come, as though there were something strange about anyone who didn't want to drink on Saturdays, and afraid she might think him a prude, he said casually that you shouldn't drink if you were in training.

'You go boxing?' Her eyes were wide again as she looked round. 'Like

Bryan and them? I'd never have guessed. Honest, it's the first thing they'd brag about if they got you up for a dance.'

He felt like a soldier ignorant of mines all around him until he sees the craters where others have stepped. With Brenda, he thought, it was wisest to say as little as possible about anything that the others might talk about.

The public house was surrounded by a low wall. In front was a sign showing a triple-turreted castle and at the back was a rough patch of grass and a few trees. Bryan and Marie had already entered when they reached it. As Walt heard the noise of bouncing music and roaring voices, excitement suddenly leaped up and crouched quivering in his belly. He said: 'It sounds all right.'

'Sure, it's Saturday, isn't it? Just a minute.' Brenda stopped in front of the revolving doors, fumbling in her handbag. Then she held out three half-crowns.

'For my drinks,' she said, and when he protested that it was all right, she went on: 'I don't let lads pay for me on a night like this. Take it—else I'll get my own.'

She was smiling, but the jut of her jaw and cheekbones warned him that she meant what she said. He decided that his judgment had been both glib and wrong in thinking he needn't fear her mind. And if she lacked the delicate, impish beauty of the dark Elaine, her toughness and self-assurance, as well as her impressive figure and bold attractiveness, made up for it. He was looking at her in frank admiration and after a moment she asked: 'Well, what are you staring at?'

'You've got nice hair. He smiled and held out his hand. She dropped the money into it, smiled back at him, and answered as she turned away:

'It gets a bit of help from t' bottle, you know.' He followed her through the spinning doors, looking at her swinging hips.

In the doorway of the concert room he stopped, as though the noise and heat and smoke had pushed him back. Leather-backed seats were all around the long walls, and tables crowded the floor, each table surrounded by young lively faces, drinking, smoking, singing and talking. The musicians on the stage sang while they played, with half their audience joining in, and waiters bustled through a blue mist to a busy bar where mirrors flashed and bottles glinted in a frame of light oak. Although the windows were opened, he felt stifled as Brenda led him between the tables, pushing away hands and smiling as she answered the calls of youths and girls: 'Who's the new boy, Bren?'—'Bryan's mate. He's all right.' 'When do I get a break, Bren?'—'When you grow up, chavvy.' 'Still third man for them two, Bren?'—'Blame Marie. She's scared of herself.'

Bryan was shouting at them, soundless in the hubbub, as he stood up with Marie beside him in a circle of a dozen youths. He thumped Walt's shoulder and pushed them around two joined tables to squeeze on to a leather seat. Walt had to lean forward slightly so that Brenda could sit back. Bryan said he had ordered drinks, and when Brenda argued that Walt was buying hers, he shouted: 'Me and Walt's mucking in, so you pipe down, Bren. Right, Walt?'

Walt nodded, hearing Brenda mutter 'Big-head'. She was pressed softly against him and he had no way of moving. In this confusion of fug and noise and smiling faces, with the girl close, excitement was pounding through him as though with his blood, racing through limbs and body and heart and, finding no outlet, racing round again. He didn't need beer, he thought; you could get drunk on this. Among those smiling at him, as Bryan shouted introductions, were Tug and Joe, the pair who sometimes travelled home with them from the pit. Opposite was Hughie Sawford, a stocky, quiet youth whose face reminded Walt of Alec Thorpe's warning: the nose was indented and the lips were swollen and purple from many bruisings. Most of the other faces had a hardened look, he thought, but they were pitmen after all and each face was friendly.

'I wanted pale ale,' Brenda said, as Bryan set a small glass before her and a pint of beer before Walt.

'Wi' me you'll have gin and orange and like it, my girl,' Bryan said, and he returned to his seat. 'Tonight we're havin' a do for Walt. Right, lads?'

As they chorused agreement, Walt quietly offered to fetch Brenda a different drink. She said he was a gentleman, but she didn't really mind gin.

'I just feel like saying something when Bryan gets lording it,' she confided, smiling, then turned to call up the table: 'At least you've got a gentleman for a mate now——that's a change.'

'Have I? Wait while I've supped this and I'll tell you summat. Straight down, Walt lad.'

Walt sipped at his beer which he thought warm and un-pleasant. As he lowered his glass everyone began shouting at him.

'Rule of the table, kid,' Hughie Sawford called above the voices. 'First one's always straight down.'

Both girls had emptied their glasses and Bryan's was tilted over his face. A waiter was setting a tray down beside them. Walt picked up his glass, telling himself he must empty it or look a fool, and with the warm rim to his lips he screwed up his face and slowly tilted back his head. The beer gushed into his throat and for a shameful second he felt he must throw it up like a blowing whale, then his gullet relaxed, opening and closing rhythmically with the fluid thudding into his stomach. He lowered the glass, empty at last, and sat back grinning, feeling like an overblown bicycle tyre about to burst. They cheered him and he felt the beer settle heavily in his stomach. Bryan pushed another full glass in front of him.

'It's all right,' he said reassuringly as Walt blinked at it. You can pay next time. I've ordered again.'

The second pint tasted a little better, as though the first had prepared his palate. While Walt was drinking some of it, Bryan, who had drunk half of his before putting down the glass, was telling the others about the scuffle with Mike Fletcher. At first it was pleasant to hear graphic embellishments while maintaining a modest smile as Brenda glanced at him thoughtfully and leaned nearer to hear Bryan, but he began to feel uneasy as two blows were made to sound like a furious brawl.

'Don't put it on too thick,' he said, raising his glass again.

'Too thick?' Bryan said they could ask Tug and Joe—ask who they liked. 'Just ask 'em. And you know me, chaps. Can I go a bit? Can I?' When they nodded he began describing the bout in Thorpe's gym, exaggerating once again: '...and I can't touch him, see? Can't even see him. And he hits me every place and ends up with a one-two that puts me on the ropes. Alec had to break us up!'

'Cut it out, Bry!' he said sharply. The flamboyant exaggeration was turning it into something that had never happened, and turning him into a mere protégé being boasted about by his patron. He raised his glass again and emptied it, face contorted as though it held castor oil, and Bryan laughed and said everybody could see how modest the kid was but not to be fooled, because he was lightning when he went. The faces now looked very impressed and Hughie Sawford leaned over to say that he had known Walt was a fighter as soon as he looked at him.

'It's in the face and the eyes,' he said, nodding soberly. 'I can tell 'em.'

In the smoke and noise Brenda asked if it were true.

'He's putting it on a lot,' Walt said uncomfortably as he paid a waiter who had brought more drinks.

'Bryan always does. Show me t' lad that don't.' As he tried to turn, her hair tickled his ear, a delicate scented touch that caused a stiffness in his neck and jaw. '...But you're not like that, are you? You're a funny lad.'

He was not quite sure how he had won this attribution of modesty and difference, and less sure of how he was to keep it, but for the moment he was highly satisfied. It was a little confusing to suddenly become a centre of attraction with this girl beside him and friendly faces all around, but it was also pleasing. And by the time, in his effort to keep up with Bryan and the girls, he had drunk his third pint and most of another, both confusion and pleasure had increased. A whirling fluffiness was spreading through his head, like the cotton-wool wisps in a fairground candy-floss machine which spin round and round as they slowly gather into a light pink mass; and many normal thoughts and feelings were being smothered like encumbrant weaklings, leaving him aware of himself in a fine new way He felt reckless, confident and invincible. He managed to turn himself and squeeze against Brenda with his face toward her.

'You're the nicest girl I've met here,' he said, as though she were the successor to many. During the next half-hour he told her about London, then his schooldays, then his childhood. He discovered that he had been lonely all his life, and told her so. He had never realized how lonely he was until now, he said. And she nodded, her blue eyes full of sympathy. Now and again Walt would smile to the others or speak to them as he drank his beer but he kept turning back to Brenda's smile and interested eyes. Bryan and Marie were huddled together at the top end of the table.

'Be careful what friends you make round here,' Brenda advised him once. 'You're not like this crowd, you know.' He felt dubious about this remark, but she had spoken too gently for him to argue. His mind, as though cringing from incessant noise, seemed to have retreated a little from his eyes, so that he was literally looking out through them as through a periscope, and there was a faint dark frame around everything he saw. By half past nine, as he kept drinking from glasses which were now lining up on the table, he could only see clearly the actual object he was focusing on and everything else was hidden in shadow.

Up on the stage a youth was singing and the audience was singing with him. It was a conventional love song about a conventional broken heart, but the youth, judging by his expressions, was singing with great feeling, though no one could hear him; and alcohol made it seem a hymn of human understanding. Walt listened as Brenda and the others sang the words and he felt that there was nothing so profound or so inspiring as the desirability of women. His own tenderness almost choked him, and through his mind, turgidly oozing out of the cotton wool, flowed the words How sweet she is... how soft... how... Until he thought of the packet Bryan had given him and suddenly laughed. Brenda frowned at him, her face close.

'What are you laughing at?'

'Nothing,' he said. 'You're a lovely girl, do you know?'

'You can cut the flattery,' she said, but smiled.

'It's no flattery. I love that blue-eyed stare of yours.'

'Bryan was dead right,' she said coolly. 'You're lightning, aren't you?'

'I mean it,' Walt protested, and she smiled again, her eyes softening as she shook her head: 'Honestly, you're a funny lad...

Over her shoulder he saw Blackie and his friends at the bar. Blackie stood with his shoulders a little forward and hands drooping, chewing steadily as he looked around. Strap two holsters to his hips, Walt thought, and put a gun in his right hand instead of a glass and he was the typical film gunman seeking his man. He was grinning as Blackie glanced at him.

'I hate phoneys,' he said. 'That Blackie's queer.'

'You want to stop staring at him,' Brenda said. He looked at her again, but Bryan leaned over the table beckoning to him.

'Come on, Walt. Let's give 'em a song.' Everyone clutched at glasses as the table rocked, and Marie cried: 'Oh, Bry, you're a real rogue, honest!'

'Come on, Walt kid. Just you and me.'

Brenda pulled Walt's arm into her breast and told Bryan he didn't want to go. Bryan said they were mates, weren't they, and Brenda said Walt had come with her.

'Wait a minute,' Walt said indignantly. 'I'm my own boss.' He frowned at Brenda and stood up, surprised at his light and easy balance.

'Go on, kid,' he said to Bryan. 'I don't let my mates down.'

He followed Bryan to the stage without difficulty, though he heard a glass topple over at a table he had passed. The musicians looked less excitedly happy than he had imagined at close range.

'Jolson?' Bryan asked, as the drummer handed them the microphone, and Walt agreed. He had seen a film about Jolson and knew most of his songs. As they began singing about April showers, he realized with amazement that he was up here on a stage with dozens of people looking at him, yet felt completely unafraid. Bryan was singing too slowly for the band, and he seemed to be singing too fast, but the audience drowned their out-of-tune voices. Walt finished first with the band and audience next and Bryan crooning the last line by himself. When they sang 'Mammy', however, Walt blinked and forgot the words as Bryan dropped to his knees during the last chorus and stretched out his arms to the delighted, roaring audience. He jumped down when it was over, but as he walked back to his table he heard Bryan singing, without waiting for the band:

'Ah-rockabye... your babee with... a Dixie mell... ohdee...'

At the table he was greeted as a good old kid, and sat down beside Brenda with relief. He immediately reached for his drink.

'I guess we looked a bit daft.' His confidence was strengthened when he lowered the glass.

'You did all right,' Marie shouted. 'Look at old Bry. He's a devil, honest!'

'It's all for a laugh,' Brenda said. 'I just reckoned you weren't the sort for that...'

'You might be right,' Walt admitted. He noticed Blackie and his friends talking as they looked at him and wondered if they were laughing. When Bryan returned more beer was ordered, but Walt could drink only a little of it. His stomach was swollen and he was beginning to feel that he and Brenda were the only stable elements in a whirling vortex. 'Your eyes are like marbles,' she told him, smiling inside a black frame.

When they rose to go, with the waiters yelling 'Time' as they bustled around, there were many half-filled glasses left on the table. In the doorway he and Brenda clung to each other while a singing, shouting crowd jostled around them, and then they were outside and he could hear Bryan shouting: 'Where's Walt? Where's my mate?'

'Go on,' Brenda called, her arm around his waist. 'We're coming!'

Walt shivered in the cold, sharp-edged air. His stomach was active, as though something were struggling to swim in there.

'All right?' Brenda asked, and he put his arm around her gratefully.

'I'm all right.' You're not really used to t' beer, are you?' She looked at his face as they began walking along the darkened road with other couples behind and in front of them. After a moment Walt admitted that he wasn't.

'I could tell wi' your face when you were gulping it. You shouldn't have drunk all that. Bloody hell! I'm tight myself.'

'You shouldn't swear,' Walt said, leaning in on her. 'A nice girl like you shouldn't swear. Girls shouldn't swear, anyway and—you're a lot too nice.'

'You are a funny lad!' She squeezed his waist. 'You're nice an' all.' Somewhere in front Bryan was bellowing a song and Marie's ragged shriek was rising above other voices, but these two walked quietly, occasionally bringing their heads together as they lurched. The struggle in Walt's stomach had been reduced to sluggish movements and the darkness was pleasant to him with the girl's waist warm in the crook of his arm. She put a hand over his as she said. 'I knew you weren't like them. I told Marie…'

Bryan was waiting for them in the arched doorway with Marie bending in his arm as she laughed.

'What you been up to, eh? Plenty time for that later. Come on, come on…'

As they entered the hall he was confused again by the heat and dazzling light, the jokes and boisterous shoulder-clouts and the dozens of shuffling couples filling the floor. Brenda tugged him into the crowd when she had put away her coat, and they danced with arms tight around each other's waists. Her face was hard against his cheek and jaw, her body pressed to his, yet he was no longer conscious of her figure, as though his own body were asleep. He closed his eyes, bewildered, unaware of what his feet were doing and only vaguely aware of repeated collisions. When the music stopped she told him to wait and then vanished into the crowd around the doorway where the cloakrooms were. Walt turned his head slowly, moving the black frame around in the hope of seeing Bryan, but what he saw was Blackie standing beside him.

'Hi, smiler,' Blackie drawled, his sallow face expressionless, and Walt looked at him disdainfully. 'Making time wi' Brenda, ain't you? You'll be gettin' black looks from Bryan's mob.'

Looking at the gunman crouch, blank face and artificial-looking wavy hair, Walt felt that there was nothing real about the way Blackie now stood and drawled. He wanted to make Blackie expose himself.

'What's up with you? Bry's mates are all right. You're the phoniest-looking thing I've ever seen.'

'That what you keep laughing at?' Blackie asked. 'That's not polite.'

'Oh, for Pete's sake!' Walt said. 'Go and play cowboys somewhere else.' He was indignant. He too had his dreams, but Blackie had no right to make all dreams childish by trying to act one out.

'I wouldn't lean on Bryan too much, kid. He's not always around.'

'Bryan?' He was experiencing a wonderful change as he moved closer to Blackie's wary face. His body was coming alive again and hardening, and he felt a magnificent pounding of blood, an adjustment of muscle, as a springy readiness tensed his legs. 'I'd manage you any time.'

'What you got against me?' Blackie's hands were still hanging. Some youths were watching Walt over his shoulder. 'What you got against me, eh? You're trying to push me.'

'I don't like you and I don't like your talk and the way you look at me. I've a feeling you're trying to get behind me.' In his mind was a clamour urging him to let go, explode, beat it out of himself, as though a savage beast with murderous needs crouched there and screeched at him. Blackie's mouth was centred in the frame and Walt's left arm was tensed for the jerk of his body.

'Any time you like,' Blackie said. 'Any time.'

Then Walt was seized from behind and his instant reaction to the touch sent his fist whipping past Blackie's face as he was jerked off balance. Blackie jumped back as Bryan clutched at Walt's coat demanding:

'What's up, Walt? What's he said?' Around them was a pushing ring of girls and youths.

'He's drunk,' Blackie shouted. 'I only talked to him.'

'You want trouble you can have it,' Bryan said. 'You and your mob.'

'A fight A fight!' someone yelled. Walt pushed Bryan away. 'I told you to play somewhere else,' he said to Blackie, and beside him Hughie Sawford added: 'I'm about fed up wi you. You're allus startin' trouble wi' our lads when they're on their own.

'I didn't start anythin'!' Blackie protested while the crowd surged and youths grouped themselves around him and Walt. 'It was him.'

'You said any time. It's going to be first time you come near me.'

'All right. All right.' Blackie suddenly threw out both arms. 'But if you want a scrap, don't pick one when all your mates is there to back you up.'

Walt had begun to say he didn't need any mates, advancing on Blackie again, when he was once more seized from behind. This time the arms were around his neck, half strangling him, and as he was tugged backwards, Brenda's voice was saying: 'Hey, love, hey, love, I want to tell you summat... His head was set whirling like a toy globe in which snowflakes dance when it is shaken as other hands helped Brenda to push him through the jostling crowd.

'Come on, love, come on. Feel bad? It's fresh air you want... Her voice was maternal and soothing. They passed a silver-buttoned blue coat in the doorway while he struggled to breathe and to see properly, and Brenda kept repeating that it was fresh air he wanted as he was pushed helplessly outside. There he staggered a, few steps and halted.

'Now, just a minute,' he began, but she tugged at his hand.

'Hurry up, Walt. Bryan'll keep the copper in there a minute or two.'

He stared at her as he gulped over a breath of chilling air. The authority of law had always terrified him; he had seen men struggling in the blue-sleeved arms on Saturday nights in the streets of his childhood, and had seen his own father carried out of the house with his nose bleeding, his mother crying after them, though it was she who had summoned the police. He snatched at Brenda's hand and ran with her to the end of the street and round the corner, their feet thudding and clicking on the dark pavement. They turned another corner and ducked into a shop doorway.

'Didn't you know there was a copper outside?' Her double-pointed sweater heaved at him and sank. 'I heard Joe shouting for him.'

He leaned his face against the cool window, panting heavily with his eyes closed. He understood why Alec Thorpe condemned drinking as he gasped and his chest shuddered.

'I'm drunk. I don't know what I'm doing, honest. I don't usually—'

'You'll feel better in a minute, love.' As he moved his face, seeking coolness, the glass grew warmly moist. His head cleared slowly and his blood calmed. He could still grin as he said:

'It's the beast in me, eh?' Then thought to himself that the lion was having his night.

'Thanks a lot,' he said, turning to put his hands on her shoulders, feeling the firm warmth and thin shoulder-straps under his hands. A street lamp shone in on them and made the contours of her face glowing curves in the shadow. Her eyes looked dark and her lipstick purple as she answered it was all right and leaned against him a little with her arms on his hips. He told her she was lovely and she pulled her head back to look at him curiously, soft against him with points of pressure.

'Honest?' she asked. She was waiting. He bent his head, and the shadow-frame closed around the blue ellipses of her eyes with the pink cheek blending into curving bone and lowered lashes. Her mouth opened slightly, soft, passive, yet clinging. In an upsurge of confusion, passions and all that called for release in him, he hugged her against him and felt them become a force at his lips as though he were creating something. Then the soft-ness and passivity became active strength and her arms tightened on his neck, her mouth closing hard on his as her face pressed demandingly against his jaw. Her strength amazed him as she pulled his head down until he was giddy. He jerked free and she clung to him, staring.

'I'm dizzy,' he apologized.

'It's the beer. We've had too much.' As she stared at him, holding to his neck, her blue eyes intent on his as though she were trying to assess his thoughts, he felt that at the end of the kiss something of himself had seemed endangered. As though she had tried to drag from him something more than his force.

'I'll take you home,' he said. They walked along quiet streets, hearing the sounds of busy traffic on the main road, with an occasional motor-car glaring at them as it passed. She shivered.

'Hope Marie fetches my things from t' dance.'

'Here,' Walt said. 'Take my coat.' She let him put it over her shoulders, and as they walked on smiled at him in a quizzical way, wrinkling her nose.

'You're a real gentleman, aren't you? And yet with what Bryan said— then going off like that in t' dance... You're a funny lad.'

They stopped at a pathway between two houses which shared an arched entry and were surrounded by the usual hedges. He looked at the lighted windows, and said: Your folk are still up.'

'Oh, they'll be up for ages gabbin'. Come on.' She held his hand as they went around to the darkened back door where she leaned against the wall and looked at him closely as she asked: 'Do you really like me, Walt?'

'Honest.' He nodded. Even in shirt-sleeves he was not cold. He could barely see Brenda's face in the dark, but he could smell the scent of hair and cosmetics blending with grass-fragrance from the gardens. He began trembling a little.

'I knew it—how you kissed me. I like you.'

His excitement bounded up, and seizing her shoulders he kissed her several times. She suggested they should go to the pictures next evening and he nodded, kissing her again.

'The Luxor?' she asked, as he pressed his lips against her ear.

'Sure.' He was not the least interested in tomorrow.

'Seven o'clock outside?' She ducked her head.

'Sure,' he said. 'Sure, sure.'

'All right, then.' She clung to him and returned the kisses. They swayed together, and in Walt's mind rose a clamour similar to that of the dance-hall fight. The girl was perfect, he told himself, and the lion was rearing, paws spread and slavering jaws wide open as it roared. His hand cupped her breast under the coat and her body twitched, then they were absolutely still for a long time, kissing. As he reached down and tugged her sweater up she caught his hand and twisted away.

'No more,' she said gently. 'Not now, love.'

'Please!' He tried to kiss her, but she turned her face away. 'Look, you've got to—'

'Not now. Not the way you are.' With finality she said: 'It's too soon, anyway.'

'Too soon?' Words gushed out of him; hectoring, then pleading. 'I'm crazy about you,' he blurted out.

'Are you?' Her interested and speculative look infuriated him. 'Why? Why me?'

'How can I tell you why? You're lovely. You're attractive...' He stood glaring at her. Did she expect him to describe this furore? He was filled by a roaring, beating lust to be accepted by her, live through her and feel through her, to escape himself and seek another ending through her body. This feeling, this idea and longing, had been more a background to his thoughts than any other since he left school. It had meant more than anything else he had read of, talked of or wondered about.

'Have a heart.' He caught hold of her, pushing his face into her hair and she patted his shoulder, her voice maternal and soothing again with a new possessiveness. 'You're going daft for a lass like the rest of 'em do, that's all. But you're nicer than them, Walt, that's why I like you. I knew I could trust you—I wouldn't let *them* see me home.'

He wanted to shout that he definitely couldn't be trusted; was less to be trusted than anyone. Yet she was right, because when she said this his excitement drained away while he held her, leaving him sulkily inactive. After a few gentle kisses in which the effort was all on her side, he left her and made his way to the main road, feeling angry and baffled because he knew he had been handled. He was a mug, he told himself bitterly. A real man would have been himself and not cared what she thought afterwards.

Yet he could not stay angry as he walked along, with the standard lamps glaring on the pavements and stretching away down the hill in a curving double row and the flashing traffic and cheerful people flowing past him. He was surrounded by talk and singing and glistening faces and could smell among the fumes of petrol and exhaust the rich aroma of fish and chips. It had been an exciting night, after all, and he would see the girl again. He was whistling as he walked along Mainby Road and only stopped when he saw dark windows at No. 13.

He tiptoed round to the back door and found it unlocked. His breathing sounded loud in the stuffiness as he bolted the door and made his way through the living-room. Since the light switches were on the opposite wall he had to cross in darkness, hushing himself each time he bumped into the furniture which was everywhere. Each stair creaked and at the top he miscounted and banged his foot down hard, crouching as bed-springs jangled in the old lady's room.

'Only me,' he called, one foot poised in the darkness as he imagined her snatching at the truncheon.

'Only thee!' Although her voice was muffled it sounded harsh enough to make him pull a face and draw up his shoulders. 'Isn't it enough stoppin' out half the night wi'out waking half the street?'

'It's not late.' He lowered his foot and fumbled for the door handle.

'Only midnight, that's all. At your age... see thee in t' morning!'

He crept into his bedroom, closing the door as he heard her mumbling to herself. Bill asked softly: 'How did it go, Walt?'

'Smashing, kid.' In darkness he found his bed and dropped on to it. He began unlacing his shoes. 'Got myself a bird—girl.'

'Good lad. You're in hot water with the dragon, though.'

'You're telling me.' He had not realized how tired he felt. His heavy eyelids had to be forced open, and the room was peculiarly active. One shoe thudded on the floor and the bed-springs jangled again next door.

'Hell!' he said, lowering the other shoe quietly. He sloughed his clothes and crawled into bed. The moving room worried him for a few moments, but when Bill asked what kind of girl was she, he received no answer except a heavy sigh.

VI

He woke thinking someone had touched him, but there was only Bill's quiet breathing, faint daylight on his pillow and the unsure chirp from outside of an over-early bird. He remembered happily that it was Sunday and he could stay in bed.

But why the disgusting bloated feeling when he closed his eyes? Why the sullen clapper in his head and why was his body sick and his tongue like a swollen ulcer poisoning his mouth and throat? The critical adult, in a paroxysm of fury at having been bundled into its dark corner and kept there, now rushed out to tell him why. Never before had it been so flagrantly defied and never had it been so wrathful, denouncing him like a hanging judge with malignant eyes and terse asides as it dabbed away spleen from bloodied lips.

Walt cringed with his eyes tightly closed. Drunk and borrowing money! Sponging on a girl! Singing—cavorting around on a stage with a horde of people watching!

God, he thought: I forgot all about that...

And had forgotten deliberately picking a fight. Forgotten slobbering over the girl, clawing her, pawing her, almost grovelling, and being neatly put in his place. Burbling to himself about the beast in him. The kind of beast—conscience presumed—that slithers over pavements on wet mornings. Such sentimentality! What would Mr. Hemingway and those other writers he so admired have said of this?

Walt made no attempt at self-defence. There was no defence against the critic in a mood like this. He opened his eyes painfully and rolled on to his back wishing he could crawl away from his weaknesses as a snake leaves behind its old skin. Nausea washed through his head as he slowly shook it. Useless to plead that the youth of last night was a stranger to the one of this morning; conscience wouldn't have that for a moment. For all his previous introspection he could only now see himself apart as he might see another; and he saw conceit, exhibitionism, a sickening sentimentality and vicious aggressiveness.

How could he deny it or hide from it when the knowledge was within and the demonstration had been made? The conclusions were a self-evident, hateful mess, bubbling and stinking in his own mind.

Sot! said his conscience vindictively, now he had been brought to heel. With a father whose life had been ruined by drink, he himself was betraying his own standards. And wait, just wait, till the old lady had her say...

So he lay, sometimes dozing, sometimes cringing under vengeful flagellation, until Bill woke up, said a cheerful 'Good morning' and sprang briskly out of bed while Walt watched with jaundiced eyes.

Over breakfast he told Bill a little about the dance, but omitted all the things he felt badly about. His eyes slid sidewise now and then towards the fireplace and the green-draped bulk of the old lady who sat drinking tea from her saucer.

'Elaine asked for you last night,' Bill remarked, as they pushed their plates aside and leaned their elbows on the table. 'D' you know what she said? She said you had a sensitive face. He frowned critically at Walt. 'I wouldn't have said you had.'

Walt grunted, his nose wrinkling with distaste as Bill blew cigarette smoke over the table. He remembered vaguely somebody saying the opposite about his face in the public house.

'She must be one of those romantic types,' he answered.

'Ah, well,' Bill said, smiling as he stood up. 'It doesn't matter now you're courting, does it?'

'I'm not—' Walt began, but as Bill walked around the table he added: 'You were calling me "kid," last night. How you've changed, dear!'

Walt told him to shut up, more aggravated by his healthy cheerfulness than his grinning remarks. Bill went upstairs. He was due to go to work that afternoon and had some homework to finish for night school. As Walt sat hunched over a cup of tea, the old lady looked at him and inquired mildly if he had enjoyed his night out.

'Yes, thanks.' He wanted the last faggots to blaze and burn out and let the *auto-da-fé* be done with.

'Bit late, weren't you?' she said, still mild, and hope fluttered for a moment. He said he had taken a girl home, and she wanted to know if he wasn't a bit young for that game.

'What game?' Walt asked innocently.

'Tarts, birds—you know what game. Better men than thee's got in trouble wi' it.' He could not tell what her real thoughts were behind the wrinkled mask and jewelled eyes, but her heavy shoulders were set aggressively forward. He remarked that if he was doing a man's job he should be entitled to a man's pleasures, thinking that this should be ambiguous enough to keep her guessing, but she only stared and exclaimed: 'A man! Humph!'

Deflated by the 'humph' he rose and went to stand by the window, his hand on the little Dutch boy's cap as he looked through the lace at some boys playing cricket in the sunshine with a dustbin lid against a lamp-post for a wicket. Behind him, she said harshly, 'It's no use turnin' your back,' and began a tirade that lasted several minutes while he clenched hard on the china head. She ended by saying:

'A workin' lad needs rest, and if you've not sense enough to know it, you mun learn it.'

'But it was Saturday,' he protested over his shoulder.

'Half past eleven's late enough for Saturday and eleven o'clock for any other night. After that t' door's locked from now on. You hear?'

He nodded and she began vigorously poking the fire.

'Right, then. That's that!'

While she cleared the table and washed the dishes he remained by the window, feeling caged and restless. He wanted neither to read nor to go for a walk; he was unaccountably lethargic, yet felt that there was something he should be doing if he could only think of it. It was one of the blank, waiting periods of life he hated, and when he recalled the previous night's excitement he knew he had enjoyed that and wanted more. Yet why did he feel so disturbed, as though the excitement had only allayed some need in him that was now becoming active again? He asked himself irritably: Well, what do you want? And there was no answer except the increasing, undirected restlessness.

He wondered, as he watched the boys yelling at the batsman who had knocked the ball over a hedge, what had happened to him when he had begun drinking. Why had he told Brenda he was so lonely? He didn't feel lonely now. Why had he attacked Blackie, whom he didn't detest now?

She thinks I'm different, he told himself. But I don't want to be. I want to be one of them. They're like me—good lions.

Later the old lady sat by the fire again with a bag of potatoes in her lap and a bowl of water by her chair into which she dropped each one as she peeled it.

'Council man came on Friday,' she said conversationally. 'Said I'd got to put garden right.'

'How can you do that?' he asked, looking at the long, seed-tufted grass and high ragged hedge. She answered that it was a rule and must be done.

'So I told him to get on wi' it. He looked young enough and big enough.'

Walt grinned and thought that if there were many tenants like her the man's job would be unpleasant. But then, perhaps the man saw himself as most of the tenants seemed to: a moving part directed by a huge self-sustaining machine divorced from the realities of streets and houses and gardens it had created. A god-machine, invisibly churning away, receiving the tribute of rent and issuing commands through its servants to its subjects. People spoke of 'the Council' with the appropriate mixture of half-awed respect, resignation and occasional defiance, and the Council man could feel impersonal about obeying its commandments. The old lady was a natural heretic. He turned to her.

'I'll do it,' he said. At first she protested that it wasn't a lodger's job, but when he insisted, wanting to ease his unsettledness, she found in a cupboard a pair of rusty shears which he smeared with olive oil. He spent the rest of the morning hacking and wrenching at the stout hedge, telling himself he could have worked faster with the bread-knife. He became troubled by the idea that perhaps he wasn't merely helping the old lady, but was trying, without admitting it, to atone for the previous night.

I never know exactly why I'm doing anything, he thought disgustedly, and the hedge was clipped to a lower, but still ragged level by the time he had decided his motives weren't really important.

That afternoon he went out with Bill, who had to be at work by three o'clock. The sports clothes and colourful dresses of people enjoying the sunshine brightened the city streets, and the trams and buses headed for the suburbs and parks were filled by couples and families as though it were a holiday.

'Best day we've had yet and I've got to work,' Bill grumbled, then nudged Walt as a pair of arm-linking passing girls smiled at them.

'Full of spring feeling, that's me,' he said. Walt asked why he didn't get a girl.

'Well now...' Bill frowned up at him, then began jauntily smiling. 'The ones I can talk with and enjoy being with have all either already got a man, are damned ugly or don't fancy me. And I do want a girl I can talk with.'

'You're too fussy,' Walt said. If a girl was attractive and a source of pleasure and occasional comfort, he saw no reason to worry about her intellect. The clever ones probably talked too much, anyway, and would want to give orders all the time.

'I can wait,' Bill said. As they walked along, the streets were growing dirtier and shabbier. Soon the sunlight had turned pale yellow on grimy walls and windows and many of the children who played on the road were raggedly dressed and dark-complexioned. Walt saw a tiny child toddling about in only a jersey and a pair of plimsolls. The house doors opened directly on to the pavements and men and women sat on the sills, smoking and talking and calling to the children who dodged occasional traffic by moving a little towards the pavements, making a narrow lane through which car or lorry could crawl.

'Surely these kids could be better dressed,' Walt remarked. 'Wages aren't so bad, after all.'

'Not for you and me,' Bill said. 'But we haven't got homes and large families to keep. Some of these chaps can't earn more than five quid a week without overtime. There isn't always overtime. Would you feel bothered in a dump like this?'

'I'd get out,' he said, and shrugged when Bill said others couldn't. He hated the sight of dirty walls, windows and curtains and ragged children. He felt no sympathy; only loathing.

'It's like where we lived,' he said. 'My old man was always out of work then, but my mother dressed us decently.'

'How?'

'I guess her sisters helped her out—they were better off. Husbands in nice soft white-collar jobs.'

Bill raised his eyebrows and then looked down again. Walt knew the remark could be taken as a slight but he felt suddenly at odds with everyone and made no apology. He told himself there was no need to be ashamed of a past he could not help, yet his feeling was very much like that of shame; shame of poverty, squalor and violence. They strolled on in silence, passing several negroes dressed in dazzling coloured shirts and ties, with wide-brimmed hats, flapping trousers and long coats. Bill explained that a lot of coloured people lived here: '...It's one of the poorest quarters and I guess it's easier for them to get a place. But, Walt—what a hellish place to live!'

From behind a high wall stretching along on one side came an incessant clang and thump of hammers, screech and clash of engines, and the clatter and ring of steel being dropped, rolled, bent, cut and handled in a dozen different ways. Pouring gusts of smoke added to the layers of soot on walls, windows and human skin.

'How do they sleep?' Walt wondered.

'Its worse during the week. Goes on all night.'

'There was a foundry right in our street,' Walt said. 'It was a pretty rough place.' As they turned a corner a few moments later, he added thoughtfully: 'I must have started learning to fight there.'

'I expect you would.' They were now walking under the high wall.

'Yeah, but what I mean is—well, my mother...' He made a grunting, derisive noise. 'Well, she was a fine woman, see? Came from a good family and all that. And she wanted us to grow up nice, so she taught us to speak politely—in that place, where the kids were dead tough and could swear like troopers!'

Frowning at the disparaging tone, Bill said: 'she was thinking of your future, surely? Making sure you didn't grow up rough like them.'

'Oh sure. Only that wasn't teaching me how to live with things as they were. Maybe that's why I'm always waiting for the future and trying to forget what's around me—' He shrugged the idea away with an impatient jerk of his shoulder. 'Bet that's how I learned, anyway. Talking like a little toff among kids like that, you'd just have to learn to scrap.'

They stopped at a pair of huge iron gates. Walt looked at the gates, at the high walls and then at a uniformed guard standing watchfully.

'It's like a prison.'

Just fancy working here as a labourer, then, and going home to that!' Bill's swinging finger denounced the squalid houses around them. Walt smiled.

'So this is why you're such a reformer?'

'No. Not altogether.' Bill leaned against the wall and explained that when he was younger his limp had been worse, and so he had been alone often and read much. He had joined a youth club in Leeds where many boys came from Socialist families, and their company, plus a few books, had influenced him.

'That's how I first got interested, I guess,' he went on. 'I didn't want to be a shopkeeper and I was good at chemistry, so I picked this. You see—I can't help being not much good for manual work, or perhaps—'

'Bill,' he interrupted, 'I'm sorry about that crack just now. I didn't mean you, honest.'

'It's okay, Walt,' Bill smiled. 'You were digging more at yourself than me, I think. Anyway, now you understand—I got into industry, made friends of people I could talk to, and read—that's all. It's all important to me—and I wasn't born in a slum.'

'It's not that I condemn you for it—' Walt began, but Bill came away from the wall, looking up at him astonished, and exclaimed: 'Condemn me for it? That's what I can't understand about you, Walt. You're a fighter, aren't you? You have life in you— I feel it and Mason felt it, and —well, you're the kind I'd expect to feel this most. You're—'

'It's played out, Bill, he said. 'It's played out. It's been talked to death as far as I'm concerned. I wouldn't talk.'

'What would you do?' Bill asked. Walt looked down at his serious face in the sunlight, then at the guard and at the houses and the children.

'I'd just come down here and build a barricade and hoist my flag. And then I'd shout to this lot to come and join me. And then I'd wait for the other side to come and get me. I'd be serious about it—not just talk.'

Bill was laughing up at him. 'I can see you doing it, too. Everything out of a book, Walt—you're an idealist, honestly. That's the easy way—the glorious, easy way. And if the other side paid attention and did come, and you won? What then?'

'What?' He shrugged. 'Who cares? There'd be someone else to look after that—we'd send for you. For me it'd be the fight—and after that they could get on with things. They could build me a statue, of course; I'd like that.'

'I'll bet you would.' Bill shook his head at him and Walt grinned back. 'You're a bit out of date, though—the days of barricades are over, surely. You said yourself it's a scientific world. They have wars now, not rebellions.'

'Always one behind, that's me,' he said, but he had suddenly found their talk no longer amusing. He was wondering if William had known what he was dying for, or what came next. Was this the world he had been defending? With the old talk and the old troubles still going on?

'You and your politics,' he said abruptly. 'I'd sooner be a good lion than a bad idealist any time.'

'Would you?' Bill glanced down at his watch and said: 'I wish you'd talk about it seriously some time. I'd like a chance to—sort things out with someone who's got no axe to grind. The trouble with my friends is they're either on one side or another, and they keep giving me opposite advice.'

'You'd think they'd have got all this sorted out by now, wouldn't you?' Walt remarked. Bill said that it was three o'clock and he must go inside, so they parted and Walt hurried off through the gloomy streets, eager to be in sunlight which had not lost its cheerfulness in filtering through smoke.

But although the streets were soon left behind, they were not so quickly forgotten, and when he was sitting in his bus, with reinforced sunlight shining through the glass on to his face, he was still thinking of them and of the streets where he had once belonged. He remembered his old home very clearly: the tall tenements on one side with flats on each floor, the cinema and the brewery opposite and the black ironworks where the houses ended. Flames blazing up at night had lit his bedroom, and the working men had looked like gnomes in fiery caves. He recalled the lumpy feeling of cobbles to feet in thin plimsolls, and the sharp edges on the stone steps which wound up and up to the flat on the top storey. There were three flats to a landing and the women took turns in scrubbing the stairs; they bustled out to scold you or to shout up to your mother if you ran up and down too often. The lavatory was shared, and if someone was using it you hurried back to the kitchen sink. Since the walls were thin, nights were disturbed by the noise of quarrelling and fighting on the stairs, and the sound of angry, drunken men and women had been the most terrifying of his childhood. In his own home he had often heard shouts and bumps, then lain with his sisters in tortured silence with darkness around them, waiting for his mother to speak so they would know she was all right.

All that, I can still remember, he thought in the moving bus. And I was only a kid—a little kid.

There had been a game of hanging on to the backboards of lorries as they drove out of the brewery, honour going to the one who clung longest. Twice a week his mother had bundled the family wash in a sheet and wheeled it on an old pram to the public laundry, where she spent the morning bent over the stone sinks. She had a tough life, he thought. All the women did... The children played in groups on the road and he remembered the voices yelling up to the windows for bread. Up would go a window and down would come sailing a newspaper-wrapped slice of bread and margarine with sugar sprinkled over, and the children would scramble for the parcel while an irate mother shouted at them to let her Jeanie or Bobby or Willy have it. He had always thought his mother the prettiest and nicest woman in that street. Perhaps she really had been, he thought. She hadn't been coarse-voiced like the others.

She was just out of her depth, I suppose, he told himself. His father had limped, but not slightly like Bill. One leg had been blown away below the knee in the first world war, so the limp, on an artificial leg which had always given trouble, was a very noticeable one. Once—he must have been four or five years old then—he had been playing with the others and seen his father leave the tenement entry and go limping down the street, a tall heavy man with thick black hair and dark brown eyes. It was curious to remember that he had always thought his father's eyes beautiful when he was not angry. Curious now, because on the day of which he was thinking he had seen the set of the broad shoulders, the clenching and loosening of the big hands, and had recognized the signs. Others had too: 'Hey, your paw looks awfy mad.'

He had run across the road and scrambled up the stairs, his heart bumping and legs straining as he went round and round and up and up. The door was open and he tumbled into the kitchen where his mother sat by the table; milk from an overturned bottle had soaked the spread newspaper and was dripping into a white puddle on the floor. His mother's apron was over her face but he could hear her crying.

'Mammy, what's the matter? What did he do, Mammy?'

'As if it was my fault…' The apron muffled her voice. He pulled at it frantically. 'Where would I get money from? Spending all his pension…' As he shouted at her and pulled her skirt, she suddenly lowered the apron. He was terrified. Her hair hung around her shiny, tear-streaked face, her cheek and temple were bruised and swelling, and she stared at him as though he were strange to her.

'Your father doesn't care about you. Only his drink and his gambling. He hates us all. He's left us.'

As she spoke she stared, without moving towards him. He knew the insecurity of floors that could fall away and walls that could tumble in; he felt their height above the street, the fearful drop, and he buried his face in her lap, shouting.

Now in the speeding bus with people around him, he told himself that in another life his mother would have been different. Yet she had taken his father back so often; she had praised him for some things even when they were apart. When he was eight his mother's father had died and her share of his money had been enough to take them to a better district. And a year later the money was all lost on a business venture of his father's, his parents were parted, and his mother was working to keep them again. And so the cycle of parting and reunion had gone on, and he would no sooner grow used to having a father than his father would be gone again.

The break-ups had been more frequent after William died. There had been a picture of William in the bedroom he had shared with Charles, and on the walls of that room had also been hung pictures of the wars in

Manchuria and Spain, and slogans like 'A bayonet is a weapon with a worker at each end.' He had often heard long arguments between Charles and his father or Charles and his friends as he lay in William's old bed trying to sleep. But Charles too had been gone by the time he was nine and his sisters had followed soon after. When only Walt was left his mother had talked for many hours, many times, about how wonderful a person William had been and how everyone had liked him. Later, as frequent moves brought them to England, where, she said, his father would never find them, she had loved to talk of Charles and how clever he was and how well he was doing. So that Walt, who felt that he was not very wonderful, cared little for popularity, and regarded himself as anything but clever, had often wondered if he were truly a member of the family.

When he got down from the bus at the cinema and began walking home through quiet streets, in healthy air and bright sunshine at last, he was wishing he had known his brothers better. But he would never know William, and Charles, who had won a commission in the Army and now had a staff job with a huge firm in the South, had spent two years abroad after the war. All that Walt had to judge his family by were the dislocated impressions, like brief scenes from a long, complicated film, of a boy more inclined to escape or ignore his surroundings than to observe or analyse.

The rest of that afternoon he spent on his bed, with his favourite books around him as he read through random passages. He kept thinking of his family and wishing he had not been the youngest; wishing he had been old enough to appreciate it when his parents had been happy together, and wishing most of all that he could have known William better. Perhaps then, he thought, he could have better understood himself and his undefined restlessness and turbulent needs.

When he and the old lady were having tea, Walt sitting at the table while she sat in her usual chair, he said he would cut the grass for her the following week.

'You don't have to 'less you want. Let them come and do it. It'll be here long after I'm gone.' He saw the scrawl of wrinkles around her pursed lips as she drank from her saucer, and it occurred to him that she was close to death. The sudden realization that he too would be like that some day almost horrified him. He asked if she ever got lonely.

'Lonely?' She came to fill his empty cup, holding the fat, heavy teapot firmly in her red-mottled hand. 'I don't. Got me own friends and me own place—not as I couldn't live wi' any o' my lads any time. They've all begged me.'

'Why don't you?' As she sat down again she said impatiently that you couldn't beat your own roof over your head where you could do as you pleased. She filled her saucer again.

'This is mine and this is how I want it. When I leave here it'll be feet first, lad. Besides—I wouldn't fit in wi' their ways now.'

'You should've been a man,' he told her, smiling. He felt that her strength justified her harshness and old-fashioned ideas. 'You'd have made a good miner.' She snorted at this, and said there was nothing a man could do a woman couldn't do better, but she'd like to see a man rear a family the way she had hers.

When Walt went to the cinema at seven o'clock, he found Bryan waiting there. He was wearing a brown suit and a black shirt with little pearl buttons on its collar points. Marie had taken Brenda's things to her home, he explained, and they had arranged to meet that night.

'Oh,' Walt grunted, wondering if Brenda were wary of being alone with him now. Bryan began praising him effusively as they joined a queue of young people.

'Me and Marie's like that,' he said triumphantly, holding up crossed fingers. Then he began describing his performance with her in the park that afternoon. 'I nearly coaxed her,' he said confidentially.

'In daylight?' Walt blinked at him.

'Behind the bushes, man. What do you think I am? Honest, you had to fight for a place, there were that many there!'

The queue was an unruly one and Walt saw many faces he had seen at the dance. They were shouting to each other, skylarking, scuffling and milling all over the pavement. Groups of youths and girls were laughing as they exchanged sallies, or called to friends passing by, and now and then those at the rear began pushing so that the whole column, like a rippling caterpillar, would crawl forward a few yards, making the same motion backward again as those at the front returned the push. Bryan had a hand on Walt's shoulder. He mentioned that Blackie was here, and Walt saw the black, wavy hair bobbing among the jostling heads near the front.

'We kidded the copper up and nobody got in trouble,' Bryan assured him. 'But you sure shook Blackie up, didn't you?'

For a moment Walt considered going to apologize and shake hands, but he was afraid this might be taken for cowardice and he preferred to make an enemy than be thought a coward.

'How did you go on with old Bren, eh?' Bryan asked, squeezing Walt's shoulder and putting his head close. Walt answered not bad, and Bryan waited, then looked disappointed for a moment. Then his look became respectful, half admiring, and he pushed Walt, grinning, and said: 'You're a deep 'un, kid. Walk off wi' old Brenda first night at the Memo and then act as if butter wouldn't melt, eh? I'll tell you this—you and me's mates.

Real mates. You've got style.'

While Walt was wondering uncomfortably what Bryan's reactions would be to an exposure of his inexperience, he saw Brenda and Marie approaching from the opposite pavement. He eased gratefully out of the grip on his shoulder, disliking the threat of being pinioned that he felt in it, as Bryan waved and shouted to them. Both girls wore sweaters, long skirts and short jackets. Brenda's blond hair flounced on her collar as she stepped short on high heels, and Walt thought to himself that she looked the kind of girl his mother would have condemned as 'fast.'

'Hi, Wally,' Marie greeted them, missing his outraged glare as she smiled at Bryan: 'Hi, Burt.' The two girls pushed in beside them as Bryan told Walt delightedly: 'She reckons I look like Burt Lancaster. How's that, eh?' Whatever his mother might think of Brenda, however bright the lipstick and blond the hair, she was good enough for him, he thought. Her teeth, as she returned his smile, were white, perfectly even and well cared for, and he admired the air of pride and the beauty of her delicately touched blue eyes.

'Bet *you* had a hangover,' she said, then looked around her. She looked aloof and mature, and he told himself that she must feel her attractiveness and know the power she had over any who courted her. She must be accustomed to the knowledge, and to flattery and fussing. He felt warily defiant and left the talking to Bryan and Marie, who teased and nudged and prodded each other, jostling Brenda and himself. Some youths behind began imitating Marie's high laugh and Bryan frowned mildly over his shoulder at them once or twice, so that Walt was glad when the doors opened and the crowd charged inside.

No one paid much attention to the old film. Pellets of paper darted overhead, people called messages over the seats, and some of the love scenes, tritely worded and conventionally filmed, were met by loud, ribald remarks. No one was impressed, either, by the attendants who flashed their torches on the rows and kept calling for order. One male attendant kept shouting, 'Quiet, or I'll put you out,' until a voice answered from the middle of a row, 'Thee be quiet or we'll put thee out,' and everyone round about applauded.

Beside Walt, who sat with arms folded, Bryan and Marie were huddled, exchanging kisses and murmuring. Walt felt he couldn't possibly make love to a girl in a crowded cinema, and, besides, there was restraint between Brenda and him. Whether she was quiet because he was, or whether she felt differently about him after a second look, he had no idea, but the silence was making him feel shy and awkward. He found the picture boring, the noise aggravating, and he was growing increasingly restless and irritable. When a torch-beam glared in his face, he shouted:

'Hey! Turn that damn thing off!'

Brenda touched his arm as he sat forward, shielding his eyes. 'Who said that.'

'I did,' Walt answered, but so did all the youths around him, and they began drumming their feet on the floor until the torch was switched off, and Walt was grinning as he settled back, his tension suddenly relieved. Brenda clasped his hand, and when he looked, she said, gently smiling and gently chiding: 'Don't go getting into more trouble.'

At ten o'clock the crowd came pouring out into the darkened street and broke up into groups, some hanging around doorways while others sauntered off shouting good nights, with single youths making last attempts at finding girl-friends on the way home. Near by stood two policemen, like staid uncles keeping a dignified protective watch over children. Bryan shouted to Walt that he would see him at one o'clock as they parted.

'If you're on afternoons we won't see you till Saturday, then,' Brenda remarked as they walked along.

'At least I won't be staggering around half asleep all week,' he answered.

'It ought to be Saturday twice a week. At least you get some fun then.' In the streets the darkness was broken by gas lamps standing in cones of yellow light. She asked about what he had been doing that day.

'Just reading,' he said, walking slowly, hands in pockets. 'I like books.'

'I guessed you was like that. Books and that.'

She was stressing his difference again, he thought, his restless irritation returning.

'Well, you read too, don't you?' he asked, a little sharply.

'Not much. Me and Marie go to t' pictures mostly in t' week. You know—' she frowned at him— 'you remind me of a film star—I just can't remember who it is.'

He was flattered until he remembered that Bryan reminded Marie of a film star and Blackie had reminded someone else of another.

When they reached her back door she leaned against the wall once more and looked up at him. He stood with his hands in his pockets, finding it much more difficult to begin kissing her cool face now than he had the previous night. He felt he should say something first, but could think of nothing to say.

'Quiet, aren't you?'

'I guess I made enough noise last night,' he answered, grinning awkwardly.

'You didn't want to come tonight, did you?' she demanded angrily, her jaw rising and cheeks tightening over the fine bones. He protested that of course he had, but she straightened up, chest indignantly presented at him, and said he'd never come near her in the pictures and hadn't said a word, and he didn't have to tell her lies.

'If you didn't want to come you should have said so.'

'I did. I just felt a bit fed up, and...'

'I'm not your sort, am I? You've changed your mind.'

'No.' He seized her shoulders. 'Of course you're my sort. It's you that keeps making me out as different.

'Because you are,' she said. 'That's why.' Then her eyes widened and she caught at his arms as he roughly shook her.

'Get it straight, I'm not. I'm the same as Bryan and the lads. I'm an ordinary miner. So cut it out.' He shook her again.

'All right.' Loose hair curled over her brow and she breathed hard. 'All right, let me go. Don't get so mad.'

'I'm sorry,' he said, quickly humble as she stared at him. He cupped her chin in his hand and kissed her. He hated no one so much as himself with his unexplained emotional violences. When he released her and smiled gently, she asked: 'Was it because of last night? Because I wouldn't let you?'

'No, it's not that, honest. You were right.'

'You haven't changed your mind?'

'I like you a lot. I don't know why you like me.' As she threw her arms around his neck and hugged him, he remembered the little rubber ring in his pocket, his behaviour of the previous night, and he thought: It's disgusting. I couldn't be like that with such a nice girl!

One lad had me on a string once,' she was murmuring, and I'm not wearing it again. But you *are* different, Walt. That's why I like you.'

He stroked her cheek, his own cheeks hard. Her body was pressed against him, yet he felt no heat, as though climax were over. He pushed his face into her hair, wondering why he got so angry.

VII

One hot Monday afternoon in June, Walt visited his undermanager before going down-pit. His training had been completed and Bryan was now a trainee himself on the coal-face. Walt had learned his job quickly because he had insisted on doing everything by himself after the first week. He was growing accustomed to a miner's life, to long monotonous weeks and hectic weekends, as he was growing accustomed to the tub-stall colliers who chaffed him like any other young driver, and to Tom, the pony who nuzzled his pockets at the beginning of each shift for the crusts and titbits he always brought. He was a good driver, but that did not satisfy him. He felt that it was the coal-face men who formed the aristocracy among miners; their work was the most difficult, dangerous and uncomfortable of all, and their wages were highest. He was no more prepared to settle for second best now than he had been when leaving home.

'You want to be a collier?' the undermanager repeated. 'Don't you reckon you ought to get your hand in first?' His name was Anderson and he was a fat, ponderous man, grunting his words as though grudging them. His stick and helmet lay on his desk beside some papers, and he sprawled across them, his fleshy face dusty and his eyebrows bristling clumps as he looked at Walt. 'A stint of coal's not like pony-driving, kid.'

'I want to be a collier,' Walt answered. 'I might as well start now.' He spoke with vague defiance because he was nervous of any kind of authority. His helmet was pushed far back on his head as he stood uneasily waiting

'I'm glad you're that keen. There's too many young 'uns won't have it!' Anderson leaned back in his stout chair to study Walt while scratching his dirty chest. 'But you're new to pit work and coaling's harder than you realize. How old are you?'

Walt told him.

'And I'm fit, honest,' he added eagerly. 'I could do it.' Two, white creases showed round the grey jowls as the other smiled and said they couldn't disappoint keenness like that.

'But we'll have to fill your job first. Give me a week or two.

'You won't forget.'

'Son!' Anderson smiled again. 'We *need* colliers—just don't come moanin' when your back starts cracking. I've warned you it's hard graft—for men, never mind lads.'

While Walt was still deciding whether to feel triumphant at getting the job or angry at being called a lad, Anderson asked if he had sat an exam at his training pit.

'Thought it were you,' he said when Walt nodded. 'Morris, eh? Well, you've passed and you'll be going to college in September when term starts.' He explained that Walt would be allowed each Tuesday to study at the college instead of working and would be paid haulage rate for it.

'You should go to night school an' all, to make sure. That's if you want to try for your manager's ticket.'

A beatific smile appeared in Walt's face.

'A day off with pay,' he muttered to himself. 'For a whole term!'

'For five years,' Anderson said. He lifted his stick suddenly and sprawled over the desk again to point it at Walt, his face like that of a mastiff on guard. 'You wouldn't be the first that took it up for t' chance of a day off. But you've got to show progress, understand?' The brass ferrule darted at Walt's stomach to emphasize each point as he was told how young ones didn't appreciate these chances and that there had been nothing like them in Anderson's day:

'I slogged nine hours a day, then went home and studied.' Walt drew in his stomach as the stick prodded. 'There were no day-school lark then, and I didn't get here from no university, you know.' Walt smiled politely and stepped back one pace while Anderson growled at him as though he were in here for some misdemeanour. He was given this chance because young ones would be needed soon to replace the older men. This was more important than filling coal so far as he was concerned.

'...Do you want to see the job run by some university boy that's never worked in. his life?'

'No,' Walt said, watching the stick. 'Oh no.'

'It'll be your fault if it is. Stick in at your studies and your work and you'll get some place. Hear?'

'Yes.'

'Nowt in a young 'un's road nowadays as guts can't shift. Have you got any guts?'

'Yes.' As the stick threatened his navel, Walt hastily added: 'I'll go. Definitely. But I can go coaling too, can't I?'

Anderson nodded, lowered the stick, and said he could get down-pit now—there were more important jobs than lecturing haulage hands for their own good.

As they travelled home in the train that night Walt told Bryan about the interview and was slapped several times on the shoulder as the big youth cried delightedly that he was a marvel.

'Tell us something you can't do, Walt. Hey, you'll be able to fix me in a cushy job when you're a gaffer, eh?'

But Walt was more elated over prospects of becoming a collier than of passing some future exams. Bryan's admiration surprised him, because Bryan was obviously going to make a good collier. He was superbly fitted for the life he would lead. The job you did meant less than how well you did it and how much better than others. Bryan was nearer to manhood, therefore, than himself.

Bill was also enthusiastic in congratulating Walt, and as he was leaving home for work next day he heard the old lady telling Mrs. Watson about it over the garden fence. 'If he don't get on it's his own fault,' she was saying. 'He's got the brains—there's no denying that...' It seemed a lot of fuss to make over something which anyone with a fair education could do. Not everyone could be a collier, yet no one seemed so impressed about his new job.

The week dragged on. Although he spent two hours at Thorpe's gym almost every morning, he still found afternoon shift utterly boring. Each day at noon he left home, and it was eleven o'clock before he returned. The journey home was pleasant, with cheerful colliers and steelworkers crowding the trams, but travelling to the pit, through sunshine soon to be left, was a joyless drag that made the mind apathetic for the rest of the day. He no longer had to be urged to visit the Castle each Saturday; he knew why it was such a special night now.

On Saturday morning only Walt and Thorpe were in the gym so they boxed a few rounds together. Thorpe was the best and wiliest opponent Walt had faced, and in spite of fierce attacks the other's guard and counter-punching were too clever for him to break down. When they were lounging, on the ropes recovering their breath, Thorpe smiled at Walt's flushed face and, sounding pleased with himself, told him:

'I still know a trick or two, I suppose.' His voice echoed in the empty gym.

'I couldn't hit you?' Walt said disgustedly. 'I'm not so good after all.'

'You're good. Don't doubt it.' For the past month Thorpe had been training him to sway and ride blows and to weave and parry punches as well as relying on his speed and deft footwork. Walt had learned all this as eagerly as he had his job; both were outlets for his furious energy and his urge for achievements he could be proud of.

'You weren't in your tiger mood, Walt,' Thorpe consoled him. 'You know, you'd do best with an audience. Lots of athletes are like that.'

When Walt insisted he would hate an audience, Thorpe shook his head and eased off the ropes to stand in front of him.

'You've never tried it, Walt. Why don't you let me fix you up for an amateur match?'

'In front of people?' It was Walt's turn to shake his head. 'I told you it was just for fun, Alec.'

'You take your fun awfully seriously, then, don't you?' Thorpe asked dryly. 'You've been training like a pro. Now, you've plenty to learn, Walt, but in your own weight you'd do well right now in an amateur contest. The clubs have matches for their funds and charities and you could go in for Clifton—I'll fix it.' As Walt stood frowning, he said coaxingly: 'You want to know how good you are or aren't, don't you?'

The thought of a crowd was more frightening than that of a serious opponent. Walt turned to lean over the ropes and said: 'Oh no, Alec. I couldn't.'

'All right.' Thorpe shrugged, but he watched speculatively as he said: 'Of course, this is a city of damned good amateurs. You'd be up against tough competition—that's why I thought it would be a good test. However...' As the trainer turned away, Walt realized that unless he accepted the challenge he would always wonder if he had perhaps been afraid of a beating. The doubt would force him to action some day and might as well be settled now.

'I'll have a bash,' he said quietly, and Thorpe was smiling as he turned again.

The rest of the morning was spent pounding a heavy canvas bag with a weight in each fist to strengthen his punching. His month of training had included some weight-lifting; Thorpe had said that any slight effect on his speed would be compensated by the increase in strength and weight. His fit condition made Walt feel happy, and as he hooked and jabbed at the jolting bag he was thinking that his life had changed a great deal. He had much to do, friends to share his pleasures, and happy weekends to look forward to. When he was leaving the gym Thorpe promised to arrange a bout for him before the month was out.

After dinner Walt went upstairs with a letter from his mother which had just arrived. Bill was spending the week-end at home, so he was undisturbed as he lay reading on the bed. After the first page, he began frowning over the sloping, sprawling hand-writing. His mother said she had spent a fortnight with Charles, looking after his children while his wife was ill, and had returned to London to find his father gone.

'We had a row about my going...' he read, turning on to his side '...He said my place was with him and I was always putting the family first. He's always been jealous because you all think more of me than of him. I expect he thought I'd be talking about him to Charles. So he does this to me when I only took him back because he was so ill. *He*'ll pay some day...' He lowered the letter, feeling the sun hot on his face and hands. No doubt his father would pay some day. No doubt his mother actually had talked about him to Charles, for she couldn't help doing that kind of thing. What puzzled him was why illness should make any difference to what his father had been and done to her. He raised the letter again.

'That clock you bought me at Christmas. You must have saved so hard to get it, and he's stolen it. Everything else too—every stick of furniture. He sold everything two days before I came back and I expect the money's all gone on drink now. So I had to give up the flat and come to live with Charles. I'm too old to start again...'

The clock came first, he noticed. The item most likely to rouse his indignation? He knew he should be feeling indignant; yet all he felt was a heaviness in his chest, as difficult to swallow as a wet clod.

'...I've forgiven him time and again when you were all against him but I'll never be such a fool again. I will never, never forgive him, and I know you won't either...'

The letter dropped on the floor as he rolled on to his back to stare up at the glowing ceiling. She needn't have tried so hard to convince him, he thought, and then wondered how people could do such things to each other. Constant forgiveness—constant betrayal. On the way out his father was everything bad; on the way back there were excuses for him: 'He's got some good points... a cripple after all... your father might have been a great man if only...'

Apart again, and this time even furniture she had worked to pay for was gone. No action would be taken. He would be forgiven in time.

'Only not by me,' he said aloud, then sat up quickly telling himself not to be so dramatic. This was that past he had rejected; it had no place in his new life.

He stood up, then began restlessly pacing, and he felt emotion much mightier than paltry indignation darkly heaving in him, like blinded Samson wrenching at his bonds. He stood by the window, looking out at children in the sunny gardens, and thinking: You did me one good turn, Pop. You came back long enough to make no room for me. And I'm not going back.

As though this were a witnessed ritual, Walt put his hands on the glass and thought solemnly: I disown him. Just like he disowned me long ago—me more than any of them, because he was never kind to me.

He was not the kind to forgive easily, whatever else he might be, he thought as he threw himself on the bed again. And life wasn't some kind of printing press that marked each rolling sheet. A person's present moved constantly into past and the only indelible record was that which time stamped on the face; the rest could be expurgated. At eighteen you had more cause to look forward than back, and he would keep only what was good. He could forget this.

Yet it was tea-time before he went downstairs, and when he was going out the old lady asked if anything were wrong at home. 'Nothing much,' he said gruffly, closing the back door. She called:

'Well, enjoy yourself, anyroad, lad. Behave, mind.'

'I won't be late,' he answered.

'Well, have a good time. The downs have to come afore the ups, you know.'

He was thinking curiously, as he walked along, that at any other time she would have jeered at him for being morose.

At the dance, in a mood of brittle, savage good-fellowship he teased

Brenda until her eyes were gleaming slits, returned vigorously Bryan's hearty slaps, made Marie laugh and mimicked her so that the others laughed. His movements grew jerkier and his voice more harshly strained, and it was he who first suggested a drink. On the way, Bryan told Brenda that Walt was going to be a manager, laughing at her when she stared.

'Ask him,' he shouted, as he and Marie hurried on in front. 'Goin' to school and everything, he is!'

Walt explained briefly and said plenty of others had the same chance. Brenda was thoughtful for a few moments, then she clasped his arm with both hands and squeezed, as she said: 'I'm proud on you, love. No wonder you're feeling so happy.'

In the concert room, at the usual joined tables, Walt told himself that he truly was happy and that he was enjoying the rowdy fellowship. He drank as fast as Bryan. Beer was good; it produced those spinning, fluffy coils which enwrapped old troubles and smothered them. Yet between drinks he sat holding an empty glass by its thick handle, twitching his wrist so that it rattled furiously on the table. He stopped for two minutes when Brenda begged him to, then began again. He answered the others when they talked, laughed with them and sang with them, but found his belly and abdomen becoming so taut that it was impossible to sit still. Brenda said he was like a cat on hot bricks and Bryan shouted that she'd better be careful: '...That's what a week on afters does to you, Bren. Watch him tonight.'

As everyone grinned and Marie screeched, Brenda squeezed Walt's arm.

'Not everybody's like you,' she retorted. Since their first meeting Walt had made no more attempts at seduction. The others now regarded them as a pair; room was always made for them to sit together and they were expected to dance only with each other. Brenda was openly possessive; she regarded it as her duty to chide him if he drank too much, and had done so several times during the first hour.

'Cut it out, Walt,' she said now. 'You'll be drunk.'

'So I'll be drunk,' he answered, winking across the table to Hughie Sawford.

'You'll be bad. Steady up!' She pushed his glass into the centre of the table and Walt jerked it back.

'Look,' he said to her, 'you drink yours and I'll drink mine. I don't need a nurse.' Everyone turned ostentatiously towards the stage to show they had noticed nothing. Brenda demanded: 'What's up? I'm telling you for your own good.'

'You do too much of that!' He stood up. 'I won't be a minute.'

Nodding at faces in the uproar he pushed a way to the doors. As he passed the bar he saw Blackie, and they exchanged sullen stares. Since their quarrel they had ignored each other. It was cooler outside although the sun was still humped over a crimson horizon and there was no breeze. He sat on the low wall with his hands in his pockets, moodily gazing up the quiet road. Instead of feeling pleasantly half drunk he was full of spiteful bitterness, and he longed for some way to relieve it or cure it. He felt lonely.

No wonder William went to Spain, he thought. I bet it's easier when it's just a case of fighting for things and keeping alive.

And thrusting through his unhappy thoughts came the meaningless words: Still not enough. Still not enough… Then: Brenda could help me if she wanted…'

'I'm here, then,' Blackie drawled, and Walt jerked around to find him a yard away, his coat unbuttoned and hands drooping. When he asked what he wanted, Blackie said in surprise: 'Ain't I what you came out for? You looked at me in there. You said that night as—'

'Oh, beat it,' Walt ordered. 'I never noticed you in there.'

'Well, well!' Blackie smiled, putting hands on hips. 'There were me thinkin' you meant it that night. "I don't need my mates," you said. You showed me up.' He moved closer, his eyes like splinters of coal in the sallow face as he said: 'I warned you not to lean on Bryan too much.' He dodged back quickly as Walt jumped down from the wall.

'You're going to be dead sorry you started this,' he answered, joyfully telling himself that this was what he had wanted.

'It was you started it!' Blackie told him. 'I'm not yellow—I don't let guys get away with that stuff. Let's go round the back where your mates can't butt in.' He added that his own friends were inside watching Walt's, then they strolled round to the rear of the public house, Blackie taking long strides with his hands hanging, and Walt thinking that they were like two gentlemen duellists approaching the field of honour. He felt that for Blackie's sake they should wear guns at their hips. They should count off paces and draw, one man to fall in the volleying smoke and the other to mount a horse and ride off towards the red horizon. He was sure this would have made Blackie happy.

On a patch of rough grass, with trees and a high wall around them, they took off their coats. There were shadows here, and the voices of waiters penetrating the raucous noise in the pub sounded like distant shouts of command.

'This do you?' Blackie asked, his white shirt divided by a black tie.

'A pint you can't touch me, cowboy,' Walt called, deliberately rousing the other's fury, and gathering his own emotions as hard as his gathered fists. Blackie came in a crouch, his arms hooked to wrestle, and as he leaped, body extending black and white, Walt dodged and struck at his face, then waited calmly while he recovered.

'You're a boxer,' Blackie complained, touching his face. 'I don't fight that way.' Walt told him to fight how he wanted, but fight or clear off.

'I'm fed up with your act,' he added, and Blackie rushed on him again, his face savage and long arms flailing. Footwork was impossible on such ground, but Walt still had every advantage. Blackie was a brawler, a roughhouse fighter, and it was the disciplined body against the undisciplined, the skilled against the unskilled. Blackie did not know how to ride a punch or put full force behind his own punches, and Walt could hit him almost where he chose without taking serious punishment. Viciously and competently he beat at Blackie's face with short jabs until nose and mouth were bleeding and the cheeks scarlet bruised. Blackie tried to grapple with him, cursing steadily and obscenely, but the close guard baffled him and the jarring punches knocked him back until he suddenly threw his arms over his face.

'Had enough?' Walt stood over him, panting a little. 'You're not that bad hurt.' He spoke contemptuously because he wanted Blackie to keep fighting so that he could go on hitting, punching and relieving himself. He was full of spite and hatred, yet the tears he saw glittering in the black eyes made him growl abruptly: 'Pack it in before you do get hurt. You've had enough. Let's—'

'Not from a big-headed bastard like you,' Blackie cried as he straightened up. 'You started it—you showed me up!'

His wild swing sent Walt staggering, but the next missed and Walt sprang to knock him back three reeling paces. His rage as furiously hot and dangerous as molten steel bursting from a giant ladle, Walt struck at Blackie like a mighty-pawed lion beating down a leopard. He saw Blackie swaying against a tree-bole as he paused for one breath before charging on him. He saw the white shirt twist sideways as he charged, and one hand dart behind as the other clawed his face; then he saw the hand come up and in at him, the brown plaited tube bending a little. He felt no blow, but in his head there was a black explosion out of which came a white core, growing and growing till it enveloped him. Then he hung in a darkness filled with invisible movement as though black clouds swirled, mated and separated. Quick painful shocks struck at his face, and he muttered: 'Cut it out.'

'Are you all right? Are you, kid?'

His eyes hurt as he opened them and saw a gaunt face move back above him.

'Christ, I thought you was dead,' Blackie exclaimed in a gush of relief. 'I thought I'd done you in.'

He put his hands under Walt's shoulders and helped him to rise.

'I forgot all about it,' Walt said, leaning on him as he swayed.

'Listen. I couldn't help it.' The worried black eyes came close to his face. The nose was beginning to swell and blood fringed the nostrils and mouth. 'I never used it before. I only carried it in case of real trouble!' There was no drawl left in the sharp-pitched voice. 'You'd have killed me there, honest you would. You went crazy. I had to... Look, look. It's gone!' His arm jerked in a white curve and they heard a light clatter on the roof slates. 'I thought you was dead—I'm sorry. Honest, I'm sorry.'

'You did right,' Walt said. He bent down, swayed for a moment, then picked up his coat and began putting it on. His rage was gone and he felt weak, emptied except for a slow pulsing in his belly. 'It wasn't a fair fight for you,' he said. As his finger touched a lump above his ear a drop of blood clung to it.

Blackie stood in front of him with his arms outstretched, his white face pushed forward in appeal.

'Listen, kid. You want to hit me one more good 'un? Well, go on—hard as you like. I've got it coming. Only I never used it before. Your mates'll murder me when they know.'

Walt peered at him. He held out his hand and said:

'Let's forget it. I told you to fight how you wanted. Let's drop it all.'

They shook hands solemnly.

'I won't tell anybody,' Walt promised. 'Was I out long?'

'No, not long.' As he put on his coat, Blackie asked worriedly: 'You won't tell? Honest?'

'It was our scrap,' Walt answered, beginning to walk away. 'I won't tell a soul.'

They reached the front of the pub and found Bryan and some of the others there with Brenda behind them. Bryan began asking questions, but stopped when he saw Blackie, and said: 'Guessed it was that.' Blackie's friends were spilling from the doorway.

'Looks like Walt did all right,' Hughie Sawford grinned. 'That's a nice red stripe to your shirt, Blackie.' Walt told them it was all over, while Blackie stood close, dabbing at his nose with a silk handkerchief and warily watching Bryan. Brenda pushed her way through. She stared at Walt for a moment, then slowly reached out to touch his temple.

'It's bleeding,' she said, frowning. 'It's a great big lump !'

'A lump?' Bryan leaped at Blackie, seized his coat lapels and swung him against his chest. 'You used that cosh! You dago-faced little spiv, I warned you—' He shook the struggling youth and began hissing obscenities at him. Blackie's mates lurched forward, then halted as Hughie Sawford and the others wheeled to meet them. The white face twisted beseechingly towards Walt, and he pushed Brenda away, shouting: 'Hold it, Bry. He's had enough.'

He clutched at the fingers gripping the lapels, but they were immovable.

'Bry,' he said, 'don't hit him.' He was terrified for Blackie's sake. He had never realized how infinitely dangerous could be the wrath of the boisterous young bear. 'We're finished if you hit him, Bry.'

'Did he cosh you, kid?' Bryan turned a glistening face.

'I fell against a tree. He doesn't carry one—search him.'

'Honest, Walt?' Blackie was hoisted up and tentatively shaken as Bryan pondered.

'Honest. It was fair enough.' Although Bryan was obviously still suspicious he took the chance to ease out of a suddenly awkward situation. Blackie almost fell as he was released.

'Don't ever do t' dirty on my mate,' Bryan softly warned him. Blackie shook his head, glanced gratefully at Walt, then joined his friends and went back into the pub. At a nod from Bryan the others followed. Walt turned to Brenda and found her staring at him with her shoulders drooping. She straightened up, blue sweater out-thrust haughtily, and her skirt flared as she whirled and walked to the doors.

'Brenda, wait!' He glanced at Bryan, half apologetically, half ruefully, and received a sympathetic grin as he ran after her.

'Brenda, don't get mad,' he said, catching her shoulders.

'You're as bad as them.' Her eyes were narrowed and outraged and her chin jerked up at him. 'You pushed me, and all.'

He began wheedling her.

'You saw how it was. I'm sorry. Let's go somewhere quiet and talk.'

She wriggled free and said he could go if he wanted to—she was going inside, where she should have stayed to mind her own business, she supposed. He knew the mood and knew long argument and pleading would be needed to soothe her. But he felt too tired for that. He felt used up, and he wanted to rest for a while without having to think or talk. He told her quietly: All right, Bren. You go. I'll go home.' As the lump began throbbing he raised his hand and found blood oozing in his hair.

'Does it hurt?' Brenda asked.

'Well, of course it does,' he said gruffly.

'I'll go get my coat and then we'll get it fixed,' she said, and hurried into the pub. Walt turned to Bryan with an exasperated grunt.

'Come round in a second,' he said. 'Just so she can play nursemaid.'

Bryan put an arm round his shoulder, more lightly than usual, and remarked that they were all the same:

'...It gets a bloody bind after a while, don't it? Tell 'em to keep their noses out and they get niggly. They want to own you.' He added hastily: 'We've got t' two best there is round here mind you—' As Brenda rejoined them he smiled guiltily.

'Look after him, Bren,' he called as she and Walt walked away. 'He's my best pal.'

They had reached the end of the street before Brenda said: 'He's a good friend to you in some ways, I suppose.' She repeated after a moment: 'In some ways!' Walt asked what she meant, but she shrugged silently and he knew she wished him to insist on an answer. Instead he returned her shrug and looked straight ahead, knowing her eyes were angrily flickering towards him in the softening light. At last she broke out:

'Well, you just aren't their sort, and you know it. Talking one minute about being a pit manager and then off scrapping the next. It don't become you.'

'I can do as I please,' he said impatiently. The ache in his head was like a repetitive scraping on a nerve. Brenda said that of course he couldn't, and he demanded why not. With a confused, angry gesture, she said: 'You can't, that's all. Do you want to be like them? Big-headed and leery and just another one in t' gang? And this boxing caper! You're going to get flashy and cocky and end up in trouble.'

'Well, that's *my* funeral.'

Brenda's lips were tight and her arms swung aggressively, the coat she carried over one of them crackling the leaves of a hedge.

It doesn't become me,' he said bitterly after a moment.

'No, it don't, and you'd do better listening to me.' They were both resentfully silent for a while. Walt glanced at her; her hair flounced on her collar as she strode along with her head up and heels clicking hard. She was full of reasons for not doing things, he thought disgustedly, but she could offer few positive reasons for doing something different. Why should he not be exactly what he chose? Would she have preferred him acting the part of drunkard's son? As a weakling without physical cause for pride?

Who was to say what was right or wrong, good or bad?

His elders? Their example was uninspiring; their motto was: 'Do as we say, not as we do and have done.'

The law? That was something you steered clear of; its function was to punish the guilty and protect, but not guide, the innocent. The policeman and judge would advise obedience to the law, but that was not enough. The Church, then?

'Do you believe in God?' he asked, so abruptly that Brenda frowned and answered seriously that she supposed so, she hadn't really thought about it.

'Then you don't... It doesn't matter,' he said.
'Why?' She looked slightly bewildered. 'Do you?'
'No. Forget it.'

It might have been something, he thought wistfully. But the lessons of those years between his ninth and fifteenth birthdays rebuked him. His geography had included Clydebank, London and Coventry, Warsaw, Leningrad and Berlin. He had learned of mass murder, the applied science of ghettoes, stalags, and the towns and villages of Europe and Asia. His history had progressed through the death shambles of streets, fields, deserts and beaches to the fitting climax of Hiroshima, and all these—as much a background to his schooling as a knowledge of the grunt of bombs and whang of shrapnel—ridiculed, so far as he was concerned, blind faith in any divine benevolence.

'I suppose,' Brenda was saying, 'you'd sooner go wi' Bryan an' them than wi' me.' She was more concerned for herself than for him, he realized, yet that was reasonable. He had made himself advocate, after all, of good lions.

'Don't let's row any more.' He touched her arm gently. 'My headache made me ratty, I suppose. I'm sorry.'

She wriggled her free hand into his and clasped his fingers.

'You're a funny lad, Walt.'

'You're always saying that.'

'I know.' She smiled, then went on: 'I only say things for your own good. I know what you're really like.'

He forced a smile and returned the squeeze. It was not worth another argument, he told himself. At her gate, however, a fresh one began when he wanted to go home and Brenda wanted him to go into the house. She finished it by saying tartly: 'You'll have to come in some time. Not scared of being in there on your own wi' me, are you?'

Walt indignantly followed her inside. She made him sit in a wooden arm-chair by an empty hearth, then fetched a bowl of warm water and gently bathed his bruised temple. Most of the furniture was becoming shabby, though a new portable radio stood on the oak sideboard. Another wooden arm-chair was opposite Walt and a long settee stood in front of the hearth. Brenda frowned as she bent over him and clicked her tongue reprovingly, till Walt said: 'Honest, Bren. Goodness help your kids when you get some.' He was surprised at her sudden flush and lowered eyes. She stood up and went to the kitchen with the bowl, saying over her shoulder: 'If I got one like you I wouldn't need bloomin' kids!'

'And you'd always be praying he'd break a leg or something so you could keep him in bed and boss him about,' Walt answered. Then he heard loud voices outside, and a moment later the kitchen door opened.

While Brenda was saying something about his falling at the dance and bumping his head, he sat waiting nervously for the ordeal of scrutiny and interrogation by suspicious parents.

'Were that afore he had a pint?' her father asked, and entered the room smiling broadly at Walt.

'How do, chum?' He peeled off his coat and tossed it on to the settee, then sat down heavily and unsteadily in the opposite chair. Walt smiled brightly and politely, shaking his head at the offer of a cigarette.

'Not got the habit, chum?' the other asked. 'Good for you!' He was tall, his smile toothless, his grey hair ringing a pallid crown. Joviality seemed ill-matched with his long face and jaw, but the alcoholic glaze over his wrinkle-pouched blue eyes explained the mood. He was humming cheerfully as he lit his cigarette. Walt could hear Brenda in the kitchen sounding curt at her mother's inquisitiveness.

'Started when I was fourteen,' Mr. Carter said, and Walt widened his polite smile. 'That were in t' old *Andrew*[1], you know. Ah, you ought to just have seen *them* fags. Duty free they was. And rum too! I still like me drop o' Nelson's...' He raised his voice: 'Ain't that right, Florrie?'

'What?' This was a cheerful falsetto. 'I say I still like me tot, eh? Nowt like it...'

'Nowt like its price, neither,' Mrs. Carter replied, just as loudly, though she was now in the room. 'Is they, lad?' she asked Walt, and walked to the table before he could answer. She was much stouter than her husband and almost as tall. Ridged on the pudgy nose of her fat face were steel-rimmed spectacles which she looked through when working and looked over when talking. Her hair was brown and frizzy and lipstick was so carelessly smeared on her small pouted mouth that Walt thought of a crushed strawberry. He maintained his wide smile while wondering how such a couple could produce such a daughter.

'Might as well have supper afore you go,' she said, spreading a cloth on the table. Dishes were clicking in the kitchen. 'Nice to have a bit company.'

'Thank you very much,' he answered, and that was his last speech for some time. She switched on the radio and hummed to the blaring dance music as she bustled about the table, while her husband sprawled comfortably and tapped a foot in time. Walt gradually relaxed his straining smile, which he was sure looked inane by now, anyway. When Brenda entered at last with sandwiches and tea, he smiled again with relief, but she said nothing and all through supper she sat quietly on the settee, only glancing at him occasionally as though uneasy.

---

[1] The Royal Navy: term derives from a notorious press ganger in the 19th century, Andrew Millar

Walt could see nothing to feel uneasy about, for her parents chattered and laughed as they ate, and talked about people they had seen during the evening. Both of them had obviously drunk a good deal and tended to laugh at remarks he couldn't understand. Their talk excluded Brenda and himself, but he was grateful that neither had asked him a single question.

'Dad, don't do that when we've got company,' Brenda said as Walt was finishing his tea. He looked at her father, who was grinning and rolling up his shirt-sleeves. He had already removed his collar and tie. His arms were covered by tattoos.

'Where did you get all those?' Walt asked, putting down his cup and saucer. He wanted Brenda to see that her remark had been snobbish.

'Where, matey? In t' *Andrew*, of course. Look here.' He rolled his sleeves tight to his shoulders and held out twin displays of coiled snakes, a dagger, a fouled anchor and a bleeding heart pledging true love to 'F'. On each thin bicep a nude moved provocatively, as he bent his arms, laughing delightedly at Walt's stare. He opened his shirt to show a battleship steaming over blue rippled waves, then opened it wide to display a navel transformed into the crutch of a horse.

Mrs. Carter was laughing and shaking her head, while her husband assured Walt there were plenty more and bent to roll his trouser cuffs to his knees.

'We don't want all that again,' Brenda said, and Walt was puzzled by her scowl. He leaned to admire out-thrust shaved calves on one of which was coiled a fiery dragon while the other showed the back of a nude who was clinging tight.

'Tha wants to see that on his back,' Brenda's mother told Walt. 'Dirty thing it is, an' all! It's like sleepin' wi' a zoo.'

'Got it done in Alex,' the man said proudly. 'I'll show you some time—fox and hounds... Aye, a real matelot I were. Thirty year o' service and been everywhere. Our Brenda were fourteen when I got invalided out. Look here —' He suddenly dropped his head and lunged it at Walt, who heard Brenda whisper something as she sat back. Tapping his dead-skinned crown, Mr. Carter demanded: 'Wouldn't know they was a steel plate under there, would you? But there is.' He straightened up, nodding gravely and shuffling forward confidentially in his chair, as he went on: 'I have black-outs, you know. Got a steel splinter right through me skull, I did. Torpedoed. Right back in forty-two and spent years in hospitals, matey, Years...'

'Dad,' Brenda said quietly. 'Don't let's have it all, tonight.'

Her father looked peeved.

'I'm only telling him—'

'We've had it every Saturday for years,' she said, as firm as a mother with a petulant son. 'Not tonight, eh?'

And Walt realized that the man's expression was much like that of a hopeful child being reproved. He shrugged disappointedly, and then the pouched eyes lowered, flickered up tentatively at Walt and lowered again.

'I were only telling him,' he mumbled, while Brenda sighed impatiently. 'Navy meant a lot to me...'

'Course it did, Dad. But give it a rest this once.'

'Best years of my life, I give 'em...' The shoulders drooped, whining self-pity in the voice, as the features lapsed into a natural melancholy. As the mumbling went on, Walt frowned at Brenda and wondered why she had to be so brusque with such a harmless weakness. Her expression of cold hauteur suggested that she had withdrawn from him as well as her father. Yet one glance came from her that was almost appeal before she looked away.

'Never did right for me, neither... Got smashed up doin' me duty...' The eyes flickered again, this time watchfully towards Brenda. Walt could feel in himself the tension that was growing in the others.

'...Give 'em my lad and all, I did!' The mumble, now a deep mourn, stopped as the grey head slowly moved from side to side. Brenda's mother said sharply: 'Now see what you've done.'

'It were comin'.' Brenda slowly rose and brushed crumbs from her skirt into the hearth. She did not look at Walt. 'It were coming, anyway.'

'No feelings!' Mrs. Carter's voice rose in pitch but lost strength. She looked at Walt. 'She's got no feelings, her.'

'Cut it out,' Brenda told her, as quiet and resigned in voice as she was proud and indrawn in expression.

'Our Ronnie were a sailor and all. Drownded, he was.' Tears brimmed suddenly behind the steel hoops as she looked up at a photograph over the fireplace of a youthful face framed in naval cap and collar. Walt also looked up, and then said: 'Oh, I'm terribly sorry.' But he was bewildered by the sudden transition from lively gaiety to complete dejection.

'We have this every week and all,' Brenda picked up Walt's cup and saucer and took them to the table.

'He was a good lad,' said her mother, staring at the picture with tears on her face. 'A fine boy. Thought more on his mam and dad than his sisters do.'

'He did that,' the father said, lugubriously nodding at the floor. 'Only son we'd got, he were.'

They sat bowed by grief while Brenda cleared the table. Flushed with embarrassment, Walt clasped his hands and wished he could escape without breaking in on their sorrow. He had no right to witness this. Mrs. Carter removed her spectacles to dab at short-sighted eyes already becoming puffy-lidded. When she spoke she was more composed: 'I'll show you some o' t' things he sent us some time, young man. Lovely they are. Thought t' world on us, did Ron.'

'Not tonight, anyroad, Ma,' Brenda told her in a brisk voice as she carried some things into the kitchen. 'It's too late, and he'll be goin' soon. Me dad ought to be in bed now.'

Silence lasted till Brenda sat down again and pointedly stared at her parents. Walt's face was slowly cooling, but a slow thudding had begun again above his ear. The couple said good night soon and went to the other door which led to the stairs. There, Brenda's mother paused to say: 'Don't be too late out on bed, will you, Bren? Don't stay up all night like you used to wi' Frank.' Her head vanished as Brenda glared.

They heard a slow tread and then muffled voices and steps upstairs. Walt sat with his hands still clasped, still studying them, and felt Brenda watching him. After a moment she said with a savagery that made his head jerk: 'The old bitch!' As he looked, she went on, her hand flicking: 'She said that deliberate to make you jealous.'

'Jealous?' He frowned diffidently, as though there had been no stiffening and stretching of claws in his belly at the mother's words, and he answered: 'Why should I be? It's none of my business.'

Brenda's eyes were troubled.

'Don't you want to know about him?' she asked disappointedly. When he shrugged, she drew up her legs and tucked her feet under her. 'You might as well,' she said defiantly. 'We got engaged when I were seventeen and he was going off to do his two years' service. We'd been knockin' about together a good while. He were a nice quiet lad. He worked in an office and—you know—well brought up and that. You reminded me on him in some ways.'

Walt grunted and pulled a face, but Brenda was looking at the fireplace. She missed his sarcastic grin when she added: 'He looked a bit like James Mason—in t' pictures, you know.' Then she said that after six months in the Army he had changed: '...He were all for goin' wi' t' lads, boozing and dancing and that. Telling me about it in letters, and I'm stuck at home never going nowhere.' As she scraped a red thumbnail reflectively across her teeth, he shifted restlessly.

'Well, go on,' he said.

'Oh... We kept having rows when he came on leave and we broke it off in t' end. They say he's engaged again now.'

She brooded, and he thought she looked tough and capable. Surely everyone must be able to see that she was older than him?

'Why were you so funny with your folks?' he asked, wanting to forget what she had been saying.

'Why? I knew they'd do it.' She was disgusted, bored. 'I knew it'd be a showing up.'

'Of course it wasn't! You jump too quick. You always—'

'Couldn't you see?' She stared incredulously. 'Mind you, that weren't the main show, but every time they've been out it's the same. Every week.' As he frowned, she leaned over, a hand outspread while the other ticked off points: 'They come home happy. He wants to show off his tattoos. So he can start about t' Navy and getting torpedoed. Then how the country don't look after its heroes because doctors keep telling him he's not as bad as he says. Then it's her turn about the blitz and bein' on her own wi' us in t' war and then it's Ron! Both of 'em about Ron, and how good he was, and how he loved 'em.' She sat up straight to look at the picture, legs folded and breasts straining at the blue wool as she went on bitterly: 'Ron weren't no different from us two. He just got killed when he were my age. But no different about them! They just want to have a moan and a weep every time they've been on the booze.'

'What's happened to your sister?'

'She had sense,' Brenda answered, her face sullen. 'She got married to the right kind that looks after his home and stays in it.'

Walt began saying gently that it was natural for her parents to feel upset. He wanted to soothe away her sullen brooding, but she flared up at him, insisting that they enjoyed their mourning.

'It's only when they're boozed up, and it's always the same. Laughing and joking and you can see t' beer wearing off and tell when they're going to start. They enjoy it. It's rotten!'

As she sulked he closed his eyes, then slowly opened them, his head throbbing. He knew her feelings. His own torment was beginning again.

'She talks about me! It's my wages save her from goin' to work. They've got to listen to me. I'm t' best piece-worker in my shop. All he gets is a bit of pension and his earnin's on light work. But he's not there half the time wi' his black-outs and such. Never misses his weekends, though!'

I know how it is,' he said tiredly.

'You don't!' She was trying to express contempt for her father at the same time as defiance of what Walt might think 'It's being at home that's up wi' him. He wishes he was still in t' Navy. Why do men all want to run around in gangs like kids and just have their fun?' She looked directly at him, and he quickly stood up and leaned against the mantelpiece, his head turned away. He told himself ruefully that she was awfully keen on settling down. Remembering his own dreams, of a home, children and a pretty wife, he wondered if Brenda were the girl, then thought that he was too young yet, knowing there were other reasons unrecognized.

'You know, anyway—about Frank and about them.' She lowered her feet, smoothing her skirt. 'Think what you want. I can't help my family.'

He turned to stare.

'You can't help... You're bothered about *your* family!'

'What?' As she leaned forward, her head tilted back, the upward thrust of her breasts increased his sense of loneliness and loss.

'Well, why do you think I cleared out?'

'Well...' Brenda's shrug was rhetorical; her eagerness was sincere. 'You said your plans and all that...'

'My old man's a hundred times worse than yours. I hate him! He's a drunken, bullying swine, and—'

'Honest, Walt?' He turned from her relief to put both hands on the mantelpiece. She said, pleased and consoling: 'Never mind, Walt. You're different. You're different from all on 'em. You're going to get somewhere, aren't you? If you just don't get too thick wi' t' gang—'

'They're my friends. The only friends I've got. You've painted your own damn picture of me, Brenda. And you're wrong.'

'Walt, I haven't,' she protested.

'You must have thought a lot of your Frank! You're trying to make me his twin. You can't be satisfied with me as I am.'

'It's not that. I like you more than him, honest.' She jumped up and he felt her hands pressing and pulling on his shoulders. 'I know what sort you really are. Sit down, Walt.'

He resisted her gentle tugs and mumbled that he must go.

'It's not eleven yet,' Brenda said. 'It only takes you five minutes from here. Don't let's fall out, love. We're the same.'

He was afraid because he realized what would happen and because he felt she might extract from him some promise to be what she wanted. He told himself he should reject her. Yet her hand touching his neck, his own endlessly wheeling turbulence and tiredness, the throb in his temple and a swelling urge towards the comforting soft assuagement of her hands and body made him turn to her and slowly sit down. Her palms were a little rough, stroking his hair and then his face with smooth rhythmic tenderness. As they kissed, her body turned in his arms and she coaxed him down with pressing lips and hands until they were lying together. She fumbled with one arm behind her, then lifted her sweater and put his hand on her breast.

'That's what you wanted, isn't it?' She caressed his face with gentle strokes, the rough nipple growing and prodding the palm of his hand while lust beat out from his loins in pounding blood. He realized, after brief effort ending in a grunt of exasperation, that she was truly his mistress now. She smiled maternally.

'All right, I'll help you.'

Then, while he thrashed out his violence and sounded the depths of his own strange darknesses, she lay passive, telling him softly:

'I know how you must feel. It's all right. You've got me, Walt. And I've got you…'

Combatant

I

An adolescent cat was making love to the paving in the warm September sun. As she bellied down, legs asprawl, to rub her black-and-white body against the concrete, she purred monotonously with her love-drugged eyes half closed. Her nostrils were twitching at the juicy smell of broken grass.

'You want to get a bloke, Walt told her sternly, squatting back on his heels in the garden. 'It's not spring now, you know.' Runnels of sweat were trickling down his chest and ribs. He had just finished cutting the grass with shears which in spite of oiling and sharpening were still difficult to use. The cat slithered towards him, swinging her tail with forceful erotic slowness, and as she arched her rump and purred loudly and dreamily, he thought:

There you are... that's it with no posing and the lights left on!

He stroked the blazed forehead while he mused, and the cat grovelled, her dagger teeth parted to show her little pink tongue in her eagerness to be caressed. Ready, he thought, to betray all dignity for the feel of different flesh. Which was how it looked inside with everyone else, too.

'You're a female,' he admonished her. 'Remember your dignity.' His mother's teachings on sex had been confined to a frequently repeated maxim that, except between two people who truly and completely loved and respected one another, intercourse was disgusting. Walt had naturally been determined for a long time to prove the opposite, but at present he felt thwarted.

When the cat blatantly nudged her nose into the roughened palm of his hand he rolled her on to her side where she lay happily purring. He picked up the shears and jerked the handle a few times as he thought about Brenda. There, now, was a girl who could keep her dignity. It was a pity that he kept forgetting his.

He remembered how she had helped him that first time after letting him learn that her help was essential. He had been very ignorant in spite of his book. But Brenda had known.

She knew all about it, he thought, clashing the shears. The most painful factor in that, he had found at first, was the possibility of comparison.

'You've got me, Walt... Had she said that to Frank too? She certainly liked to talk while it went on.

He stood up and walked across the grass-strewn garden to the hedge, where he wrenched half-heartedly at a few tough branches, squinting against the sun's reflection in the windows opposite. It was Sunday afternoon and the street was quiet. Walt was not on speaking terms with the old lady: she had locked him out all night because he had been late home. He had walked the streets until eight o'clock, when she let him in, and then gone to bed until dinner-time. Cutting the grass and the hedge was an excuse to stay out of the house until it was time to visit Bryan, and a way of working off his feelings. While he worked he was thinking angrily that, had he not been arguing with Brenda until midnight, he wouldn't have been locked out. A long argument over the same old things, after another instalment of her father's unending monologue on Navy life, her mother's usual recital of the hardships of grass widowhood[2] in wartime, and the joint requiem for 'our Ron', this time blessedly tearless. Until recently he had not minded too much being bored by her parents; not with the heartening prospect of himself and Brenda alone together. But now, being alone together produced another boring cycle: of brittle words, challenge and reply, demand and refusal.

'Look, Bren,' the latest had begun. 'I've got to go to night school. Mondays and Fridays are out.'

'When it's over...'

'My homework, and I've got to get to bed. I have to be up early!'

'Well, you don't have to go to that rotten gym so much!'

'But I've got to train. I've a fight coming in a—'

'What do you want to fight for? You don't get paid for it. What about me?'

'I'll see you right after the gym...'

'And go home early!'

The thing is, he thought, she doesn't want me to have any life of my own. She doesn't understand...

He threw down the shears and plucked a sprig of privet, beginning to tear it in his fingers. Weight-lifting had thickened his shoulders and arms, but he was still slender-waisted, his movements still fleet and sudden. His black hair was now longer and thicker above a toughened, harder-edged face. His coal-face training was almost completed. What he was blaming Brenda for not understanding was that he found himself still compelled to keep doing those things he did best. Having begun boxing again, he must keep it up; he had fought four contests and won each time, two of the fights being stopped before the last round. Having begun day school because authority said he should, he must attend night school too, for,

---

[2] Widowed by husband's absence: term derives from an original meaning of discarded mistress

although mathematics and science proved a little easier when he knew what they were related to, he would have to study hard to pass his exams and he was not going to be humiliated by failure.

'She just thinks she's got me,' he told the purring cat, and scowled at her. What troubled him was that he was not sure how much he had conceded; how much loyalty he owed for the gift of her body.

'The gift of her body,' seemed to him the perfect phrase. Passed from her to him and never shared by both. She withdrew to wait until his frivolous enjoyments were over and he could return his attention to her, and he felt half ashamed then for having exposed himself to such critically maternal eyes. He sometimes fancied Brenda mentally shaking her head and clicking her tongue while smiling indulgently on him, and he would be disgusted with himself. But only in retrospect. He would grow furious at her, for her pride in her beautiful body and refusal of participation.

She makes it like my mother said, he thought sourly as he turned and went into the house, leaving the shears lying. It's not what it's cracked up to be...

Having fetched his coat, pointedly ignoring the old lady, who sat in one easy chair, and nodding curtly to Bill, who sat reading in the other, Walt walked the few blocks to Bryan's house. In spite of his bad mood it never occurred to him that he could find fresh lodgings. Sometimes he felt that he received slightly better treatment than Bill. A meal was always ready when he arrived home from work and the better of the two easy chairs was reserved for him if he wanted it. As soon as he entered the house with his snap-tin under his arm and cap perched on the back of his head anyone in that chair, whether Bill, Mrs. Watson or the garrulous insurance agent, was ejected. '...T' lad's been graftin'. Give him his chair.' Each day she wanted to know what he had been doing, and he often felt there would be less point in trying so hard to be a good collier without her shrewd questions. Even though he did curse at times her frequent criticism and her ability to deflate his confidence and make him feel clumsy and callow...

Bryan was sprawled on his bed, shoe heels resting on the baseboard while he lazily flicked cigarette ash over pillows, eiderdown and carpet. Walt and Hughie Sawford sat in chairs beating their feet in time to the music of men who had been idols now for two decades: Miller, Goodman and Shaw, the Dorseys, James and gravel-voiced Armstrong.

'None of that slow blue stuff for me,' Bryan said when the last record was put away. 'I like the hot ones.' The other two nodded. There was the tepidness of popular music as played by dance bands; there was bebop, along with several other new forms which were mainly abortive from the first; but they could imagine no kind of music which might replace swing.

Before returning home Walt told of how he had been locked out.

'I had another row with Brenda and all,' he said. 'She's been worse since you packed up with Marie.'

'Kid, I've told you,' Bryan said earnestly, swinging his legs down and sitting up to lean towards Walt. 'You've got to pack it up. She don't like you going wi' us. They always do this to mates, Walt.'

'It don't seem right to pack up just because you did,' Walt said defensively. He pronounced many of his words as Bryan did. This had begun through mimicking others in the pit because it was the easiest way to make himself understood, but it was almost habitual now except in moments of stress. 'It was you that got me started with her in t' first place!'

'Well, sure, sure,' Bryan admitted reasonably. 'But enough's enough, eh? We don't want to get tangled up. Love and leave 'em, eh?' Since breaking off his courtship with Marie a month ago he had been continually exhorting Walt to leave Brenda so that they could begin going to larger dance halls in the city.

'We've got plans for really banging things up this winter, Walt. The whole gang. Gee, I thought you were the smart one with birds! She'll have you for a lapdog, Walt. They're all saying that, aren't they, Hughie?'

Walt flushed quickly and Hughie grinned and shrugged non-committally.

'I'm sayin' nowt. I hope tha comes wi' us, though, Walt.'

Walt growled that no one would break the three of them up. He liked Hughie almost as much as Bryan. He was the softest spoken and gentlest of the gang and usually tried to avoid trouble, though he always supported Bryan. Over his right eye he wore a plaster from a contest he had fought and lost three nights ago. Walt had learned that Hughie had lost more professional fights than he had won.

'I guess there's a blow-up coming,' Walt muttered at last. He asked Bryan: 'Who said I was her lapdog, anyway?'

'I just heard it—you know.'

Walt grunted and then rose. Bryan followed him downstairs and put a hand on his shoulder as they stood at the front door, frowning over him like a concerned older brother.

'What about it, Walt? Break it up—we want to get around a bit, don't we? Boy, we'll have some fun this winter...'

Walt rubbed his face perplexedly as he nodded. He felt that Bryan was right but didn't understand his problem.

'Good kid! You'll tell her, eh? Tell her tonight. Next week-end we'll be free. And, anyway, you don't want bothering wi' this wi' your fight comin' up next week.'

'All right. I'll tell her tonight.' He had decided as he spoke.

'That's my mate talking. You won't go wrong listenin' to old Bry.'

As Walt strolled homeward, his shoulder still tingling from a last hearty shoulder-clout, he told himself it was time to do this. He was too young for courting.

I want to study and train and to... He did not know what else. He did know, however, the blind frustration of an inchoate restlessness which past excitements had sometimes allayed but never consummated. He knew that Brenda meant to shape him and that he must shape himself. And knew fiercely that he wanted to be free to go on.

Yet his decision brought little relief. It had not been always bad with Brenda. They had been close, sharing confidences and experiences, becoming involved in one another's lives. To break away? To hurt her?

It's a pretty rotten trick...

But like echoes of that music recently heard came thoughts of other dance halls, other girls, of the companionship and freedom from responsibility combined in gang activity.

...Bryan laughs a lot, and beer feels good when you're at a dance with others around you. And when you know you can get a girl... You like that kick when other girls stare, don't you? You want to see how many you can get... big-head!

He had been triumphed over again. The part of him which loved to act the sour adult had been driven into semi-exile by his growing defiance. It hid itself away like an outlawed knight brooding in his dark castle, and Walt would be lulled into forgetting it until suddenly up would fly the black portcullis and out would sally Sir Critical, pennon of honesty flaunted on sharp lance. A few quick thrusts, a shout of triumph, and before Walt could organize the skirmish would be over, the portcullis closing and he, the loser, left behind.

Tea was ready when he reached home, and when the meal was over he sat opposite Bill in dogged silence, determined to take the same time and act the same way as always. But he could not help seeing the green-draped bulk on the edge of his vision sitting just as dogged and more stolid by the hearth. He hooked his elbows into the tablecloth and thought that she could go on for ever if she wanted, sitting with her jaw stuck out and eyes almost quelling the fire, but he wasn't going to apologize first.

Bill was being ostentatious about reading his book, but he glanced up warily now and again, as though hoping there wouldn't be a quarrel but ready to witness its start. Walt thought maliciously that he might be reading for answers to his latest batch of problems: the Yugoslav breakaway from Russian alliance, and the Russian blockade of Berlin. But his real worry, that which included all the others, was that Communism was being blamed for everything. He was constantly, anxiously, trying to explain the Russian viewpoint. It seemed never to occur to him that most people were so tired of recurrent crises that they took them for granted, and were more interested in sport than in the cold war.

'You think the Russians have got a plane that can break the sound barrier yet?' he asked. Bill took a magazine about life in Russia.

'I don't know,' Bill said, looking at him over the cup, plates and fruit-dishes. 'Probably not—yet.'

Walt said it looked as though the West had everything. He wanted to tease Bill a little and was only half serious. Recently he had refused to hear Bill's account of the breach between the two Communist countries, but now he said: 'This row with Stalin and Tito. It's proved I'm right, hasn't it?'

'It has?' Bill put the book down, prepared to listen seriously. 'How?'

'Are you dumb? Look at them—one good lion in Yugoslavia turning on another in Russia! What happens to their countries is a side-effect of which lion's to be boss.'

'You and your theory,' Bill said with disappointment. 'I'll grant you Tito's one of your good lions—he's an opportunist. But that doesn't make both sides the same...' He went on talking earnestly for several minutes, proving his point to his own satisfaction, but when he finished Walt merely said, 'The trouble is, Bill, you're too biased!' then went upstairs to change, leaving Bill looking mortified after him. He was combing his hair when Bill entered the bedroom.

'I was only kidding,' Walt said, as the other perched on his bed. He was half ashamed at Bill's rueful look. 'Don't pay any heed.'

'Oh, I'm too darned serious, I suppose.' Yet Bill still appeared jaunty as he cocked his head at Walt. 'You're in a bit of a mood, boy! I guess walking the streets is no lark.'

'You should have opened a window for me.' Walt pulled on his coat and began counting his money. Bill looked so shocked that he grinned, and said:

'You're real scared of her, aren't you? I'd have said I did it.'

'She'd have chucked you out!'

Walt shrugged and went to the door, halting as Bill called worriedly:

'Walt—don't get in a fight or something. I know the mood you're in, but try to keep out of trouble, boy, huh?'

'Trouble?' He looked as bland as though there had been no nights when Bill had seen him creep to the bathroom to bathe a cut lip or marked knuckles. Resentful at the fatherly tone, he demanded: 'What are you on about?'

Sitting up on the bed, leaning on his hands and trying to keep his expression inflexible while his eyes remained diffident, Bill warned him that he had changed since making friends with Brenda and Bryan.

'...I mean, you seem to be getting pretty reckless. I haven't seen you read a book or talk about serious things for ages. You seem awfully hot-headed and stubborn. It's this boxing thing, too, I suppose...'

'Is that so?' He opened the door.

'I'm saying that as a friend,' Bill added quickly. 'Just as a friend. You do want to keep your friends, don't you?' He blinked in surprise as Walt jerked around and glared at him. The door handle creaked in his whitened fingers.

'If my friends would try all giving the same advice,' Walt said slowly, 'if they'd stop all pulling different ways, I'd be okay.'

'I didn't mean anything.'

'I'm not going to be pushed around all the time!' His mother, Thorpe, Brenda, Bryan—and now even Bill had begun. Like eager sculptors clamouring around him as they brandished chisels.

'Your temper, Walt! What's eating you?'

Walt released the handle after a moment and shrugged.

'Oh, I guess it's Brenda with her bossing me around. I'm going to settle that.' Bill agreed that he had better, and Walt clattered downstairs and went out.

As he walked on he was thinking of the coming contest and wondering why he was so eager to fight above his natural weight. He was forced to do almost as much weight-lifting as boxing in his training to keep it up, whereas Ford would be training to keep his weight down.

But being a welter made him a bit bigger and a bit more important, the hidden critic remarked. Only Jack Ford was heavier, and he was going to feel that when the time came.

Walt grunted disgustedly as he turned the corner, trying to remember the name for people who argued with themselves.

Brenda was talking to Marie and two other girls as she waited for him in front of the cinema. She wore her usual Sunday clothes: blue sweater, skirt and short coat. Although she saw him halt and wait for her at the corner, she continued talking to the others for a few minutes. Still angry, Walt thought. He nodded to a few youths in the unruly queue and noticed that neither Bryan nor the others were there. No more Sunday cinema for him either.

When Brenda strolled up to him he suggested a drink.

'Picture'll be starting soon,' she objected and Walt said they weren't going to see it.

'Let's go in t' Cross Keys,' he said gruffly, his shoulders hunched as he stood looking uncomfortably at her, the noisy crowd behind him. She began arguing that it would be dead in there on a Sunday and that she wanted to see the film, and he knew that so long as they stood here the advantage was hers because she didn't care about an audience. He turned away.

'I'm going, anyway,' he growled. A moment later she was striding beside him, her hair bouncing on her collar as she stared straight ahead. Eyes in the queue were turned to her face and sweater and legs, and Walt thought reluctantly that at least it was good to have a girl like her walking beside you and other youths looking envious. She accepted their stares calmly as her due.

'I'm going out wi' Marie tomorrow night,' she informed him. 'Seein' you're going to be so busy!'

He said that was fine and they crossed over to the large public house on the other side. The doors stood open and in the huge empty concert room a waiter lounged on the bar reading a paper as they passed. They went into a small lounge; its tables were well apart and the windows were frosted. As private as they were likely to be. He went to the bar and Brenda sat in a large leather chair at a table in one corner. She said loudly: 'We're going to a dance.'

'All right,' Walt said over his shoulder. 'That's fine.' He bought beer and gin and orange—treating the girl generously to the last, said the critic.

'Glad you don't mind,' Brenda said as he sat down.

'I'm not your gaffer.' The stone floor and shining walls added a ring to their flat, clipped statements. He should tell her now while he was angry, but this was precisely the stiff and haughty attitude Brenda always took up after a tiff, and she was so obviously sure that this was simply another tiff which she would win by being vigorously independent that he thought: It's going to be rotten to kick the chair away and let her choke...'

She emptied her glass quickly and Walt finished his drink, then brought two more. He knew she was working up to an outburst and that he should forestall her; yet now she was here, the familiar blue outrage in her eyes and the familiar toss of blond hair opposing him, he had no idea of how it was to be done. It had sounded matter-of-fact when Bryan was advising him: plain sensible talking it over and parting with no hard feelings. They hadn't taken Brenda's reactions into account.

Two women entered the room, nodded to Walt and Brenda and sat down by the bar. They talked cheerfully in low voices while Brenda looked down at her fresh drink, her tight lips thin and pale. He decided he couldn't do it and keep his self-respect, and reached out for his drink with relief.

'You could give the gym up,' Brenda said. 'You don't have to do all those things.'

'We had this last night.'

'We never settled it.'

'Listen, I got locked out through this carry-on. All night!' They were muttering, a hissing slur edging each fierce word.

'Honest, Walt? Why didn't you come back? You could've slept at our house.' She looked filled by contrition for a moment, until he said that didn't matter, he wasn't giving anything up.

'I'll have my fun on my own, then.' Her jaw was clenched and rigid as she scowled at the orange glass.

She could have had a baby through that first time, he thought. They had taken chances and she had depended on his loyalty. It wasn't her fault that he was so dissatisfied.

...But it's going to come some time—or it's you who'll choke.

'I just bet if Bryan and them told you to come for a boozing night you'd find a way,' Brenda said without looking up. He's the one behind this. Got you boxin' and everythin'.'

'No, he isn't. I can think for myself.'

Brenda looked up, smiled scornfully in almost the same way as the old lady might do, and said: 'Don't kid yourself.'

He admired her most in this tough and independent mood; ashamed underneath of parents she despised, constantly trying to dissociate herself from their weaknesses, and therefore allied to him. Yet they were really apart now, bogged in sullenness which prevented them from moving apart as it did their coming together.

'This is just about what busted you up with Frank,' he said. 'Isn't it?'

She picked up her glass and barely opened her lips to say: 'You're jealous about him.' They both drank silently as an elderly couple entered and passed them. Walt waited till the couple were seated near the two women, who were talking to the barmaid. Then he lowered the glass and muttered that she was jealous of everything he did. Brenda put her glass down empty and looked at him. Then she leaned nearer, her face smoothing and softening, and said earnestly: 'Walt, I only fight wi' you over things for your own good. I'm better for you than that lot are.'

The bright depth of her eyes made him frown and raise his glass again. While the beer flowed into his throat, he thought once more that he couldn't do it. He would stick it. She was a fine girl, and he would stick it and be damned.

...Or stick it and be a girl's lapdog. Lions roared, but lap-dogs whined and snivelled, and pined without the soft, comfortable, treacherous lap that shamed them while it cradled them. The lap of a true mistress.

'It's no good, Bren,' he said, putting the glass on the table. 'We'll never stop scrapping. Let's pack it in.' He sat waiting with his hands on the glass while her eyes grew larger, bluer and more furious. Several seconds passed. As he saw her arm coming up he thought, Jesus, she won't do that with people here? and was so sure she wouldn't that he checked an instinctive parry as her hand swung in, so hard that his face was jerked around to see staring eyes and mouths forming Os. His tears kept him seated for a moment, dabbing at his eyes, and she was at the door before he sprang to his feet, outside before he reached the door, with an empty glass still rattling on the table as it rolled.

He ran after her around the corner. Her heels were clapping on the pavement, her head down and her hair, tawny in lamp-light softened by dusk, was over her cheek like a mourning statue's. Catching her shoulder he forced her into a shop door-way and pushed her against the glass.

'If you were a man,' he said, his cheek stiff when he spoke. 'By God, if you were a man, Bren...'

'I'd knock you flying, you dirty ram,' she cried, and he caught her hands as she clawed at him.

'You got what you wanted, didn't you? Didn't you?' she hissed as they struggled.

'I knew you'd say that. No!'

He was used to profanity, since everyone used it in the pit, but it had never sounded so foul and obscene as coming from her red mouth while hatred glared from the blue eyes and softly curved face. It had not even occurred to him that a girl might know all these words.

'Listen, listen—' He shook her till she was silent. 'I wanted to tell it you different from how it sounded. It's me that's just no good at courting. It's not you, Bren. I still think you're a fine girl—a lovely girl. It's just me.' Trying desperately to convince her, he blurted out his real age. '...I never even told you that.'

'Bryan told you not to!' She pushed him away with spread hands. 'You're his little pal and he looks after you. If you stuck to me you'd have to stand on your own two feet—and you can't...' Her mouth quivered and swelled, and tears clustered her eyelashes. 'Go on, go wi' him. I wouldn't want a two-faced rotten crawler like you, anyroad.'

She whirled and was gone and he heard the click of her heels quickly fading in the darkened street. A couple passed the doorway, glancing at him as he leaned against the glass, and when they too were gone he drew himself up and stepped on to the pavement.

He walked home with his head down, past the silent shops and past the cinema which looked deserted for all the life and liveliness inside. Now she would be going home to wait for her parents and look at the picture above the fireplace. It hadn't been like this in the Hemingway story where boy and girl parted.

That made you feel sad, he thought. But not cheap and dirty and guilty. Not too traitorous to look at yourself... At the bottom of his own street he met the old lady and Mrs. Watson. David and Goliath in black coats and white buns, he thought.

'I've something to tell you,' he said, and the old lady stopped with Mrs. Watson's spectacles peering up eagerly at him as she waited beside her.

'That girl who kept me out late—' he stared into the creased, expressionless face— 'I packed her up.'

'Tha's done right.' She began moving on, Mrs. Watson following reluctantly.

'Just like that! Chucked her up when she wasn't even expecting it.'

The old lady paused again to say calmly that any girl who'd keep him out till that time was no good to him. He saw her slight warning jerk of the head towards Watson, but answered heavily that he was glad she was pleased.

'It shows tha's got a little bit o' sense, anyroad,' the old lady said, and walked away with Watson already chattering curiously to her.

In the house he found Bill curled in an arm-chair.

'Gosh, you're soon back.' After a quick scrutiny of his face, Bill returned to his book. Walt threw his coat on the sofa under the window and dropped into his chair. After a while he leaned forward with hands clasped and began gently rocking while staring at the fire. He was quiet for a long time. The pages occasionally rustled and Bill's eyes flickered up to glance at him now and then, but it was Walt who first spoke.

'If you've been with a girl—the lot, you know—and you pack her up—it's pretty rotten, isn't it?'

Bill put his legs down and faced him.

'So you did break it off?' When Walt nodded miserably, he asked: 'And you feel bad about it?' Walt nodded again, and Bill sighed and shrugged.

'It's not in my line, boy. But didn't you plan to do only the things you felt good about?'

'I'd have felt just as bad if I hadn't packed her up,' Walt protested. Bill frowned, and said that this seemed to make a hole in his theory. The frown lapsed to a grin.

'Go on,' Walt said. 'Take the mickey out of me. I suppose it's only fair.' But Bill grinned for only a moment before he shrugged again and was serious.

'I can't pass any opinion. You set up your own rules, and you and I use different ones, don't we? I mean, you told me I had to do what I thought, and—'

'All right,' Walt interrupted. 'Don't start getting anxious about me. You've enough worries. I was only asking.'

'Well, I think you wanted me to condemn you because you've condemned yourself,' Bill explained. 'But I only go by facts and I don't know yours. Only you didn't expect this idea of yours to make things easy all the time, did you? Or aren't you sure about lions and deer now?'

'Don't worry,' Walt stood up, disgruntled. 'I can sort this out.'

'Good old Walt,' Bill said flippantly. 'No easy way for you, eh?' He added as Walt reached the door: 'I'm realizing that yours is the toughest way there is. Do you know that?'

'I couldn't care less,' he answered. But when he was in bed he could not stop thinking about Brenda and what she had called him. He thought of the past few months, then of the vicious profanity as her eyes glared, and then of the white flash as her hand came over to point his face at the round-mouthed watchers. A piece of gossip for the Cross Keys. The old lady might hear and guess it had been him. And if Mrs. Watson learned, then the whole estate would soon know.

He rolled over, softly swearing into his pillow at himself. While he worried over that, Brenda would be at home with her unhappiness, and it was she who had been wronged. When Bill came upstairs he pretended to be asleep, but he was still awake when Bill was breathing heavily and the bed-springs next door had quietened. Another hour passed while he tossed and wriggled, his body infected with the turbulence of his mind, and round and round wheeled Brenda's glistening tears and swinging hand and hoarse profanity.

Until at last he heard the thudding of the distant forge-hammer which beat even on Sundays and was slowly soothed by its monotony. He lay with eyes tight closed, and, as his drowsiness thickened, imagined himself in a high-vaulted place of sterile cleanliness. He stood before the cool magnificent mystery of a great altar and felt at peace. He was not there to pray or worship, but for peace.

A shame I don't believe, he thought. Just a few moments... turn everything over... They knew what they were talking about with their rock to hide in... As the slow incessant thudding stroked him to sleep.

II

When Walt was on morning shift, the alarm clock became a fiendish machine. Cleaving his sleep at quarter past four, its sudden clangour always brought him flailing up, full of calamity as though the earth had abruptly stopped spinning and pitched him off. Having found and stopped it, with Bill's grumbles muffled in the darkness, he would lie back thinking how tired he was and how hard the work before him. He would wish he were on afternoon shift, though when it came to trudging to work at midday he would be wishing he were on morning shift.

By the time Bill appeared downstairs, still yawning and blinking tight eyes, Walt had eaten and was ramming his snap-tin into his coat pocket. He put on cap and scarf, grunting to Bill, who yawned back, as he went out. It was dark and he dug his hands into cold pockets as he hurried along with shoulders hunched to keep his neck warm. The steel rims and hobnails of his boots rang and clattered on the oily pavement and echoed hollow and staccato from the dark walls and sleeping windows as he passed. At the cinema he joined a group of huddled shapes in caps and overcoats waiting for the swaying oblong of chequered light climbing the hill. They greeted him, but except for a couple discussing football with red dots flaring and dimming at their lips they hardly spoke.

Bryan was just inside the tram, looking outrageously rosy and cheerful as he squeezed along his seat and grinned up.

' 'Mornin'.' Walt slumped down beside him and was immediately given a lively description of a club the gang had visited the previous night.

'...Gee, you should've been there, Walt. You have to pay to join, but there's beer and dancing and stacks o' birds, kid. Honest...'

'Not now,' he pleaded, but Bryan was quiet for only a few minutes before he almost crowded Walt off the seat by turning confidentially and asking: 'Did you tell her, kid?' When Walt nodded he squeezed his arm, then waited for details, but Walt sat silent and empty-eyed like most of the other passengers, while the tram swayed and rattled down the hill and collected its pale-faced, coughing and grunting cargo. He was sure he had not slept for more than two hours, and Bryan's gusto was too much at this early time. Mention of Brenda had made him wince and close his eyes as though at the opening remarks of a nagging shrew.

Once reminded he could not forget. In the steel cage he thought of her as black wind whipped past his fluttering trouser cuffs, and he thought of her on the long journey inbye, walking bent up with a water-bottle in one hand and powder-bag in the other, his mates breathing heavily as they trudged along behind him. Crawling down the face towards his stint he scraped his back twice on the low roof because of his preoccupation, and cursed softly as the skin was abraded by the rough stone. He recalled the jolting slap while he was shovelling, his head down on his chest and his shoulders touching the roof, and remembered her profanity when he was helping his mate to set a prop and bar where their coal was cleared.

'Tha wants to shake out on it,' his mate said at snap-time. 'Tha'll get lamed dreamin' like that.' They were sprawled on their sides hurrying to finish their sandwiches before the conveyor belt began moving again.

Walt thought glumly that he just didn't feel any kind of man any more.

His work was not yet too hard, for he was shifting only half of what would be his stint when his training finished at the end of the week. The coal-face was no longer so confusing to him now he understood the pattern of its cycle. Thirty men worked on this one, which was almost three hundred yards long and barely a yard high. Each day they stripped the face to a depth of six feet, setting steel props and thin bars to hold the roof. When they came next day the face belts would have been moved up to the coal, the trunk belt in the middle roadway extended to keep up, the props and bars left behind withdrawn and thrown forward to be used again, and the face would look exactly as it had a day ago, a week ago or a year ago. Each day exposed the next day's work, leaving behind the wreckage of stripped earth. When Walt looked behind, over the belts, he saw the past: shambled stone and rubble crushed into a solid mass as though coal had never been there. In front was the future: a long shining black wall of days, weeks and months of coal. Above was the roof which in two days would be rubble, unless luck ran out and it became rubble today, and on either side was the present: men hewing and hammering, lifting and shovelling as they used out today's sweat and strength to expose tomorrow's work. This seam was deeper and hotter than that Walt had worked in at first, and the colliers wore thin pants or worked naked. After two years as a filler, Walt himself would be a collier.

Until this morning it had needed only the thought that he would soon be a filler to rouse pride in himself, but Brenda's contempt and his own guilt had combined in too rancorous a poison for this antidote; he had to prove her wrong.

On the way home that afternoon Bryan was making plans for the week-end. He tried to cheer Walt by his constant talk of 'banging things up', but as the tram was nearing the Luxor Cinema he said a little worriedly: 'Is it this fight that's on your mind, Walt? Might as well be straight—I don't reckon much to t' idea mysen. Ford's about the best amateur welter Mantywood's had in years.'

'You want me to pack up because they've matched me with him?' Walt asked. 'It's not that, anyway.'

'But you're not even gettin' paid.' Coal dust was traced faintly in the lines of Bryan's frown. 'Just for a youth club...'

'Alec Thorpe fixed it with Clifton for me to fight for 'em,' Walt said doggedly. 'I'm not letting them down because this one's tough. It's the first time Clifton's had a welter in the tournaments for...'

'But you're a lightweight by rights. Ford's too heavy...' They rose and clattered down the iron steps as the tram stopped, the people on the platform warily moving back from their steel-toed boots. On the pavement Bryan clasped Walt's shoulder and said gravely:

'Ford's turning pro soon, Walt. It's all right for Clifton and Thorpe bragging they've turned out a lad that...'

'Now you're down on Thorpe, eh?' Walt shrugged the hand away. Bryan was right about his weight against Ford's, but the persuasive tone and older-brother attitude ignited the memory of Brenda's '...Bryan's little pal... crawler...' and he thought bitterly that she had seen what he had not.

'Take it easy, kid. I'm not down on...'

'Well, leave Thorpe alone, then,' Walt said, and began walking away with Bryan calling forlornly after him: 'Well, I only said it as a mate, Walt. Don't be mardy...'

Walt's dinner was waiting on a white cloth folded at one corner of the table. While the old lady sat by the fire he ate hungrily, dust making his eyes look hollows with damp hair tousled over them as he bent to his plate. For once there was no inquiry about the day's work, but when he had finished she asked why he had eaten so little breakfast.

'It were there for thee to get. Do thee no good going to thy job on an empty belly.' He grunted he hadn't been hungry, then, seeing her slowly raise the poker and realizing more questions were coming, he quickly drained his mug of tea.

'What did she say o'er you packin' her up, then?' She thoughtfully stirred the fire and raked ash from a sparkling bar, watching what she was doing.

'Not much. Wasn't much she could say, was there?' He stood up and went to the door. She remarked he had seemed upset, then looked up to demand: 'Were it thee as got t' slap in t' eye in t' private bar?'

Trust her to know, he thought, swinging the door back and forwards as he nodded dumbly.

'She sounds a nice 'un! Or had you been takin' advantages?'

Walt began to blush, then at her grim nod and 'Humph!' he shrugged and said: 'I got what I deserved. She called me some names and showed she didn't think I was much of a man.'

'That don't take a lot o' workin' out. A man takes making, and you've nobbut started yet'

His glare and angry answer were checked by Bill's opening the back door. The old lady went to the oven, remarking casually that he'd best get some sleep, hadn't he? and Walt went upstairs, telling himself, as he climbed, that, if he didn't know what he was, he certainly knew all the things that she was...

At the evening classes and at college next day he sat staring at black patterns of logarithms and chemical formulae, and wondered what it boded that the first girl to take him seriously should be made so unhappy and should end by despising him. Having left home to make something of himself, he'd come as far as banging things up and letting girls down. What should he be doing?

That afternoon his technical drawing master pointed to a line on which Walt had made three extra attempts and remarked that the idea was to describe an arc and not an archway. Walt nodded humbly, began erasing, and argued to himself that his idea had been to shape his own life, which was something Brenda would have stopped. At least boxing and the gang left him free to break away when he chose.

Freedom! That was the point; he must be free. No more entanglements with girls.

If only—he thought, adding further smudges to the grubby paper—if only I didn't feel she was right about me... A two-faced crawler, she said...

That evening one of the professional boxers who sometimes used the gym offered to spar a few rounds with him. Afterwards, Walt sat at the ringside with a towel around his shoulders while Thorpe lectured him on ringcraft. Finally Thorpe said: 'Ford's going to be a real test for you, Walt. He's tough and he's a deadly puncher when he gets in. He'll bring out the best you've got—' Walt broke in, remembering what Bryan had said, to demand if he had any chance.

'Chance?' Thorpe looked startled and then a little angry, standing up to frown down on him. 'If you're that nervous, you'd better call it off! Sure, you've a chance—if you really fight and use your speed. Your speed could do it.' He turned away, then quickly turned back:

'Look, Walt, it's a case of whether all this training is just for you to go around feeling pretty tough, or whether you want to find out what stuff you're made of. You said you wanted to train for welter and I—'

'I only wanted to know what you thought,' Walt apologized, adding half ruefully: 'I'm all for knowing what I'm made of, believe me. It's important right now.' He remembered once saying a good lion must be a good fighter, and thought to himself: We'll see how good a lion you are now...

On Thorpe's instructions he had his hair cut next day.

'Take it really close,' he told the barber. 'I don't want any flopping about.' In the mirror at home he saw a bristling black skull-cap above a face all knobs and eyes; he avoided mirrors for several days after that.

At the pit they called him Fritz for the rest of the week, and the old lady said he looked like a worn doormat. When Bill saw him he frowned and then reached up to gently rub his flat hand over Walt's head. 'I just wondered what it felt like,' he explained as Walt gaped indignantly.

The men on Walt's face knew about the coming fight from Bryan, who also worked there. Most of them mentioned it to Walt and many promised to come and cheer him. Although he was still a trainee he would work on this face when a filler, and he was therefore one of the team. Among themselves there could be petty feuds, but they thought of themselves as one team and any member had their support against outsiders. They had their own private pride in themselves and their work, their own private jargon, even their own nicknames for themselves and their superiors. Bryan had been seen one Saturday in gaudy splendour and named 'The Tramp', while Walt's mate, a long-faced, gap-toothed collier of middle age who seldom spoke or smiled, was called 'Happy'. 'The Colonel' had spent six years in the Army as a private; 'Samson' was the smallest and thinnest among them, and the bald-headed charge-hand who looked after the men's interests was 'Curly'. Originality was of no account so long as each name had that touch of happy inspiration which delights everyone except the recipient. Walt found it unnerving to imagine the title they might finally bestow on him; one filler who talked in rapid, high-pitched sentences had been dubbed 'Yap-yap' years ago and was never called anything else now.

Men tried to keep their personal lives secret, for if a piece of scandal or gossip about which anyone was embarrassed became known the colliers would compose crude verses and set them to the tune of a popular song, to be chorused in the crowded pit bottom at shift-end and in the busy bath-house for half the pit to hear. If no other subject were at hand then Walt, Bryan and other unmarried fillers were treated to obscene lectures on women and on the dangers of living a loose life while working with a shovel. Bryan was the favourite butt, because he often boasted of his experiences. Sometimes one collier would encourage him with affected admiration, and the others would nudge each other and grin as they sat or crouched, with Bryan waxing more and more eloquent in his descriptions. On Friday morning, as Walt squatted down before the shaft gates in the large, dusty pit bottom where runs of loaded tubs stood ready to be thrust on to the cage when the next shift began, he could hear Bryan being teased.

'Look at him,' said a doleful voice. 'Big lad like that and he'll not be able to lift a shovel in two years, road as he's going.'

'The women, lad—drawin' all t' marrow out on him, they are.'

'Can't lift t' shovel some mornin's as it is—I don't know about later!'

'Grunts every time he lifts t' hammer up. Fell o'er three times trying to hit a prop.'

Bryan began retaliating; Walt envied him the way he could hold his own. He was a collier ready made; he could fill his stint almost as quickly and set his props and bars almost as securely as the best men on the face. Already he spoke to those who were slower with a touch of good-humoured superiority, however much older than him they might be. This was accepted as natural; it was right for a good filler to have pride in himself, since coal was what paid their wages.

'Gi'e o'er,' someone said, as the cage crashed into its supports and the crowd trooped forward. 'He's never had nowt in his life. He wouldn't sleep wi' me were I a lass.'

'No,' Bryan shouted as he squeezed on to the cage behind Walt; 'And if tha were a lass, I wouldn't *want* to sleep wi' thee, neither.'

In the smoky tram Bryan offered to call for Walt that evening. When Walt told him Alec Thorpe was taking him in his car, he said: 'Anyroad, we'll all be there to cheer. So'll half the lads on t' face.' The contest was being staged during the city amateur tournament at one of the biggest halls in the city and Walt was afraid to think of how huge the audience would be.

'Happy told Curly and Slogger this morning as you was a good lad,' Bryan told him. Slogger was the deputy in charge of the face; the men claimed he had never known a hard day's work, but he was popular for his good-humoured repartee. 'I heard Curly say as he's having you signed over for your own stint.'

Delighted that the taciturn old collier had praised him, Walt said joyfully: 'Hey, I'll be a filler on my own, Monday!'

'Sure,' Bryan said. 'Now we're both t' same again, eh? Together, lad.'

All the way home Walt kept repeating to himself: 'I made it. A coal-face man on my own. At eighteen... A full collier when I'm only twenty...'

When he told the old lady, she said: 'Now that's summat as you *can* feel pleased wi' yourself o'er.' And grateful for even this grudging recognition, Walt went upstairs to lie down. But not to sleep. First he was excited about becoming a filler, then he began to think about the coming fight, although he knew this to be a mistake. The city tournament was the biggest amateur boxing event of the year; there would be many in the audience accustomed to professional boxing, and since Walt's bout was the last before the middleweights and heavyweights everyone would be there to see it. He might be knocked out in the first minute, or so hopelessly outclassed that the fight was stopped; he might lose his nerve and be unable to climb into the ring when that great audience roared...

Let me do all right, he thought desperately, lying as still and relaxed as he could. Let me do well...

Because, said the critic, he wanted to impress the crowd. To impress himself, Walt answered. He had repaired the pain caused by Brenda. Less than a week, and he felt that although Happy had praised him and the colliers befriended him, they would feel about him as Brenda did if they saw what was inside.

A bad thing to do to a girl... Cruel. She told me *he* was sometimes cruel when they were young—and he did some boxing before he got smashed up. They say it comes out. It comes out. It comes out in you... She once said he was a dirty beast and couldn't go without women. Me too? Is that what I really miss Brenda for? Was it that I didn't want to give up? In the pit they say their wives always win arguments because they can go without longer than men can... But that's black-mail! I'd get somebody else before I'd give in.

Like your father, said the critic, and Walt sat up, swinging his legs down. His belly was tightening and thighs fluttering. For a while he paced up and down, then he began prancing about in stockinged feet, throwing quick punches and reminding himself not to try riding any blows, because Ford had the weight. His shadow boxing finished when he bounced off the drawers on to the bed, where he sat up wondering if it were nearly tea-time yet. He could hear them talking downstairs.

I bet I'd have liked William, he thought. Maybe he'd have liked me and helped me. If I were a Catholic I could have Masses said for his soul, and if religion were true he'd be watching me now... They can't confess *all* their sins! How could you remember every little thing you'd done for a month?

After tea Walt paced up and down by the window, waiting for the car. It was infuriating to see the others behaving as though this were a normal Friday night: Bill was going to Atwell's as usual and the old lady was washing the dishes in the kitchen.

'Tha can buy me some new lino if tha wears that out,' the old lady said when she came in for more dishes. She had never commented on his boxing but he felt she regarded it as something to be tolerated until outgrown. Bill was also unenthusiastic.

'Well, I hope you win, Walt, but I'd rather not come and watch.' The look on his pert round face was not enough concerned with the matter to be distaste; it was flat rejection. 'It just isn't in my line. But they'll all be digging for you at Atwell's.'

'Enjoy your coffee,' Walt muttered as the door closed.

For another hour Walt paced up and down, telling himself this was a nice way to prepare for a fight, and he had decided Thorpe must have had an accident or the tournament had been called off, when he saw the car draw up outside. With a yell he ran out by the front way, cleared the hedge easily and reached the car door as Thorpe opened it.

'Hi,' Thorpe said. He sat in shadow which darkened his white hair, making him look youthful. 'What's all the excitement? I've timed it to get you there just right.'

As they drove off he saw a pinched face and spectacles peeping from next door, and then thought he glimpsed a green overall at the curtains of his own house. But surely she wouldn't watch him go, he thought. Not the dragon.

'Ford might be cagey at first,' Thorpe said. 'You're a dark horse who's suddenly appeared, so he'll watch you. A lot of people will be—'

'Don't talk about it,' Walt pleaded. Thorpe looked round and then smiled. 'Easy, boy. I'll be in your corner. It's all fixed up. Think about Ford and nothing else. Be as scared of him as you like once you're in there —it'll make you faster.'

He began humming quietly to himself, and Walt watched the headlights slicing into the dark to splash the rears of trams and buses and to spotlight people crossing the road. Everyone seemed to be moving deliberately slowly when they waited for them to cross; no respect for motorists at all! Funny, you never noticed it till you were in a car. There were people everywhere in the city centre: people and headlights and bright moving windows, and a traffic policeman tall in a shining white cape against a low dazzling background.

'Nearly there,' Thorpe said.

The strolling groups of men, talking and turning to one another on the glistening pavements, were probably going to the tournament at the drill hall, he thought nervously.

'Alec.' Thorpe looked round momentarily. 'I've never properly thanked you. It's you that gave me all the training...'

'Thanking doesn't mean a thing, Walt. I wanted to do it. It means as— ah, well...' Walt stared at the smooth, smiling profile with its flattened nose.

'You just make a good scrap of it, Walt. So I can think that it's one of my lads up there—that'll do...'

'Is that what it's all for?' he asked doubtfully. 'So you can say it's one of your lads? Is that why you train?'

'Not quite, son. I try to make it pay. But a good lad's different. I don't want to say it to anyone but myself. One of my lads and I helped him.' The car slowed and eased to a stop. Thorpe took his hands from the wheel but still looked ahead for a moment. Then he turned and said: 'It puts a certain obligation on you, Walt.' And when Walt assured him he would fight his best, he interrupted: 'Not just that. If people treat you as someone different, remember it, will you? Now Bryan and the others have all used the gym some time. They're wild lads—' He forestalled Walt's interruption with a raised hand. 'Sure, sure. They're all right. That's all they'll ever be, though. You've your wild oats to sow, but when I spoke about saying you were one of the boys—' He broke off to smile suddenly, his whole face changing. 'To hell with this. You'll learn for yourself. Come on, son.'

Walt wasn't quite sure what he had been advised against, nor sure that Thorpe knew exactly what he meant. But even Alec had brought it on to that embarrassing level—the tough no-nonsense sportsman—reaching out in that peculiarly tentative, roundabout way people seemed to reserve for this.

'You should have a son of your own,' he said, as Thorpe tugged a canvas hold-all from the back seat. Then he remembered Bryan's story of how Thorpe's family had been killed, and in the darkness he blushed furiously.

'Come on, we haven't much time,' the trainer answered cheerfully, as though he hadn't heard. He led the way to a brick side-entrance, and stopped where a lamp bracket burned yellow above a large white poster lettered in red. He pointed the hold-all, and Walt read the poster which described each bout. Then, among those marked 'Special Contests', he read:

WELTERWEIGHT
W. Morris (Clifton) v. J. Ford (Mantywood).

It was strange to read his own name and know many others had read it and perhaps discussed his chances against Ford.

Me, he thought. It's me. Reading my name and talking about me and they've never seen me...

'Come on,' Thorpe smiled. 'Turn pro and you'll be used to your name on posters—in *big* letters.'

They hurried to the dressing-room, where the Clifton trainer was waiting among his charges. He was a heavy cumbrous man, huge in a knitted, roll-collar sweater.

'I thought you'd had it,' he exclaimed when he saw them, dabbing his face with a large handkerchief. It was warm in the dressing-room.

Most of the dozen youths there had already fought; clothes were piled untidily on benches and tables and a half-dressed group gathered around Walt as he changed.

'A night like this can give them nerves without being kept hanging around here,' Thorpe was explaining to Prestcott, the Clifton trainer.

Walt had no time to be nervous as he changed into singlet and trunks and laced up his boots with Thorpe telling him to look slippy.

'Your boy ready?' someone called. 'Just ten minutes.'

As Walt straightened up Thorpe held out a dressing-gown for him to slip his arms into.

'Gee,' Walt said, staring. It was of blue silk with yellow collar, cuffs and tassels. 'That's a real boxer's gown.'

'It's mine, and don't you nip off home with it!'

Walt managed to grin at the youths who cried encouragement as he left the dressing-room, and at the officials who told him he looked a champion in his robe. But waiting at the gangway, with the long aisle stretching before him down to the brilliant ring, he could grin no more. Mouth and stomach had dried up and his legs were trembling. He heard steps behind him and knew Jack Ford and his second had come out, but kept his head still. The lights went on in the great hall as the pair who had just fought returned through a lane of seated people, a mass of faces turning to look after them.

'Let's go, son,' Thorpe said, and walked with a hand on his shoulder down the aisle. The ring in front of them was high up, with arcs blazing down on it and packed seats stretching away into the shadows all around. There was no recognition from the audience; only the echoed roll of murmuring hundreds. Cigarette smoke trailed across the ring, grey under the arcs.

Walt climbed up and through the ropes, and everything else was immediately cut off. The four lengths of ropes were his boundaries and he could barely see the referee and the time-keeper. He began scrubbing his feet in the resin-box to disguise the trembling, and grinned at Thorpe as a few indistinguishable yells were followed by a ragged clapping.

'Bet I know who that is,' he said. 'Forget 'em. Just Ford—just think about Ford.' Thorpe made him sit on the stool and began kneading his calf muscles as Ford climbed in, and there was a long roar from the Mantywood boys. Feeling happier while Thorpe was hiding him from the crowd, Walt looked across at a youth almost as tall as himself and heavier in the chest and shoulders. The slightly flattened nose and tender lips were evidence of his experience.

He looks a stone heavier than me!' Walt gasped.

'Well, he's not.' Thorpe's digging, kneading fingers were easing the fluttering from his thighs. 'Remember he's trained hard to get his weight down—you've got the edge on footwork and it's what'll win for you. But don't let him get you where he can hit you, hear?'

The referee was announcing the contest while Thorpe kept repeating: 'Make him chase you. Don't get reckless, he's crafty. Make him chase you.' A burst of applause greeted the announcement of Walt's name and a bigger one greeted Ford's. Then the crowd was quiet, and Walt thought to himself: It's because he looks so much heavier and they think I've had it before I start, and if I think about that I will have... but look at those shoulders and biceps... I'll bet I'm like a ladder turned sideways next to him...

'Seconds out...' The hard gum-shield slipped up under his lip. He always wondered what damage might be done if his two false teeth were torn out by a punch.

'Easy the first round—let him chase you...' The bell clanged and Walt moved out to touch Ford's glove and begin circling. The crowd was quiet, hundreds of red spots flaring and dying in the darkness behind Ford. He had a square-jawed aggressive face and narrow intent eyes; his fair hair was cropped almost as short as Walt's, his guard deceptively awkward-looking. Elbows tucked in with both fists near his jaw, he was tight-knit and dangerous, and Walt felt this danger in every tensing muscle. He would never get Ford with in-fighting and Ford showed no eagerness to attack. To draw out, Walt feinted with his left and dropped his right glove a little. Ford's feet shook the canvas as he moved in so fast, his gloves like chopping pistons, that Walt had to duck from the waist, swing around, and throw a wild right to recover. Ford whirled to follow up and stopped as Walt's right bounced off his gloves. There was some yelling from the darkness outside.

I'm faster, Walt thought. Definitely faster. But the way he chops—murder if he gets you on those ropes...'

In no hurry, Ford moved after Walt, sparring and breaking away and watching the gloves with a deadly intent look, as though he knew exactly what he was waiting for and that it would come. Walt was compelled to retreat steadily, for to force the pace he must either go in to meet those chopping jabs or try another dangerous feint. It must look hopelessly slow to the crowd, he thought. They didn't realize the fight would be over with one mistake. Yet the crowd waited patiently. Now and again came a call, but he was concentrating too closely on Ford to understand the words. He saw that with each left-hand feint Ford was swinging around a little, exposing his jaw to a right hook as his shoulder drooped. It was probably a ruse, Walt thought, to draw him in, but he was trying to calculate a way of using it. He must try something, because each time Ford came close he could feel the danger so overpowering that he would lash out involuntarily soon, which was what the other wanted.

Weaving and bobbing all the time and making Ford have to work out how to keep him still for a moment, Walt backed towards the ropes. He knew he was close when the narrow eyes flickered to his jaw to gauge the best punch. The brief touch was icy because of the sweat under his singlet. Ford came in, hooking low with the left to hold him there as Walt had wanted him to do. He twisted, the punch glancing off his chest, drove his left for the ribs and brought the right hook over as Ford's guard dropped.

A grunting shout exploded as Ford reeled, and Walt drove him to the opposite ropes with four punches which he knew would satisfy even Thorpe. With Ford pinned to the ropes he drove fierce jabs at the cradling arms, and yelling burst over them. Ford was bending.

Down... Walt thought frantically. He's going down and who's a crawler now?

But Ford hung on, taking the fury on his rigid shoulders and arms, and suddenly had twisted away, flailing wildly as Walt charged after him and almost stumbling backwards in his helpless retreat. Then he dodged one swing and had time to cover up before Walt came again, leaning in, with his left raking forward to meet Ford's glove and the next taken on the shoulder. His nose beginning to bleed and his eyes blurred, Ford steadied himself. He had finished retreating.

They heard the bell clang through the yelling, and had to pass each other to reach their corners. Walt dropped on to his stool, going limp as he took a mouthful of water from the bottle Thorpe held up.

'You young rip! Is that taking it easy?'

Walt spat out the water and began saying excitedly: 'I nearly had him, Alec. I nearly...'

'You don't have to tell me!' Thorpe rubbed and kneaded his legs. 'A touch of the tiger, Walt. A touch of the tiger. If your Freddie Mills had seen that hook, he'd be up shaking your hand right now. You followed up great, too—but don't do it again.'

'He's too strong for me.'

'I know. Keep away till I tell you. Now let him wear himself down a bit. He's saving himself and we've got to weaken him—'

'Seconds out.'

As Thorpe whipped the stool away he was hissing urgently: 'Straight lefts and keep him out. Weaken him... You're in front, remember.'

He meant to stay in front. As he met Ford, who was now crouching more and looking very wary, Walt was thinking:

If I could just do this... You see, Brenda—as Ford came in and darted back from a feint, then dodged a whipped-out straight left—you could be right and I don't know and I must have *something*... It's been like this most of the time, I suppose...

Ford was now retreating and Walt was following, left foot shuffling lightly, all his weight on his toes.

...Only if I did this really well tonight I could stop feeling that and wouldn't have to fight so much, and maybe forget about her... And Ford saw his eyes inattentive for a second, lunged and had him on the ropes, pounding short-arm jabs into his ribs so that the breath exploded from his nose. Walt clinched Ford's arms and put his chin on his shoulder until they were ordered to break. As they parted, he ducked a fierce hook and landed a swinging right, with pain wrenching his sides as he struck.

Jesus, that hurts... Because he had been badly hurt for a moment, and because Ford's increasing confidence made him more strongly and indomitably dangerous as he advanced, Walt's body rebelled and he met the next rush instead of side-stepping. Ford's punches were too heavy for him to take very long, and he gave ground quickly, striking back fiercely all the time as the blows jarred his ribs and spine and made his head jerk, though Ford had not hit his head. At the ropes, Walt ducked and dodged so suddenly and adroitly that Ford stared out bewildered before he whirled round, blood trickling from his nose again. The crowd was yelling, but Walt fought at long range for the rest of the round, keeping the other off with his raking lefts and dodging so fleetly that he was impossible to hit.

Thorpe began scolding him as soon as he dropped on to the stool.

'But he's running at the nose, Alec,' Walt protested when he had swilled out his mouth. Already his breathing had steadied.

'That's nothing,' Thorpe said after a quick glance. 'He's not hurt at all, but you will be if you let him use that weight. He'll be after you now—keep away.'

For all the next round Ford attacked fiercely, but it was Walt who landed most punches, weaving, ducking, tricking the other into charges and jabbing in viciously as he side-stepped. He was beginning to move less nimbly when the bell clanged.

'I'm starting to feel it,' he told Thorpe. 'should've done road work or something.'

'You can't do everything. Listen, you piled up points there. That was real boxing—and don't think this crowd doesn't know it.'

'He's strong...'

'Just hold on and keep away.'

He went in again, repeating to himself that he must hold on. Hold on and hold off this juggernaut who should make a very good pro because it looked as though only a six-pound hammer would knock him down—or one really smashing straight left.

That was the chance he waited for while dodging and ducking the quickening hooks and swings. Ford seemed to be getting stronger; he looked full of confidence, methodically working Walt on to the ropes, and patiently beginning again after each baffling swerve, his inexorable pursuit infinitely menacing. Walt let the rope brush his back and repeated the ruse he had used before. As Ford's shoulder dropped he hooked with the right, and knew he had been outwitted as the skull dropped also to nod the blow away, and Ford's right glove slammed in under his ribs to fold him and the left whipped up.

His head was snapped back and the shock shuddered his spine as though an iron spike had been driven through his jaw. As he struck and rolled over, the wood-canvas floor shivered and the smell of resin was strong in his nostrils.

He didn't knock me out...

He began counting and felt his body suddenly weightless, a flowing and swirling in his head, but the smell of resin and canvas helped him fight. As he opened his eyes, he thought:

Four...

Thorpe was signalling to wait, but with his head blurred and body half afloat he must start now. One knee came up, with the floor wavering under it as the count reached seven. He found the top rope and was up, leaning on it, for nine, and then away, his head clearing with the bound. As Ford came in swinging, he clinched and held on.

'Break...' They parted, and Ford rushed, crowding him on to the ropes again, while he fought dizziness and hooked his elbows over his ribs, his gloves at his face. He heard furious snorts and was jerked in tight arcs by repeated explosions on his arms, but he hung there, the rope sagging out, until the bell clanged.

He had to look carefully for his corner, and dropped heavily on the stool when he reached it, letting Thorpe ease the gum-shield out and pour a little water into his slack mouth.

'Spit!' His head was forced forward until he spat the water out.

'They're making some racket...' he said vaguely.

'You should see how it looks from out here.' Then Thorpe's face shrank as it rushed away, and sight blurred until an intensely bitter smell had him coughing and he could see again except for tears in his eyes.

'You've met another tiger, Walt. How d'you feel?'

He waved the bottle away, and as his head cleared and he became properly aware of the stool under him, Thorpe's anxious look and the noisy crowd, he answered: 'I'm okay now.'

'You want to go on? There's two more rounds.'[3]

He nodded. His weakness had gone.

'Sure?' As he nodded again, Thorpe leaned over, chafing the nape of Walt's neck, and murmured: 'The referee's just looked at his nose. He'll have to watch you now. The blood on your singlet's from his nose, and another hit stops the fight. Give him all you've got if you get one chance.

---

[3] The special contest described is presented as a six-round bout. I would like to make it clear that under A.B.A. rules, bouts are normally fought over three rounds or four. LD

Hear?'

'Yeah,' he mumbled as Thorpe slipped the gum-shield back. The din from the darkness was like the immense rumbling of many engines.

As the bell went he rose fairly slowly, testing his legs, but Ford charged like a rushing bear, all swipes, cuffs and smothering weight, determined to finish it. A left hook, which would have ended the fight had it caught Ford's nose, thudded on his mouth and made him cover up quickly, warily guarding his face.

He's mad, Walt thought, as he waited instead of attacking—mad because he's hurt and he's a tiger, and since he's not the kind that crawls he'll try to murder me...

He fought well with that knowledge, holding Ford off by vicious swings and hooks, all whipping at the face and tender nose. Three times he ducked abruptly to let a murderous swing beat past, and the third time saw Ford's chest unguarded. Walt's straight left, first move in his most instinctive and best attack, drove forward as his left foot crashed on the canvas, and as it struck under the breastbone he saw Ford's mouth loosen, the white gum-shield briefly exposed under the puffy lips. His right swing went for the ribs, and, as Ford desperately dropped an arm, a left hook hammered on the side of his jaw. He lurched on the ropes, arms rising too slowly as Walt's feet twitched and a straight left hit the same place, then began bending as Walt pummelled his body. He dropped to one knee as Walt backed away, then sank to rest on his hands, staring at the canvas.

Walt could scarcely keep count for the uproar. As he crouched in his corner he glimpsed Thorpe's strained stare at Ford, as though the trainer were trying to hypnotize him into staying down, but he was not surprised to see Ford rising at seven and holding the ropes as he swayed upright at nine.

Muff this and I've had it, he thought. I can't hit any harder than that.

He swung fiercely as he charged and crowded the other on to the ropes, taking furious jabs for the sake of increasing Ford's dizziness. Then a wild swing landed on his right eyebrow and he was blinded for one moment; long enough for Ford to land another swing which threw Walt so hard on to the ropes that he thought he was going through. As he fought for balance another punch exploded against his face, and he clutched giddily at the rope which slithered away as another punch drove him down.

Ford's feet backed away as though in slow motion. To have almost won... Now the sour smell of canvas and resin. The smell of defeat... For those last three punches had done it—driven out, completely, his strength.

Three... four... This tiger crawls... this lion—he was good when he thought he was winning—but he crawls in defeat.

Because he could have got up. Once more.

Seven...

Give the girl a coconut... a bull's eye...

Eight...

There was no rope to help him this time and he was still straightening up as Ford attacked. Walt clinched immediately, and still hung on, shaking his head vigorously to clear it, after the order to break. Ford grunted and snorted against his ear and tried to free his arms.

'Morris—break!'

He doubled up as they broke apart and Ford's swing almost toppled him over. Then he chased Walt and forced him to the ropes again. Without looking up from his crouch, Walt threw punches as Ford pounded him. He made no attempt to cover up but wildly hooked and jabbed, until his right arm jolted and he was free for a second to dodge away. He had no chance of an orderly, collected retreat, but he could keep hitting out and fighting for every backward staggering pace, and he could see the arms, like the body, living up to their training and natural skill, Ford's mouth stretching in a pained grimace as they exchanged punch for battering punch. As his back touched the ropes again, one final effort, one surge of frantic strength, called out because he must live up to the body and to his training and because in being damaged he must wreak the utmost damage he could, fetched him down, sideways and clear, while Ford leaned out to the darkness, helpless after a mighty swing. He had no idea of where Walt was. And Walt's right swing, up on his toes with his mouth open as he sobbed, struck the shoulder and Ford clutched at the ropes to save himself, one leg jerking up.

Three times the bell rang, and when the fighters had found their corners the crowd was still cheering and clapping. Walt almost swallowed the water and most of it trickled down his chest. Thorpe was working on his right eye.

'Swelling, isn't it?' he panted. It felt as though the eyebrow were a huge lump.

'It's not cut.' Thorpe held his singlet away from his body and wiped at the sweat on his face, neck and shoulders. His legs were quivering, and from the waist up every muscle and bone was wincing under pain as though the beating were still going on.

'How about it, Walt?'

He looked up as the referee approached to bend over him with Thorpe.

'How about it?' Thorpe asked again. The rules were strict and he realized they meant to stop the fight before he was hurt again.

'I'm not bad hurt, honest.' He sat up straight, steadying his legs and his breathing.

'How's your eye?' the referee asked, looking close at his face.

'Oh, fine.'

'It's not cut, anyway…' The referee moved away. Thorpe smiled and dabbed at his face again, then ducked away as the call came and the bell rang.

It isn't just for the crowd, he insisted against the critic. You know what it is. All you do is stab me in the back…

They touched gloves and began circling, Walt's legs too weak now to skip and carry him out of danger. He bobbed and weaved and flicked out his left incessantly like a cobra cornered by a mongoose. Each time Ford rushed he rode what punches he could and allowed himself to be forced backward. By the pounding force of Ford's punches and the vigour of his movements, Walt knew he was beaten, but he kept jabbing for the face and warding him off. A glancing hook caught Ford's nose and drew blood, and as he immediately looked worried and guarded his face, Walt threw himself forward and aimed for the body with a flurry of punches.

One last time, he yelled in his mind as he chased after Ford with his arms pumping, and met an upswinging, well-timed glove which took him under the chin and sent him backward in a whirl of dazzling white light, darkness, ropes and the smell of defeat on the canvas, with his gum-shield clattering across the ring. The sour humiliation of resin dusted his face.

Just to beat the count would be something, he thought. To finish the round and the fight on his feet…

The count reached six as he distinguished a rope in the blurred darkness. Raising his head cleared his eyes, and he saw Thorpe's face, then his signal to stay down. Still counting, he drew a knee under him and got his body half up, seeing Thorpe shake his head worriedly and shape the words: 'Don't try it.' His eye must have been hit again, for he could tell the hot slowness of blood trickling down his face. The noise and giddiness had made him lose count.

He crouched by the ropes and turned to see the whole ring with his left eye, beginning to weave as Ford came again from his corner, but the bell clanged repeatedly and the fight was over, and Ford lowered his guard as he approached. He took Walt's arm and turned him towards his corner, where Alec Thorpe was coming through the ropes.

He let himself be bundled on to the stool. A towel was thrown over his head and Thorpe knelt silently to work on his eye with gentle fingers.

'In accordance with the rules…' the referee was shouting in the middle of the ring, while Walt sat with his chest heaving, looking down as he felt pain shudder through his torso.

'If I'd even finished on my feet,' he mumbled stiffly.

'...from further punishment...' the referee called, and Walt looked up.

'You did finish on your feet. They stopped it.'

'...Jack Ford of Mantywood.' A cheer broke out and went on and on, as Ford stood up once, then sat down while his second worked on his nose. Cool sticking-plaster clung to Walt's eye-brow, and as the referee went on about the gallant loser, Thorpe tapped his knee and said: 'Go and shake hands.'

He rose just as Ford did, and they met in the centre with the applause rising to break over the ring like thunder rolling down from chasmed mountains.

'Give 'em some sport, didn't we?' Ford grinned as he shook hands, holding a sponge to his nose. Walt said he hoped Ford would win a title.

'I'll have to get bone took out o' this first,' Ford answered cheerfully.

As they made their way back along the gangway, clapping, yelling and whistling continued in the hall and hands reached out to touch their shoulders as they passed. Walt let Alec Thorpe guide him, leaning on his arm a little and looking down dizzily at the blue robe flapping about his slender ankles, glad to have such a splendid robe with everyone turning to look. There was confusion in the dressing-room until Thorpe had chased the other youths away and made Walt sit quietly for ten minutes. Prestcott mentioned that a shower had been rigged, and it was under the shower that Walt properly recovered. The aches in his body increased, and his jaw and eye felt grossly swollen, yet he began to feel happy. As he was dressing, Thorpe told him to come to the gym next day for a rub down.

'And now I'll take you home,' he said. They left the dressing-room, with the youths still shouting praise and consolation to Walt, then in the dim corridor Thorpe said: 'You know how proud I am, don't you?'

'You taught me. Anyway, I didn't win.'

He kept his head down, hoping Thorpe would leave it at that and dreading embarrassment. They walked towards the doorway.

'How does it feel to have the crowd roar for you like that?' Thorpe smiled as he swung the canvas hold-all.

'It's—' Walt frowned. 'I couldn't tell you.'

'It happens to good pros all the time.'

'I'll think about it,' Walt answered, and grinned in spite of his sore jaw. At the doorway an attendant asked: 'Are you Walt Morris? Well, a young lady asked to see you.'

Thorpe was frowning at him quizzically.

'Look, Alec—' If she were still waiting and Alec took them home they might be arguing before they got out of the car.

'I'd like to see some of the heavyweights, anyway,' Thorpe smiled.

'Sure you're all right to go home alone?'

Walt nodded, and when he had promised not to stay out in the cold and to visit the gym, Thorpe left him.

I'm not getting entangled again, Walt thought firmly as he went outside.

She was standing under the lamp, reading the poster, and as Walt stopped and looked she turned to smile, hair glistening, brown eyes twinkling and teeth sparkling in the light.

'I don't suppose you remember me.'

'I wasn't expecting you!' His mind still befuddled by the beating, he stood staring foolishly, then moved under the light to look more closely.

'You're all bruises. Is your eye very bad? I asked for your dressing-room but they wouldn't let me in.'

'It's all right.' He touched the plaster self-consciously, feeling shy of her. She was smaller than he had thought her in Atwell's; no taller than his shoulder. Under a smart black costume she wore a pink blouse with a froth of lace at the collar. She carried a small black handbag.

'Good,' she said, as he began scraping a shoe toe on the pavement, his hands thrust into his pockets. 'It was a marvellous fight—you were marvellous, Walt.'

'You saw it? On your own?'

'Certainly.' She laughed up at his rounded eyes. 'Bill told us about it last Wednesday—terribly proud of you one moment and shocked at the idea of men fighting the next—you know Bill. So I decided to see it for myself. But that other one was far too big for you!'

'Not really.' She looked too small to want to boss people around, he thought. 'He just looked bigger—but he's a fine boxer.'

'Oh, you were terrific.' She squeezed the bag in both hands and Walt thought her face very soft and lively compared to Brenda's. She was prettier. Then he remembered his decision about entanglements and said gruffly that he must catch his bus.

'So must I. At the station.'

As he walked, with his legs stiff and ribs aching, the pavements shining underfoot, he felt huge beside Elaine. The street lights sparkled on her glossy crown as she tripped along, hurrying to keep up with him and talking in a voice he told himself was 'upper class'. She had seen him at the college on the previous Tuesday.

'I called you, but you didn't notice,' she said. 'You didn't have such short hair then.'

Ruefully he touched the thick bristle, recalling the face in his mirror, and answered: 'I'm going to let it grow again, you know. I know it looks funny.'

'It makes you look very young,' she said, looking up at him judicially: 'young and vulnerable…' He remembered she had told Bill he looked sensitive. He grinned.

'Considering I got knocked on my back three times in twenty minutes I suppose I am.'

'So you *have* got a sense of humour,' she remarked. He frowned at her note of surprise and said of course he had.

At the huge square from where the buses started they stood on a corner, the blue arc-lights making the girl's lips purple and her eyes as black as her heavy hair. People strolled past while they talked, and from the lines of buses opposite came the rumbling and muttering of engines. Elaine glanced at his hair several times and Walt kept rubbing his hand over it in embarrassment.

'Would you tell me all about your pit and your friends and your boxing some time?' She asked. 'Please?' When he offered to take her to a professional boxing match she shook her head with her small nose wrinkled in pert distaste. 'I'd rather not. It's different with someone you know—I wanted to see… I don't think I'd go again.'

He dug his hands into his pockets again, finding them suddenly large and awkward.

'You were marvellous, anyway… Won't people stare at your face on the bus?'

'Who cares?' Walt asked. She looked up at his hair again and said she really should go, holding out a hand and smiling. He leaned over her a little, squeezing the tiny hand.

'I hope it doesn't hurt too badly.' The black handbag rose and she gently touched his brow where the plaster was. Walt shook his head and leaned nearer, thinking it no harm to end their meeting with a mere touch of romance. She freed her hand, raised it, and rubbed it gently over his bristling hair.

'Honestly!' She smiled and stepped back. 'I've been dying to do that since I saw it.' And before he had his other hand out of his pocket she was tripping across the square like a schoolgirl in wedge heels, moving through light and shadow until she was gone. Walt was left to stare, and rub angrily at his stubble.

III

'But, Walt,' Thorpe urged him next morning, 'you've got the talent, son. In a year's time you could be on your way as a pro—your whole life could be different.'

He thought of the cheering audience for a moment, but repeated that he'd think about it. That kind of future would prove nothing more than his fight had, and less than some day becoming a collier might. Though free to choose, his choices were limited, for he had to keep faith with the dark, blind sources of his restless force.

'I'm not sure it's worth getting your face flattened for and maybe ending up tapped,' he told Thorpe. Which was also sincere.

He arrived home from the gym to find that Bryan had called and braved the old lady in her chair to pin her there while he related every gory detail of the fight. She passed several disgusted comments while Walt and Bill ate their dinner, and ended by remarking: 'Eh, well, you young 'uns are daft enough for owt.' Yet she had already given Walt a pot of soothing ointment for his bruises.

'What I can't understand'—Bill shook his head across the table at brown-wealed cheekbones and a slitted, purple eye— 'is how men can sit and watch, and not jump in to stop you.'

Walt listened to all this in disdainful, injured silence. When the old lady had taken their plates into the kitchen, however, he remarked that the women's section of the Atwell's club seemed to have stronger stomachs than the men's. Then he told Bill about Elaine.

'She never told anyone she was going.' Bill frowned. 'I've heard she's like that...' With a slow, sly smile he looked up to say: 'Of course she has asked about you. So you're next on the list, eh?'

'Oh no, I'm not.' Walt left the table and said from the doorway that one entanglement had been enough and he wasn't going on anyone's list.

'Don't be so sure,' Bill called, as Walt went upstairs. 'I bet she's quite a little lion-killer on safaris!' And Walt could hear him still laughing from the bedroom.

In the city that night the gang so competently banged things up that they were refused entry to a dance hall because most of them were drunk and rowdy. Bryan had begun demanding to know who was going to keep them out anyway, when they were told police were on the way and hurried off to the bus station, where they stood jostling each other in a large waiting queue and sang at the tops of their voices. On the moving bus they were ordered to be quiet or get off, but they kept on singing, and the conductor saw eyes steadily regarding him from tough, young grinning faces and went to stand on the platform as the bus rumbled up the darkened hillside.

On the Sunday night too they drank a good deal. Walt had discovered that the best way of avoiding the critic's reprisals for the body's brief triumph was to meet the others early and occupy yourself with fresh plans for evening. Shun solitude until Monday, then rely on the anaesthetic monotony of routine work and fatigue. Soon you began looking forward to Saturday again.

The week-end proved less hilariously diverting than Bryan had promised, however, and Walt was left feeling slightly disappointed but reluctant to admit it. The Sunday-night club was a large hall above some shops. It had a bar, a stage with a small band, and a fair-sized dance floor surrounded by tables. Elderly groups and couples as well as young people went there, and there were more girls than youths. Walt and Bryan escorted a pair home, but once they left the club and the gins and oranges, Walt's partner became more dubious of his bruises and black crop. To his disgust they said good night while lingering at a drab street corner, with Bryan trotting out old dirty jokes and the girls giggling coyly as they nudged one another.

'We ought to've made a date wi' 'em,' Bryan said, rebuking Walt on their way home for having leaned in silence against a wall. 'Can't get far wi' a woman in one night.'

'I couldn't stand a giggling pair like that for *more* than one night,' Walt said.

Monday cheered him. The morning edition of the local paper carried an account of the tournament and described the special contest as the best of the evening, praising both Walt and Ford. At the pit he received boisterous congratulations from the young ones and brief, approving remarks from older, quieter colliers which gratified him more. For the first time he cleared his own stint and set his own props, and the colliers working on either side of him came to look, tapping the props with their hammer heads, then nodded and said he'd make a filler yet. He went home too pleased with himself to heed his aching back and knees.

At the college next day he walked from one classroom to another with his head erect and chest out, and asked himself why he bothered with this studying, since he had no wish to be a manager but wanted to be a collier like the rest. Some of the colliers had invited him to their club the following Saturday, a signal token of acceptance.

At lunch-time he left the big granite building and at the gateway found Elaine waiting for him. It was a bright, cold day and she wore a thick green sweater under the coat of her tweed costume.

'I thought I'd see you here.' She smiled up, books gathered under one arm, her hair bound back by a red ribbon, as they were jostled in the gateway. 'Like to go to Atwell's for lunch?'

He thought of lists and safaris and took his time over shrugging and saying he supposed so, but a quick, saucy upward glance at his hair made him wince.

'Your poor face looks much more like its old self,' she remarked cheerfully and chattered about her classes on the way to the cafe. She was taking a commercial course at the college because she wanted to work for a woman's magazine some day. Walt told her very briefly about his own studies, and while he was talking she touched his arm and interrupted, 'Don't walk so quickly, Walt. You're making me trot,' in a breathless voice while smiling appealingly upward. He slowed down, thinking that she did this little-girl thing pretty well, and also thinking that she was smartly dressed each time they met while he was always wearing the shiny blue suit and white shirt open at the collar. For even in winter a tie to Walt was like a pink bow to a disreputable tomcat. It was worn only at a dance, and plucked off immediately on leaving.

In the cafe Elaine bought two buttered rolls and coffee, then went to the secluded corner table at which she had been sitting when Walt met her. A few women sat at other tables in the blue-walled room, chatting and smoking over their coffees, but a quiet listlessness filled the place and the swarthy woman seemed preoccupied, her black eyes gazing idly past him as she said they didn't cook meals, then heaped his plate with small pies and scones. As he brought this load to the table, Elaine stared.

'Gosh! I can see you don't have to worry about your figure,' she exclaimed. Walt, who usually bought a larger meal at less cost in a cheap restaurant, decided her remark must be bait for a compliment, since he could not see how a girl so diminutive need worry over her figure, either.

'They won't do you much good,' he grunted scornfully, nodding at the rolls. No energy in that!'

'I've got plenty of energy—I've cut lunches out.' She watched him eating for a while, nibbling while she looked and smiling each time he glanced up. It was a frank inspection, and he began unconsciously holding his food and his teacup in such a way that his broken, grimy nails were hidden. No amount of scrubbing could fetch all the coal dust out from under them or from the cracks and scratches on his hands. When she asked if he would tell her about his friends, he nodded and asked what she wanted to know.

'Anything. What you do with yourselves and what they're like.' She pushed away her plate and cup, wiping her fingers on a tiny crumpled handkerchief. 'Bill told us you had a girl and then that you broke up.'

'He does a lot of talking about me!'

'Oh, don't be angry. He likes you. He respects you in lots of ways.'

He shrugged and sat back as she lit a cigarette. 'The way he sticks that limp of his, all right. He's hardly ever grouchy—and I would be if I was him.'

Elaine nodded absently, toying with her cigarette case. He admired her slender, supple fingers, the nails glistening, but not red, and cut fairly short and round.

'What are the girls like?'

'Like? They're just girls... They like dancing, fun—a drink.'

He frowned downward and said tartly: 'Like their boy-friends to look like film stars, and if they can't find one he looks like they say they've forgotten which but he reminds 'em of it, anyway. You always remind them of *some* film star!'

'Was your girl like that?'

'Sure. Pretty much like the rest.' She had to be put away for good, he thought, yet wanted to make it girls in general and leave Brenda alone. 'Somehow the bloke they've got's never enough—never right for 'em—so they watch it on the pictures the way it ought to be and then they have him looking like the film star and—so they work it out with themselves some way. It's complicated—but it makes them half contented.' And that was not merely girls in general but some more of putting Brenda away, he realized, growing angry at himself, then angry at Elaine because she was laughing. She had a soft, shining-mouthed merry laugh, yet it made him say sharply: 'Don't laugh at me!'

'I wasn't—I thought you meant me to.' She watched him, curious, the smile easing. 'Suddenly you're angry. Why?'

'I'm not.' He put his hands on the table, careless of grime or rough nails. 'It's nowt to you what my kind of girl's like,' he said, defensive now.

'Well, you pretty well included all girls. I didn't mean anything Walt. I didn't know it was painful.'

'You're hell of a romantic-minded,' Walt told her. 'Painful!' He raised his cup and sipped a mouthful of tepid tea and tea-leaves, admitting to himself that he had been angry, and not merely about Brenda, but because Elaine aroused a quick resentment in him.

'Talk about you,' he said as he put down the cup and manfully swallowed the last sticky leaf. But while he listened to her he was also wondering why she caused him to feel vaguely suspicious, ready to hit back verbally at any time. There was more to it than Bill's lion-hunting, he felt.

She told him she had been in the city for almost a year, living with her sister and her brother-in-law, who was a teacher at the college. About her ambitions she was vague, except that they were connected with magazine work.

'I'm learning shorthand and typing. I used to think of designing, but I'd rather like editorial work—I'd like to do stories or articles, too... Don't you feel there are several things you'd like to try, Walt?' Her father's business kept him either in London or abroad. '...My mother's in London, too. They're divorced and she married again three years ago. Her mother was part Spanish.' Each item was mentioned as casually as the other, smiling over at him while the cigarette case slowly revolved in her fingers. 'I like living with Judith and Donald. They're not awfully well off, but they're buying their own house—a lovely, big one. Donald's teaching night school and they let me pay my share. I get an allowance from Daddy, but Judith doesn't. She wouldn't take it, anyway.'

What puzzled him was that daughters of a business-man should be mixing with Mason's group.

'They're Reds, I mean,' he said.

'Well, Pinks really. Except for poor Bill. Judith's *much* fiercer than any of them.' She explained that Judith had garnered her political ideas during the war, partly through meeting Don and some of his fellow Socialists. They were Labour Party members. '...She had a fearful row with Daddy over marrying Donald, but she's not so strait-laced as people think, you know. She's more my friend than my sister, and—'

'Yeah, but why?' he interrupted. 'Why should two like you be political?'

Elaine shrugged and said surely they had a right to their own ideas. '...Judith picked it all up in the Services, and with Don, and she passes it on to me. Well, I have to listen, you understand—but I don't feel terribly fierce about it all, the way Judith does. She loves meetings.'

'I'll bet she does,' Walt agreed, stifling comment.

'...So you see I'm not simply nosing into your life, Walt. You know all about mine now. And I can meet some of your friends, can't I?'

'Sure.' He decided she was a nice girl when not being coquettish. He leaned on the table. 'Is your sister happily married?'

'Of course. Why?'

'Nothing.' He sat back and glanced up at the clock. It was time to go. 'You just don't seem to see many happy married people around.' He was thinking of her parents, his parents and Brenda's parents as well as grumbles he had heard at the pit. 'I was just wondering.'

'Well, of course,' she said gravely as they stood up and went to the door, 'they haven't been married all *that* long.'

As the door closed behind them he asked her age.

'Eighteen.'

'So am I,' Walt said, and felt she was curious again while she smiled. He added carefully: 'I packed up with this girl because I think eighteen's too young for steady courtship, don't you?' Elaine said she didn't think so, and he wished he knew whether that quick sauciness meant she was smiling to or at him.

'It's a marvellous age for making lots of friends, anyway,' she added, and he agreed. She suddenly laughed. They were turning a corner and Walt whirled abruptly and demanded: 'Now' what's funny?'

'It's nothing.' She scarcely broke step, but walked on, saying: 'I was just remembering that boxing contest and thinking it was a jolly good thing poor old John didn't decide to punch your nose or something that evening in Atwell's. He didn't like you very much. Making friends!'

'Oh,' he said sheepishly, and after a while said: 'I could show you better fights than that at professional matches.' He added proudly: 'I've been asked to turn pro.'

'But you're not going to, are you?' She looked up quickly. 'It must be a horrible life.'

'Your picture in the papers and crowds cheering you?' He wanted her to see the temptation he had resisted. 'A lot wouldn't think it was horrible! But I'm not, anyway.'

'I suppose it would be quite a life for someone who was good at it and liked that crowd and all that...' she admitted, thoughtfully nodding. They came to the college wall and turned another corner into a busy street as she asked why he had refused the chance.

'It's just not for me.' Then, after a moment, to his own surprise, he was saying: 'If I told you the best thing about that night—you wouldn't blab about it?'

'Oh no. Do tell me.' As they stopped near the gates where groups and couples stood around talking, she turned up a small, eager face and waited.

'Well, it wasn't the crowd.' He pocketed his hands and leaned against the wall, frowning at his scraping shoe. He was not suspicious of her honesty; he knew he could trust her with this. Since Friday he had been longing to tell someone and know what they thought of it. 'It wasn't them at all. I was surprised how that seemed not so important afterwards. It was getting up that third time.' He frowned up earnestly, then asked himself how a girl could be expected to understand, and why he had chosen a girl to tell. Yet what man could he have told? 'You see, my mind —well, not my mind exactly—yes, my mind had chucked it in. It wanted to stay down and I wouldn't—my body wouldn't. *I* wouldn't! And when I got up I knew a bit more about—well, about the *kind* I am. *I* was right, you see—doing what my body really wanted to do. Because it was right to get up...' He grinned, flushed and awkward. 'You don't know what I'm talking about, do you?'

'Oh, do go on, Walt,' she said seriously. 'Please. I'm trying, honestly.'

'No, that's it, really...' He hunched his shoulder on the wall. 'Only it's not as simple as mind and body—sort of. It's one part against the other, you know. Anyway, what I was going to say was, it made me feel a bit easier about things I'd felt bad about. That's all, really.'

Yet there was more, he felt. More he could have groped a way to had he waited, instead of trying to frame movement and wheeling into fixed, limiting words too soon. He shrugged.

'You're always doing that,' Elaine said.

'What?'

'Sticking your hands in your pockets and hunching up your shoulders or shrugging. As though to say you couldn't care less.'

He said it was habit and they stood quietly as people do when conversation has gone too deep for the time and place, yet it is impossible to talk lightly again.

'I'll see you again, then,' Walt said gruffly.

'I'll be in Atwell's on Friday.' She hitched her books under her arm and they strolled to the gates. 'I do wish you'd let me see some of the places you go to and meet some of your friends.'

'I'm working on Friday,' he told her, with other people now milling around them and other voices breaking on theirs. 'But I'll look you up. So long.'

'See you soon.'

Once she was gone he wished he had arranged to meet her that evening. Yet he felt he should be careful. A girl was friendly or attentive or sympathetic, and, before you knew it, you'd talked and sentimentalized yourself into another entanglement through little confidences and agreements on ideas, and feeling she was too nice not to be nice to. Which wasn't fair to either of you. He would ask Bryan what places would be interesting for her if she was so eager to see the lusty life.

At the prompted thought of how Bryan's size would impress Elaine, Walt felt a rush of jealousy, not for her, but for Bryan's s gift of strength. However hard he might try, he would never equal Bryan in size and strength—would never be the man Bryan was without effort. It didn't seem very fair when he thought of it, and he thought of it often during class, reflecting that a knowledge of science and mathematics wasn't enough to balance against far superior effortless strength and manliness. Hard to admit there were better classes you could never enter.

He was bored that evening because all his friends were on afternoon shift, including Bill, and he had grown unused to spending evenings idle and alone. He decided to go to the gym, then went upstairs to put on a tie, donned a blue military-style raincoat bought a week ago, and went to Atwell's instead. She wasn't there and the nonchalant entrance and slow stroll to the counter under the neon lights were wasted. Only Andrew Mason was there, smiling pleasantly and waving to Walt, who reluctantly took his cup of tea to the table.

'A pleasant surprise,' Mason greeted him. His shirt, knitted tie and corduroy coat looked to Walt like the same ones he had been wearing last time. As Mason pushed aside a sheaf of papers he had been marking, he inquired if Walt were looking for anyone special and was vigorously assured that Walt wasn't.

'Well—very nice of you to drop in. We've been hearing of your boxing success. Congratulations.'

'It's no success when you get licked.' Walt looked away uncomfortably. This gaunt-faced, fulsome-voiced, over-toothed intellectual wasn't the kind he could talk with. Most of the tables were empty with tilted chairs clustered around them. He look back again at Mason. 'On your own, eh?'

'I finished an early class and thought I'd drop in before I went home. A bed-sitter becomes dull enough. I spend a good deal of time in here.'

He was a lonely-looking man seen without the others, and the constant unsuited smile and carefully pleasant voice made Walt think him a little pathetic, then tell himself sternly not to be mushy. Yet he returned the smile and they talked about the college for several minutes.

'You have quite a devotee in Elaine Stewart,' Mason said, his smile whimsical to just the right point of no offence. 'She asks about you.'

'She seems awful interested in me and my friends—I don't know why,' Walt answered guardedly.

'Don't you? It's natural, Walt. She's had few chances of mixing with your kind of friends. And after all—' the smile was slightly teasing for a moment—'if you can stomach the politics?' When Walt nodded curtly, he continued, hands spreading outwards: 'If Elaine's sister is right, and such friends as Bill and I and a few others are right, you and your friends are society's future inheritors. You're the future world-shapers—our hope, you might say—and Elaine wants to see how you're all developing towards this huge historical responsibility.'

'Is that so?' Walt said flatly. It was a guide-book Elaine needed, not him. In Mason's speech had been a light dryness that could have been continued teasing or perhaps self-mockery. He nodded.

'When I said we were observers, I shouldn't have included the others. I expect these young ones will eventually get involved. Your friend, especially.' The last words were grave.

'If Bill wants to be a Red, let him be one,' Walt said, irked by Mason's air of omniscience. 'Your lot haven't any right to shape his life.'

'Except that we're his friends.' Mason removed his glasses and rubbed them with his handkerchief, then went on: 'Bill is a nice boy, Walt. He has very high ideals—more tender than he thinks.'

'Bill? He called me an idealist!'

'Bill is a rank idealist. He could be very badly hurt.'

'That's your opinion against Bill's You're against them, it seems, so—'

'I was a member—once. Didn't Bill tell you? Ah well—he isn't too proud of my performance.' Mason smiled, hollow eyes once more

139

twinkling behind the horn rims as Walt stared over the papers and brown-stained cups. 'A member, and resigned—to Bill's disgust.' Walt wished he would stop talking as though it were all slightly contemptuous and laughable. It was like listening to a man making a fool of himself to win applause from an otherwise cold audience. 'I sympathize with you young people. At your richest time you're set in a postwar world of austerity, goods under the counter, spivs making black-market fortunes and people getting through how they can. That struck me last time you were here, you know.' He paused and asked politely: 'Do you mind my talking about you? You interest me because I sense something—with your good-lion exuberance and so on—probably Elaine senses it too, for she was impressed... she was impressed... I feel you should be helped, but we're all inadequate. It's not us you need...'

'I know that,' Walt broke in. 'You go on about why you're anti-Communist.'

'I'm not.'

'Well, anti-Russian, then.'

'I'm not that either.'

'You're not for anything,' Walt said slowly, 'but you're not against anything. And you talked to me about—'

'Wait, you have me wrong!' Mason was growing as excited as Bill would have done; he was defending himself with more heat than Walt saw need for. 'I meant I'm not blindly anti-anything. But I can see the faults. I can foresee how Bill could get hurt in a future time of putsches or trials or so on. I can say that this isn't our way, without refusing that way to other countries. You see, Walt, I don't like how it's going in Europe. I don't like many actions of the East any more than many of the West. I'm no more happy about the Communist position than the Socialist one...'

'God!' Walt said dramatically. 'You're in a bloody mess, aren't you?'

Mason sat back, his wry grin making his face less cadaverous for a moment. He remarked that it all sounded like tripe, didn't it?

'It's played out. You've no right to stop Bill doing what he wants, anyway.'

'Ah, if you could see...' Mason sighed. He studied Walt, taking his time. 'Walt, my defence is that I personally refuse to take those courses open at present. Lots of people aren't satisfied with the Socialist Left, but won't go Communist. We're waiting for something else.'

'Well, folk are sick and tired of hearing about trouble and being on the brink of war,' Walt said determinedly. 'Just sick and tired and couldn't care less!' Mason nodded quietly until Walt sat back.

'And so are you, Walt?'

'I'm fine. I don't mind working hard and plugging along if I can get to bang things up now and again and if I'm left to live my own life.'

'We'll drop the politics. Let me buy you a coffee.' He rose slowly.

'Tea.'

Mason smiled down on him for a moment, then nodded and said:

'Tea it is.' While he was gone Walt looked around at the photographs and shadowed corners, a few murmuring couples, and wondered how much less lonely than a bed-sitter it might be. He understood why Mason was so eager to talk, and although he was sure Elaine would not come now, he decided to remain with the teacher a little longer.

'You look an extremely smart young man in that raincoat,' Mason said when he returned and sat down opposite. They sipped gingerly from the hot cups, then Mason said, as though suddenly making up his mind: 'Walt, is this conscious toughness a personal trait or does it apply to your friends too?' As Walt stiffly lowered his cup, he went on smoothly: 'I mean there's such a need to conform nowadays—a dread of individuality—do you know what side you're really on?'

'I told you where I stood,' he said, warily and half angrily. 'I've finished poking into things too much!'

Mason scratched a fingernail thoughtfully over the sleek papers. 'Do you read much poetry, Walt?'

'Me? No!' Once in school, at fourteen, he had been called to recite before a crowded mixed class. One of his favourite poems, he remembered. A real soldier's poem:

'If I should die, think only this of me...' And when it was finished and the teacher asked did he like poetry, he had to blurt out 'Yes, sir,' because it was that poem. And the whole classroom resounded to scornful laughter at anyone liking stuff you had to spend hours learning by heart, while he stood in scarlet-faced, miserable shame for his own gushiness.

'We did some at school, of course,' he added, while Mason's long fingernail scraped faintly. He always remembered, 'I have a rendezvous with death at some disputed barricade...' but only that line. For William, perhaps. Bill had said the days of barricades were gone and it was scientific war now. No people in the streets nowadays. Scientific war. I'd give ten years to get the one that killed him...

'What on earth are you thinking about?' Mason asked. 'Is poetry that bad?'

'What about poetry?' Walt asked irritably. He finished his tea as Mason explained: 'I was thinking of a great poet who once said that one law for lion and ox is oppression.'

'I don't want to oppress—'

'He meant oppression against the lion.' Mason gently smiled, his head on one side. Walt frowned, wondering what that meant.

'At least somebody was sympathetic...'

'Oh Lord—you're not the first by far to blazon a lion on your standard, Walt. Many others have—one of the most famous ended as a madman after doing that. The beast of prey! But I gather you don't feel the lion should be master of the deer? You don't feel some kind of superman?'

'Not superman!' Walt struggled between exasperation and hatred of being misunderstood. 'I just said that's the way it is. What I want to do—' He remembered the talk that morning with Elaine and frowned because he was about to heave up a tide-like rolling in twitching, dying struggles once more. 'Look, I don't want to hurt a soul. But I'm going to live my own way as my own way comes, and I'm not going to be pushed into what other folk want me to be, see? That's all. It's that simple.'

'Simple?' Mason lounged back till his head touched the blue wall, smiling, yet frowning, and still studying Walt. 'Lucky you're not trying to spread that creed if you're so determined on honesty. How young you are, Walt—probably young enough to contradict yourself ten times a day and neither know it nor be harmed by it. You have your own beliefs. You're determined to be honest. And you refuse to be coerced or persuaded, what?'

'I'd *like* to be like that. Who wouldn't?'

'Most people—underneath. Walt—' the smile puckered around the convex teeth, eyes turning downward, face whimsical— 'there are accepted ways of being nonconformist and they all demand conformity. Everywhere and anywhere. The lands of the free, Walt, the homes of the brave... every country has lots of accepted ways of rebelling which are recognizable, nice and can be handled. There are some no one will stand for, and simply being your own self, honestly following your own beliefs, is one. Bill's way isn't popular. But it's more acceptable than yours...'

Walt stared at the smiling, now enigmatic face for a while.

'I've no idea what you're on about, he finally admitted.

'Ah, you would have if you tried preaching your doctrine. You don't realize how deadly it might be if you began making converts and teaching disciples. Good Lord! Then the soldiers would lean on their spears till your marks were made in the sand, or perhaps here they'd allow you a high tower where you could see the stars...' He paused, and went on, as though flippantly: 'But not the dignity of a Calvary—mankind's that much changed today.'

'You don't understand—I don't want to make anybody else feel my way.'

'That's rather a pity,' Mason said. 'However, even alone—but no, I'm day-dreaming. Public retraction or the poison vial, Walt. Or perhaps—'

His face changing to keen shrewdness he leaned in towards Walt, who was thinking that the sentence about day-dreaming had been the truest. But this was to be expected of intellectuals, he supposed.

'...I suppose you've read some of these shocking statistics on juvenile delinquency, Walt? These ways of conforming I mentioned. After all, most young people have ideal types in their minds they try to live up to—agreed? And don't the standards of modern cinema and modern writing tend towards the tough, batter-his-way-through type?'

I'm not breaking any laws!' Walt protested, tightening the belt of his raincoat.

'I wasn't just thinking of you. Isn't this rebellion that conforms the kind of thing that's raised the rate of juvenile crime since the war? Don't you think so?'

'Maybe.' Walt shrugged. 'They say it always happens after a war.

'True,' Mason nodded. 'That knowledge doesn't cure very much, does it?' As Walt smoothed his coat, he inquired: 'And you don't feel any of this—this of your own age group—concerns you?'

'Look, I don't know what you're thinking I could do, but there's nothing I know of. And if it's all a lead-up to politics, forget it.'

'No, I just wondered what you thought of it all... You know you're an ancient Greek of a good lion sometimes, Walt?'

Walt rose, pushing his chair back. 'Haven't you read Homer, Walt? He knew some good lions too—not altogether like you, but fair specimens. I'll send you one of his stories some time.'

Walt thanked him and said good night. He was relieved to get away from the lonely hollow eyes. At home he remarked to Bill: 'That Mason—queer sort, but you have to feel a bit sorry for him somehow, don't you?'

Part Two

A man's worst enemies are those
Of his own house and family;
And he who makes a law a curse
By his own law shall surely die.

    From Islington to Marylebone
    Jerusalem, WILLIAM BLAKE

Rampant

I

The world rolled towards the year's end with Western statesmen giving thanks for their Bomb and urging greater unity against the predators, Eastern statesmen giving thanks for firm leadership and urging greater unity against the aggressors, and the nations on either side of divided Germany checking their armour and forging new weapons. Closer to, the bickering of industrialists, union leaders, parliamentarians and other politicians waxed and waned like a sporadic snarling. Walt occasionally raised his head, sniffed, shrugged, and continued padding along his own way.

One Friday, a few weeks after his promotion to filler, brought a small triumph. He arrived home at dinner-time, put his usual board money on the table with an extra ten shillings beside it, then took off his coat and casually sat down to eat.

'Hey-up,' the old lady said when she had counted it. 'What's this?'

'Get paid a bit more—pay a bit more,' he answered, bending over his plate while she frowned down straddle-legged with her bulk above the table like a green mountain threatening a white plain. The note crackled in her red fingers.

'I'd tell thee if I needed a raise...'

Walt lowered his knife and fork and pretended to be examining his bared left arm, which was blackened by several long scratches where some falling coal had struck that morning.

'You've kept me pretty cheap all this time and I know how dear stuff is. Besides—' he knew this would appeal to her—'I want to know I'm paying a fair whack. Fair enough?' He glowered up and impatiently lifted his fork again. She put the other money in her overall pocket and studied the note, then remarked that he'd be paying more than Bill: '...I can't make more nor one nor t' other, you know!'

'Bill gets less money than me, don't he? Bloody hell, ten bob's nowt, is it?'

'No need for language. As she walked over to the fireplace and he heard the tea-caddy clatter Walt chewed hard on his food and kept his face stern. Five shillings more, he thought, and she would have refused. She would prefer to sit in the public house for an hour with her one glass of beer turning flat before her. You had to learn how to handle women.

As she sat down in her sighing chair she said: 'I suppose you'd only chuck it away on your beer and lasses, anyroad.'

Before he went to bed Walt mentioned that he was going dancing that night. He had arranged this with a girl at the club on Sunday.

'It's alls dancin' nowadays,' the old lady commented. 'Have you done your studies?'

'Sure,' he lied, after a moment. He had been neglecting his homework recently to go with Bryan and the gang. He would skip next Monday's classes, he decided, and go to the gym. Alec Thorpe must be wondering why he was staying away.

'This dance finishes late,' he added, as he opened the door. 'I might be a bit late getting home.' He returned her long, thoughtful scrutiny with a brief, innocent smile. Not the dance nor the girl's hints that an evening alone might produce a more exciting climax than mere kisses were the real causes of this challenge. He was eighteen and getting around a lot and meeting lots of girls. And might as well get some return for his philanthropy. '...I'll try not to be too late, mind you.'

She stared a moment longer, wrinkled and inscrutable, then bent over to lift the poker. The eleven o'clock curfew, he told himself while keeping his face blank, was over.

'Just don't overdo it,' she grunted, raking down a shower of ash and crackling cinders from the gleaming bars. Just a question of learning how to handle them, he told himself, going joyfully upstairs, and even though the girl that evening proved more inhibited about excitement than he expected, Walt still felt he had learned a thing or two about women in the past few months.

Yet he was never over-confident about Elaine Stewart. He took her out several times during the next two months and never felt completely at ease with her; though, except for her flirtatious and consciously provocative moods, he could not define what made him uneasy. Once they went to a dance and during the interval visited a public house which was notorious for its uncouth clientele. Elaine stayed close by him, and asked as soon as they left: 'But that's not the kind of place most of your work-mates go to, is it?' And Walt had to admit that it wasn't, realizing that she wasn't seeking sensation and that Mason might have been right about her. Conferring honour, he said: 'Some Saturday I'll take you to see our colliers in their own places.' It was a point of pride with him that he was asked to go for a drink with his workmates more often than Bryan was. Bryan would have scoffed at the offer, anyway.

On another night Elaine took Walt to Atwell's and introduced him to her sister and brother-in-law. Donald was fair-haired, pleasant and growing plump; Judith was stockier than Elaine though almost as small, with a deep, quick-talking voice. She was pretty, but her black hair was bobbed and she looked so intelligent, he thought, that he was a little afraid and spoke gruffly. He felt afterwards that he had been looked over for signs of promise, given a second chance, and rejected, all in a few minutes. That was his last visit to the blue walls, neon tubes and continual drone of Atwell's.

Most weekends were spent with the gang at different dance halls and pubs; most free nights were spent with casual girl-friends. Walt was saving up for Christmas, having told himself that money hard earned should be spent sensibly, yet two pounds a week on drinks and cinema seats never seemed senseless. With five or six days of hewing and shovelling coal to live through, a bright week-end was something to think about. He visited the gym less frequently as his passion for boxing waned and the disappointment in Thorpe's looks irked him more; since his fight with Ford, since his success as a filler, entering a ring had lost its unique challenge.

Twice Walt gave up the more riotous pleasures of usual Saturdays to take Elaine to meet older colliers and their wives. The club squatted among the blackened walls and roofs of a heavy industrial district, its members mainly miners or steel-workers, who were prepared to put some hard effort and hard drinking into enjoying Saturday nights. The concert room was huge, a dozen white-aproned waiters serving the long ranks of tables, and a piano and drums on the stage to accompany different professional entertainers every week. There were more than a hundred such clubs in the city and every week-end saw them crowded with miners, forge-hands, cutlery-makers, grinders and a dozen other kinds of hard-working men and women.

'If you want to see the working class,' Walt told Elaine the first time they went, 'it's the clubs you want to visit.' She seemed to enjoy the noise and bustle of the smoky tables, the brisk waiters and the singing, joking and laughing. The club was noisy, but not rowdy; too restrained for the tastes of Bryan and the others. Elaine smiled and talked to the men who came up to Walt's table, bought them a drink and teased him slyly for a few moments. He thought her as carefree as any other girl that evening, and she never talked of class developments or historical roles the way Bill and Mason did. He liked her, though he felt she was enjoying the evening and seeing her surroundings in a private, reserved way as well as openly. The idea of something kept back and hidden from him was slightly baffling and irritating, and two or three weeks usually passed between one evening together and another.

He never troubled to analyse his reasons for keeping her away from Bryan and the gang. They were a tough crowd, after all, and would all be making up to her once they knew she wasn't his girl. Bryan tried to interrogate him about these evenings spent away from them, but had to be satisfied with a brief just a girl, that's all.'

'I guess we've got to go wi' 'em on us own sometimes,' Bryan would grudgingly admit. Then beg Walt with concern not to let one come between himself and his friends. '…They all do it, kid… Can't help wanting to split lads up, somehow.' To which Walt scornfully replied that none was getting hooks into him again and he needn't bother about that!

In Elaine he had someone who could be shown the people and places he was growing proudly fond of; someone who might see and admire what he saw and admired, and with whom he could act differently from the way he did with the gang. Sometimes it was necessary to rest from hectic fraternity, to sit quietly and talk with a girl. So long as the girl understood that this could only continue if they avoided romantic entanglement. When she showed genuine interest and asked questions, he approved of her. He never needed to explain anything twice about the pit and the work. When she grew playful or coquettish, he became sulky and disgusted. She sometimes adopted the pose of an innocent with a wise old man and listened meekly to his lectures or his advice on how to behave in such places, yet a suspicion of being gently mocked would begin nagging at Walt and have him feeling as though she were the older.

A week before Christmas he took her to the working men's club again. They arrived early, had several drinks with half a dozen of Walt's workmates at a large table, and by eight o'clock he saw she was in flirtatious mood. As the older men questioned her about college and university life and she answered, Elaine laughed a great deal, rolling her eyes and leaning back to show off her figure.

'I reckon they's some right capers among these students,' said one collier with a sly grin. He was a pleasant-faced, sandy-haired, burly man, fifteen years older than Walt, who called everyone his 'old flower'. He was nicknamed Sandy.

'I've heard that too,' Elaine agreed, laughing.

No one else seemed to mind; they tended to lean a little too close to Elaine and talk a little too confidentially, if anything, but Walt sat silent and uncomfortable, his anger slowly heaving. When he felt that she was posing, overdoing mysterious-eyed seductive glances and languid postures, he always became embarrassed for her sake. She had a way, too, of looking as though she were sizing you up which reminded him of her sharp-eyed sister, but he was sure it was not intelligence potential that Elaine was looking for in her audience. She was trying to gauge them as men, but lacked the necessary experience.

'Walt, my old flower,' Sandy told him, with a leer at Elaine which Walt considered disgustingly lecherous, 'this is a nice little lass tha's got here. Real style.' Elaine thanked him very much and smiled brightly. She was wearing a pink wool dress which clung tightly to her high breasts and neat hips, stretching when she moved as though under considerable strain.

When a singer appeared on the stage, the lights were dimmed, the waiters rested at the bar, and everyone turned to watch through a mist of waving smoke. In the near darkness, Walt jerked his chair against Elaine's and gripped her arm above the elbow. She had turned to the stage and her back was towards him, her scent a tenuous fragrance.

'Knock it off,' he murmured angrily. 'These blokes are old enough to be your father. And they're married.'

'What am I doing wrong?' Her head tilted back against his jaw and he saw the upward curve of one dark, gleeful eye. If they'd had a few more drinks, he thought, he would have believed her half tipsy. Tightening his grip, he whispered: 'Don't muck about, smiling at 'em as if it was your honeymoon or something. And stop leaning back so your—and stop fluttering your big eyes.'

Elaine turned, and one or two of the colliers looked round to grin at them. 'I can't help my eyes,' she said, disarmingly widening them. 'Or what happens when I lean back!'

'Well, you'd better,' he hissed savagely, as he saw grins and nudges around the table. 'Because their wives will soon be here and they won't think you're cute. And they could pull your arms off and bash you round the ears with 'em!'

'All right, Walt,' she said humbly, as she turned again. 'Whatever you say, my old flower...' And for the rest of the night she was modestly quiet and still, answering people and smiling politely and succeeding in making Walt feel a bullying lout. He was sure she enjoyed this, and enjoyed his embarrassment at teasing about whispering and squeezing in the dark from the colliers.

When they left the club and joined a long queue at a tram stop across the wide, busy road, she told him he had hurt her arm. He mumbled that he was sorry, rocking gently on his heels with his hands in his pockets as cars and buses flashed and rumbled past.

'Why were you so furious?' She swung round in front of him, looking up from the high, raised collar of her coat. 'It was only fun.'

'Forget it, will you?'

But when they were on the tram, Elaine holding to a seat-back and Walt an overhead strap, jostled together in the crowd by the swaying motion, she was studying his face carefully as she remarked: 'These tempers of yours puzzle me. I wonder why they break out so suddenly?'

Walt glanced uncomfortably around at the standing and seated people.

There was a general aroma of alcohol and chips.

'Would their wives really bash my ears?' She smiled as though the idea were wonderful.

'I only said they could if they wanted to. And they *could*.'

She appeared to be thinking this over for the rest of the journey. At the bus station he took Elaine to her stop, but before she got aboard she asked: 'What's their love-life like, Walt? Are they very passionate, or just sort of routine about it all?' She often asked such questions.

'I don't know.' He knew that in the pit the men often talked obscenely and even made jokes about their own wives which caused him, the listener, to feel uncomfortable. Yet he suspected that this gross and brutish attitude was merely a formula for covering something else.

'Well, are they really jealous of each other?' Elaine prompted him.

'I'm sorry,' he said, slightly embarrassed. 'I just don't know about all that. They don't talk to young ones like me about their private life very much. Just—jokes, you know.'

'Well, you should try to find out,' she said as the bus began shuddering. 'After all, it's your life.'

At the pit on the following Monday Walt was finally christened. Since he kept company in such high society he deserved recognition. They called him the Marquis.

Two days before Christmas he went home, leaving Bryan and the others disappointed but full of plans. On the table he had left a tie and socks for Bill and a bright new head-scarf for the old lady, though he reflected in the train that the old lady would probably never wear her present.

Looking out at the bleak, snow-dappled countryside, he realized that it was only nine months ago since he had been travelling the opposite way. That was hard to believe. It seemed to him that back in the grimy-blocked city with its boiling pressure of hundreds of thousands all life should now be suspended until he returned to join in. The carriage was crowded and filled with smoke and talk, but Walt sat still and quiet. His body had learned patience.

I feel ever so much older, he thought, his breath grey on the glass. He felt he must have changed immeasurably, yet, when he tried to word these changes, could only look at his horny-knuckled fingers and calloused hands, consider the calm endurance of his limbs, and think: Well, I have changed... He was happier, that was what it was. He might still have that gathering restlessness which ensured that no period of peace or happiness would last long, but he felt happier

...About me, he realized.

Charles lived beside a village near London; a cluster of farm labourers' cottages around a post office and public house. The cottages were lit by oil lamps and water was fetched in buckets from a pump beside the post office. Farther along, set well apart, were privately owned houses, some of which were used only at weekends. These had electricity and running water and were surrounded by trellis-work and hedges; not the privet Walt was used to, but tall, graceful bushes of varying kinds, smoothly level or clipped to artistic patterns. His brother's house was the third Walt came to, after trudging past the thatch-roofed squat cottages where snow had been piled against the walls in hard-crusted dirty heaps by the road-plough's passing. In the doorway he saw his mother, a fairly tall, slender woman in a brown dress, calling over her shoulder while she waved.

'He's here, Joan, he's here,' she called excitedly as he walked up the path, and her over-high voice raised sudden tenderness in him. He reached her, and in a great burst of affection dropped his suitcase and crushed her against the leather buttons of his raincoat, laughing as she hugged him.

'Good old Ma!' he said, then saw she was crying. He patted her shoulder gently, but she continued sobbing as she clung to him.

'Oh, I'm glad you're back—so glad you're all right. I've been so worried about you.'

He stiffened, blood pounding up in his neck and face, as she clung frantically. He had forgotten how her emotional cascades overwhelmed him with a dread like that which comes when stone creaks and grates and the muscles are paralysed by thought of suffocation.

'I'm fine, Ma. Honest.' He broke away and retrieved his case while she stood looking at him and dabbed a handkerchief to her eyes.

'What a size you are! You've grown three inches, surely.' Her elocution was good, careful and devoid of accent. Putting it on just a bit, he thought, mildly amused. She had always done that when there was company. White was seeping over the grey hair, but you knew she had been good-looking before the hard lines of work and creases of worry were filed in her oval face.

'Not an inch!' Her avid stare, with more tears imminent, made his smile self-conscious and made him feel more gawkish than he had for months as he entered the house. Joan, his sister-in-law, was standing by a wide hearth where a gas fire blazed, the plush out-of-date furniture in the large room matching its oak panels and low, glowing black beams. She was a slight, handsome woman of thirty, with curly brown hair and pale, Roman-nosed features. The two boys sat close together while they looked up curiously with toys around them on the floor. One was six, the other four. A year-old girl slept in a pram by the fire. As Walt greeted them all, then looked down at the fat, rosy face, his mother said: 'Oh, of course, you've never seen Margaret.'

The two boys were soon climbing over him as he sat near the fire, answering his mother's countless questions after she had fetched in a laden tea-trolley. Each time Walt reassured her on one point she began asking worriedly about another: his lodgings, the food, his pleasures and the girls he met—his studies, his wages and his work. And while she interrogated him she broke off questions to remark on his growth, how he had changed, and to ply him with more tea or sandwiches or cakes. He was allowed only brief answers, yet she made him feel breathless. Apart from rebuking the boys and eventually making them return to the toys on the floor, Joan watched quietly from another chair. Gradually the questions slowed and the high pitch eased in his mother's voice. When she remarked with a hopeful smile that she'd been thinking he might have tired of the life by now, he answered gently: 'No, love. It's my real life now.'

'Of course—' she smiled again, patently being brave— 'you're going to have a superior position eventually...'

'Maybe. In a few years.' But he was thinking how snobbish the remark sounded. Then he saw the flutter of a nerve in her cheek, something he had often seen, as she said: 'If you just knew how it worried me—with you in a job like that...'

She managed not to cry, but he noticed how Joan looked away with distaste in her grey patrician eyes. Since he knew his mother would fail to understand his feelings about the work, he tried to comfort her by making it all sound ridiculously easy and safe, becoming effusive himself and flushing a little when Joan looked at him sceptically.

His brother came home after the children were in bed, the curtains drawn and all the lights switched on. By this time his mother was cheerful again, using her hands as she talked, explaining to Walt—as though she had never scrubbed stone steps or sweated in a laundry, he thought—that the farm workers here were very quiet types and rather simple, but quite nice. They heard Charles drive into the garage, then he entered rubbing his hands briskly.

'And how is the family's mole?' He was a little smaller than Walt, but plumper, with short hair neatly parted and smoothed down like a schoolboy's. His features were regular, and in spite of rimless spectacles his smooth, oval face, faintly yellowed from his two years in Egypt, was attractive.

'If they keep turning out these bigger and better bombs,' he said as they shook hands, 'I may come and join you down there.' He turned to kiss Joan's cheek. 'Sorry I'm late, darling—tidying up before the holidays.'

When Charles had eaten, Walt suggested a trip to the pub, reassuring his startled mother by telling her: 'I only drink an odd pint, of course.' Charles apologized and said he had work to finish.

'Surely we can go out for a little while,' Joan urged him. 'Surely tonight.'

'Well, we can ...' Charles nodded with an amicable shrug. 'Only I'd have to do it tomorrow, then, or Boxing Day. And I promised you I wouldn't.'

'I don't see why at Christmas you have to do any work at all,' she said testily.

'I don't have to.' Charles rose and walked over to the cabinet. 'It's just advisable—as you should know. I'll have it all done for tomorrow.'

Walt stood by the fire wishing he had said nothing. Joan and Charles were both trying to conceal brittle anger and his mother was looking on with unconcealed disapproval.

'Let's you and me go,' he suggested to his mother. Joan said she would go too, and while the women went for their coats Charles stood by the cabinet with a glass in his hand.

'Like one now?' he asked. Walt refused. Seeing the sheen of a few grey hairs at the temple, he thought that Charles looked older than thirty-one. He resembled his mother and sisters, but not Walt nor his father.

'Forgive this unsociability,' Charles said. 'I'll see you later.'

One room of the public house was full of men with red, roughened faces, drawling their words slowly and lengthening the vowels. The other was small, with a log fire and a few tables, empty except for Walt and the women, who sat talking quietly at first.

'How's Charles doing?' Walt asked when he had heard all his mother's family news.

'Oh, very well,' his mother answered proudly. 'His firm think very highly of him; very highly indeed. Don't they, Joan?'

'Oh, *very* highly!'

Walt frowned at her. 'He's being promoted soon—taking over a new branch in the Midlands.' His mother sounded at her most genteel. 'It's a very good move for someone so young.'

'They usually promote someone who's organized and managed a branch in some hole abroad for two years,' Joan commented. Walt could understand annoyance at his mother's proud, proprietary tone, but the bored bitterness surprised and dismayed him. He worked hard to make it a gay evening, still buying fresh gins when they insisted they'd had enough, questioning Joan about her life in Egypt, and even flattering her a little. By the time they returned home they were laughing hilariously at jokes he had heard in the pit but would never have told them sober. In the warm living-room, as they took off their coats and scarves, Joan said she was going straight to bed.

'I'll pay for this tomorrow, but it was lovely to go out with you for a while. It's been fun.' Her languid coolness was replaced by cheerful charm.

'My pleasure,' Walt assured her, gently swaying. His mother sat with him on the green plush settee as they ate supper in front of the fire with the tea-trolley beside them.

'Charles is still working away,' she said. 'He's very conscientious. He's got a fine future. She thought for a while, then looked more cheerful, turning to say: 'Still, you have too—you seem to be doing well. I knew you'd be a success at whatever you took up, you know. You're all like that.'

He grunted, abruptly leaning forward with his hands clasped. From one in imminent danger of being a failure, he was promoted to a success whatever he took up. It was said so casually, now it was said too late.

'It's so grand to be together in front of a fire again!' Her happy, affectionate survey of him made criticism seem cruel. Yet to say that so easily... He could imagine her casually informing someone that her other son was also doing very well—very well indeed—moving into a superior position soon...

Only her other son liked to drink and mix in rough company and behave with girls in a way she'd call disgusting, was thinking of all that and missing it, and wishing he could explain it without her being terribly hurt. But she would be hurt. So he must try to appear as whatever she wanted him to be while he was here. Which meant he would never be coming back to stay, because he didn't want to stay with those who expected him to live out their ideas. The trouble was, he felt unhappy about it. About not being what this loving and genteel mother wanted him to be, not giving what she wanted him to give, and being critical and impatient to boot.

That makes me not much of a son, he thought, body gently rocking on the edge of the settee.

'Charles and Joan aren't too happy. She demands too much of him.' His mother had lowered her voice, shaking her head confidentially. '...But Charles is too soft with her. He tries to please her far too much and she takes advantage.'

'There's a curse on this family! There's Charles—there's you. What's wrong with us?' He turned to her.

His mother sighed, shaking her head once more as she leaned back. 'Don't ask me.' She closed her eyes, her head against the green velvet, and looked much older so; the flesh looser on her cheeks and the creases wider. 'These young couples today. If they'd had my life with your father…'

'I know, Ma. It was tough.' He felt the same chest-aching heaviness that news of his father's last betrayal had caused. He wanted to stop her, but she was going on: 'You'll never know how bad it really was. You were too young…' She sat up, hands jerking into action at this chance of relief. 'He was unfaithful to me time and again. In secret at first, but he even boasted of it to me, later. Oh, he was a ladies' man—long before you were old enough to—'

'I don't know why you stuck it,' he broke in.

'He loved to talk down to me in front of others and show how much cleverer he was. Because I came from a better family than him and he was jealous. His people were nothing. Nothing. He hated my background.'

Walt saw the nerve fluttering in the hollow of her cheek as she stared past him. Why had they married? To torture one another?

'He's come home time after time with all his wages spent. He's beaten me black and blue.'

'I know—I know!' He raised a fist. 'You've told me. I saw it!'

'I brought you up—all of you. I worked my fingers to the bone to do it.'

'Ma!' He put out his hand desperately. 'Why did you keep having him back? You could've had a divorce.'

'I couldn't afford one.' She frowned at him, then looked at his hand. 'But why keep on taking him back? Why did you?'

'For you, of course.' She moved back a little, then stood up and put their cups on to the tea-trolley, watching what she was doing while he stared up.

'How do you mean—for me?'

'Well, not just you.' She began pushing the trolley away. 'All of you—children need a father.'

'A father like that?' He stood up slowly. From the doorway of the kitchen she answered: 'He was good sometimes—he could be all right when he wanted. It was when…' She shrugged.

He heard her rinsing the cups in the kitchen. There was sweat in his upturned palms. He should have expected that. The old theme. Now you hate him, now you don't. Now he had good points, now you're the son of a swine. Now tear down the middle and want to run away from your other half…

He was leaning over the fire when his mother returned and suggested cheerfully that they could do with some sleep, both of them.

'I'll stay up a bit,' he said, keeping his back turned.

'But you must be awfully tired. You should really—'

'I'm not tired!' he cut in on her concern.

'Oh, very well... I see you haven't lost your funny moods.'

He knew that tautness: last stage before emotion crashed out, in rage on both sides at first, then sullenness on his and broken-hearted tears on hers. Leading to the agony of reconciliation, which he couldn't endure at this moment.

'Travelling gets me jumpy—and then the beer and that,' he explained, smiling pleasantly as he turned. High on her face were two vivid spots and her cheek pulsed with the fluttering nerve. He bent and kissed her hair, inhaling a faint odour of gin with the stronger fragrance of lavender.

'I know what the life did to you,' he told her.

'You're very like him,' she answered, after looking at his face for a long time. 'Be careful of yourself.'

When she had said good night and gone, he thought miserably of how unhappy he must have made her. But this—this was the very core of the sudden, tensing blind antagonism that often overpowered him—this smothered rage that set him against his own mother. What evil essence had imbued his father's seed?

He was sitting on the settee, biting his thumb-knuckle and staring at the fire, when Charles quietly entered and walked to the cabinet. 'Like a night-cap?' As Walt whirled round, Charles held up a bottle which glowed amber against the dark panelling. 'You were lost in thought.'

He brought bottle and glasses over to the hearth and sat in a deep chair. The drink tasted vile to Walt, but he smacked his lips and said: 'Not too bad...'

'No. And now you can boast you've tasted whisky.' Charles smiled, his face looking pale, with dark shadows behind the spectacles. 'Your facial contortions rather gave you away, Walter.'

Walt smiled sheepishly—he would have liked to impress Charles—and remarked, looking around him, that he had a nice place.

'Owned lock, stock and antimacassars by the company. I always think it's like a scene from one of those Queen Victoria films. Now relax.' Charles smiled musingly as he studied Walt and drank his whisky. Unlike the rest of the family his movements were smooth, his face calm—almost grave—and he spoke in a clipped, authoritative way.

'You work pretty hard, don't you?'

'Have to. Competition's keen. I'm sorry about tonight—about the touch of domestic strife, too.'

'That's all right.'

'I imagine Mother has told you life's not running too smoothly for us just now?'

Walt nodded, finishing his whisky with a scowl, and Charles put his glass on the arm of his chair.

'Just one of those things, you know,' he said, lazily leaning back. 'We have our differences, Joan and I. I married her because I had developed a taste for civilized and sophisticated people and surroundings. Apart from the fact of loving her, of course... Unfortunately, Joan shares with our mother the distinction of coming from a good home and good parents and being unable to forget that.' The words rolled out pontifically. 'Her father was born near the ladder's top and has never moved up or down, and she'll never be reconciled to the discomforts of these lower rungs.'

'I thought you were fairly well off?' The amused pomposity sounded brittle and hollow to Walt, so he spoke seriously.

'We're not poor. I'm regarded as highly promising for my age, but I'm not the young genius Joan expected. If it weren't for Mother, Joan would have all the housework to do and three children to look after. A little tough after two years away from the good life—and definitely not in Joan's line.'

'She's not my type,' Walt confided, warmly fraternal from the whisky. 'I can't say I take to her much—give me a woman that can...' He looked up anxiously. 'You don't mind me saying that?'

'Not a bit—free speech for every man, I always say. Do you mind if I turn out these lights?' He reached up and the room was snapped into darkness except for where they sat before the white, blazing gas fire. 'My eyes ache after these long spells.'

With the darkness came the beginning of a gentle drowsiness. It was easier to talk into the hard-edged shadows. 'I had a row with Ma. We seem to flare up at each other like—'

'You shouldn't when she's had a few drinks,' Charles said, his oval face suddenly lit by a match spurting over his pipe. 'That's how it was with your father—flaring up.'

'Well, I was only asking why she kept taking him back. She shouldn't have—it was wrong.'

'It was her choice, surely?' The match went out and Charles was a dim figure, lounging back with a leg over the chair-arm.

'She said it was for our sake, though,' Walt protested. 'But we were happier without him, so that's not true.'

'Perhaps not,' Charles agreed after a moment. 'Perhaps not in your time—you never saw him at his best.'

'No. No, he wasn't quite at his best in my time!' The shadows supported his scorn, until Charles slowly answered:

'He wasn't always in mine—but he was good when I was a kid. I could never hate him...'

'I could—hate his hide and guts.'

'Sure?'

Walt clasped his hands, beginning to rock as always. Instead of answering, he asked bewilderedly: 'But why? Why lose us all through it, and go on doing it time after time?'

'I hate to sound trite, but couldn't it be love?'

'Love?' Walt peered through the curling blue smoke.

'Why else sacrifice like that? Isn't it good to have a mother with that much love in her?'

'And he loved her too?' If Charles were being funny, it was a risky joke.

'He kept coming back.'

'When he was broke!' Walt threw himself back disgustedly, shaking the whole settee. 'When he was down and out and needed a good touch! Or a good belt, maybe! Maybe it was that...'

'That's part of love.'

'Jesus ...' He jerked forward again, but Charles continued to pull easily at his pipe. '...She spoiled our lives for that? That's your idea of love?' Perhaps Charles had been too old to get caught up as he had; and had never lain with his head to the wall and heard the shouts and bumps of one night, the mumbling and creakings of another, with an equal dread of both. 'Love!' He stood up. 'Coming together so they could torture each other! I'd call that a pretty queer sort of love.' His strengthening rough accent harshened his contempt.

'Sit down, old chap—getting upset doesn't help.'

Charles filled his glass as Walt slowly sat down again. Then he leaned forward with the glass in one hand, pipe in the other, and said mildly:

'Love has some queer shapes, Walter. One partner often has to endure a lot of pain and prefers that to being apart. People can love each other while they're tearing each other's guts out half the time.'

'Well, God help the kids in your kind of love,' Walt muttered, and Charles abruptly leaned back.

'That's a point you have to watch, of course.' He raised his glass.

'I haven't been bothered with all this for ages till tonight,' Walt said bitterly, wishing he were in some dance hall with Bryan, playing rough and laughing, and sizing up the girls.

'I just don't want to be like he was,' he added.

'That's natural.'

'But she says I am...' Walt scowled.

'You're yourself and no one else. Remember that.'

'I do,' he said, suddenly pleased, 'I do remember that. And I won't be pushed into anybody's idea of what I ought to be.'

'Quite right.' Charles finished his drink, then said thoughtfully. 'You'd better watch the girls, old chap. They can get awfully frustrated if you marry them and then won't be moulded into the appropriate shape!'

'That's just what I think.' He had found a fellow mind. 'I'm a good lion.'

'Pardon?'

'Good lion.' He waved his hand vaguely. 'Personal-survival value and functional value. The lion that kills a—' He saw Charles slowly shake his head, so he stopped and began explaining about Bill and his politics first, then Mason, and his own argument. It took some time, but Charles smoked with quiet patience, occasionally nodding, until Walt had finished: 'So—I'm a good lion.'

The fire hissed and a clock ticked on the mantelpiece.

'Well?' Walt prompted at last.

'Let's get some sleep.' Charles knocked out his pipe and stood up. 'This could last all night.' He switched on the lights.

Disappointed, Walt followed towards the door, halting as Charles turned to frown.

'I can understand Bill,' he said slowly. 'The Communist patient fitting of one piece to another, using its own special logic—that might tempt. The answers are all there—your framework, with the rules all laid down for you... Like the Catholic... This lion thing, though—' shaking his head perplexedly—'I don't see what it solves.'

'Well, it makes sense to me,' Walt said stoutly.

'Yes...' Charles scratched his head, blinking at Walt. 'Maybe I'm getting old. With us it was Socialism.'

'By the way,' Walt said, squaring his shoulders, 'up home they call me Walt. I—don't like Walter, see, and—'

'Oh...' Charles gravely inclined his head. 'I understand perfectly, Walt. I won't forget.' Walt put a brotherly hand on his shoulder as they went upstairs. In bed he could hear from next door Joan's low voice and a mumbling answer; the conversation went on for some time.

Awakened next morning by whoops and shouts of delight he rose and went down to admire the boys' presents and give them some money. In his pocket was a necklace of bright stones for his mother. She was in the kitchen with Charles, preparing a turkey for dinner, both of them cheerfully busy.

'Joan didn't feel too good—she stayed in bed,' Charles explained as Walt ate his breakfast.

'I hope it wasn't last night,' Walt said, but his mother briskly assured him it was nothing unusual. Seeing her laugh with Charles while they worked and hearing the noisy children, Walt wondered if Joan's absence had anything to do with this light-heartedness. When he had finished eating he gave his mother her present, and was handed a slim oblong box in exchange.

'I didn't want anything,' he protested, with his mother and Charles standing close together while he opened it.

'Charles and I bought it between us.'

'Nonsense—I was allowed to chip in, but it was this girl's idea...'

In Walt's hand lay a chromium-braceleted wrist-watch with his initials engraved on its back above a stamped '15 jewelled'. He stared at it with his eyes blurring.

'You were always talking about one,' he heard his mother saying brightly. He raised his head, the watch clasped in his hand, and Charles said:

'One request. The first speech of thanks would spoil it, so don't try.'

'I couldn't ...' His throat ached. It was painful to see their delight and painful to hold the present while his mother praised her one-guinea necklace.

You shouldn't give people things like this without warning, he thought confusedly. Its too much. Too much...

'You always buy me something pretty,' his mother was saying, while Charles leaned over to help as he fumbled with the strap.

At noon he and Charles visited the pub. Frozen snow crunched underfoot and cold edged their faces as they walked, with a gusty wind plucking snow from eaves and bushes to hurl at them.

'Honest—' Walt raised his watch to admire it— 'I didn't know whether to laugh or cry.'

'That's a trite remark for such a professedly unconventional type,' Charles said. He glanced round with his head bent against rough spray. 'Look, she got you that because she seemed to feel you'd never had a really good present. It's partly with your being away now, I suppose—to make up a bit... So take it that way, will you?'

'But how could she afford it?' They were passing the squat, snow-aproned-cottages.

'I helped, and she saved the rest out of what we pay her. She does most of the housekeeping, you know.'

'What's wrong with Joan, Charles? Is she ill?'

'She's not strong.' The clipped tone was marked. 'I didn't marry for a housekeeper.'

'Yeah...' He saw a slight contraction of the fine-edged lips, a tiny crease above the white-dotted spectacles. 'You know, my landlady's seventy, near on, and looks after two on us...'

'Must be a very fine old woman,' Charles answered dryly as they reached the pub door and began kicking wads of snow from their shoes. Inside, square bottle-glass windows kept out light but the snapping fire flickered over the dark wooden walls and warmed every corner. Charles bought their drinks and they sat down opposite two old women and an old man who nodded politely.

Charles sipped his whisky and told Walt: 'I notice your accent increases when you talk of things that don't please you.'

'I notice you can't half down that stuff.'

'One learns to abroad.' Charles finished the whisky and reached for his beer. 'I don't think you have much time for my wife at all, eh?'

'I'm sorry I said that last night. He saw Charles looking at him over the rim of his glass, his eyes not so much shrewd or sharp as thoughtfully interested, 'It's just that these—intellectual women aren't my sort. I mean —well, my mother comes from a good family too, but she's a good worker.'

'So you are proud of some points about her?'

'Well—yeah, of course.' Walt raised his own glass. 'If she keeps pinning her more snobbish ideas on to you and leaves me out of it, I'm happy. I'm not—'

'Oh, this family stuff! You're quite obviously not happy.'

Walt shrugged and emptied his glass in long slow swallows, then fetched more beer and another whisky for Charles.

'How much family history do you know?' Charles asked as he sat down.

'Only what a swine he was, or how clever!' He watched the yellow flickering in his glass, troubled by the long calm scrutiny. He grunted: 'Beats me how two like them got hitched up in t' first place!'

'You don't know? It's quite a romantic story—no, I mean that.'

At Walt's bitten-off jerk of laughter, he put down his glass. He began unbuttoning his heavy overcoat, and nodded seriously at Walt.

'All right, tell me.'

'Well, I don't know if it's good to open old graves—but I detest hate and bitterness—perhaps it would help you see it less starkly.' Charles lit his pipe, puffed until he was satisfied, then leaned back. 'You have to picture more than thirty years ago—most of the characters might have come straight out of a film or a book. Stock characters are usually based on what was once typical—'

'Get on with it,' Walt urged him.

'All right.' Charles smiled a moment. 'Stock character one is a tyrannical, God-fearing, God-abusing, Scottish Calvinist cotton-mill manager. His son is given the best, his daughters the cheapest of educations. Spirited but naive youngest daughter has a teenage romance with third stock character—a gallant, handsome young rebel worker who has educated himself brilliantly in some things, advocates Socialism eloquently, and defies the villain openly. Naturally he's already marched out of his own God-fearing home, but having met through both being compelled to attend the same church, these two continue to meet. And eventually elope. Excursions and alarms! "Never," says the incensed Calvinist, "darken my door again." He means it, too.'

Charles shrugged and leaned forward to drink, his smile dwindling. 'Then what?'

'You don't want any more. I've told you how—the good bit. Someone got the plots mixed up after that.' He finished the whisky, sighing as Walt insisted: 'Tell me what happened next.'

'Well, instead of becoming the first Socialist Prime Minister and wife, forgiving the old Calvinist on his death-bed, they have six good months. The rebel is then old enough to fight, and is called upon to do so—returning in 1916 short of a leg and other bits and pieces, and with the seeds of a whopping chip nicely germinating on his shoulder. He still rants about Socialism and tries very hard, and they commence producing offspring to enjoy the coming Utopia.' Charles laid his pipe on the table and stood up. He smiled briefly at Walt and said: 'The tough going had started—and the rest is too full of unemployment, depression, strikes, blacklisting and alcohol for you to enjoy.'

He went to the bar and stood there, his lips a little puckered. He did not look at Walt until he returned with fresh drinks.

'Come,' he said as he sat down. He looked amused. 'Drink up. Alcohol's always been the general cure-all for the male side of our family.' Walt's startled look made him smile more widely. 'Don't despair! You might be different.'

When they had drunk some more beer Walt asked to hear more. He was trying to connect his nervous, fussy mother and morose father with this defiant couple, but it was difficult.

'I don't know that I want to tell more,' Charles said, lighting his pipe again. 'When I was a kid we wore board-suits and board-boots and there was the dole and soup kitchens. We didn't mind too much because we were all in the same boat and didn't know how different it could be. Only they did. She did and he did. Oh, he stayed a rebel for a long time and took lots of beatings...' He raised his glass slowly.

'But he changed,' Walt said, loudly enough and harshly enough to make the old people look curiously across at him.

'Yes... Lost the way at some point and then lost himself. Yes...' Charles looked suddenly defiant. 'Oh, it was his own weaknesses and hellish, self-reliant pride that did a lot of it, certainly. He was that kind. Could take some punishments, but not others.' He paused to regard Walt thoughtfully. 'Like most of us. And she stuck to him while he fought his way up and when he crashed. She stuck years of poverty that never touched some parts of her and destroyed others, and she brought us up her own way.'

'Middle-class,' Walt said. 'In a slum!'

'Agreed. She never faced parts of her life—never really *lived* in that place. She lived in dreams of an impossible future where we were all one big, well-off happy family. Only remember that her husband by now was a worse tyrant than the one he'd rescued her from—'

'And you say I should understand him!' Walt sneered.

'It was his own guts he was gnawing—his own youth...' Charles looked angrily away. Then he turned again and told Walt: 'And in her place you'd have tried to prove yourself a lady and you'd have turned snob. Or perhaps joined him in his degradation?'

They sat quiet and tense, Walt staring over at the fire while Charles drank. At last Walt said, unconsciously plaintive: 'It's just that she kept taking him back. It's like—betrayal.'

'We had this last night,' Charles said, without raising his head. 'What was done to you was done to all of us. You've suffered more evidently because you saw the worst—or because you're still young. But leave it alone.'

'I *can't* leave it alone now it's all started again. I've got to sort it out!'

'Why, in heaven's name?' Charles snapped, jerking around.

'Why?' Walt stared back, slowly frowning, then lowering a raised hand with a hopeless grunt. With every solitude filled by confusing questions, inexplicable yearnings and dark, strong urging to things he did not know —when he knew only what he did or felt but never why... 'Charles— didn't you have to sort it out?'

'Whatever's biting you ...?' Charles jerked his hands in exasperation. Then he stopped. 'Let's take it easy. Just look how steamed up we've both got over this. Walt, accept things like we all have to and try to live calmly. Now, no more of this, old chap, please...'

They talked little after that, and both were thoughtful. When they returned home Walt was affectionate and attentive with his mother, as though to compensate for his own troubledness over her past. It was late afternoon before Joan came downstairs, and the evening was spent drinking by the fire, Charles and his mother doing most of the talking. Walt kept covertly watching the lively eyes in the work-impaired, time-impaired oval face, and he thought: Even as she sits chattering now, even as her hands jerk and weave and she smiles—even so she was as young as me and loved him and never dreamed of it ending like this... And time seemed to swirl around him, a vast nebula where individual sparks were all combined in a misty shimmering that hid each minute speck.

Where? he wondered, frowning in his chair and oblivious of the others.

Where from and where to? How much do they count, or William or Charles in me? Are we one piece, or can I break away?

'He was always like that,' his mother said, laughing, and he realized Charles had been talking to him. Joan went to bed early and Walt excused himself soon after. He lay wakeful and thought of the city a great deal. Joan stayed in bed again next morning, and he and Charles revisited the pub. The small room was empty, though the large one sounded as full and noisy as before.

'I've proved a disappointment to you, haven't I?' Charles said, as they sat near the log fire. Although Walt denied it, Charles smiled and said they would be jollier today: he ordered drinks in quick succession, and told self-bantering stories of how it had felt to begin commanding soldiers much older than himself. While they were laughing, he put his head on one side and remarked: 'You look very much like your other brother, you know. I wonder how much like him you really are?' He shrugged and would have talked of something else, but Walt touched his arm and asked:

'What was he like?'

'A nice kid.' Charles smiled again and went to the bar. When he returned with two whiskies, he said: 'I knew you'd be asking some time.' He sounded lightly rueful. 'It hurts just a trifle because I lived under his shadow while he was alive, and in his ghost's shadow till I left home. And I was the oldest, after all.'

Walt nodded slowly. He remembered how his brothers had been held up to him.

'Did you hate William, Charles?'

'No. No one hated William.' Charles shook his head, still smiling. A burst of laughter shuddered over the bar. 'He was the romantic, mind you, and I was the realist.'

Thinking of Bill's ideas on barricades, Walt asked:

'Why did he go to Spain? Because he was a romantic? An idealist? Was he wrong?'

'Wrong?' Charles frowned. 'I wonder what makes you—'

'Was he, though?'

'He was right. For himself. You see—' he looked down, toying with an empty glass— 'he was that kind. Men were fighting evil—embodied at last in one tyrannical force. The great act William was born for—another Byron charging off to—'

'Don't say it like that!' Walt's fingers started tightening, but he relaxed as he saw the slight twist to his brother's smile and the crease wrinkling the forehead.

'I'm simply being frank, Walt. Even though I was a bit of a cynic, I preferred helping my fellow men by other means than getting my head blown off. But William was quite prepared to get his head blown off. Besides which—' the smile widened, but he looked down again—'my eyes and my being the eldest bread-winner kept me at home. William wanted me to take your father's place altogether, you know. Yet he was your father's favourite. Perverse, eh? Son hates father who favours him—perhaps because he hates him. I seem incapable of hate...'

Walt watched him muse again. He said nothing. He felt that Charles was remembering more than what they were discussing.

'...William just wasn't cut out for the dirt and disappointments of politics. When they gave him a cause he fought for it. That suited William—he did all right, too.'

'I remember how you all used to go on about all that stuff...' Walt was puzzled. Socialism, dying in Spain, causes; all their talk and slogans and pictures. 'What happened to it all, Charles?' Charles looked up blankly and Walt repeated the question.

'Oh!' Charles roused himself and fumbled inside his overcoat, fetching out his pipe. 'Those days must seem strange to a good lion, eh?' He smiled, lounging back as he tamped down his tobacco. 'Gosh, we believed in it. Socialism was round the corner—a brave new world! He lit his pipe, then snapped the match abruptly. 'It didn't come, I'm afraid. We had Spain and we had Hitler. But the brave new world didn't come. Yet it was always the class conflict for us before the war—everything hinged on that.'

'But not now, eh?' One of the foremost of the quoters was justifying his arguments to Bill.

'Somehow I lost much of that view,' Charles admitted mildly. 'A bit when William died, I think—perhaps that's the kind of punishment which *I* can't take. A bit more in the war, a bit more afterwards—it was a hell of a knock to find the brave new world still far away, and the old one much bigger and more complex than I'd realized. I began to see all that as the shadow of life, and I deserted it for the substance. Now I'm pretty busy without revolution.' He grinned, the pipe cocked upwards. 'Your Bill would say I'm corrupted by an officer's life and success. Perhaps he's right—a new framework. Still, I could say your Bill was corrupted too.'

'I think politics stink,' Walt said, fervently glad that William had not been so political after all.

'You're absolutely right,' Charles agreed, but his eyes were vacant again and smoke wreathed his face in thick coils before he looked up.

'Our Socialism and idealism and so on...' he murmured. 'To your fellow-traveller Bill and good lion Walt. What then?' He shook his head, amused. 'Good lion! Lord, what a reflection on humanity. Never mind, let's be jolly.'

They continued drinking and talking pleasantly, with Walt becoming so charged with good-fellowship that he offered to call his brother Charlie, if he wished. '...That's what we'd call you up there.'

'Thanks all the same,' Charles said graciously. 'I've got used to the full name now, and it's quite all right. It was a nice thought...'

On the way home, Walt walking with careful correctness over the ridged snow, Charles told him: 'By the way, old man, don't let's go too near Joan. She detests the smell of drink when she hasn't had any herself. You know how it is...' Walt saw the contraction of lips and silently put a comradely hand on his shoulder.

Yet Joan seemed in good spirits at dinner-time, and his mother was so pleased by Walt's demonstrative affection that she told stories of girlhood pranks in a Victorian home. Afterwards Walt lay on his bed, feeling bloated and resisting a sensation that the bed's foot was rising while the head dipped, until he fell asleep.

That evening the others prepared to sit by the fire again, but Walt went alone to the pub. Two such nights were more than he could stand, and the continued talking bored him. He also wanted to avoid another moment of real intimacy with his mother, for he sensed that her emotions were clouding and crowding up again, and dreaded another outburst, however sorry for her he felt. Even among the red-faced drawling men in the smoky, low-beamed pub he found himself bored, and glad that tomorrow morning he would be returning to the city.

When he returned the others had just finished supper. Charles and his mother were washing dishes in the kitchen while Joan sat near the fire.

'Well,' Joan stood up, stretching her arms lazily. 'May as well go to bed. You go back in the morning?' She had been courteous but generally quiet towards Walt since their evening out. When he nodded, standing before the fire to warm his hands, she said: 'I'll bet you're bored stiff.' She smiled, yet he noticed uneasily an almost hostile hauteur in her grey eyes as he mumbled that it had been all right.

'You probably detest this place as much as I do.' Joan turned and began walking to the door, then looked back, still smiling with a fine eyebrow quizzically arched at him. 'You probably think I'm an idle bitch who spends half her time in bed.'

'It's got nowt to do wi' me,' he answered gruffly, bending over the fire, his face growing hot.

'That won't stop you thinking it. However—' he heard the door click open— 'since you don't much care for me and my kind, that hardly matters, does it?'

Walt's head jerked round. Charles was standing in the kitchen doorway looking at them.

'It's like this,' he said slowly, he and Joan watching each other across the room and ignoring Charles. 'I don't know much about your kind. I'm used to women as work and have a proper place in things. I don't just see where your sort fits in.'

He stood up, his face hot, but the sense of betrayal reinforced his anger.

'I'll bet you believe in being lord and master in the home.'

'Yeah, sure...' His shoulders were hunched, clenched hand digging deep against his thighs. 'Beat 'em every week to show 'em who's boss. Runs in the family, see?'

They stared at one another. Joan's lower lip was nipped between her teeth. Charles said abruptly: 'Good night, Joan.' His mother was behind his shoulder. Joan looked at him coldly then she nodded.

'Good night,' she answered, and went out. Charles followed her.

'Good night, Walt.'

'Yeah, sure,' Walt grunted, smiling thinly as Charles turned to look. Then Charles closed the door behind him.

'She'll ruin him!' Walt's mother came over to the fireplace. 'She's got him under her thumb and she'll ruin him.'

'She's done it,' Walt said. 'No wonder he's so full of excuses for other folk...'

She touched his arm and, still scowling, he looked down. He saw her eyes glittering and the nerve fluttering. He brought out his hands to gently squeeze her shoulders.

'Now, don't you worry any more about me, eh?'

'Oh, I wish you'd give up this—'

'Don't!' he interrupted. 'Please, Ma...'

'It's all your father's fault—all of you.'

'Well, it's not yours,' he consoled her, and kissed her cheek, bending stiffly to the fresh scent of lavender and quickly moving back again as he saw tears.

'I'd rather see you married to some working girl, however common, than be a slave like Charles.'

'Yeah...' he mumbled. If the girls were common, so was he. His mother was urging him, to get on as quickly as he could.

'...I just hate to think of you—I know you can... I mean, you won't be an ordinary miner too long, will you?'

He was sorry for her unhappiness over him, disguised as sadness over his leaving again, and he was sorry for her past unhappiness even more. Yet now he was determined, once and for all, that the dragging anchor of their unhappy past would not be shackled to his own life. The exchange with Joan had sickened him of all this.

In bed he could not sleep, and Charles, when he came tip-toeing into the dark room, jerked him out of an agony of impatience for morning.

'Look,' Charles whispered, sitting on the edge of the bed. 'Call me what you like—but she has a way of getting things out of me.'

'You have a right to tell your wife everything,' Walt said. 'Forget it—' But his temper broke through and he blurted out: 'She's really got you nailed, hasn't she? However can you …?' He rolled over disgustedly.

'She's the kind that likes to hear about herself… I was pretty enthusiastic about you and it didn't please her, I suppose. She demanded to know what you thought of her—'

'Let it drop,' Walt grunted.

'She has ways of getting anything out of me. I didn't know she'd throw it up at you.'

'I couldn't care less.' He pressed his head into the pillows. 'It's what it makes you look. Boy, no wonder you stuck up for them! We're a different kind.'

'Yes…' The weight left the bed. From near the door Charles's voice said: 'I just wanted to explain…' The dry tone made Walt imagine the twisted lip and tiny crease. '…I realize there isn't any excuse.' He said good night, the door closed and Walt lay eager for the city. He heard wind soughing through bushes and trees, branches rattling and quick gusts beating against the windows, and he longed for the comforting thudding monotony of nights at home.

II

Over the city, like the eternal smoky pall, had settled a jaded depression which lasted until New Year's Eve. He talked with Bill across the supper table, listening to the latest analyses of dissension without argument because at least you knew that all of Bill was presented to you in the rounded, anxious eyes and bobbing forelock and that his pomposity was over-eagerness at work, not knowledge of a fingertip touch of rot slowly spreading with plenty of time and no opposition. With delight he saw the old lady wearing the bright head-scarf when she went out, and with interest he listened to Bryan's account of a roistering holiday. Yet he remembered, in spite of his wishes, the story of his parents' youth, the emptiness of his mother's snobbish pride in her sons, and the subjugation, the cancerous pain, covered by his brother's shrivelled smile.

'You're awfully quiet, Walt,' Bill remarked. 'Nothing wrong at home, I hope.' Walt answered that there was nothing wrong. Nor was there—apart from what had always been wrong. He had chosen to return to his past for a while, and had got what he deserved; just as his mother had put her conception of love before her pride, as his father had turned crawler, as Charles had played lapdog, and as each had got what they deserved. Love that meant surrender or abasement, suppression or pain, was the only kind his family had found, it seemed.

This was a time for resolutions.

'I'm going to cut out the talking and act more,' said Bill. 'It's a time for big decisions—time to choose.'

'Somewhere different every week, kid,' Bryan planned. 'It's the time for all the best fun is winter.'

Walt was satisfied with resolving to become immersed in his chosen life again as quickly as possible, and to forget his morose brooding. He knew that he was dull company at present.

The last morning of the year came and Bill had a message from Elaine.

'When are you two going to paint the town white again? she wants to know. She says not red, because you're so resolutely non-political that she doesn't want to offend you.'

'You notice,' Walt smugly pointed out, 'she don't mind spending time with a non-political, anyway.'

'Tell me something—' They were sitting up in bed, the clothes around their shoulders, while the old lady was kindling a fire downstairs. 'What the heck do you two find to talk about?'

'All sorts. She asks tons of questions.'

'About you?' Walt thought Bill's shuffle and eager peering better suited to a schoolgirl.

'Me and other things. She's interested in everything about people—especially their sex life. She's dying to know if they're romantic!' He grinned, then threw off the bed-clothes.

'Some day,' Bill remarked, 'she'll just have to find out about that for herself.'

'Well, not with me!' Walt was dressing, cringing in the cold.

'Why not? A lovely girl like Elaine? I'd have thought you'd be...'

'She's got some funny ideas about it, I bet you. She'd expect too much. That romantic sort...' He shook his head sagely, struggling on one leg with his trousers. He remembered remarks about looking sensitive and vulnerable, the languid seductiveness that surely only innocence would assume, and the estimating way of looking at men with the occasional hints of private judgments. 'She'd look down on a bloke if it wasn't just what she'd expected.'

'I can see one thing,' Bill sighed. 'I've an awful lot to learn about girls!'

That night the gang celebrated the New Year at a village dance hall not far from the suburbs. Walt was still moodily quiet but Bryan was in his most reckless mood, and when they returned from the crowded local pub he devoted his attentions to a girl already engaged to a village youth. The girl seemed not to mind, but her fiancé and two friends followed Bryan into the cloakroom to prove his error. Bryan kicked the legs from under the first to strike, seized the second with his left hand and hit the third with his right. Walt and the others had no idea of impending trouble until the cloakroom door crashed outwards before a backward-flying youth, who was followed by a sprawling friend and then by Bryan himself bellowing rage and swinging at the first men to approach him, while the gang came bounding across the hall.

The ensuing fight involved most of the young men there. Many were miners and as loyal to one another as were Bryan's friends. Girls screamed and clambered on to chairs to watch the battle which took place in the doorway where Bryan, Hughie and Walt made a stand, with the other five behind them in the short narrow corridor. There was space for only four abreast here, and since the villagers attacked in a bunch, hampering each other so that some could scarcely raise an arm, while the three defenders had space to fight properly, the city lads held their ground. Walt took the centre with Bryan on his right, Hughie on the left, and as each charge came they struck out at the massed, shouting faces, those behind seizing anyone who grappled, to drag, punch and kick him, then throw him down the stone steps into the road.

In spite of fists pounding on his face and body, Walt enjoyed the fight; a magnificent defence, to him, by a few against many, as heroic and blood-heating as anything in his books. At each pause they yelled taunts and defiance at the crowd, but when one rush forced them back with other arms and faces pressed against their own, he forgot his enjoyment and fought blindly violent. Bryan's rage was immense: he cleaved into the throng like a bear breaking his chain to scatter a pack of baiting hounds, his fists and great shoulders swinging, holding his blond head down and cursing incessantly. Hughie fought silently and competently, taking each blow with an unfeeling head-shake and stolidly, accurately aiming his punches. Walt fought in a frenzy, when there was no room to swing his arms, using knees, head and feet, and clutching at the rumpled hair of those who lunged at him, sidestepping when he could, to throw them at the ready feet of his allies. Men shouted deeply, youths yelled, women and girls screamed excitedly, and above all this din was some terrified girl's hysterical whooping, chilling Walt's genitals and goading him to bloody-minded viciousness.

'Find me summat to hit 'em with,' Bryan roared over his shoulder. 'I'll clear the whole dump, I will.' All eight of them were bunched at the brink of the steps, immovably pressed together as they grappled and wrestled.

'Gi' o'er, gi' o'er,' an attacker was shrilling near Walt. 'Me ribs—you're crushin' me—' Maddened by the punching, pressing and outrageous buffeting, Walt spat and grunted as he fought. He was clutched at and felt his shirt rip to the waist band as he tore free. He saw a small wiry youth, hair tangled and ear bleeding, come lunging through the crowd at him with a full lemonade bottle glittering and flashing as it swung up.

'I'll shift 'em.' The bottle came for Walt and he tried to dodge, but his body was trapped and it cracked down on his shoulder, the jarring agony making him yell. He seized the slender wrist and fought for the bottle, with the youth clawing at his face and trying to bite his hand. Grunting, features stretched in effort, Walt eased an arm around his neck and bent him cruelly, still twisting the wrist and set on capturing the bottle if he had to snap the other's neck. The upturned face stared at him with first effort, then fear. The face, bottle, his own squeezing hands and everything else were red-suffused. With the bottle once in his hands he would smash everything in the doorway.

Sheer pressure forced the crowd to retreat at last, and the faces eased backward, with two youths shakily rising from the floor and a third slowly leaving the wall to stagger after them, hands pressed to his sides.

'Oh, me ribs,' he gasped, 'me ribs is broke, chaps—help me...'

His friends caught him and passed him through their ranks into the hall. Then they began moving forward slowly and determinedly, to stop abruptly as the youth at Walt's knees groaned and opened his twisted hand, then threw up an arm to protect his face and head. But Walt merely pushed him aside with his foot, too powerful now for concern with revenge, as he straightened up and began advancing with the heavy bottle swinging in a small arc.

'Back up,' he ordered sharply, as though handling a recalcitrant pony. Without looking to see if he were being supported, he walked towards the crowd, prepared to strike the first who stopped retreating. They saw his face, and those nearest pressed, shrinking, against their friends.

'Back up,' he said again, contemptuous and implacable.

'Don't,' a staring youth pleaded. 'Tha'll kill somebody...'

Walt felt Bryan jostling on one side and heard Hughie panting on the other. The crowd retreated out of the doorway.

'Bring some chairs,' a youth shouted, his eyes watching Walt like those of an animal trainer retreating from savage menace. 'Bring us summat.'

'Come on,' Walt invited him, raising the bottle and tensing to leap and scatter them with flailing sweeps. 'What's holding you back?' His shoulder ached intensely and he wanted to plunge in and strike about him before they could disperse, yet while they obeyed him and retreated, his rage was controlled by a sense of mastery. The hall was quiet except for some activity behind the crowd.

'Let's smash the place,' Bryan growled, his head down, and Walt had begun going forward when he heard some girl's sudden, indrawn yelping sob and the anguished, terrified suspense in it made him pause. He looked at the white faces and fear-hollowed eyes, hands rising palms out while some of the youths struggled against their companions in a frenzy to get other bodies and heads between them and the lethal bottle. The youth who had shouted flinched as Walt looked at him, then the bottle was heavier and Walt knew himself to be bluffing; the time when he would have used the bottle was past and horror of what he might have done was already sapping his courage.

'Get the coats, Hughie,' he ordered, and as Hughie and two others ran into the cloakroom he told the crowd: 'You lot hold still and you're all right. But don't shift either road or we'll start.' He moved the bottle a little and the crowd stood motionless until Hughie and the others appeared with the gang's coats.

'Let's smash' em up,' Bryan hissed, but Walt shook his head.

'Come on, Walt, we've got 'em all,' someone called nervously from behind. 'Come on, Bry.' They began retreating, Bryan warning the crowd: 'Don't try and follow us—else we'll come back wi' enough mates to tear this place down!'

'Don't never try it!' A man answered and Walt involuntarily jerked up the bottle, causing someone else to plead: 'Don't throw it, kid—you'll kill somebody...'

At the top of the steps Bryan said: 'You go first, Walt,' but Walt insisted they descend together.

'...We'll run like hell once we're down.' In spite of trembling, he could not leave Bryan to guard his own retreat. Slowly and crabwise they shuffled down the steps, watching the crowd, while the others waited in the roadway menacing those who recently had come tumbling out and were now recovering against the wall. At the bottom Bryan snatched the bottle from Walt's weakening grip, brandished it so that the following crowd disappeared in a mix-up of shoulders, heads and arms, then cried, 'Hop it, lads!', and the bottle crashed on the steps as they pounded down the lane in a bunch, with knees jerking and arms tucked in. When they reached a main road and shop windows, they risked brief backward looks and found no one following. Walt examined his watch and found, to his relief, that it was unbroken, then took his raincoat from Hughie to cover his ripped shirt.

'If they've got a phone we've had it,' someone gasped.

'What'd a place like that be doin' with a phone?' Bryan demanded. 'Just dive for cover if you see a squad car.'

At the bus stop they kept outside the yellow cone, sweating and panting, with clouds spraying from their mouths in the cold air.

'Come on, bus,' someone prayed. 'The cops'll come straight here.'

'Once we're away, we're safe,' Bryan said. 'They don't know none of us.'

'Think that kid's ribs were broke?' Walt was so full of nervous vitality that he kept rocking from one foot to the other. His bruises and grazes were stinging, his shoulder still painful.

'Nah, he were all right.' Bryan stayed calm while the others waited for the bus in anguished impatience. When it came they clambered aboard, then sat on the rear seats upstairs, exchanging tense looks without speaking, eyes uneasy and frequently flickering aside or downward, as they watched every pair of headlights approaching from behind. Yet once the bus was trundling through the bright, standard-lit suburbs, with home-going people on the pavements to look at, all of them began grinning at one another settling back more comfortably and starting to talk.

'That was a fair scrap!' Bryan slapped Walt's shoulder. 'Owd Walt wi' t' bottle, eh, lads? That shook 'em.'

'*Soon* quietened 'em down,' another commented, and Walt wondered what this was going to seem like in the morning. Then he suddenly thought: Wait a minute—cut out that morning stuff!

They had held their own in a wholesale battle—he should be proud of himself. What were these sudden attacks of betraying conscience or these morning-after self-accusations but the illogical, genteel training of his past trying to destroy the achievements of the present? To the others he dryly remarked: 'You know, that's what you really call banging things up,' and he joined in the roar of laughter while a few passengers turned curiously to look at soiled clothes, mauled hands and gleeful bruised faces.

Walt was on afternoon shift next day and slept until the old lady called him down for dinner. He ignored immediate memories of the brawl by leaping out of bed and dressing hurriedly, but he was jerked to stiffness, eyes closing, with a shirt dangling in his hands when he remembered the bottle's weight as he advanced on unarmed opponents.

You'd better watch yourself... if you'd used it... and you were going to use it, didn't care for a minute, wanted to beat them down... He told himself that someone else had attacked him with the bottle first and that he hadn't begun the fight, but he knew exactly how murderous his rage, his determination to subjugate his enemies, had been, and he was afraid, hurrying downstairs to stifle his fears by busily washing face and hands at the kitchen sink. The lather stung his face and knuckles, and his shoulder was still stiff.

'Strewth!' Bill sat up in his easy chair and stared as Walt returned to the living-room. 'What happened?'

'Fell down some stairs,' Walt answered, then his temper flared as Bill regarded him with growing distaste and finally shook his head, turning away as he muttered disgustedly: 'Well, if this is part of your theory, Walt...'

'My theory?' Walt glared, the towel still dangling from his hand. 'What about yours, snooty? Where's the big decision? More action and less talk?' He dropped into a chair at the table as the old lady took a plate out of the oven. To the back of Bill's head he said: 'It'll make a meaty bit of gossip for your hen-party at Atwell's, won't it? You're all so bloody nosy about what I—'

'Don't you swear in my house!' The old lady banged his heaped plate down, and he knew he was in trouble as he looked up at her eyes puckered to opal splinters, jaw cocked and shoulders backward drawn.

'All right,' he said sullenly, reaching for knife and fork. 'Folk just want to mind their own business. Telling me what's—'

'I'm mindin' mine! I'll say what goes on here, an' no young tearaway's bringin' trouble home...'

He tried to eat, hunched over his plate, but his lowered face grew ruddier as she berated him, towering above his chair. His mouth was full of food, his jaw too stiff to masticate, as she finally said: 'Look at you, just look at you, you damned young imp!'

He put down his fork and looked up silently. They glared at one another while Walt's face slowly cooled and even grew cold, then her temper erupted and she banged a hand flat on the table with her face now turning red. Bill's body twitched at the noise but Walt sat still.

'You'll change your ruffian's ways or get out,' she said, harsh voice thickened and low. 'I've took more off'n you than ever off me own. Next time you've been brawlin' you've got to go.' Muscles twitched and gathered in her wrinkled cheeks while he waited and looked, silent. She drew a slow breath. 'I don't know *how* you'd go on anywheres else, but you're out next time. Now think on it.' Then she stamped past him and into the kitchen with her hands clenched. A shudder began in his legs and went up his back to his neck and jaw, then he sighed, sweat in his palms, and continued eating while ignoring Bill.

That night he returned home, ate a silent supper and went to bed, while the old lady sat by the fire, occasionally stabbing at it with the poker, and read the evening paper with grim concentration. Next morning brought a brief letter from Charles hoping he had enjoyed his visit and would return some time. He sensed that he was intended to read more than the letter actually said, but he was in no mood for empathy, so pushed the letter into a drawer and tried to forget it. A day later there was a fatal accident at the pit: a stone-ripper on morning shift had been buried by a fall of dirt, suffocating before he was rescued. The men on afternoon shift were discussing the accident as they trudged in towards the face, and Walt heard one of his mates behind him saying: 'Well, that's an early start to t' year.'

'Let's hope it's us first and last,' another said.

Walt was buried the same afternoon. With two other colliers he was working at the centre of the face where it opened on to the middle roadway, and the conveyor belts on either side delivered coal on to the larger truck belt which carried it away. The motors were roaring and the coal—rumbling and crashing on to the truck belt—filled the low face with black, swirling clouds of dust in which lamps flashed thinly. The roof was weakest here and heavy girders were set over the supporting props.

'She's actin' up today,' Walt's mates warned him. 'Keep plenty o' catch-props up.' The roof continuously, ominously creaked and bumped, showering dust on to their wet, naked backs. Walt took their advice and set extra props under each doubtful section of roof exposed as he worked. By now he could clear his stint of coal as quickly as many of the colliers, kneeling with rough stone brushing his moving shoulders, the dust swirling in the yellow beam of his helmet and thickening in his nose and throat as he swung his shovel in powerful long sweeps. He glanced up when the roof grumbled, and when dust trickled on to his shoulders he rolled over to examine by yellow-splashed light the cracks from which it was sifting out.

The three of them were setting a heavy girder, Walt under the middle and pressing it to the roof by his shoulders while the other two eased a prop under each end, when the biggest weight-bump[4] cracked like a snapping hawser. It broke up the roof above the girder, props groaning sideways out and dirt pouring, then with a brief, snarling roar it brought the girder collapsing down under a great slab of stone followed by rubble. The men at either end were flung clear, but Walt's steadying left arm was caught and when the rumbling and buffeting ceased he lay pinioned.

He breathed and nothing reached his lungs. He was covered by dirt and stone. He strained for air against solidity, screaming inside a closed mouth and wildly thrashing without moving a limb. Mad, he wrenched and tore with his head and teeth and felt stone giving, ragged-edged, with pain slicing along his cheek as he broke through and heaved at dust-filled air. Then he lay sobbing and gasping, hearing the chug-chug of the motors suddenly stop and the rising shouts of men. He was in utter darkness, his

---

[4] mining term: sudden collapse

helmet and lamp gone, stone crushing his body and the roof menacing him with creaks and groans and showers of stone which rattled on his bleeding cheek. The girder was wedged on his arm, painfully twisting it just below the shoulder, yet the relief of being free to breathe again, even though his face was twisted sideways pressing on rubble, made him curiously calm.

If the roof went, he thought glumly, he was a dead duck. And hadn't made things up with Bill and the old lady.

Oh, damn it all, it's not fair to happen now...

But it wouldn't go. Of course not. Him dead? Extinguished? Walt Morris simply not here any more to see and feel and think? It was like the world falling into the sun and human life burnt up—might happen some time, but certainly not now...

The pain in his arm was wrenched into agony and a groan shuddered out before he could stop it. He felt he must scream in a moment, but lights flashed over him, which meant the others had come. There could be no screaming now.

'Hold back, chaps—' Curly's voice, that— 'see to t' top first. Are tha all right, kid? Can'st hear us?'

'Yeah,' he grunted.

'Hold on lad.' He heard hammer heads clanging and ringing on steel props. Curly ordered some colliers to break up the great slab resting on the girder, but Walt had to stop them because of his agonies when they hammered. He knew the rubble was being cleared from his legs, but could see only the lamp-beams. They kept clear of the rotted roof directly above his head which kept showering stones and trickling dirt on to his face and shoulders.

'For God's sake, thee keep off, Bryan,' Curly was shouting. 'We want no elephants here. Does tha want to get buried an' all?'

As bad as that? The slab must certainly be a long one, since men were working on it at either side. You heard of them having to saw men's arms off...

Don't let them have to do that, he begged. Not my arm, please. Begging whom? God? A bit late...

Don't sell out now, he told himself. Be the only one to see it through how you kicked off. Except William—he did too, didn't he? But no crawling now...

'How goin', Walt?' That was Bryan, worried.

'All right.' A piece of stone struck his face. 'Don't come too near. She'll go in a minute.' Never let him be remembered as the one that So-and-so got killed trying to help—yourself was forgotten in remembrance of the rescuer. 'Just look sharp!' His voice rose too high and he stopped.

'Shan't be long, my old flower. I shan't let that little lass o' thine down' ...Sandy... 'She'd ne'er forgive us, and her a Duchess an' all.'

Pleading now, selling out, would make every claim to Bill, Charles and Mason, to himself, a lie. There was a Hemingway story about the one in a bombardment, praying and promising all sorts and forgetting everything once it was over and he was safe again. But there went your whole life when you did that...

With the pain beating in ceaseless waves through his shoulder and neck into his head, he lay thinking desperately that once it was written down and read, it was changed.

...He knew, you see ... he knew about this and that it was selling out and crawling... and if you've had it once shown to you there's no excuse for doing the same thing...

His arm was freed. The girder and great stone had been levered up by grunting men with bars. Lumps and rubble were being roughly brushed from the lower part of his body, then he was dragged out by the legs, holding his face off the stone, neck curved and back rasping. Bryan strained between two lamps in a dazzling ring to peer anxiously down at him while a tin bottle was tilted against his mouth, brackish water swilling dust down into his throat and choking him for a moment.

'I'm not bad hurt,' he told Curly as the charge-hand examined him. 'Just my face and shoulder.'

'Thy legs and back is cut an' all,' Curly grunted, his black, sweat-streaked face close as his fingers probed painfully at the shoulder. 'Fetch t' stretcher, chaps. Let's get him out.'

In spite of protests that he could walk, they laid him on a stretcher and manoeuvred it under the stone lip into the roadway, where Curly attended to his cuts. On the face someone called: 'Better down now than wi' somebody under it—' A prop was thrown at the ragged roof. Walt heard the clatter of it striking, then a rumble as dust billowed out, to slowly settle, with a new white cairn crowning the girder which had trapped him.

On the surface an ambulance waited to speed him to the infirmary. He began to feel dazed and unsure of what had happened, as he was bathed, then wheeled on a trolley to the X-ray room and to another ward for treatment.

'A dislocated shoulder and multiple lacerations,' the doctor told Curly, who was waiting, still black and smelling of the pit, when Walt was wheeled out of the casualty room. 'He's a lucky lad—I'm surprised the shock isn't much worse, but we'll keep him here tonight, anyway.' Walt was given a sedative and tightly wrapped in an iron bed, where he lay with his arm in a sling trying to remember what being buried had felt like and insisting to himself that he couldn't really have lain thinking about books.

I'm not that crazy, he thought before he fell asleep. Next day he was taken home in the ambulance. Everyone made a fuss of him and Bill kept describing how his heart had turned over when Bryan brought the news.

'...I just stood there, Walt, and my heart turned right over...'

The old lady had to be assured that the accident hadn't been caused by his carelessness, but after that she kept Mrs Watson and other visitors away from him all day so that he could rest, and Walt realized with relief that they were on friendly terms again. He was glad of her protection as he began to remember what had happened and how lucky he had been. He wanted to forget it, not to tell others about it.

III

For a while being a semi-invalid was quite enjoyable. The mixed sympathy and admiration of everyone around him, the grim strip of plaster stretching from brow to jaw, made him feel slightly heroic, while the sling kept his shoulder comfortable and fresh dressings applied each morning at the infirmary soothed the cuts and grazes on his back, ribs and legs. When Bryan and Hughie called they brought fruit as though he were in sick-bed instead of comfortably reading by the fire, and Bill brought from Andrew Mason a translation of the *Odyssey* with a message from Elaine hoping he would soon recover.

'They were awfully cut up about it,' Bill said. 'Elaine wants you to call her when you can.'

The old lady lectured him for wanting to go out, and it took some firmness to prevent her from accompanying him to the infirmary each day, but she was very solicitous, and, as he told Bill, it was almost worth being injured to see her face gentle for a change.

But on the Thursday night a week after the accident he dreamed of being pinned in darkness by the shoulder while dirt dribbled down on him. He struggled and screamed, but he could not move and no one came, and the creaking grew louder above him, the dribbling coming faster, then he heard the bump and the roar that would end it. His grunting efforts at screaming jerked him awake. For a moment he lay shivering, his pyjamas stuck to his body and limbs, then he leaped out of bed and switched on the light. His shoulder ached, his back smarted, and under the plaster his cheek seemed to be oozing blood. He changed and lay down again without waking Bill, who snored comfortably with his mouth half open in the other bed.

He remembered the frantic effort to breathe when the dirt shrouded his face, then thought of the ripper who had died, not quickly from the heavy stone but slowly under suffocating solidity. He thought: It nearly happened to me...

The thought was now terrifying, and he dared not rise to switch out the light in case the dream returned.

Bill was on morning shift, and when he returned home from work on Friday afternoon he asked Walt, who was sitting by the fire, if he had been reading late.

'...Only you left the light on,' he added casually.

'Must've fallen asleep,' he mumbled, glancing across at the old lady, who was usually strict about lights but now merely inquired: 'What's up? Couldn't you sleep?'

'I was a bit restless.' He almost blessed his injuries for her present mildness. Bill said he shouldn't read too much, as he looked pretty pale, and the matter was dropped, but Walt felt so uneasy about the dream, having been reminded of it, that he decided to go out that night. Bill had given him Elaine Stewart's phone number, and before tea he went to the telephone box at the corner.

'Walt!' she answered. 'Are you better, then? I'm so glad.'

He assured her he was fine. He was unused to the telephone and its way of making casual talk sound forced; for him such conversations were a series of brief phrases and long pauses. When he suggested going out she answered: 'All right. I'd begun to think you'd tired of my company...' She sounded in provocative mood, he thought irritably.

'Would you like to hear jazz, Walt?'

'Can do,' he grunted. 'For a while.'

'And then a drink, I suppose?'

'Well, sure...' He felt certain she was wearing that impish grin as they arranged where to meet. Elaine and her private jokes!

Bill travelled with him on the bus, both wrapped in coats and scarves, with Walt still wearing his sling and sticking-plaster. People on the pavements wore rubber boots and heavy coats, and frost was laced over the windows shimmering in the electric light.

'Come up to Atwell's later,' Bill suggested, slyly adding: 'If you're not otherwise engaged.' His efforts at teasing about Elaine were always clumsy and almost embarrassing because liable at any answer to develop into earnest questioning. 'I've got something to tell old Andrew that'll shake him. You too.'

'A secret, eh?' Walt smiled. Bill looked so full of new importance that it was easy to guess the cause.

'I did it, Walt.' Bill turned to him, beaming under the dull yellow light. 'Acting instead of talking, boy. And I feel great—I've made up my mind and I know where I'm going and why.' He cocked his head, forelock tumbling. 'Are you surprised?'

'Not really. I reckon Mason won't be, either.'

'I joined a group at the works.' Bill bobbed restlessly in the leather seat, urgently wanting to talk about it. Walt sensed the difference between past excitement or agitation and this present exalted personal triumph. 'And we're going to start a branch on the Clifton itself. There are some comrades up there I haven't met yet.'

'Comrades already?' Walt grinned. Mason might prophesy and Charles might sound rueful, but Bill looked happier and more self-confident than ever before. 'It won't cause trouble in your job, will it? I mean—being a Red, after all…'

'I couldn't let that stop me, could I?' Bill demanded. 'I believe in it, Walt, you know I do. Isn't it what you'd do?' He had begun to argue. 'Look, I know what I'm doing, now, at last. You just have to look for the truth and then stick to it when you find it, and that's what I'm doing. Don't you think I'm right, Walt?'

He could not argue; not with Bill determined, yet still pleading, delighted with himself, yet needing approval too. 'Sure you're right. It's right for you, and that's what counts.'

'I knew you'd see it like that,' Bill answered happily as the bus lumbered up to the terminus stop. He was grinning broadly as they parted.

Elaine was waiting outside the post office, standing in a blue radiance under the clock, reaching up on tiptoe now and again as she tried to see over passing heads. The hood of her red coat was pulled up, framing her delicate face in a ring of black curls, and he thought she looked much prettier than those other girls who stood there or who hurried past, with bent heads and coats held anxiously close to protect silk stockings or long dresses from the splash of feet on the wet, snow-raddled pavements. He sidled up and prodded her back. She whirled, mouth open and brown eyes wide.

'Oh, Walt—you fool.' She laughed at him, catching at his right arm, then suddenly frowned and said: 'Oh, your poor face—and your arm!'

'You should be used to seeing my face this way,' he said, and she smiled again as they joined the crowds. He answered very briefly her questions about his accident, then changed the subject. 'You've changed your hair-style, haven't you?'

'Like it?' She pulled back the hood and he stared at a tumbling mass of black curls till she said doubtfully: 'Well?'

'Sure, sure, I like it.'

'I'm flattered that you noticed, honestly.' She took his arm. 'I thought you led much too rich and varied a life to remember any individual girl so well.'

As though, Walt thought, she herself were utterly unused to a change in boy-friends…

'I'm pretty much of a what-you-call-it—doesn't like women.'

'A misogynist? Oh, Walt!' She laughed gaily, hugging his arm. A moment later she was saying quietly: 'I'm awfully glad your accident wasn't too bad. It was quite a shock when Bill told us—he was pretty excited, you know…'

Doggedly changing the subject again, he told her of Bill's news.

'Good for Bill,' Elaine said.

'You're pleased?'

'For Bill's sake—yes.' She shrugged at his frown. 'It was simply a matter of making up his mind, and they were only keeping him in a perpetual dither by their arguing against it. He had to do this.'

'You think the Reds are all right, then?' he asked, slightly bewildered.

'It's not that, Walt. Bill will only be satisfied when he's been one of them—otherwise he'd never be sure and never be happy. I don't think he'll stick it long—he's too gentle underneath. Let him find out for himself.'

'You're a smart lass,' he said, but frowned when she went on: 'I don't say I'd like to see a really close friend or one of my own family mixing up with them, but I think it's Bill's solution.'

'If it's right for him, it's right for anybody like him, however close to you they were,' he said gruffly.

'That's all right, but—' she tossed her head carelessly—the subject was unimportant—'our own affect us more deeply, don't they? I mean, all sorts of emotions are attached to decisions concerning them.'

All sorts of emotions attached … That sounded like a book. He remembered Charles remarking how women got frustrated if you wouldn't be moulded. Thoughtfully looking down at Elaine, he grunted: 'I reckon you were right the first time.'

The jazz club was in a cellar in a dark side street. They descended stone steps to blink in dim red light at tables crowded under an arching roof; the walls decorated with murals of musicians caught at inspired moments: trumpets raised, trombones extended, drumsticks bouncing and saxophones parallel to the floor. Smoke drifting through the red glow veiled the low stage on which a band was playing a slow blues rhythm, the music contained by the stone curving walls and echoed mournfully back on the seated audience. It was warm, airless, and some youths sat in shirt-sleeves, some girls bare-armed in blouse or frock. Everyone listened to the music, rarely talking as they nodded in time or tapped hands and feet, but smiling approval at some special riff or long-held wailing note.

Elaine helped Walt with his raincoat and they sat alone at a table at the back of the cellar.

'Like it?' The light, caught in pockets and spirals, glittered and twinkled all over her hair as she inclined her head to him.

'It's a dreamy sort of...' He looked around doubtfully. 'Hey, look at that bunch with the beards—they're no older than me, I bet.'

'Hush!' She chided him. 'Do you like the music?'

'Yeah...' he said vaguely, studying a counter in one corner. He could see only bottles of soft drinks behind it. Sighing, he looked around him again.

'Beards!' he grunted disgustedly. 'University types, I suppose...'

'Don't be a roughneck, Walt. You sound too disapproving to be true.'

He snorted. Piano notes tinkled alone, weary, depressed and yet philosophical, then a muted trumpet growled sympathetically and all at once he felt the rhythm of the music rather than listened to it, and he began to relax. But he had to add:

'I think beards look daft. It could have something to do with the fact that he shaved only twice a week, he privately admitted, but the idea of her admiring bearded men disgusted him. With a sideways, teasing look and smile, Elaine sat back, murmuring: 'Perhaps they feel the cold more than a rugged type like you.'

When the music ended, brighter lights were switched on and three of the musicians joined friends at tables while the others drank beer out of bottles, leaning back with them tilted over their faces, legs astraddle. He asked her if he could buy beer.

'You have to bring it in yourself.' As he grunted and looked sourly at the students again, she said: 'Poor Walt—no fun without beer?' Her red coat hung open, displaying a white fleecy sweater and sparkling pendant which swung outwards over the table as she leaned on her elbows, saying: 'Don't resent their being students, Walt. A lot come from poor families and it's very hard for them.'

'Who said I resented?'

'They have to find work in the summer, and they have to study awfully hard to—'

'But I don't resent them,' he protested. 'Why should I?'

University, he thought; years spent learning all kinds of things; an ingrained scholastic wisdom which would mean no doubts, no hesitations when more learned men talked, no sense of inadequacy when he read books which appealed to a knowledge simply not in his own mind... To have been at university must mean a huge confident power that made you equal to anyone in argument and conversation... Yet this had never occurred to him seriously before. And Elaine's sympathy, her understanding smile, made him bristle as she said:

'You'd have liked to go yourself, I imagine—instead of having to work and study too. I wish you could have gone, Walt. It would be exciting to see.'

'Well, I don't.' He was prouder of what he had. She was romanticizing; turning him into a figure of pity; that was what he resented. 'You don't know me, Elaine. You can't scribble me down on your list like the rest of 'em.'

'What?' She frowned, and he was sure the wrinkled nose was intended for effect, like the widened eyes.

'And you can't sit there wishing things for me when you've got them nice and comfortable and I'll never have them—because I don't want them!'

'I didn't mean to be patronizing, Walt,' she said, hurriedly and anxiously.

They were quick, this girl's 'interested in you' kind, to apologize for the slightest error in approach; nervous about it, he thought.

'But what did you mean about lists?'

He tilted back his chair, a toe hooked around a table leg, jerking the white sling at her.

'You've had more than me to show you around—they're smiling to you now.' Some of the young people were looking over shoulders to smile at her and glance curiously at Walt.

'Oh, so that's it.' She returned some smiles and greetings, looking back at him eventually with a different, an arch smile. 'What's so wrong with that?'

'Nowt. Just remember I'm a different kind. You're not turning me into something out of a woman's book.' His accent was deliberately being increased. Incognizant anger was making him glower at her. 'Your sort like to do that, don't they?'

'What are you talking about?' Her small hand—shapely, he thought, smooth through care—rose to clasp the pendant as she stared. 'You're trying to hurt, aren't you? You nurse some kind of grudge against me, Walt—we shouldn't go out together, really.'

She looked sad about it, and his anger immediately began turning on himself. Why did he pick victims to hurt as a way of hurting himself when he did not know why he wanted to hurt either?

'You just resent all I stand for.'

'No, wait a minute.' He made an impatient confused gesture, seeking time to order his ideas, but Elaine joined both hands, holding them still, and said judiciously: 'Yes, that's what it is. Because when you take me among people I feel all the time you think I'm an intruder—'

'I do not!' A few people turned again at his sharp words.

'Oh, you explain them and everything, but I'm there on sufferance. You keep me out in ways and you resent my wanting to know more or wanting to talk to them—but it's not me you're jealous of.' Her hands broke apart. 'It's them! You keep as much of yourself held back from me as you can.'

'It's you that does that,' he said indignantly.

'Me?' demanded Elaine, equally indignant. They stared across the table at each other, watched by a few couples who knowingly looked and smiled among themselves. 'Why, you're always picking quarrels!'

'You're always passing judgment underneath. It's all "terribly, terribly interesting and all that" to you, isn't it?'

'You pig!' she said, her eyes brilliant and fierce, her shoulder jerking, so that, remembering Brenda and himself furious, he prepared to ward off a slap.

'You swing at me and you go over my knee,' he warned her.

'I wouldn't demean myself.'

He teetered back in the chair again, determined to stare her out, but, as the staring lasted, asking himself why he gave way to these flashes of temper. Why the suddenly boorish manner, the calculated insult, as though merely by talking like a woman, looking like a woman, being more subtly a woman than Brenda ever could, she infuriated him? The loss was Brenda's, not his. He was growing ashamed, and was slowly easing down the chair as her eyes suddenly filled. He was about to tell her not to cry when her small, rich mouth began curving and widening. She tilted back her head, her laughter tinkling out, then bent forward. 'I can't help it, Walt; we're so ridiculous—glaring!'

As she laughed helplessly, pressing her hands over her mouth with her tight little body shaking, he stared a moment longer, then ruefully grinned.

'We're like kids,' he muttered. Her eyes rose to his rueful look and she burst into fresh, helpless peals, with people glancing again at them. Her head bobbed, red and yellow light rioting over her tumbled hair, and Walt leaned over to tousle it with his right hand as he would have done with Bryan or another good friend. He trusted her suddenly. She looked up, her tanned face glowing, smile helplessly wide and eyes lambent with dark glee.

'Don't be affronted. But you're not—are you?'

'I like you a hell of a lot,' he told her. 'You're the best girl I know, Elaine. I blurt things out to hurt, and then. I'm hurt too. I don't know why. I hate myself for doing it.'

'You didn't mean it?' She watched him. The music suddenly blared out again, the lights dimming, as Walt shook his head. She reached over and caught his right hand, squeezing it and smiling at him as the music stamped and pounded around the fiery walls and set the young people's bodies twitching, feet tapping briskly. He was so full of trust, so affectionate for her gift of laughter, that he went on impulsively: 'You're the only girl I keep wanting to see again.' Knowing uneasily that temporary emotion was being granted too much: 'I don't really go out with other girls more than a couple of times.'

'I soon get bored with other boys, too,' she replied, releasing his hand and sitting back, but looking content. Half an hour later they left the club and picked a cautious way through puddles and crusted slush out of the side street and on to the busy pavements of the main road. They entered the first pub they came to, a comparatively quiet one, and sat in a corner of the large, dark-walled saloon bar opposite a pianist who was clanging out old-fashioned tunes on reluctant keys.

'Does this suit you better?' she asked, looking at some men in working clothes talking at the bar, all unshaven and dirty-faced.

'It was just I wanted a pint.' He put a gin and orange before her and had to return, one-handed, to fetch his own drink. There were some couples at the tables, but there was no harmony in this parquet-floored, cold room; each group was tightly self-contained, and he did not like the place. It compared badly with the jazz club and its lively unity of appreciation. '...Some time I'm taking you with our crowd, Elaine, to the Memo. You'll enjoy that.'

'Fine.' She pulled her coat tight around her, curls spread over the red rumpled hood. 'Walt, why do you always buy me gin and orange?'

'What?' He looked at her astonished as he sat down. 'You like it, don't you? Girls always drink that, don't they?'

'Do they?' Her teeth sparkled as she raised the glass and peeped at him, hair untidied by his hand and now clustered above her arching brows. 'Remember that first time we went out—that horrid pub? You pulled me through an absolute mob of people, all looking drunk, right up to the bar —then dumped me on someone's shoes and said...' She hunched her shoulders, comically aggressive as she growled: 'Pint an' a gin an' orange! Then you pushed it at me and looked around as though you expected someone to try stealing your drink. The place and the din scared me so, I daren't say a word.' They laughed softly, then she went on: 'I daren't tell you either that I didn't drink very often.'

'But you ought to 've done...'

'I daren't.' She laughed again at his concern. 'It's all right, Walt. I'm acquiring a taste for it now. But that place scared me and you looked quite the readiest for trouble there.'

'You were safe with me,' he said glibly, and she answered quietly: 'Yes,

I knew that. It was a nice feeling.'

'Look, it's not that I'm so brave.' He felt guilty over these continual efforts to impress her with toughness, as though that were all he could offer, as though he felt it had to be made obvious or might not be recognized. 'It's a way of covering up, Elaine, I'm scared underneath—I'm shy, really.'

'Why, Walt!' She lowered her glass, dark sober eyes regarding him. 'Be careful—you're exposing yourself.'

'Cut it out.'

'Sorry.' She sat back. She said gaily: 'Bang goes another iron regulation—I'm always doing it.' Raising the glass and cheerfully saluting him, she sipped some gin, then began teasing: 'It shows your confidence with the girls—just push a gin and orange at 'em, and no answering back. I bet they love it.' She cocked her head, curls bouncing. 'You get around a bit, don't you? According to Bill, you're a bit of a masher.'

'Bill's that kind,' he said gruffly. 'Exaggerates!'

'I think he does it to test my reactions as much as anything else.' Her voice was still light. 'He's that kind too, I suppose?'

Walt nodded.

'Old-maidish,' he agreed. 'Always making something out of things. He tries to tease me—I told him we're just—sort of good pals...' He ended doubtfully. Elaine murmured, 'Yes,' and there was a silence which grew more and more awkward as each moment passed. He finished his drink while Elaine looked at her glass. This kind of silence left you half committed, he thought, uncomfortably touching his cramped left arm. The action was purely mechanical, a substitute for thrusting hands into pockets, but Elaine noticed.

'Does it hurt, Walt?'

'No. No, it's okay...' They smiled brief smiles and she sipped slowly at the remainder of her drink. The pianist was now resting at the bar, a florid, fat man obviously too keen on the beer. Erratic conversation started and stopped around the room, jerking into droning life and petering out casually.

'You look quite a wounded soldier all bandaged up, Walt. Why haven't you told me about it?' She wanted to share it—wanted to share his being a miner and being injured. Was she using him to feel all the life?

'Bill said you were really trapped. Were you trapped for long?' She leaned a little closer, touching his arm gently. He screwed up his eyes and shivered, remembering his dream.'

'Not too long.' He was shocked by the strength of his fear, the skin-shifting cold sensation over his back and shoulder-blades.

'Were you unconscious? Do tell me about it. Were you?'

'No.' It took effort to shape the 'N'. She frowned and he let his lids droop, seeing her through the dusky filter and feeling that he, the himself, could no longer be seen. It was like wearing sun-glasses; you weren't shy of looking at girls passing in the street then.

'Walt—' she pressed his arm, her high-boned little face concerned —'was it really terrible?'

He sat with fear clenching his gullet and lungs collapsed, heart bruising its knuckles on his cringing ribs. He heard slow groaning and creaking, felt dirt dribbling, smelt his own sweating terror.

He stared, trying to snap this rigidity, while she said: 'I was —we were all awfully upset when Bill told us,' and suddenly he had broken free. But his body was frozen from within and he had no strength left from the struggle.

'I wasn't scared at the time.' He opened his eyes wide at her, felt a rolling globule skirt his eyebrow and lengthen down his cheek.

'Walt, what's wrong?'

He stood up, gathered the glasses and went to the bar. While the beer was drawn he stared into a silver, bottle-framed reflection of a white face, stark under black with black archways over dark round entrances to fear. He ordered a whisky, gulped it down neat, scowling ferociously, and felt more composed when he returned to the table with warmth radiating out from his stomach.

'I'm sorry,' Elaine said, when he sat down. She took his arm again, her humility arousing tenderness. 'I'll never learn what to say and what not to. I'm awfully stupid.'

'No, you're not. It's me.'

'I'm just ignorant about your work.'

'You're not. Why shouldn't you be, anyway? What do you want to get mixed up with it for, Elaine?' He turned, moved his arm so he could catch her hand while he looked at her. The piano abruptly began pounding out determinedly, jerkily cheerful ragtime music, like sacrilege in the temple of tired talk.

'Not mixed up.' She had to raise her voice. 'Believe it or not, I'm *really* interested in people who do that kind of work—what their lives must be like and how it must be down there, and what it must be like for their wives.' Her shoulders lifted. 'I mean—well, just because it's not my own life doesn't mean I can't appreciate how brave and how—how fine they must be. To live and work like that. The women too, Walt. My heart would break every day, I think, to see you going off...'

He failed to notice the 'see you', because he was imagining how his mates would have received such a speech. They would have answered courteously, smiling, turning as she left them to grin at one another and cock their thumbs at her back. Even sincerity could only partly combat her otherness, her difference from them.

'I thought it was all romantic, too, before I was living it,' he said gently. 'You have to change a hell of a lot, Elaine. You have to stop feeling things in some ways.'

'But you could do it—you did it. And you're sticking it...'

He moved his shoulders uneasily, less sure than he had ever been.

'...Even when Bill first mentioned you in Atwell's—he was so impressed, so full of you—and I thought: Someone brave enough to go ahead with what he wants—even taking on such a job. I thought someone like that can do anything he really—*really* wants to...' She looked up, flushed, and smiled, saying more briskly: 'You were awfully good for Bill, you know. At Atwell's you stood your own ground instead of being—well, sort of nice about things and humming and hah-ing the way Bill had been doing.'

'You've got me all wrong!' This love they had for painting their own picture! 'Elaine, you make me ruddy well ashamed. Look, I set out full of dead-romantic motives and no idea what it'd be like. I got them knocked out of me, but if I'd known...' He shrugged. 'Well, maybe I'd never have taken it on; I don't know. As for Atwell's, I went off half-cocked because I'd got my back up. But this way you're trying to see me, Elaine, its...'

'They all see you that way, Walt. You're going to be something fine. Andrew Mason said...'

'Because they're intellectuals,' he insisted, but they were interrupted by the barman bawling 'Time, please!' with more energy than he had shown all evening. They rose and left, Elaine leaving a half-empty glass on the table. He realized now why a few drinks had made her hilarious and half tipsy before.

They were nearing the bus station and Walt was slowing his pace when Elaine asked: 'Why do you never offer to see me home, Walt? It's not very gallant...'

'I will if you like,' he offered, and she laughed up, remarking that this wasn't very gallant either, as they crossed the square. On the bus they were quiet, Elaine humming softly to herself, while Walt thought that taking the girl home once, just once, needn't lead to entanglement.

They got down together in a quiet tree-lined street where each large house stood detached from its neighbours in an orderly garden.

'Posh,' he commented as they walked up a dark path. 'Do you need a ticket to get in?'

'Don't be snobbish, now,' Elaine answered. The house was in darkness. 'They're at Atwell's.' She unlocked the front door. 'They won't be back for ages.' He followed her in, feeling that events were moving too fast too casually, remembering that Brenda had been the only other girl to take him home like this.

And we'll be alone, he thought, a light thrill kicking in his loins. Then he firmly, sternly, took his irresponsible impulses to task. A nice girl... all very well... but if Brenda had caused entanglement what on earth might Elaine create?

'It's not properly furnished yet—they're getting things bit by bit...' The lights clicked on, bright on heavy blue curtains already drawn, a large blue carpet, a long modern settee and a few matching chairs. Elaine shrugged off her coat and switched on the other two bars of an electric fire in the hearth.

'Like some coffee?' she asked as he unbuttoned his raincoat and stood in the middle of the room, arm in one blue sleeve, with the left sleeve neatly tucked in a pocket, the coat draped over his shoulder. 'Let me help you with that, she said, but Walt shook his head.

'I'll have to be off soon.'

'The last bus isn't for ages yet,' she protested, standing with her back to the fire, hands clasped behind her. He avoided her look by walking to the wall and glancing at some reproductions of paintings, but they were mainly still-life and Walt preferred storms at sea, nudes, ancient battles or even a good crucifixion, so he turned his attention to the books lining the wall on a shelf.

'You needn't rush off,' Elaine said. He looked round. She was watching him with her head cocked inquisitively. He began to blush and turned back to the books without speaking.

'They're Don's books,' Elaine told him, crossing to the corner and touching some books level with her head. 'These are mine here.' She looked along at him, calm and appraising, a small smile beginning as his blush increased and his free hand sought his pocket.

'I mean over here.' She waited. He knew he was being teased but knowing made no difference to the blush. He was growing confused again, unable to match her with words, and feeling that for her as well as him there was antagonism mixed with attraction. She looked so pleased to have him at a loss, he thought. He strolled over to her slowly, and when he was at her side she smiled and reached past his head.

'I'll bet you've never read Katherine Mansfield, have you?' Her scent rose around him, faint and intangibly provocative, and he grasped her in his right arm, bending over her. She was so light that her toes almost left the floor. He saw the quick widening of her absorbent dark eyes, then they closed as he pressed his mouth down on hers, his left arm pinned between them and suffering a wrench of goading pain as he pressed harder wanting to hurt. He felt the hardness of her teeth and the more cruel his pressure the more painful was his arm; the more fierce his kiss became till a blaze of pain racked his shoulder and he released her.

'Don't be cruel,' she whispered. 'What's hurting you?'

Her hands cupped his face and she pulled his head down. Her smallness and lightness made him abruptly change and wish to be gentle. Her lips gathered and swelled, moving slightly, her hand pressing the nape of his neck, and he let his eyes close. He was aware of the world's movement through immeasurable space, dark space and endless time, with all of the circling and wheeling and aeons of dark flowing pivoting for a brief unreality on their connected bodies and then passing through them and away as they slowly parted.

He would have promised anything, pledged anything while she smiled up, but a moment later she had whirled away, chuckling gleefully as she stood by the fire.

'We're getting to be really good pals, aren't we?' she asked wickedly.

He stayed by the wall, forcing his right hand deep down in the stiff pocket of his raincoat, pulling with the other till the sling hurt his neck. The fury passed, and he said slowly: 'Was it all worked out?'

'I wanted to see if you would. I wanted to know what it was like.'

Like a cat licking cream off her whiskers, he thought, and said: 'You know! You've been kissed before—plenty of times, I'll bet.'

'Oh, but not by somebody experienced like you, Walt.' She smiled, turning casually sideways, but still watching over a fleecy white shoulder as she rocked contentedly on toes and heels. 'It was terribly, terribly interesting...'

'Yeah.' He began buttoning his coat. 'I'm frightfully pleased. It's time I was off, anyway.' Delighted, he saw her self-esteem vanish as he turned towards the door.

'No, don't be angry. I was only teasing.' She hurried over and caught his arm. 'It was fun having you at a disadvantage for a moment.' She pouted as he looked down. He grinned slowly and shook his head.

'You're nothing but an out-and-out little flirt. I'm not really angry. But I've got to go.' True, his anger was gone. But she worried him.

'All right.' She went with him to the front door. As she opened it, she said: 'Anyway, a few cracks have shown in your armour tonight.' As he turned, she ran her finger-tips over the lapels of his coat, smiling shyly up at him. 'A girl's manoeuvred you into seeing her home when you hadn't meant to—kissing her—even made you blush. You ought to be careful... I mean if you met some other girl who wasn't just a pal—well, anything could happen.'

'Look,' he said firmly, ' just because...' She tucked one lapel neatly under the other, patted them, and said: 'Kiss me. Quick, someone's coming.' He kissed her pouted mouth, and as he moved back she said delightedly: 'You see? You're no misogynist!'

'Hey-up,' he said to the closing door, and heard her call good night. He stared for a moment then slowly turned and walked down the path. The memory of the kiss was spoiled now. He wondered if she was playing with him, tormenting him, determined merely to show him he wasn't what he pretended...

I deserve it, anyway, he thought; I've acted big-headed with her... Or was she showing she could handle him?

That brought him to a halt, hand emerging from his pocket. What had she said about emotions attached to decisions concerning one's own— with its implications that she would make the decisions?

You nearly walked right into it, he told himself reproachfully... Always getting entangled with girls, somehow!

In bed he lay thinking of her, with the hammer-beat coming low and distant, Bill quietly breathing near by. He tried to recall and relive the moment of the kiss with its knowledge of and its affinity with the elements. He thought he must love her, then thought how young he was.

What do you know about kisses and women? What do you really know apart from your back-alley adventures?

Not for a long time had the critic been so scornful. This must be his first experience of those sirens who abounded in books; able in strange and subtle ways to coax or coerce men into anything. No one could explain how it was done... But come to think of it, what girl didn't try to be like that? With Elaine it just showed more because she was so romantic and loved to dramatize herself.

What man could live up to the kind of notions she must have?

He slept well that night. On Saturday evening he met Bryan and the others, everyone wanting to buy him beer because he was off work, and he slept very heavily when he finally got to bed. But he woke suddenly in darkness, fighting to free his shoulder, grunting in terror and then breaking off a loud scream as he jerked straight up with the bed-clothes tangled at his feet.

'Good God, Walt! What is it?'

He held his shoulder, his teeth locked, and then slowly, as Bill's feet padded, his body eased out of rigidity. The light blinded him and he cringed for a moment, sobbing sharply.

'What is it, boy?' Bill asked gently, peering heavy-eyed at him with his hair corkscrewed out over his sleepy face.

'Just a nightmare.' He clutched his shoulder, staring at Bill.

'About that?' Bill nodded.

'No, no.' He dropped his hand, ashamed. 'Leave t' light on, will you?'

'Sure, sure, boy.' With occasional anxious glances, Bill went back to his own bed and climbed in. Walt lay looking at the ceiling until dawn changed the harsh yellow to a pale pink. I have to go back soon, he repeated to himself time after time. I've just *got* to go back...

When he woke again and went downstairs, Bill had already eaten his breakfast. The old lady rose from her easy chair, with Bill looking up quickly over a shoulder as Walt entered.

'Sit thisen down, lad—there's some bacon here for thee.'

He knew by the bacon, which was scarce enough to be a monthly treat yet was put before him, a week's rations for three people, and he knew by her frowning quietness, that Bill had told her. His own silence rebuked Bill and warned her to ask no questions.

He tried very hard to overcome his fear, not by evading it but by meeting it; evoking it and arguing against it. It was like pitting his own strength, toe to toe, without skill, against a heavyweight. He could tell no one because Bryan had over-exaggerated as usual to everybody about how calmly, how heroically he had behaved during the rescue, and now he could not expose this cowardice. He was bitterly ashamed; for all its effort and endurance, his body was being defeated.

On Sunday night he stayed home and scarcely slept. On Monday morning he decided to visit Alec Thorpe after he had left the infirmary, rather than go home to brood alone.

Thorpe had his own quarters on the third floor of the many-roomed house. There were carpets everywhere and furniture which made Walt walk carefully for fear of knocking against it.

'This is all I need,' Thorpe said, in a small comfortable room with a fire blazing in the hearth and boxing photographs patterning the walls. 'The gym's my real home.' As Walt sat in a deep, square leather arm-chair and looked at a framed photograph on an occasional table beside him, Thorpe said: 'Yes, that's me.' He went to a small cocktail cabinet. 'Twenty years ago when I was a real boxer—even better than you, Walt.'

Walt smiled and looked at another photograph of Thorpe in shirt and flannels, one arm holding a small boy, the other around a woman in a sleeveless summer frock.

'They were my family, just before I lost them, actually.' He put a small glass in Walt's hand. 'Here, sherry, it won't hurt you.' He looked at the photograph and said 'Cheers, Walt.' As he lowered the glass he went on: 'It was one of those damned railway accidents, you know. Nancy and Colin had been on holiday, and the train was derailed. A lot of people were killed—but you wouldn't remember it, of course.' He perched on the arm of the other chair.

Walt did not remember it. You never did remember such things very long, he thought, any more than you remembered any particular bombing raid in the war. You read in the papers that it was a catastrophe, thought how terrible it was for the poor people, and forgot after a few days. Looking at Thorpe's smooth rosy face and white hair, he thought: You never realize it's all real, real and sudden for somebody; an ending...

And for a moment a newspaper headline and paragraph were a real experience in his own life, more real than those of civil wars, starvation and menaced destruction, as he shared Thorpe's remembrance of loss and grief without hope. He thought how paltry his own trouble was.

'Tell me about this accident, then,' Thorpe said. 'I only heard a couple of days ago.'

'I just got buried, Alec.' He emptied the glass and put it down. Then he looked up at Thorpe, grinned, and said wryly: 'I'm too scared to talk about it.'

'Bet you weren't scared at the time!' Thorpe took it as casually as it was said, laughing for a moment. 'Trust you to be scared before or after—there should be some way of not thinking about our trials, eh?'

He would have told Thorpe then, but Thorpe also put down his glass, leaning forward to ask seriously: 'What happened to the tiger, Walt? You don't seem to care any more...'

'I don't know really.' He looked down at the toes of his new suede shoes. He and Bryan had bought matching pairs. 'You could be out of the pit before long, son. You could do all right.'

He started and frowned, and Thorpe went on persuasively: 'Walt, you'll get farther using your natural talents than in any other way. Don't you want to make some mark for yourself? You could, you know. You don't want to spend your life an unknown, digging coal, do you? When you could go so far?'

He stood up restlessly. Now he no longer needed the sling he could pocket both hands.

'What young man wouldn't like to make his mark?' Thorpe asked, watching him face about.

'Oh, I want to make my mark...' Did he? But with whom? The crowd's cheering had meant less than beating one more count in his fight with Ford, so with whom? 'We'll talk about it some other time, huh?'

'Okay.' Thorpe shrugged ruefully. 'But be sure you can afford to chuck away such chances, Walt. I don't know anything else you've got better...'

When Walt went home he was thinking of Thorpe's loss and scornfully berating himself for being so involved in such selfish fears. He wrote to his mother without mentioning his accident and went to the cinema that evening to keep his mind occupied. He slept peacefully and was happy all day Tuesday. He thought of phoning Elaine, but he was still worried about her and confused about entanglements and being handled, so decided to stay away until he was more sure of his ideas. He woke that night gasping in a darkness become tangible, suppressing his breath. He had not dreamed, merely woke in utter panic to blunder to the light switch and stand with his back to the wall staring round the empty room. Bill was on night shift and he would be alone for three more nights. His fear was not something he could contain any more; it had a malignant life of its own, and its confederate was darkness. After that he slept with the light on, but Thursday brought the whole dream again and he was grunting and struggling when he awoke. In the moment of wakening he heard the clatter of a striking prop, saw the dust explode in mushrooming thunder and then the new white-crowned cairn with the end of a girder protruding. He cried out 'It isn't fair...' then choked as bed-springs jingled next door. He lay back and looked at the light bulb, letting his eyes be dazzled so long as there was fierce light.

He had never been afraid of the dark before; he had respected it. It was not the darkness he feared even now so much as the malignancy which used it, warped it into an enemy. In the pit your body was only a shell separating the darkness within, the live darkness, from that without, the surrounding sterile darkness. Light did not create life; it only drew it out of rich fecund darkness; light could be harsh, it dazzled now and hurt the fearfully wide eye, but darkness was never harsh. Darkness had always meant strength and sometimes peace for him; he felt that to ever find his sources he would have to go deeper into it than was possible for him now. If fear kept up this vendetta then it would never be possible, for he was growing to abhor the darkness and cling to the harsh protection of light.

He slept no more, and when Bill arrived home from work he found the fire lit, his breakfast ready and Walt curled in an easy chair, weary-eyed. Walt said that he was so unused to all this rest that he couldn't sleep, but Bill's false jocular envy and the old lady's silent frown when she came down made his excuse sound sheepish and silly even to himself.

When the two were left alone, the old lady handed him a mug of tea and sat opposite to drink her own. Her unbound hair hung thin over her shoulders, changing her so that, with her eyes still tightened by sleep, he could almost visualize the young woman she had been. Not a very pretty young woman, he admitted with a proprietary reluctance, not with that heavy jaw and the solid build—her husband must have been a brave youth. But he added quickly: He must have been one hell of a boy too, to get her love and respect...

'Tha knows Mrs. Burrows down t' road?' She settled herself, comfortably, spreading and filling the chair, pouring tea into her saucer.

'One of those old—one of them you go out with.'

'Aye. Well, her man were in t' pit an' got buried once. Had nightmares o'er it for months after...'

Walt swirled the tea around, holding the mug in both hands and looking silently into it.

'My Abe's told me afore now as it can happen any time. Gets on top on any man one time or another—he'd say. It's wi' bein' shut in—the best is forced to feel it some time, eh?'

'I'll be fine when I'm back at it again.' They glanced at each other, she over the saucer's edge, he over the cup. As she lowered the saucer, she nodded, saying: ' 'Course tha will. Tha's been too long at home, that's all.'

'I'll be more tired. I'll be able to sleep.'

'That's it. 'Course tha will.' She put the cup cheerfully into the saucer, and he thought sadly: No, I won't. Because I can't go back. I'm not the man your Abe must have been...

He rose, washed and prepared to go to the infirmary. The mirror showed why Bill had avoided looking straight at him over breakfast. A white face pleaded for relief, with imprisoned eyes large with dark yearning inside brown rings, cheeks grooved under sharp bones.

'Tell t' doctor o'er not sleepin' well,' she advised as he left the house.

The doctor had not arrived when he took a place among the brown benches in the long green-walled room with little cubicles opposite. Walt disliked the place with its rows of listless sufferers, its stone walls and floors, antiseptic smells and general atmosphere of benevolent intimidation. What interested him were the other injured miners to be found there every morning, all of whom had been struck or buried or crushed at their work. They came from the city's perimeter; from a ring of pits where coal thundered down the chutes from washeries into wagons, to be carried all over the country and abroad. The name of every pit was familiar to him as to anyone in the city, and he knew a few names by now among this pale-faced, limping or bandaged handful who were digging no coal for a while but were recovering so that they could return and begin digging again.

A new doctor arrived that morning, tall, young, with horn-rimmed spectacles and a blond moustache. He went briskly into the cubicle, cheerfully wishing everyone a good morning, and called: 'Right oh, Sister; first patient, please.' A cheerful man; a brisk, hearty, benevolently intimidating young man who made the waiting patients look warily at each other and sit straighter on their benches, listening to the conversations in the cubicle.

'Ah yes, the leg. Let's see... Yes, fine... Let's see you bend it, eh? Come on, bend it, old chap.'

'Ah can't!'

'Well, let's see you try. Just try... Here, let me...'

'Hey-up! Ooo... Now then!'

'That's the stuff. Fine! Come back Monday, will you?'

Out hobbled the elderly little patient, face twisted in exaggerated agony, with the doctor calling for the next one before the first had closed the curtains. Behind Walt a man muttered: 'Bet he's had his morning pint o' bull's blood!'

'Next patient,' the doctor called a moment later, as someone else was ejected. It was like waiting hopelessly for interrogation with the verdict already decided, the firing-squad overworked. Walt knew his own time of recovery was over.

'Bet he's ex-Army,' someone said. 'M and B and duties...'

In the little cubicle Walt took off his coat. The doctor read his record card at a littered table, then smiled up: 'Ah yes, how's the shoulder?'

'A bit stiff.'

'Needs using, old chap. Shirt off.' There was nothing unkind about him, Walt realized. He was simply bursting with healthy vigour he wanted to share. 'Yes, they've healed nicely. You'll have some scars, but that one on your face will soon be gone. You can start work Monday.'

Walt pulled on his shirt and dumbly watched the flourished signing of card and medical certificate.

'Only wrenched your shoulder, really. Not too bad, eh?' The doctor smiled as he put the papers in Walt's hand.

'No.' Only a ten-ton slab of rock and a twelve-foot girder. Only scared, sick.

'Don't let it happen again, eh? *Next patient...*'

I've lost my nerve, he thought at the doctor as he picked up his coat. Could you help me? Or grin and say it needs using...

When he reached home and the old lady asked questions he replied: 'I start Monday. It's a good job it wasn't my behind I trapped or he'd have chucked me out with no trousers on!' And stalked upstairs disgusted, to doze on top of his bed. That evening he went to the telephone box, but it was Elaine's sister who answered the call.

'I'm afraid Elaine's out. She's going to the university dance tonight with some friends.'

'She's got lots of friends, hasn't she?' he muttered sourly, a finger jammed in his left ear, with darkness pressing around the cold booth.

'Well, of course she has...' He scowled, hunching his shoulders. He had not intended to comment aloud. 'Elaine's very interested in people, Walt. A girl as young as her needs lots of friends, anyway.' It was a hint, he thought: Judith disapproved of him. He gave her a message for Elaine to meet him on Sunday and then went home.

'Sorry,' Bill said, when Walt suggested going out before he went to work. 'We're meeting to discuss our chances of starting a new branch up here.' Walt stayed at home. At nine o'clock the old lady put her coat on and said gruffly: 'Tha can come wi' me if tha wants. I'll buy thee a pint.'

'I've got some money left.' He stared at her as she tied her scarf before the mirror. He was tempted to go—the invitation was so novel—but he shook his head when she turned, thinking of her friends.

'Just as well, I suppose,' she grunted. 'Watson's enough to give a man earache wi' her natterin'.'

He went to bed early and was tired enough to fall asleep with the light on, but he woke up much later and found that it had been switched off by the old lady when she came to bed. He tried to lie still, but the fear of suffocation twitched and sprang to life. The darkness, the bed-clothes grew heavier, lying on him at first and then applying pressure which slowly increased, with sweat prickling out on his chest and belly, gathering, filling his navel and trickling down his ribs and thighs while he began struggling to breathe. He clenched his hands and held himself down, grunting and panting with his teeth closed, but at last his body threw off this restraint and he found himself bounding to the light switch and sobbing in anger at the same time.

For some time he sat on the bed, his shoulders shaking. He realized how much he was alone. Cold made him shiver and he crawled under the covers, curling up his body with a hand between his thighs, thinking with his eyes open. There were many fears: fear of the first moment underground with half a mile of earth between himself and life, of the first toppling lumps of coal when the shots had been fired and the pick chunked in, of the first roof bump, the first trickle of sprinkling, gentle, deadly dust. He was afraid that others might see his fear, but more afraid that he would yield to it and be for ever subjugated, losing everything. He had so little to fight back with; the weight of his life, his self-respect, his willingness to continue as this puzzling person Walt Morris, was balanced on so few supports that with one destroyed the others would crumble. His fear made him afraid, in an incognizant way, of life itself. There was nothing outside he could appeal to.

On Saturday he stayed at home again. Constant tension was making him ill. He had a headache nothing would relieve; a fierce ragged thrusting through one side of his skull which bright light intensified, so that they drew the curtains down-stairs and moved in dimness while Walt sat hunched before the fire. Bill inadvertently patted his shoulder as he was going out that evening, and the shock blurred Walt's vision, his face screwed in pain like a baby's. His eyes burned, and like a man flayed, every vibration was a small agony.

'Tha's got a real dose o' 'flu,' the old lady said determinedly, and just as determinedly Walt agreed. Both said it must be put right before Monday morning, and he went to bed early with a hot toddy, having taken a variety of powders she had bought and submitted to being rubbed gently with goose grease. Worn out by a cycle of magnified worries and horrible depression, he fell asleep, with Bill snoring long before he did so, and it was late Sunday afternoon before he woke up.

'Tha were better off sleepin' it out,' she said, fetching his dinner from the oven. 'You'll feel better now, eh?'

'Stacks better,' he said dismally. As he was going out she warned him not to be late home: 'Never ought to be goin out wi' t' cold as you've had. Don't forget you've an early rise.'

'I might not go tomorrow.' He watched his fingers fastening leather buttons. 'I could have just one more shift off—to get really fit.'

'Aye... An' another, then another, then another, I suppose. You want to snap out on it!'

He closed the front door with relief. His headache was less intense but his limbs felt heavy and he thought he would burst into childish tears if anyone shouted at him.

'Walt,' Elaine exclaimed when she saw him. 'You look awful!' It was not encouraging. Instead of a noisy club he took her to a quiet public house which had an opulently furnished best room, a sedate clientele and a huge fire to keep it warm. They sat on comfortable leather-seated chairs in a corner by themselves, with well-dressed men and carefully coiffured women talking around them and exuding perfume and cigar smoke. The carpet was thick.

'This isn't your line at all, Walt,' Elaine commented. 'Are we slumming, or something?' She smiled at light-grained walls.

'I've as much right to drink here as any of them,' he grunted, and she frowned, withdrawing a little. She had taken off her red coat. Around her throat was a triple row of pearls, gleaming where they vanished in her dusky hair. Her pink, low-necked blouse was trimmed with lace.

'You really don't look well, Walt.'

'I've had 'flu.'

'Oh—I wondered why you didn't call all the week. I thought you were shocked with me.'

'That wasn't why,' he said, and then shrugged. He had wanted to merely sit and talk and relax, but she was recalling that night and she was smiling provocatively, and so he felt irritable. A waiter brought beer and gin.

'Bring a whisky,' Walt said. Perhaps that would relax him. He looked round at Elaine, who sat composed and natural, tanned, lovely, liquid-eyed, so manifestly not out of place.

'It's your line,' he said. 'Isn't it?'

'I liked the jazz club.' Elaine frowned again. She added: 'Those other places were all fun, too.'

'Was the dance on Friday fun?' He paid the waiter, watching the silver slide out of a calloused hand, still rough despite its rest, into a soft plump palm. For a moment he hated everyone who had never known underground, heard stone bump or knelt on gritty ground.

'Oh, they're always fun,' Elaine said when the waiter had gone. 'I went with John and some friends.'

'The hairy one...'

'I'm sure if he knew how much the beard bothered you, he'd shave it off at once, Walt,' she answered, toneless and abrupt.

'Does it tickle when he kisses you?' He raised the whisky.

She said: 'You'll have to ask John—it's his beard.'

He emptied the glass, scowled, shuddered and put it down. Then he turned and said humbly: 'I'm sorry, Elaine, I'm a—' He checked the word, but she smiled brightly and nodded.

'Yes, Walt, you're a bit of a bastard sometimes.' She smiled more brightly at his horrified stare. 'But you can be nice.'

'You—you shouldn't *say* things like that!'

'Why not?' She looked innocent. 'I'll bet you do.'

'Not in front of girls.' He reached for his beer, shocked out of his sombre mood. 'Honestly, I'm surprised at you.'

'Oh, Walt!' She laughed softly, raising her glass. When she put it down, still shaking her head with amusement at him, she said: 'You look so funny! You're such a prude in some ways.'

'Me?' He frowned over his drink, thinking to himself that she had him really tied up this time. He was worried again about her.

'Yes, you. It's the same when I ask you about girls or about people's sexual relations. You go all queasy and uncomfortable like some Victorian old maid. Another night, I suppose, you're doing your best to seduce some girl in a dance hall.'

'You think far too much about all that stuff', he said primly, trying to win back some advantage.

'Well, don't you? About girls.'

'Well...' He hunched up his shoulders, half exasperated. 'It's just that I'm sure you romanticize too damned much. I reckon you build it up too much in your head.'

'Do you?' she asked, eagerly leaning forward. 'Do tell me why.'

'I just think you do.' He was fumbling for words, but words could not frame vague intuition. 'You bother me. I reckon you're making too much of it—expecting too much...'

'Well, if that's as clearly as you can put it...' She sat back, lips pouted, disappointed as she looked at her drink on the glass-topped table. 'But then you're what they call experienced, aren't you?' Slightly hostile, her slanted eyes rose. 'You know all the details. I don't.'

He ran his fingers around the rim of his glass, thoroughly embarrassed. 'I didn't know men could be prude and wolf both, for instance,' she said after a moment.

It was amazing, he thought, to find barriers spring up with such speed. They were sitting together, talking together, just as they had often done, and now suddenly each was self-contained and there was no exchange of understanding. He wished she were not so intense. Or was it he who was intense, made so by her? He had paid for more drinks and gulped down a second whisky before they spoke to each other again.

'You really aren't well, Walt,' she said. 'Are you? You're so pale—your eyes look so unhappy.'

'It's just me.' He felt a spasm of revulsion at himself and his unceasing conflict. 'I've made myself like this, Elaine. It serves me right. I'm a neurotic!' His head was a little clouded by whisky fragrance.

'A neurotic? What on earth do you mean?'

'You know... It was another word he could not define—to him it meant a repugnant type of person who thought too much about himself —but people used it very vaguely and loosely and he was not sure. '...I'm too self-centred, I guess. I'm always occupied with myself. Every time I'm not actually doing anything, just day-dreaming, you know.'

She nodded, leaning her elbows on the table and listening attentively.

'Well, it's always about me. I'm always thinking of myself. I mean—I think a lot of dopey stuff sometimes, but it's still me in the middle of it. I'm always in my own mind, and that's what's ended me up like this—neurotic.'

'Nonsense,' she said, waving the idea away. 'Everyone does that. You just don't know enough about psychology.'

'You do?' He was reluctant to trust her, but her confidence, her abruptly adult firmness, were impressive.

'Certainly. Judith gave me a huge book on it which covers everything. I've studied it carefully. Well, I have to if I'm to be a good magazine-woman some day...'

He agreed, and she went on briskly: 'All people think of themselves practically all the time—it's perfectly natural. Dopey things too. It's your ego—you only stop focusing on yourself when you're distracted by some outside stimulus, you see? Like a book, or work, or someone talking—outside stimulation. Do you see what I mean?'

He nodded. He knew little about the subject, except for advertisements on the backs of cheap magazines accusing him of nursing an inferiority complex.

'We're all like that, Walt, and when something bad happens we can get very introspective.' Her knowledgeable delivery reminded him of her sister, but he was eager to believe what she said. The repeated 'we' was comforting and made him grateful.

'You really ought to study all this, you know. Especially as you're a pretty emotionally unstable type.'

'I am?' he asked humbly, feeling like a shy student with a kindly, sagacious professor.

'Well, I mean, Walt . . She pointed out the obvious as gently as she could, putting her warm hand over his. 'Your reactions are a bit cock-eyed at times—you say so yourself.'

'Oh yes...'

'People have complexes and things—most of us would benefit by psychiatric treatment... He hoped she didn't think he was slightly mad, but he was almost prepared to agree with her if she said so. 'It's the conflict in the mind that makes us do things. We have to accept some of it...'

He looked admiringly at her and then sat thinking, while Elaine sipped her gin with sage dignity.

'What's troubling you, Walt?' she asked at last. 'You can tell me.' And he began talking of his family, of his last visit, and ended by telling her about his childhood. While she listened and nodded, people talking quietly around them, he murmured reminiscences of his father, past homes, and of general unhappiness. He realized he was remembering only what was bad in his past. But there was a great relief in talking it out, letting the stories surge up from memory and express themselves. As he grew more conscious of what he was doing and that he was seeking her sympathy, his voice mumbled into silence and he stared at the hand she was still pressing on his.

'Oh, Walt, there you are!' She obviously understood everything about him now, he thought, more than he did... 'It's what happens when you're a child that counts. There's enough there for a dozen complexes!'

He nodded glumly, full of regret for himself.

'What can I do?' He was prepared to put himself, completely submissive, under her guidance. To be a mass of complexes without any choice...!

'At least you understand the cause of all this now.' She thought for a while, ripe lower lip pinched delicately between teeth which gleamed in the wall light like the triple choker around her throat. 'Look, I'll lend you that book next week. That might help.'

'Next week?' he said, disappointed. 'Elaine, I haven't told you it all. Something's happened to me.' He removed his hand, looked at her and looked away. 'I've lost my guts—my nerve's gone.' He told her of his nightmares and his fears, remembering details till he began to sweat and clench his hands, but going on and finding gradual coolness and easing of his limbs when it was all told. He ended by admitting simply: 'I'm just scared to go back and it's eating me up. And I hate it. I hate being yellow.'

'You're not.' She reached for his hand again and clasped it, smiling as he looked at her shamefaced. 'You can't help what the shock did, silly. It might wear off.'

'You don't understand,' he said slowly, surprised. 'I've got to lick it while it's there. And I'm supposed to start work tomorrow.'

'But you mustn't,' she said, aghast. 'That might do you fearful harm.'

'But if I don't,' he explained patiently to be sure she understood, 'I might lose my nerve altogether. I might *never* go back.'

'All right. Then you'll be something else instead of a mine manager.' She squeezed his hand and looked firm—had he not been so concerned with his troubles he might have thought how funny it was to see such matronly brusque wisdom in a face shaped by a spry love of laughter. 'You could be lots of things—you've shown how good a miner you could be, and that's enough, Walt.' She smiled, her eyes repeatedly moving from one of his to the other. 'I'd rather see you doing something else. I think you're made for something else. And it's such a risky job—you could have worse accidents than this.'

'But I'd be quitting. Elaine, would you want a man that packed it in when it got too tough?' He studied her gravely.

'I saw that fight of yours...'

'That was different.' He freed his hand again.

'You're not a quitter, Walt. Anyone who knows you could tell that. It's only you who can't see it just now. That ego of yours—that's what it is.'

'I *could* be a professional fighter,' he murmured doubtfully. 'Thorpe said—'

'Oh, no, Walt. Something else. Something worth while—you'd find it.'

He sat back, trying to think. But he had no thought, only feelings. He was not surprised that she urged him to leave the darkness. She belonged in the light, bright, happy and careless in the light where everything was seen and known, and she must see that as his salvation. And it could be... It was possible...

'I don't know,' he said. 'I thought it was my life...'

'Walt, what you really need is to feel you belong somewhere. I know!' She turned away for her glass, drank, then turned back, her eyes candid.

'You need a person too. Somebody to help you and look after you…' As a suspicious frown gathered his brows, she added: 'Oh dear, that's no kind of an advance—you're so afraid of that. I'm telling you what I know jolly well for myself.'

'You're not so bad placed.' He looked straight at her to say one of the things that vaguely troubled him. 'You get money from your father—he looks after you. And you don't seem to need to pay him back.'

'But why should children have to pay their parents back? We'll be parents ourselves some day. That's not the point, anyway.'

It was hard to argue against such a common-sense attitude, especially when his arguments were so vague, mere bubbles from it at present submerged.

'Is it any comfort to know I'm on your side?' she asked.

'Sure it is. A lot.'

'Do me one favour, then.' When he nodded, she said: 'Don't go to the pit until you feel better. Please?'

'All right,' he promised. Who else cared? Who else deserved a promise from him? She was trying to protect him, like the light that blazed over his bed at nights and cut him off from all kinds of darkness.

There was no more talk of the pit before they left the public house and strolled down, between looming black-faced buildings, to the bus station. There, on a corner, Elaine said she would go home alone: '…What you need is a good night's sleep, Walt. I'll see you on Tuesday at the college. I have to go out tomorrow night. She looked up into his face. You look so haggard,' she said gently. She reached up and her fingers brushed the faint weal on his face, tracing down it, cool and light to his jaw. 'Poor Walt… I'm so glad you told me everything. Good night.'

He watched her tripping demurely across the road to her stop. He felt better and he felt stronger, but he was worried. If he were in love with her, why the half-afraid uneasiness?

He reached home before Bill and found the old lady pouring boiling water into the teapot on the hearth. She looked round, her green-swathed bulk bent stiffly at the hips, and said: 'Changed your mind, have you? Get a bit o' supper, then, afore bed.' As she straightened up he saw that the pit clothes which had been fetched from the infirmary were folded in the hearth.

'I haven't.' He crossed the room, feeling, as she banged the kettle down, that each ancient piece of furniture, each china figure and statuette, the wedding group and even the bayed stag, had become charged with dim disapproval. He took off his coat and sat down at the table. 'I'm thinking of chucking it up!'

She kept her back turned for a moment, stirring the tea in the pot, but he saw how her shoulders rose and seemed to grow broader. At last she put down the pot, turned and came towards him, the spoon glinting as it bobbed.

'Well, now, thee listen to me. If there's owt to make me sick—' almost leaning on him, she waved the spoon over his defiant, upturned face—'it's a brawler, a tearaway, wi' no heart to face his own work. Tha's said tha'rt a man afore now and I've said tha's a long road to go. Get back to t' pit and start learnin' again.'

'I can't...' he said. His head dropped. This time he could not face her stare. 'You don't realize...' he said feebly.

' 'Course I realize! I've had lads o' me own. I don't like seein' a lad suffer. But it's you what picked this job and bragged you could do it. You thought you could, didn't you?'

He nodded, clasping his hands together. She looked down a little longer, then she pushed a mug in front of him and stumped over for the teapot.

'I told you as t' pit's got me own man down afore now. But he allus said you had to take t' bull by t' horns...' She leaned over the table again, a curving brown jet splashing into his mug. He watched it. As she returned to the fireplace she went on, less fiercely: 'He had to do that because there was nowt else to turn to in them days. You said you was a pitman, now. If you pack it up afore you even try again you'll be nowt... You'll never be owt.'

'I know...' He let her put the milk and sugar in his tea without moving to do it for himself.

'Tha's been a fair lad at times—tha's been thoughtful now and again.'

He looked up and in her hard, jaw-prowed old face saw that this was of great importance to her, but could not tell whether it was merely for his sake or for something in herself. 'But I'd have no time for me own flesh and blood that stuck his tail atween his legs and run off. It's not fair when you've claimed you was a pitman—it's not a bit of a game to take to an' drop when you want...' She sat down by the fire, grunting as she bent for the poker. Hefting it, shining in her right hand, she muttered: 'It just i'n't fair to men as had to stick it for life if young 'uns can chuck it up as easy as that. It's wrong.'

There was no doubt in him of the justice of her claim. He did not need to think; he knew she was utterly right. Men had been forced to endure the life of the pit. Men had died. They had been crippled and limped back for casual work. They had gone on with it, however hard and wearying and soul-depleting it became, and all this death and endurance and effort had gone into the tradition he had chosen to be part of. He could not desert without spoiling the tradition, however infinitesimally and without spoiling himself. To leave the job when all went well would have been one thing; to be chased away by fear was another.

'You're right,' he said, reaching for his mug and looking up at her. 'I'll start tomorrow—I can always say I tried again.'

'Thi clothes is out ready.' She attacked the fire vigorously. 'I'll bet you come home wonderin' what was botherin' you.'

Soon after, he went to bed and lay with the light on, the whisky fumes making him drowsy. He had broken his promise to Elaine, he realized. I can't help it, he thought. He recalled the old lady's speech; her mind must work as his did, that was all... Elaine couldn't understand this, but the old lady could. The old lady was used to the darkened side where men worked. A promise to one woman against a promise to another—a woman in it either way, and he had meant to keep free of entanglements...

IV

Next morning he woke with such a headache that he prepared for work mechanically and scarcely thought of where he was going. By the time he reached the pit he had begun wondering at the absence of fear, but at the pit-head he was surrounded by colliers who welcomed him back, chaffing as usual, while one or two promised to help him if he found this first shift difficult. The swooping, swaying blackness of the shaft was bad, but he told himself that this was natural after two weeks without practice. Even the worst moment was a lesser ordeal than his nightmares, because fear at last had shape and could be understood.

It came when he crouched on the coal-gummings in his stint, sweat easing him after the long trudge through low roadways, while he hung his tin water-bottle over a roof bar. He twisted his sprawled body, flashing his cap lamp around, and saw that the roof was not good, heard the coal crackle and grunt under weight, and felt afraid. There was scarcely room to raise his head with the loose coal eighteen inches thick under him. He was enclosed—he felt entombed—and he clenched his fingers into the sharp coal, his eyes shut while his heart pounded. He told himself: Come on, it's not so bad. You just can't go home and tell her you couldn't face it...

A collier scrambled into the next stint, removed from between his teeth the string of his round bottle, and called cheerfully: 'Are we all right, then, my old Marquis?'

'Yeah, fine.' The voice drove off his fear. He reached for his shovel, the lamp flashing white.

'Don't kill thisen wi' scufflin' first shift, mind. We'll gi' thee a pound if tha has it rough. Two weeks wants catchin' up, eh?'

He knew he would be truly all right. This was not the darkness of nightmare, that hideous darkness where no one ever came; this darkness was that of his mates, a part of their lives and his. It was full of their past and their strength.

The belts jerked and began moving. He took up his shovel, its shaft smooth in his left hand, crutch hard in his right. His muscles gathered as he knelt with legs spread wide, buttocks pressing the coal between them. The big flat blade drove smoothly into the loose coal, his arms tightened, swung, the lamp flashed round on coal, props and moving rubber, and the first load thudded on the belt.

'Get your head down, boy!' he yelled to his mate.

'Make it crack, lad. Watch thi back is all...'

And the sweat came oozing, thick and rolling and satisfying.

When the shift was over the darkness and the work were natural to him again. He cleared his stint with such enthusiastic speed that he was in time to help the collier who had promised to help him.

'How did you go on, then?' the old lady asked, and with his cap pushed jauntily back, dust flecking his eyes, he was able to answer nonchalantly: 'Oh, not bad. Same as usual.'

'Told thee!' She bent to the oven speaking her last word on the whole matter: 'My man 'd've been back a week sin'!'

At lunch time next day he met Elaine in the college courtyard. They stood under the rough brown walls while students passed with scarves tossed over their shoulders, faces rosy from the cold.

'Oh, Walt! So you did go... She pushed her books into his hands and pulled on black woollen gloves without looking at him the first startled, disappointed moment.

'I had to. I shouldn't have promised—but it went great, love.' He told her about it, hands excitedly jerking, when she had taken back the books.

'Yes.' She nodded and sighed. 'I can see you're yourself again.'

'But—you're glad, aren't you? I did it—'

'Of course I am, stupid!' As he blinked, she began walking away, leaving him to hurry after, frowning. When he caught up, she said: 'It's just that on Sunday—' she shrugged without looking at him— 'oh, it doesn't matter.'

'Look, Elaine—' His gentle hold of her arm was rebuffed by a quick jerk. 'Well, don't think I'm not grateful about Sunday. This doesn't make any difference. You helped me, don't you see?'

'I was a good listener... Anyway, I brought that book if you can be bothered to look at it.'

'Elaine, I'm sorry I had to chuck out your advice. But I had to! Sure, I want to read it...' But she was very quiet over lunch, and when he suggested a date said she would be busy all week. When they were back in front of the college gates, she looked up reproachfully to say: 'After all, Walt, you did promise me you wouldn't go. I believed you. I mean—it's all right you're going, and you're better now, but—you did promise.'

Had promised—he told himself, with hurt eyes like brown elongated tears regarding him—when she believed herself his only helper and adviser... had thrown aside a moment of deep intimacy and unguarding trust.

'I'm terribly sorry—try and understand, love. I just had to.'

He felt they would never be close again.

'Yes, I know you did. Forget it, Walt.' As she turned away and he watched her run quickly into the building, he thought desperately: But she'd have changed you... she wants you to go her way—and she had to be shown...

These protestations did not ease his shame. He should never have let her share his trouble in the first place, he realized. Intending to prove how seriously he took her advice, he began reading the thick volume on psychology she had given him. He never finished it; in fact he read only a little of it. Much of the language was technical and difficult, and instead of reading through from the beginning he opened it at random passages, reading what he thought might affect him. It was the catalogue of mental disorders which appalled him, for he discovered that at one time or another he had shown symptoms of not merely one, but at least three-quarters of them. He had displayed both manic and depressive tendencies, been prey to phobias and obsessions and possessed most of the significant traits of the hysteric. He read each passage with horrified fascination, but when he finally learned of schizophrenia beginning with nervousness, increasing irritability and voices heard in the mind, he slammed the book shut and reached for the *Odyssey*, which was now his favourite.

A week later he returned the book. They had not lunched together and he had to wait at the gates for her returning. She was wearing a bright red-and-white knitted stocking cap over her curls, the tassel flopping at her shoulder.

'You can't have studied it already,' she protested.

'I don't want to. You could go nuts just realizing all the things you might have. I talk to myself all the time in my head. Do you know what that means?'

'What?'

He nodded, sombre-faced, at the book in her hand.

'Just read up on it. But you're better leaving your mind alone. I just wish my mind would leave *me* alone a bit more.'

She looked down at the book. 'You're an idiot, Walt.' Then she looked up. 'You never called me, did you?'

'You said you'd be busy,' he protested indignantly.

'Well, of course I was, but you could have called. I wondered if you were all right...'

He dropped his eyes and mumbled he was fine. She waited, then said brusquely: 'I want to be sure we agree on one thing, Walt. This friendship of ours—we have fun together, now and again, and all that, but it's what they call platonic, isn't it? You don't really mind my going out with other boys and being free to fall in love, or things like that?'

He shook his head, shoulders hunched, shoe toe slowly scraping. ' 'Course not. We're too young to get—seriously entangled.'

For a moment longer she watched him, sighing when he would not look up. 'Fine, then. I wanted to get it straight, because a rather nice boy at the university asked me to go out with him.'

'Maybe he'll be more in your line.' He looked up, surprised at how much this hurt, and saw her quick anger at the remark. He added hurriedly: 'Anyway, there's a lot of things I want to do.'

'Well—I'm not stopping you am I? I'll see you around, then?' She had gathered dignity.

'Yeah,' he said. 'Sure...'

For some time it was hard not to think of her. He saw her at the college occasionally and they even went out together again once: to a cinema, so that they scarcely talked. She was not warm any more, nor in any way flirtatious or provocative; they were like good, old, cool and hostile friends. He learned that romance can end in oblique remarks, growing awkwardness, unspoken reproach and guilt, as well as in a slap and swear words, and he found the first not much happier than the second. But it seemed the damage was done, and in his own defence, guided by the same dark, undefined motives that had refused Thorpe's suggestions, he told himself she had been wrong in the crisis that followed his accident. She would want him to go her way; sooner or later that would have been proved.

Yet when anything interesting or exciting happened, he often thought: I'll tell Elaine about that, and at night, sometimes after kissing or fondling or trying to sound his own rebelling depths with some girl casually met and casually mated with, he would think of her for a long time, wondering why they made each other angry. He saw less of her as weeks passed, and even began avoiding the college gate she used at lunch-time. Girls, he decided once more, were too complicated to know for longer than a night or two.

In the main, during the first half of that year, he followed his own advice to Elaine. He left his mind alone and tried to construct around his perception and emotions a mesh of carelessness which would filter disturbance from outside and hold down an occasional inner heaving of turgid dissatisfaction. He roamed freely like the lion selected as his symbol and he was seldom alone. He was different from some of his companions, for as his weight and strength increased, as his skill at his work improved, as he became more confident of his own powers, he grew fierce and aggressive only when forced to defend himself. So long as he stayed with the gang, however, it was impossible to keep out of brawls—and lions are savage creatures when roused—all he could do was ensure that the old lady never found out about them. A cut lip which might swell now worried him more than the combined scrapes and bruises of all his earlier fights.

Trouble came to the gang as a natural consequence of drinking for two hours before visiting the kind of dance hall most likely to attract youths and girls as reckless as themselves. At the night's end a few would break away to court, perhaps mate with a free-and-easy partner, while others went homewards in a noisy bunch, ripe for any excitement. Walt clung to his friends because of his affection for them and theirs for him; because he, like each of them, gained confidence from the group; because his broiling vitality always found outlet in the places they frequented, and because it was easier in their company to ignore what disturbed him. They cared for little; they knew of little yet to care for. Their common bond was a frantic liveliness and a rarely mentioned defiance of cramping, shaping authority. They wanted to show their strength and that they were young men to be reckoned with; violence was often the handiest way. Their brothers or fathers had been soldiers, returning now with tales of war and a camaraderie that good-humouredly looked down on them, and it was necessary for them to hit out at times.

Yet they were fiercely loyal to their own, bought beer for and gave money to the unlucky one unable to work for a while. They lavished drinks on girls, not always with motive, and they treated well any casual pub stranger who attracted their respect or liking. They tipped taxi-drivers heavily after late-night dances, tossed hard-earned half-crowns into the caps of street artists and blind or crippled beggars—anyone who aroused their sympathy—and they sometimes sat with moist eyes and full throats while watching the unhappiness of some child star of the cinema. Their future could be seen in that individual member who at some point saw some girl more than once, slowly dropped out of their activities, and would be eventually shaking his head at his unruly ex-companions while he danced or sat sedately with his sweetheart; his ex-companions meanwhile sadly shaking their heads over him and asking each other how a bloke like that could let a lass like her get the hooks in.

By the spring Bill's forelock was almost permanently between his eyes and Walt had warned him to have it cut off: '...if you don't want to end up cross-eyed.' Bill was less tolerant of Walt's casual attitude to politics. He even got angry sometimes, arguing with the zeal of one who knows beyond question that he is right and will soon be proved so while his critics are disgraced. When he was not arguing, or attending night classes or political meetings, he was reading books whose very titles made Walt pull down his brows and groan. He had a habit of suddenly looking up from a book, marking his place with a finger, to hurl accusingly such questions as: 'Did you know two-thirds of the world's children are suffering from starvation, disease and ignorance?' ... 'Two-thirds, Bill? Surely not as many as that?' ... 'Facts, Walt.' Bill would stare for another accusing moment, then look down again, as though conscious of wasting his time: 'I wish you'd read the papers now and again.' Walt would protest that he did, but since his method of reading a newspaper was to glance at the headlines and the first paragraph in large print, guessing the rest, he never protested too strongly. Apart from politics, they almost quarrelled over such basic issues as: 'Walt, did you know it was once natural for brothers and sisters to have sexual relationships?' ... 'Brothers and—Don't talk daft!'... 'Who's talking daft? What do you know about prehistory. Sons and mothers did once!'

'Oh, now look!' This philosophy held nothing sacred. 'It's against nature. Honest, I mean—propaganda's one thing, but when you start—'

'It's not against nature at all.' It was Bill who kept calm, self-possessed, rolling out arguments while Walt grew more shocked. 'Merely against social conventions which we've developed because we had to. It's all social conventions.' Walt could see in this the insidious undermining of human decency and believed some of the stories told of revolutionaries in the past.

'Well, if they're the kind of ideas you're preaching...'

'Oh, you're so ruddy ignorant about philosophy!'

'You've got dead big-headed lately. Know-all!'

Bill used him as a sounding-board for all his ideas, and was so sure of himself—so damned smug, Walt would think—that Walt always retaliated, even when he knew scarcely anything about the issues.

'The Reds can't do anything wrong now, can they? They're just as ready for trouble in Europe as we are!'

'They have no long history of political rottenness and colonial oppression and assassination behind them as we have. They're young and trying to grow and have to protect themselves.'

'Like locking up anybody that speaks out of turn.'

'That must go on as long as the West creates counter-revolution inside their countries.'

'Counter-nuts! What about the Communist spies they're trying in America now?'

'Oh, blimey!' Bill would brush aside his hair impatiently and blink as it sprang back. 'They're being tried for their political opinions. The West only believes in political freedom in countries abroad—not in their own.'

'Well, I wouldn't want to live where secret police could nab me whenever they liked, and shove me in a dock the week after, all ready to confess.'

'And I wouldn't want to live where negroes get burned and lynched, and you get life imprisonment for being a revolutionary—and trade union leaders get bumped off by gangsters if they don't sell out!'

'I've always said politics stink, haven't I?'

'That was all very well at seventeen. But you're nearly nineteen now. You can't get away with that good-lion tripe now, you know...'

'Oh, can't I?' There would follow a long silence, studious on Bill's part as he resumed his reading, sulky on Walt's as he pulled scowling faces at Bill's bent head.

'In the East people get locked up because they're spies,' he would say triumphantly, after some thought about all the answers he should have made. 'In the West it's because of their politics.' So would begin a fresh argument.

'...If people like you insist on leading selfish, ignorant lives it will all take longer for us who do care!'

'You're a fanatic. You'll be growing a moustache like Joe Stalin's next.'

On Bill's set of drawers shortly after that appeared a photograph of the Russian leader, benevolently looking across the collar studs and hairbrush and *History of the C.P.S.U.* at another of Maxim Gorky. The old lady, who read only local news on the inner sheets of the evening paper, asked Walt who they were.

'His grandfather and great-uncle on his mother's side,' Walt told her confidentially, and Bill frowned up from his supper later on being informed casually, as she sauntered out to, the kitchen, that 'thi mother must have been a fine-lookin' woman when she were young'. Walt caught him studying himself in the mirror upstairs as they were preparing for bed that night.

April brought blustering winds which chafed his face after bathing at the pit and made him glad to reach home each afternoon or night. He grew more restless, still thinking frequently of Elaine while buying drinks for other girls at the club on Sundays or taking them home from dances. His studies irked him, and although he attended day school every Tuesday he stopped going to night classes. He started smoking because most of the gang did and it looked more adult, but he spent occasional weekends with the colliers and their wives in the cheerful clubs and sometimes went home with one couple or another for supper. Because he went to school the charge-hand on the face began teaching him how to reckon the men's earnings and allowances.

'If you never get to be a manager,' Curly said, 'maybe you'll make a charge-hand some time or a union man. We want some brains on our side an' all.' Walt respected Curly so much that he held back his thought that surely, in a nationalized industry, everyone was on the same side. The men talked of gaffers and there were arguments with officials, but in spite of newspaper reports of strikes at other pits, there was seldom trouble at the one where Walt worked. He was content to do his job and draw his pay, leaving union affairs to older men. In this he was no different from most of the young ones at the pit and many of the older ones.

On a day early in April when both he and Bill were on morning shift, a letter came from his mother which he began reading as he ate his dinner. Bill sat down at the opposite side, looked up from his plate at Walt's face, and asked: 'What's wrong?'

'My father's ill,' he muttered, reading. He was in a sanatorium half-way between London and the city.

'He's got consumption,' he added, and Bill and the old lady glanced at each other before looking at him as he pushed away his dinner and bent over the letter. It went on:

> 'His condition is serious, I understand. So his past has caught up with him...'

Over the pages were scrawled old charges and demonstrations of how such an ending was just. He understood why she wanted to prove this to him. He knew by the tone, the sentiment, the run of phrases and words, that she was bitterly unhappy. He knew this as surely as if she were talking to him, the taut vibration of the truth in her voice, the nerve fluttering in her cheek.

'I'm terribly sorry.' Bill's tone irritated him at that moment. 'What are you going to do?'

'Nothing.' He looked at the old lady longer than at Bill. She was silent, turning away to punish the fire. He had never explained his home life to her, and after his first day she had never questioned him.

'Try and forget it,' he said, standing up, his dinner steaming unwanted between himself and Bill's shocked stare. 'It's nowt to do wi' me.'

Upstairs he went to the bed as to an understanding friend, sprawling with the letter crumpled.

...If he dies, he thought, I might like him better. Let him get it over with...

Was he so evil? he wondered, when he understood what he wished. Was he cruel and selfish, only seeking peace for himself? Better to admit his hate than evoke false feelings close to the genteel sentimentality and weakness of his family. To disown was to disown, and they should leave him out of their sufferings.

He raised an arm, bare to the elbow, big-handed, scratched, with sinews corded and muscle a long smooth swelling. He had grown strong; still lean and light, but strong. Strong in the back, they said, weak in the head. That made a good collier. That was what they said. It didn't do to think too much, with a job like that...

The wind buffeted the window and he rolled on his side, agony struggling up and flopping back, clutching as it sank.

...I hate him. And yet I must be like him in a lot of ways... He was tough... I should be all for him...

He reached out for the *Odyssey* on the chair beside him. It opened, accustomed by routine, at the meeting of Odysseus and Telemachus, but their tears and embraces made him now grunt in disparagement and he turned to the killing of the suitors, then of how they faced the avengers.

Imagine him coming home, he thought, putting down the book much later—coming home to kill all their enemies and sort everything out... And finding Telemachus was a fighting man.

He could not rest. He went to the cinema alone that night, and when he and Bill were enjoying a last cigarette in bed, Bill's diffidence, his unspoken but still obvious sympathy, roused him into starting an argument and making insulting remarks about Stalin.

Bill refused to be angered, however, and shaking his head wistfully as he sat up in bed, his hair dangling as usual, he mildly answered:

'Walt, if I could make you see. If you could only be made to understand the self-honesty, the tremendously high ideals, unselfishness and plain common sense in all this...'

The old Bill, he thought, eyes round with visions, sure of them coming true. He asked quietly: 'What does Mason say about you now?' For if Mason were right, then how could Bill be so proud and happy? Someone was making a mistake.

'I keep away from that crew now.' Bill slid down, covering himself up. 'They only want to change my mind—Mason and the Stewarts and a few more. They're corrupt and want me to be.'

'You used to like them.'

'In politics you have to make up your mind,' Bill said, calm and resolute. 'They're corrupt and they're no good to what they profess to support. Don't you see?' His head turned; a round-eyed, hair-tousled, pleading look at Walt: 'It's not that I'm rotten or anything, Walt. But they get me confused—Mason throws stuff at me about the past which sounds terrible—he says things about Europe which worry me. Then, when I check up with the Party they put me straight and show the reasons for things. But it isn't right I should have to keep pestering older comrades to explain all these accusations to me. That's why I'm keeping away from Mason.'

Walt decided to switch off the light. Sitting up, shivering a little, he could see Bill's face. You couldn't stay scornful at a bloke as sincere as him.

'If they start doing what they've been doing in America,' he slowly pointed out, you could end up in gaol, Bill. I'd hate to see you—'

'That wouldn't worry me!' Bill peeped over the blankets. 'Our party's always been lied about and persecuted. The Nazis tried to crush the German Communists—beat 'em up, threw them into concentration camps, tortured them and killed them—but they couldn't stamp us out. Just as the Romans couldn't stamp out the early Christians!'

As Walt went to the switch, Bill added: 'They can do all that to me if they want—I'll stand it.' He was smiling upwards.

Stand it? Walt thought as the room vanished in darkness. Little, limping, jaunty Bill suffering martyrdom and standing it? Yet as he climbed into bed, remembering the preoccupied smile, he thought: The way he looked he'd half like something like that to happen... He felt, with a touch of concern, that Bill was committing himself too eagerly now, as though to make up for his previous vacillation; he was leaving himself no way of retreat if anything went wrong. But since he himself had advocated action instead of talk, and since it was Bill's life, anyway, he could not argue with such wholesale dedication.

...I'll bet his 'comrades' get fed up with him spouting at their hen parties, he thought, grinning in the dark as Bill said good night.

Yet on the following morning, a Tuesday, he defended Bill against Andrew Mason, whom he met at the college gate which Elaine usually used. Walt was casually lingering there, refusing to admit to himself that he actually wanted to see her, insisting that he had as much right to use this gate as she had, when the teacher stopped in front of him.

'How nice to see you again. Let's lunch together, shall we?'

'Not at Atwell's.' Mason's hand was on his shoulder, jostling as some students hurried by, his thin hair flapping in the gusty wind. Walt was annoyed. He told himself Mason always turned up when you were looking for Elaine, then remembered he wasn't supposed to be looking for Elaine.

'Atwell's? Good Lord no, their coffee is the only thing I go there for. I know a cheap place—very plain.'

It was very plain indeed, Walt discovered. Bare wooden tables were separated by partitions all along one side, with steam from the counter opposite clouding the windows and forming little beads on Mason's thick spectacles. People were eating on stools at one end of the counter and there was a great deal of shouting of orders behind it to the banging of plates, but they found an empty table and sat on unsteady chairs to eat. Mason was a hurried eater—perhaps because he lived alone, Walt thought —bending over his plate and scooping up food on his fork as though it were a chore to be performed as quickly and with as little attention as possible. He used a large red handkerchief to wipe away casually the specks and splashes left on his trousers.

'And how is Bill?' he asked, when they had both finished and Walt was lighting a cigarette. 'Still seeing red?'

'He's got pictures of walrus moustaches all over t' place.' Walt grinned. 'He says prayers to them when he thinks I'm asleep.

'I'll bet you tease his life out,' Mason said, his horse teeth displayed. 'You shouldn't do that, you know. He's in the sensitive stage.'

'It's you lot that want to leave him alone,' Walt said sternly. 'Bill's dead keen and he believes in good things like—well, like helping starving kids and that. He says you torment him.'

Mason's spectacles were clouded by steam and he had to remove them, wiping them in the red handkerchief, the steam condensing and glittering on his corduroy coat.

'I only told him some truths he didn't like.'

'Well, he didn't believe you.' Walt related how Bill had gone to others for advice.

'Yes, I expected that.' Mason put the spectacles on again, his sunken eyes enlarged. 'I told him because of my own experiences. However, his new friends impress him most at present—they're strong. And Bill feels he belongs to something fine and invincible, which makes him invincible too. But he's only beginning!'

'If they're all like Bill, he'll be all right. Let them stuff him up all they like, and let Bill spout his head off...'

'The very idealism that makes Bill such a hell-driver now,' Mason answered, tapping the table with a long finger, 'will take him into a head-on crash over something or other at some time or other.'

'Is that why you resigned?'

'Oh, I'm old history—' Mason began wiping his eyes again and Walt looked away from the squint. 'You know—it's quite the fashion for young intellectuals to join them and then quit later in life. People forgive them for it, eventually...' The cynical flippancy gave way to quiet regret: 'Not many try to imagine how much both decisions have meant to the young intellectual in question.'

If you were going to mock yourself, Walt thought irritably you should keep it up. Not almost burst into tears half-way through. He said gruffly: 'Who cares about intellectuals? There must be more like Bill in their mob.'

'Oh yes. Bill is a type.' Mason smiled, talking wryly now as though mentally shaking his head at Walt. 'The young dedicated idealist who reads avidly, questions eagerly and plunges into Party work—there's no stopping him. He's read of all their noble aims and thinks only of the end product—recognition of the real means comes later. Bill's type grasps only those ideas which bolster up his own convictions that he's right. They surround politics with their own idealistic aura and move around for a while in an exalted haze—with every problem knocking them on their backs so that some "stronger" comrade has to pick them up and comfort them. They always get the worst of an argument with a *real* Communist.'

'A real Communist?' Walt repeated. Mason regarded him solemnly.

'A pretty determined chap, Walt. He'd make Marxist mince-meat of your good-lion theory.'

'Would he have me locked up if I kept believing in it?' Walt asked, remembering Bill's arguments. 'Would they do you in for not agreeing with them—fighting them—if they ran things?'

'Some would.' Mason smiled again, leaning over the table and manifestly enjoying himself. It seemed to Walt there was something feminine in this enjoyment; not the blunt anger which he attributed to men, but the pleasurable malice of a Mrs. Watson, with the same smooth delivery and glinting spectacles. 'The scary character is the left-wing Communist. He believes he belongs to the chosen, and that the chosen are born, not made by signing a Party card. He'll give a little rope to fellow travellers, but he'd prefer to hang them, really, unless they're frightfully close to the real thing. His war-cry is "No sentimentality—obey the line"—and believe me that covers a multitude of sins.'

As Mason sat back, still smiling, Walt insisted that Bill would never be that kind: 'Not old Bill.'

'Let us pray,' said Mason, and lowered his head. But if it was all so funny to him, Walt wondered, why go on so long? His instinctive dislike of the teacher was returning after their talk, and he glanced at his watch ostentatiously, then said they should go.

When they were outside, leaning back against a rough wind which chased through the streets and buffeted them, Walt said bluntly:

'There's something funny with you and all this party stuff—you say you're down on it, but you're always talking about it. Like a bloke that's been jilted.'

'Jilted?' Mason looked round, his long hank of hair blowing out over his face. 'That's a shrewd remark. But say I was betrayed, rather.' He put his head uncomfortably close to Walt's, his voice tattered by sudden gusts:

'Once you've been in, you know, you can never be quite objective about it again. Like old schooldays—you look back half affectionately, however bad the thrashings you got and however glad you were to leave.'

'Like a widower,' Walt said, studying him, wondering what the man did with his life. 'Sorry she's dead, but glad as hell she's not coming back!' They reached the college gates.

'What a very hard young man you are,' Mason rebuked him. 'Nothing is sacred to you except personal liberty!'

When he had gone, waving back over his shoulder, Walt decided he wasn't really such a bad sort—just acted womanish at times, that was all. But then—he was an intellectual, which might account for it.

A week after this Walt sat his exams, passing to his own surprise, by the minimum number of required marks. He told Bill that he must have been squeezed through because of a shortage of second-year students. The delight that would once have filled him at such success was now lacking. School meant little to him, though he was sorry that end of term meant he would have to work on Tuesdays, but Bryan made the news an excuse for a celebration that weekend which would have taken place in any case as normal routine. They were always celebrating something.

Walt felt slightly disloyal at being the only one of the gang who felt bored at times with drinking, dancing and banging things up. Each week they went to a different dance hall—they would not have been allowed in a second time at some they visited and left in uproar—and the kind of girls who sought their company made him think wistfully of Elaine. His aimless restlessness was never appeased by these girls—who borrowed their repertoire of slick clichés and hackneyed ideas of romance from cheap films—though sometimes his lust was.

Occasionally he went to the gym, but Alec Thorpe was obviously losing interest in him. He looked at Walt's hand one night, examining his fingers and remarked: 'Started smoking, have you?' After a long look at Walt's face, he finally said: 'Well, I hope it all did you good. It's a pity to see talent wasted, though.' Then he walked away to supervise two youths vigorously sparring in the ring.

In the middle of the month a fierce argument arose between Walt and Bill over a British warship which had been fired on by Chinese

Communists and was trapped up the Yangtze river. Walt was furious at this presumption—after all, your country was your country and even the Japanese had conquered China—but Bill defended the action.

'She was going about her lawful duties,' Walt insisted as they undressed for bed. The phrase was one he had read in a newspaper. When Bill argued that the Chinese had issued an ultimatum, Walt said indignantly: 'It hadn't expired! Anyway, who are they to issue their ruddy ultimatums?'

'The Chinese,' Bill answered calmly. He crawled into bed and asked: 'Do you know how many of them there are?'

'Who cares?'

'Six hundred million, Walt. More than we've got all put together.'

'They haven't got the atom bomb, though. Neither's Russia. If that had been an American ship they'd have dropped a couple on them, you can bet.'

'I wouldn't want to start throwing *them* around,' Bill remarked. 'There'd be an awful mess if we gambled wrong!'

'You wouldn't care—' Walt got into bed—'so long as the Communists won.'

'You don't understand.' Bill switched out the light and Walt closed his eyes against a sudden change to pleading.

'...If only you would, Walt. I imagine if you and these friends of yours with your vitality and daring—if you all stuck together and fought for a fine, different life... I mean, if you have to fight in the streets make it for something worth while—'

'You said fighting in the streets and barricades was over,' Walt accused, him but he was imagining Bryan and himself behind a barricade opposing a street full of cruel-faced steel-helmeted attackers, and he was thinking it would take a regiment to shift the two of them.

'I said your idea of it was over.' Bill was being very patient with him, and making that clear by his tone. 'But when we've won the life we want we may have to defend it in the streets. We may have to defend ourselves against forces both inside and outside. The British capitalist has powerful friends, you know.'

'You mean the Yanks, of course.' Walt sighed rhetorically.

'Well, I certainly don't mean that Russian troops will ever move against working people! You know I'd be against any country using force on another. Socialism has to come from inside a country, because its people want it—Lenin laid it down that every nation has the right to self-determination. So if there's a fight here, we'll have to sort it out on our own.'

'Fair enough,' Walt agreed. 'Send for me and Bryan when the talking's all done...'

In May good weather came. Bill grew even busier—he seldom went home at weekends and had little time for arguments with Walt. One Sunday morning Walt went downstairs to find the old lady waiting with grim impatience. She had been venting her anger on the fire and stood facing him, straddle-legged, by the hearth, with the poker dangling. He smiled, feebly and uneasily, trying to guess what he had done.

'Where's Bill?' she demanded, and he mumbled, just coming,' slipping into his chair with relief. As soon as Bill entered, the poker rose to point at him, and he stood staring at it with his eyes popping.

'What were tha doin' yesterday afternoon?' The blue veins pulsed under the transparent skin of her temples.

'Me?' Bill glanced at Walt, who concentrated on pouring milk over his porridge.

'Aye, thee, sirree!'

'Oh—I know...' Walt looked past the old lady's head, and saw in the mirror how Bill leaned against the door's edge in a passable imitation of one of his own defiant stances. But in spite of the waving distortions he could also see the plump little hand clenched tight against a thigh as Bill answered casually: 'I sold some papers with a couple of other chaps.'

'In the street?'

'All over the estate, actually...'

'What paper?'

'The *Daily Worker.*'

'Aye!' Walt flinched as the poker clattered on to the fender. He had drunk a lot of beer on the previous night and his head was aching.

'First thing I got from Watson last night—all night. It's a Communist paper, isn't it? Goin' round from door to door and makin' a sight o' yourself. You never even asked me!'

'But why should I ask you?' Bill's voice was too high, and Walt looked up, sorry for him. This was not the kind of martyrdom Bill would be good at.

'Why?' The old lady moved forward, her whole bulk quivering and Walt swung round, half prepared to leap between her and Bill. It was Bill who he felt needed protection. '...Showin' me up like that? A Communist paper? If ever tha does that again—'

'Just a minute,' Walt broke in. 'Look, Bill is a Communist. That's one of their jobs. There's nothing—'

'Thee keep out,' she told him curtly. 'Tha're bad enough, but tha never got up to strokes like this...' She faced Bill again. 'Whyn't you tell me about this?'

'I didn't think you knew what they were.'

'I know they're a wrong lot,' she assured him. 'I know that, sirree!'

Bill pushed nervously at his hair, but he said boldly enough: 'You don't. You only know what you read in the cheap Press and what stupid old gossips like Watson tell you.'

'Thee dare!' She stepped back, tilting her head, her eyes large for once, full of green outrage. 'Dare talk back to me and call my friends?'

'But she *is* an old gossip,' Walt protested, turning from one to the other in his chair. 'You've said so yourself.'

'Tha's been told to keep out—else tha'll get summat'll not forget in a hurry!'

Walt was so astonished that he sat blinking with his mouth open. She had spoken without even looking at him. She looked silently at Bill for a moment. When she spoke, as though her anger had risen too high to exist, she was quiet-voiced and calm:

'I know what folk say about 'em. If you're mixed up wi' 'em keep it away from here—else pack up and get out.'

'I've lived here years,' Bill protested. Walt saw his eyes glisten in the light from the window, the lock of fair hair dangling across them as he stared at the old lady, half furious, half beseeching. 'It isn't fair. I've a right to follow my own beliefs without people butting in and ordering me not to...'

'Don't bandy words wi' me,' she said, still calm. She sat down, mechanically reaching for the poker as she watched Bill. 'Not another word—it's my house, this, and I'll not be defied. And no more o' that carry-on or you mun find some place else.'

Walt watched his hands open and close. He shook his head in warning as Bill glared down at him for a moment and whirled out, banging the door behind him. His halting step sounded up the stairs and Walt slowly turned to say reproachfully, ready to defy her: 'You were wrong; you shouldn't have done it. He thinks a lot of you.'

'I've nowt against him,' she said tiredly, putting down the poker. He saw how pale she was, how the blue veins throbbed, and realized how much these outbursts exhausted her. She looked very, very old, her eyes dull and almost hidden, and he could not start arguing. He said persuasively:

'He's not doing any harm—honest. You know old Bill's all right.'

'Leave it be,' she muttered. 'I'm ashamed on him mixin' wi' that crew and I'm not havin' it in my house. Now leave it be.'

He finished a miserable breakfast and went upstairs. Bill sat on the bed with his head lowered, the cold sunshine filling the room.

'Come and have some breakfast, Bill.'

'I don't want any.'

Walt closed the door and moved towards him slowly. With the

jauntiness gone, his round eyes vacant, he made Walt think of news-reels he had seen showing cattle stranded by floods, their heads wearily drooping as they listlessly watched the eternal rain.

'Cheer up, boy.' He sat on the bed beside Bill, putting an awkward hand on his shoulder. 'You know what she is...'

'If it had been you, she'd have gone on for a while and then let it drop. She wouldn't have talked to *you* like dirt for standing up to her!'

'Course she would. She's chucked me out and let me off half a—'

'No, but not like that. Not like that. I'm all right with people, me, as long as I behave and act nice—but they soon show what they think if I cross them.'

'You've got plenty of good friends, Bill. Now take it—'

'Don't, Walt—' Bill knocked his hand off, turning his head away. 'Don't baby me. You stopped people pushing you about, didn't you? But look at me—they think I'm not a bad little chap when I'm nice to them—but nobody thinks I'm really their equal, nobody ever respects me...' Walt moved uncomfortably, looking at the bent head, listening to the low spate. '...I'm the odd man, me—a sort of hanger-on who's got to watch his step. I've got to fit in with *them* all the time. I can just *feel* they're all together and I'm odd man.'

'Well, I've felt like that,' Walt said. Conquering some reluctance he put his arm around the shaking shoulders again. 'It's just how you feel...'

'Yes... and you can fight and go with your gang and take out good-looking girls. You can take the mickey out of me too—look at when we went to Atwell's; you didn't talk half as much sense as me, but they all made a fuss—'

'Ah...' Walt said contemptuously. 'Because I insulted them!'

'Because you're not a bloody cripple—'

'Oh no. Now, Bill, listen. Don't start—'

Bill jumped up, knocked his hand away once more. He brushed past Walt, and stood before the set of drawers, jerking a hand at the tilted mirror. He glared at Walt.

'Don't start what? Take a look. I've never had a girl yet!'

'You could get one easy. Don't talk daft, kid. You're as good-looking as anybody else.' He swallowed in embarrassed discomfort. He hated to see this exposure, felt repugnance at the glistening tears. Yet he was deeply sorry for Bill and wished he could offer comfort.

'Look at your comrades,' he said, speaking the word with deliberate esteem. 'They wanted you bad enough.'

'Yes.' Bill looked in the mirror for a moment. He knuckled his eyes hastily, then he passed Walt again between the two untidy beds without looking at him. He lifted a book from the table as he sat down and leaned back on his pillow. 'Yes, and listen, Walt...' Dignified, he opened the book. '...You've scoffed and made fun. But they judge a man by how sincere he is and how willing he is to work for the common good. They're not concerned with personalities.'

'I'll never kid you again, Bill,' Walt promised solemnly. 'I wish I'd bitten my silly damn tongue out first—I'm your mate, too, you know. And she'll get over this.'

'I don't really mind you,' Bill said, but there was no smile and he was looking down at his book. 'But she can't stop me for good—I may not stay here much longer...' He began reading, drawing up his knees.

Walt felt like saying that his politics seemed to have brought only unhappiness. But it seemed Mason had been right and Bill's life was already centred on his group. So there was nothing to say that could help. He went back downstairs and left Bill reading.

V

June was a hot month. The city sprawled in fiery sunlight and panted out heavy clouds of black and brown smoke which hung above the roofs until evening coolness lifted them to drift away over the hills. The heat made work unpleasant for everyone and Bill remarked that he felt faint when he watched the steelmen working in front of giant, oven-shaped furnaces, or perching on platforms and casting down manganese or molybdenum into huge ladles of white-hot, boiling steel, with sparks erupting and black-plumed flames belching up fifty feet to the iron roof.

'It's just murder in there,' he told Walt, who said: 'I can guess.'

Afternoon shift at the pit was something of an ordeal. The colliers stood in the pit yard with heavy powder-bags in one hand, water-bottles dangling from the other and snap-tins clipped to their belts, and they watched the morning shift pouring happily away from the shaft with the sun removing the stale odour of the pit, and they scowled up one last reluctant time at the hard sky. It took effort to make the first move towards the black, windy shaft, the cage, the dark, dead stuffiness of the low coal-face.

'Roll on home-time,' someone always said, and someone always answered 'Roll on sharp...' And so, shuffling on to the steel-floored cage, the long shift would begin, with the sun dying when they returned.

The kids had it best, Walt thought. School holidays meant they could run about in pants or knickers, and you saw them clambering into the rattling trams in whooping bunches, off to the outskirts where rivers and ponds were all free for those who could outrun park-keepers or farmers.

But on morning shift you could lie in the garden every afternoon and let your starved body enjoy the sun. Beer tasted good, though tepid, at weekends, and the girls were more attractive in their bright, revealing summer frocks. A lot of those afternoons in the sunshine were spent thinking about girls, and peculiar floods of sudden, objectless tenderness often made his throat ache when he did this. He wanted, he told himself; a *nice* girl; a girl with whom he could talk; a girl to go around with, protecting her, of course, and sharing tender kisses or holding hands, but primarily a girl who was quiet, likeable and nice to be with. Not the kind who wanted to boss you. If you could keep sex out of it—and with this girl it definitely would be kept out of it, since she would be a *nice* girl—perhaps the friendship wouldn't turn over-complicated or go sour. What she would look like or talk like he had no idea, but he was sure he would know her immediately when they met. In the meantime there were always other girls, different girls from her, who need not be taken seriously.

This vague, ideal girl, frequently insisted on assuming Elaine's shape, in spite of self-arguments that she had probably had another half-dozen boy-friends by now—almost equalling, though he never considered this, his total of casual girl-friends.

One Saturday a letter came from his mother to say that she had visited his father, whose condition was worse. She wrote:

'He'd like to see you and Charles. Charles is going next week and I wish you would try to visit him as well. It broke my heart to see him suffering so. He is in great pain and he's only the shadow of himself. You remember how big and strong and fine-looking he was...'

The letter went on like this for a page; an elegy, a lament for his father's lost greatness. He tore it up slowly, then burnt it, refusing to feel or think anything, rummaging in the kitchen cupboard for the shears, with the old lady protesting: 'You only cut it last week, you loon...'

That evening he was so objectionable with two strangers in a pub that Bryan had to play peacemaker and prevent a brawl. He drank so much that Bryan and Hughie insisted on seeing him home.

'Long time since I've seen *you* actin' up,' Bryan commented, but added cheerfully that it was nice to see he'd still got plenty life in him. Next evening at the club Bryan announced that he would be twenty-one on the following Saturday and that this time they were going to have a 'real' celebration and 'really bang things up'. There was to be a party at his house after the dance. 'Anybody as wants can bring a bird—I've got one lined up. My old man's been paying an endowment policy years for me and next week it's all mine. So you can get ready!'

Their cheers made everyone in the club turn to stare. Since it was such a special occasion they agreed to confer the benefits of Bryan's father's endowment policy and their ability to bang things up on the Memorial Hall and the Castle. Just like old times, as Bryan said, with all the old gang and girls. On Monday morning at the pit he wanted to know if Walt were bringing a girl: '...Make it a bird as can really enjoy herself, Walt. I mean—you're only twenty-one once. We want to let ussens go...'

Telling himself that it was only because he'd once promised to take her there, Walt phoned Elaine. He had to try two more times before, on Wednesday, he found her at home, and immediately informed her, sounding cross, that he had been calling all week.

'Why, I thought you were dead,' she answered. 'It's been so long ... But how are you, Walt?' Clear and cool her voice, he thought. The lady's voice that could rely on itself to stress and pronounce every word correctly and never become discomposed. When he told her about the celebration, she was silent for a few moments. Hunched over the telephone, finger well implanted in his ear, the sun flashing in the small mirror before his face, he impatiently urged: 'Well? Want to see it?'

'Why do you want *me* to come?'

'Because I want you to, that's all. You don't have to, of course.' He went on persuasively: 'I'd love to see you again, though—and I mean you always used to ask about it. There'll be a good time—you'll enjoy it.

'But I'm going out on Saturday,' she said, after another pause which decided him that she was merely being evasive.

'Okay,' he answered. 'I guess we *are* a bit rough and ready round here, and it'd be a rowdy— Only all the others are taking their girls.' He kept changing from persuasion to disgruntlement, reluctant to put down the phone without winning her agreement, then angry for having called her in the first place. 'But I suppose you're interested in more intellectual things nowadays.'

'You really want me to come?'

'Well, of course.'

'A lot?'

In the booth he rolled his eyes upwards and stifled a sigh.

'Ever such a lot.' He could not resist mincing the words slightly, pulling an exasperated face at the dazzling mirror.

'Well, I'll come straight to the post office at seven. I'll make some excuse.'

He was so delighted that he said 'Elaine...' and when she asked 'What?' went on seriously: 'I'm dead glad you're coming. I've missed you.'

'Well, I've missed you a bit,' she answered before the receiver clicked.

He came out of the booth wearing an inane self-congratulatory smile, thinking, at the same time as he told himself how pleased he was, that he was dying to see the faces when she walked into the Castle with him.

That Friday he withdrew all the money he had saved since Christmas and bought himself a cream shirt and grey-flecked sports coat to match dark blue gaberdines he had bought two weeks before. With his week's wages and the remainder of his savings, he had over ten pounds in his pocket on the Saturday evening as he studied himself critically in Bill's mirror. His clothes were impeccable, he decided, his lean face close-shaven, thick hair well creamed and carefully combed. He was not thinking of his effect on his friends. He was thinking: I bet I'm just as well dressed as any of her better-off boy-friends... He had spent fifteen minutes in alternately scrubbing and examining his broken nails until he heard the old lady muttering about 'turnin' into a pansy if you ask me...' as she stamped out of the kitchen.

'Don't wait up,' he called as he went out.

'I'm not likely to,' she retorted. She had given permission to stay out very late—Walt would have stayed out and risked hostilities in any case. She never locked the door on him now, and he had bought her a new string shopping bag that afternoon to put her at a disadvantage.

In the city he left the bus and took a taxi for the five-hundred-yard journey from the railway station to the post office. It was a warm evening with no breeze and the streets were amber and silver as rags of low cloud drifted under the sun; even the black sides of tall buildings glimmered bright for once. Elaine was already at the post office, not even glancing at the taxi as it pulled up, but watching those who passed. Her skin was tanned deeper, and this, with her black hair, which was still short and curly, made her dress conspicuous. It was of white linen, cut low across her breast, with a pleated skirt, and over it she wore an open, short-sleeved white bolero jacket. He saw two passing youths look over their shoulders with long, low whistles, but she coolly ignored them, except for a slight tilt of her chin.

'Hey,' he shouted. She looked round in surprise. 'Come on.' He helped her in, then gave the driver his directions. As they were pressed back into the seats, she said: 'Goodness, we're doing this in style, aren't we?'

'I can afford it,' he said airily. They sat well apart as the taxi sped along and Walt explained about Bryan and his party. 'I wanted to take the best-looking girl,' he said finally with a grin. He turned. She was clasping a small white handbag in her lap, smiling quietly as he looked at her face and at her frock, dazzling on the smooth brown skin with a tiny shadowed cleft where the sinuous rise of her breasts began, then took her hand. 'You'll blind 'em all, honest.'

'So that's what it's for?' Still smiling blandly, she glanced at his hand and then up at his face. 'I half guessed that. Even when you said you missed me.'

'But I did miss you...' Her brown stare was too calm, too knowing and self-communicant. He insisted anxiously: 'Sure I missed you, honest. Stacks of times—I said you were the only girl I liked taking out often—I just didn't call you because...' Since there had been no valid reason for not calling he could only shrug.

'Because you were jealous about the others?' she prompted him. 'We agreed that was all right...'

He shrugged again. He did not want the night to become complicated at its very beginning, but did not want to offend her either. He said evasively: 'It's a special night—it called for the only special girl I know. We always have fun, don't we?' Then he leaned back as the taxi climbed the long hill, purring past terraced houses and little shops, with people strolling and the klaxon honking at those who dared cross the road. It was like being in a cushioned cave with the breeze through open windows striking cool on their faces and plucking at their hair. Elaine turned, leaned on him for a moment with a hand on his shoulder, and kissed his mouth.

'You should have called,' she said, moving back and opening her bag. 'I missed you too.' She took out a compact, holding the mirror at arm's length as she skilfully applied a touch of lipstick. Her mood was changed: her eyes sliding darkly sideways at him while she smiled at her reflection. 'Why must I always make the first move, Walt? Sometimes I think you're half frightened of me...'

'Sure I am,' he grinned. 'Who wouldn't be?'

'One reason I came tonight'—she snapped the compact and put it away—'is that I go on holiday next week—for two months. So I may not see you for a while.'

'Oh.' He moved slowly, sitting up, hands clasped, full of disappointment. 'Oh well—it's a good job I called, eh?'

'I'll be in London some of the time, but I'm spending two or three weeks travelling abroad with my father.'

'Your father?' he repeated, then sank back and said: 'Well, that's fine for you.' Outwardly casual, he was resentfully tense.

'Well, you do approve? He's really going on business and I'm sneaking along—you know. Walt, don't frown like that.'

'Sorry,' he said, looking out of the windows. 'Didn't know I was.'

'Yes you did.' They were far apart again and becoming hostile. 'You've still got this damned thing about—my father and so on.'

'No, honest; I'm sorry. It's none of my business. He turned and spoke sincerely. The night was going to be spoiled if this started; already it seemed less special. 'I brought you out to enjoy yourself and see—' he grinned and touched her hand again—'see working-class youth on a binge, as Bill'd say. Forget the other stuff.'

'All right—I was going to suggest you try to see me in London.'

'Maybe.' He refused to think about what kind of life she might lead in London. 'But we've got all night together first, haven't we?'

'*Mister* Morris!' She rolled laughing eyes at him as the taxi swung into the yard of the public house. 'What a suggestion—and in a taxi, too!'

'You're not going to start tormenting?' he pleaded, as they got out.

'I wouldn't risk spoiling our platonic relations like that, Walt. Not when they're just beginning again. But I never know if your sense of humour's working or not.'

The taxi-driver glanced at them both before reversing his car through the gateway. She was off with her private jokes again, Walt thought as they entered the pub. Ready to lead him a dance. She took his arm, however, when they were inside the revolving doors.

In the middle of the concert room, which was not yet crowded, four tables had been joined to seat two dozen youths and girls. Bryan sat at their head, too busy yelling to a waiter at the bar to notice Walt. He was resplendent in a loose-fitting silver-grey suit, fawn shirt and polka-dot bow tie. The red-haired girl beside him was fairly pretty, but she wore too much face powder in a vain attempt to disguise a profusion of freckles on her nose, cheeks and brow. Walt knew her; her name was Myra. There were two empty chairs on Bryan's left reserved for them, and as they walked to the table the crowd around it were already singing with the band:

'*I'd like to get you... on a slow boat to China...*'

'How do you breathe in here?' Elaine was asking.

'Wait till it fills up!'

'Walt! My old marra!' Bryan stood up, already half drunk, bellowing so that everyone turned to welcome him, then ignored him to study Elaine, who carried on walking to their places, smiling brightly at Bryan. The girls looked her up and down, then glanced at one another while the youths kept on looking. Walt's chest swelled, until he saw long blond hair on the collar of a blue two-piece as Brenda looked once, Marie straining forward to see, then looked away. They were sitting between two of the gang.

'Hey-up, hey-up...' Bryan was murmuring, pulling out a chair for Elaine and gaping at her. 'So this is why he keeps duffing us, eh? Walt, lad, I don't blame thee.' Walt introduced them, hoping Elaine hadn't noticed Myra's stiffened shoulders and flat-eyed look as Bryan fussed over her. He saw everyone still staring and demanded: 'What's up with you lot? Seen a girl before, haven't you?' His friends grinned broadly, reached for their glasses, and continued to stare.

'No wonder they called him Marquis!' Bryan was leaning over the table, ignoring Myra, to fawn on Elaine—his film-star technique, Walt commented silently. In a plaintive voice Bryan asked what Walt had got that they hadn't, rolling his eyes at her, his hands flat on the table holding his weight. Elaine was obviously enjoying herself, but Walt wondered if she were laughing with Bryan or at him.

'Walt has lots of talents...' Her eyes darted sideways. 'I bet he has lots of girls he never tells you about—lots...'

'I wouldn't want another girl if I'd got you.' Bryan was almost crooning, his red-haired partner's eyes growing smaller as she pretended to be listening to Hughie Sawford. When the drinks came Elaine was made to swallow hers straight down, which she did with a grimace, and Bryan paid for more. Around the tables they were talking or singing in little groups—there were too many of them for a general conversation— and three waiters were being kept busy. Walt covertly watched Brenda, who was acting very vivaciously, chattering to Tug Henderson and Marie without looking once at him. At the same time he could hear Bryan: 'My party's made now you two's here... Yes, my best marra that is—I could tell thee some tales, Elaine... He's a lucky lad, though, findin' one like thee...'

And tomorrow, Walt thought, would bring earnest warnings not to let her get the hooks in...

'I think you're nice too,' Elaine said. 'We should tell Walt.'

'I've been waitin' five minutes for a drink,' Myra frigidly interrupted, 'if it isn't too much *trouble*... Bryan bawled at a waiter, slapped some money on the table and ogled Elaine once more. 'Thee and me'd get on fine, lass. But we'd best not get the old Marquis wi' his rag up. He's a terror when he gets goin', my mate, you know...'

'He isn't the jealous type, are you, terror?' Her eyes flickered gleefully as she patted Bryan's huge hand and asked Walt: 'Why didn't you tell me you had such nice friends?'

'He does this as a matter of principle,' Walt informed her, and leaned in to whisper: 'You're doing fine, love—but watch the redhead...' She merely laughed, her eyes brightly flecked, and continued flirting with Bryan in spite of Myra's malicious looks. He talked to her about the gang, their girls and adventures, while Walt sat feeling proud of her every time some youth turned admiringly to look at her face or quick-moving hands or when a girl regarded her thoughtfully. A dainty leveret unconcerned among large birds, he thought, who ruffled their feathers but dare not attack. He glanced again at Brenda because he was trying not to, and found her watching him. She nodded curtly when he risked a tentative smile.

'Tug and Joe brought them two,' Bryan said. 'I didn't know they was coming.'

'Who?' Elaine asked, and Bryan explained, not even noticing Walt's frown.

'So that's Brenda!' Walt uneasily emptied another glass as she looked with interest down the tables. 'We always wondered what she was like when Bill—'

'Who the hell's "we"?' he demanded roughly, banging down his glass. 'Stop staring and finish your drink, will you?' But he could not prevent himself turning, and saw Brenda meeting Elaine's stare, bosom and jaw both proudly raised and out-thrust, the blue eyes suddenly flashing to him. He stopped thinking that Elaine was much finer than these other girls. He felt she had no right to look at Brenda or comment, as she did: 'She's quite attractive... A terrific figure...'

'Them two was no easy catch,' Bryan boasted, waving his hand so that it was quite obvious whom he was talking about. 'It took a pair like me and Walt to get them interested.' He nudged Elaine and she lurched against Walt, her eyes widening. '...Only they got too interested, kid.' While he laughed, Walt broke in suddenly: 'Shut up, Bry—Brenda's a good lass.' He felt like going to sit beside her so that she would know how he would never demean or mock her this way. 'She was fair enough to me when I went with her. Just because we chucked —'

'I know she was fair enough!' Bryan shouted, and his laughter roared again. Walt and Hughie Sawford exchanged significant looks as an empty glass went toppling.

Elaine kept him happy for some time, with the large room filling and smoke gathering and curling around the tables, empty glasses lining up until a waiter would collect them and carry them off. When Bryan went to the cloakrooms with some others, Walt made excuses for him to Elaine: '...the best thing'll be if he gets too drunk to be awkward. But it *is* his twenty-first, after all.'

'But I like him,' she protested. 'He's what you'd call'—her eyes twinkling mischievously up at him, three small empty glasses before her —'colourful, Walt.'

'Bry's all right. Look, if he starts bragging me off...' He frowned, embarrassed, turned wholly round on his chair close to her. 'He does it, you know. I guess it's him being so big and sure of himself, you know. He seems to want to look after me with girls. He brags me off in case they think I'm nowt—nothing special. Don't pay any attention, will you? Because it makes me look a bit silly when he really gets going.'

'Of course I'll pay attention. I want to hear about your hidden past.'

'Well, you'd just better watch Myra!' She was in that mood, he thought. The less he said the better. 'She's not a redhead for nowt.'

At half past eight Bryan clambered on to the stage, a little hurt because Walt had refused to make it a duet, and treated the packed, noisy audience to 'Twenty-one Today'. The musicians gave up the attempt to keep time with him, but with his usual enthusiasm he sang four more songs before he decided he wanted some beer and got down. On his way back he knocked over a stool, sending the girl on it sprawling, and he stayed there for five minutes apologizing and buying drinks for the table, thumping everyone's back. Walt and Hughie kept a wary watch over him, but neither of them was quite sober since Bryan had been plying them with rum and the two girls with gin. Walt was full of taut exhilaration, while Elaine had developed a tendency to lurch on her stool when she laughed and bump against him when she turned to speak. Members of the gang kept coming, ardently ogling and out to make an impression, bringing her a drink and asking to be introduced, so that she sat with a variety of mixtures and colours before her, reaching for whatever took her fancy. Walt warned her about mixing drinks and was told not to fuss: '...I'm only taking a tiny sip of each... When Bryan returned, he and Elaine kept their heads close together and Walt knew he was being talked about, especially when she turned, laughing, to say: 'Poor Walt, did I get you the name of Marquis?'

No use trying to stop them, he thought, as she turned again to Bryan.

At the crowded bar a face smiled, but it took a moment to realize that this was Blackie; Blackie in a Royal Marines uniform, white cap and white belt against dark blue, hair cut short and shoulders pressed back as though he had never slouched with drooping hands. He came over to talk, bringing drinks for Walt and Elaine and leaning for a while over Walt's chair. When Walt asked how long he had been a marine, he said: 'A few months. All my old mates has been called up now.' He hooked a thumb in his belt. He still drawled, though not so lazily. 'I'm in for five years.' When Walt demanded why, he shrugged. 'Well, why not? I hadn't much on a job and I were fed up wi' it. Fed up knockin' about here, an' all. You can do all right as a regular, you know. I could be a sergeant afore I'm thirty, maybe!' When he returned to the bar, straight-backed, Walt noticed, wearing the uniform and sticking out his chest as though proud, Walt thought: Now he'll be able to carry a real gun sometimes... At least Blackie was doing something about his life. He looked around him in the smoking, roaring, clinking and clattering, shouting din, at laughing or drinking or talking faces, and he thought of how casually Blackie had said: '...Fed up knockin' about here, an' all...'

I'm getting fed up too, he realized, then looked up to watch Elaine steer a graceful if slightly off-course exit to the cloak-rooms, with people turning to watch the swaying white frock on the small, bronzed, black-headed figure.

'Boy, she's worth looking at,' Bryan commented. 'Th'art a lucky old ram, Walt lad.'

'You stop telling her things,' Walt ordered him, receiving an amicable, mollifying pat on the shoulder while Bryan grinned obscurely. He was angry, imagining the teasing Elaine would be inspired to after all this. 'Stop telling her everything about me—and stop making cracks about her being my girl. She's not a steady—I just brought her like you brought Myra.'

'Is that so?' Bryan asked, looking quite pleased. Then he narrowed one eye and murmured: 'You'd better tell old Bren that. She keeps looking up here pretty niggly.' He grinned again before turning to the neglected redhead.

Walt looked down at Brenda, telling himself that she was too proud to start any scenes with another girl. She smiled at something Tug said, Marie's falsetto whooping over all the other laughter, and, watching her composure, he thought: I always admired her, anyway. I gave up a lot, in one way...

He was half regretful, and therefore guiltily quick to take offence when Elaine patted his shoulder, standing behind him and smiling mock sympathy, glancing down the table as she inquired: 'Memories, Walt? You look full of regrets.'

'Don't talk like a sloppy film,' he answered as she sat down, brightly regarding him.

'Sorry,' she said. 'I didn't know you were touchy about it.'

'Well, I'm not, really,' he said more gently. 'I'm sorry I—'

'Why didn't you tell us you weren't his girl?' Bryan demanded, beaming, with half the heads around the table turning. 'Honest, thought you was till he just told me, love. Not as I mind, like ...' He leered.

'I didn't think it was so important,' Elaine replied. She picked up the glass Blackie had brought. 'I thought I *was* his girl tonight —for tonight.'

'Well, she's not *thine*, is she?' Myra pointed out to Bryan, so obviously prepared for battle that Bryan decided she was the only girl for him and began assuring her of it. Walt drank his heavy-odoured rum, then said to Elaine: 'Look, don't pay any—'

'You were quite right, Walt,' she told him, regarding him with partially glazed dignity. 'Don't let other people push you into anything.'

'All right, don't get all haughty,' he muttered. They sat quiet, drinking with careful concentration. With her beside him, finding the beer and rum had not made him drunk, and with the others rowdy all around, he thought: *She's* all right! She doesn't need to push it all into one night; she doesn't have to grind it out at anything. She's got her old man to keep her and push her through a university she's not that bothered about going to —and take her abroad for holidays and...'

'Stop mixing your drinks,' he snapped, and she said: 'They're my drinks, aren't they?'

'What do you want to drink like that for?' he demanded.

'We came out to have fun, didn't we?'

'You don't have to worry,' he said. 'You've a couple of months doing nowt in London to look forward to.'

'There are times,' she said slowly, looking in front of her face smooth as she raised a glass, 'when you bore me...'

He flinched. His muscles locked, and across the table Hughie, Sawford stared and then frowned at him. Elaine sipped and put the glass down calmly.

'All right, Walt?' Hughie asked. 'You're dead white, kid.'

'All right.' He nodded as his limbs painfully eased. Then he said to her, 'We've got to stop this, haven't we?' and she smiled immediately; innocent, amenable and manifestly part withdrawn.

'I will when you will,' she offered.

'It's me,' he said repentantly. 'I know it is.'

She nodded and said that she knew that, too. 'Maybe you'll outgrow it,' she suggested, and he went stiff again.

The party broke up at this point because most of them could drink no more, and some wanted to dance. With Bryan raucous-voiced in the lead, his arm around Myra, they poured out into the twilit streets and walked to the dance hall, a noisy, straggling crowd which spread over the pavements and roadway destroying the peaceful dusk.

'You don't mind my holding your arm, I hope,' Elaine said leaning heavily on Walt. 'Only I feel a bit woozy.' He slipped an arm around her waist and told her: 'Ten to one you'll be sick.'

'You shouldn't do that.' She was mumbling her words a little. The fresh air, he thought. 'People will only get the wrong impression...' He looked down at her bobbing head without answering. While she went on talking, aimlessly it seemed, about hating the idea of compromising him, he wondered why his drinking had affected him so strangely. His body felt drunk—full of undirected turbulence—yet his mind stayed detached to watch. All the wildness and noisiness of the night, like Bryan's over-boisterousness, seemed unnecessarily exaggerated. He felt as though they were all play-acting; pretending that they wanted only this, yet ensuring that no doubts could penetrate by discharging a constant screen of energy and noise.

In the dance hall the lights were dimmed for a waltz and the floor was crowded. Elaine said she felt much better. One of the gang came to ask her for a dance—the news that she wasn't Walt's girl had spread quickly—and as they moved away she winked over the youth's shoulder at Walt, calling:

'See you later, Marquis.'

The place hadn't changed, he thought, even though there were many new faces. The strange youths grouped around the hall or slowly shuffling in a revolving mass of dancers under a weaving spotlight looked no different from those who had always come here. Crowded floor, stuffy air, coloured lights in the gloom, and the same clash of gaudy clothes with sober, the same sprinkling of hard faces and tough expressions, the same expectant-faced girls and exchanges of sidewards, estimatory glances between them and the young men. A hundred other places like it, ten thousand other young dancers, scattered all over the hills and valley of the city.

'I'm getting fed up with it all,' he remarked, nodding as Blackie appeared beside him. 'I don't know why. It's always the bloody same, though.'

'You see more life in t' services,' Blackie said.

Below the stage Bryan was sprawling in a chair with Myra on his knees and a group around him laughing and joking. He did not want to join them. He saw Brenda standing alone, looking among the dancers for Marie, and impulsively walked over to her. When he greeted her, she said, 'Hello, Walt', and looked at the dancers again, not hostile but seemingly indifferent, while the coloured lights glistened softly on her chiselled cheek, then left her in shadow again.

'You're looking great,' he said. He wanted to touch her shoulder and say that she was still a lovely girl, that it was hard, a little hurtful, to see her as a girl like the other indifferent girls who passed, strangers in an endless wheeling of indifferent strangers.

'You're doing all right yourself.' The blue eyes surveyed him, from suede shoes to creamed hair. 'You didn't turn out so leery after all. Still tailing on wi' Bryan, I notice.'

He saw Elaine smiling at a fresh partner as she went past; a youth he had not seen before.

'Bryan's my mate, that's all. How's your family, Bren?'

'Just the same,' she answered, watching the dancers again, and he was ashamed of knowing what was a cause of shame to her yet of sharing nothing else with her now. An outburst of laughter made them look down to where Myra sprawled on the floor, having been jerked there from

Bryan's knees. Bryan was as convulsed as the rest of the gang while he tried to hoist the indignant girl up again. Brenda's look made him move his shoulders uneasily and say, as though in apology: 'Well, you're only twenty-one once.'

'You'd nearly be that if you'd been tellin' the truth that time, wouldn't you?' she remarked casually, and he said he'd see her later, sheepishly hurrying back to Blackie.

'Your judy's doing all right.' Blackie's buttons glittered as he shoved out his chest at some girls glancing. 'Been excused four times...' Elaine drifted past, smiling up at a talking, tall partner, but winking archly at Walt when she saw him.

'I'd better watch her. She's a bit tight.'

'That's what they're all thinkin',' Blackie drawled significantly, and Walt looked at him sharply, then moved nearer the edge of the floor and watched. When the waltz ended, Elaine's tall partner kept hold of her hand, urging her it seemed, but before Walt had moved some of the gang casually surrounded her, talking as they guided her to where Bryan was sitting while her ex-partner stared after them. When Walt joined the group she was laughing, a sheen on her brown skin under the bright lights, her eyes merry. She greeted him: 'Well—you must be the only boy in here I haven't danced with.'

Triumphant, Walt thought. Triumphant, with a tendency to lurch if she rested too long on one leg. He pointed out that Bryan wouldn't be dancing with her: '...He's not capable of gettin' Myra off his lap.' Bryan joined in their laughter, almost knocking Myra to the floor again with a boisterous thump while he bent forward, shaking his blond head. Music began and Walt adroitly moved Elaine on to the floor, with disappointed cries coming from behind as they danced away.

'You're in big demand, eh?'

'Everybody knows I'm no one's property, you see,' Elaine answered. 'You're compromising yourself again, you know.' She looked around her airily.

'Now look—'

'I saw you talking to—is it Brenda?' Her eyes gleamed up, wicked, then she looked around again. 'She really has got a terrific figure, hasn't she? Fine shape...' He began saying he had only been polite to the girl, but she interrupted: 'You don't have to make excuses, Walt. You've every right to...' She lurched out of step, smiled as he steadied her, and went on thoughtfully: 'You know, they say it's an unconscious wish for babyhood that attracts some men to big-breasted women...'

He looked over her head, his face red and stiff, and she inquired: 'Do you think you want to return to babyhood, Walt?' As though, he thought furiously, she were asking if he liked to rumba. She pouted at his continued silence.

'I suppose her performance wasn't up to appearances—since you did give her up. They say that's common...'

'Listen a minute.' He squeezed her shoulder with his right hand until she winced. 'I know you're tight, but this is a tough place—behave, will you?'

'I'm not doing anything,' she protested, wriggling till he moved his hand. One of the gang tapped his shoulder, and as she danced away, Elaine called: 'Lecture me later. Besides, look at the bodyguards I have.'

'It's them you want to watch,' he retorted, and then saw Brenda dancing with a stranger. He cut in, and she took his hand, moving against him without smiling as they danced. He held her close, quiet with the old resistant softness gathered against his chest, and he remembered her—moments of tenderness, albeit maternal—when she had proffered comfort if that were what he wanted, then he wished there had been a little more to it; just a little more. She was such a fine girl—and she was such a handsome, shapely girl...

'I'm fed up with all this, Bren,' he said over the shuffling and music.

'Happen you're growing out on it at last.' When she looked up, he pleaded impulsively: 'You don't still think I'm rotten, do you? A crawler and all that? Do you, Bren?'

'No.' She looked over his shoulder. As composed as Elaine, he thought, but not naturally so, like her. Brenda's was a conscious, guarded composure; she held herself down. 'You'd've been all right if you'd listened to me. I told you what was best for you.' And if they were reunited, he wondered, would she be advising him over things in a week, mothering him in a fortnight and bossing him in a month? Would she still shame him?

'You don't belong wi' 'em, Walt. Your new piece doesn't, either.' As they passed Bryan they saw him, his head close to Myra's, pass a caressing hand along the girl's thigh, and up her waist to rest on her breast. Others had also noticed, and Walt felt Brenda's silent judgment.

'I know, Bren,' he said. 'It's a bit rough. I'm getting fed up with it all.'

'I knew you would.' Her hand tightened slightly and he put his face closer, the fragrance of her scent, cosmetics and hair capturing him with the memory of dancing so, bodies joined and a silent promise for later. She felt it also, her face touching his and arm around his neck, but he knew it was momentary and would vanish if they spoke. Even when the music ended, and they waited, both were quiet until, as another tune began, Brenda exclaimed:

'Huh—your new piece is doing all right now.'

As they moved, he looked and saw Blackie teaching Elaine the new bop steps, swinging her out to arm's length. Her bolero coat was removed, her naked back and small round shoulders glistening, and as she spun round her skirt flared in a white swirl high above her knees. A moment later he looked again and saw her still laughing, body curved backwards with her high breasts strained against the upward cup of her dress.

'Look at 'em drooling.' Brenda tugged him into correct step as he faltered. The youths around Bryan were fixedly staring at Elaine's legs or shoulders while she whirled. 'She's a tart! I don't care how she puts it on and trips around—she's a real tart.'

'No, she's not,' he said fiercely, and she raised her eyebrows, scornfully smiling after a moment, relaxing away from him: 'She's got you hooked!

'It's not that. But she's a decent lass—she's used to places where they can dance like that.'

'I've been to plenty decent places—but I know better than to dance half naked in here.'

'Only her shoulders...' he muttered. He looked no more, but all the turbulence that had ranged free in him now quickly coalesced into the fighting urge. He grew tense, and Brenda remarked: 'So you haven't grown out on that? Walt, you're a dope to get in trouble over a tart like her.'

'Cut it out, Bren,' he said softly, and she shrugged, but only paused before adding: 'Anybody can see what she is.'

They were moving down the hall again, and he saw Tug Henderson tap Blackie's shoulder, then whirl Elaine in a faster, more frenetic dance that made her look a little bewildered. As he released Brenda, she said: 'She's no more your sort than they are...' She turned away and he pushed through the dancers as Elaine almost stumbled at the end of a wild turn. Tug was a stocky youth, but not much of a boxer or fighter, so that his prestige was less than Walt's, and Walt could seize his left wrist in one hand, catching Elaine in the other as she was flung outward. Half surprised at his own fury, for she was not really his property after all and his ability to defend her had therefore not been challenged, he released Elaine, and said to Tug, 'Have this one wi' me,' his voice automatically roughened to a growl.

'Hold on, Walt,' Tug protested in alarm. 'What's up?'

'She's not a show-piece. She's not here for you to see how fast you can chuck her about and how much leg you can make her show. I know you, Tug.' Since he had stood before now watching other girls' legs when Tug danced with them, the last remark was irrefutable. 'She can dance wi' who she likes...' He looked around them, wanting an argument from any one of them. '...But there's none o' that stuff, see?'

Hughie Sawford watched quietly, nodding assurance, but the others evaded his eyes. Bryan, only now dimly realizing that something was wrong, was gaping over Myra s shoulder, preparing to rise.

'Okay, Walt,' Tug said. 'I'm sorry.'

When Walt released him, he turned away with a non-committal shrug. Disappointed and full of aggression, Walt turned to find Elaine looking perplexed.

'I don't think he really meant...' she began, though she looked dubious.

'Elaine,' he said, like a patient father, 'you know nowt about this place.' He made her sit down beside Bryan, who had to be reassured that the trouble was over. After some rumbling and vague threats Bryan wrapped his arms around Myra, and Walt leaned over Elaine, lecturing her on dancing like that in a place like this.

'Well, you should look after me,' she defended herself when he was finished. 'You brought me.'

He pointed out that he couldn't help others cutting in and she pointed out that he could stand near by and watch her.

'With you dancing with every wolf in the hall?' he demanded.

'Well,' she said, sweetly smiling, 'I can't help people cutting in, can I?'

He tried glowering down with his jaw thrust at her, his eyebrows pulled down. Most of the gang would have been subdued, but the sweet smile persisted. So he leaned in, close to her face, demanding: 'Why don't you put your jacket on?'

'Because it's hot.' She touched her brow where there were mere glistening pin-points in the dark hair-roots. A very smooth brow, he saw; a tiny ear peeping from under curls, a soft hollow where the shoulders cupped her throat and a shadow between the swell of her breasts against their white curb; the whole brown and smooth and supple, evoking an image of her naked. He was confused, bashful, and the blood throbbed in his cheeks. He found that she was looking at his eyes, the smile more sincere, but as she started to speak he straightened up again.

'You are frightened of me, Walt,' she said lightly, and he waited for his face to cool, without answering. When he looked, she said immediately:

'My hero'—clasping her hands with an expression of adoration —'rushing to my rescue.'

'Glad you appreciate it.' He frowned suspiciously.

'And even breaking off his necking party to do it.' Her expression helplessly broke down into that wicked grin and he wanted to smack her. 'I had time to notice that before Blackie excused me, you know...'

Her smile or laughter could rouse him more than any tirade of

Brenda's, he admitted, as he grunted and turned away. She evoked from him the same intense over-reactions as his mother. They were both able to consistently probe his blind spot; blind because he could not tell why they aroused such violent furies.

'I'm getting you out of no more scrapes tonight,' he said distantly, and broke his vow only ten minutes later. Blackie asked if she could dance with him, and having received Walt's stern permission, Elaine overdoing the meek expression, he thought grimly, they went off into the crowd. He was talking with Hughie Sawford a few minutes later when there was a scuffle and chorus of shouts in the middle of the floor.

He knew that Elaine must be in it, and knew he had been waiting, perhaps eager, for this. With half the gang following he bounded across the floor, thrusting his way through the ringed watchers to where Blackie was tussling with the tall youth who had partnered Elaine earlier and tried to hold her in talk. Standing alone as though the audience held aloof, Elaine looked frightened as she watched the fight, a disarranged curl dangling over her eyes and her hand before her mouth.

The tall youth swung at Walt as he jumped between them, but Walt ducked the blow and struck him twice in the face, open-handed as though invincible with no need to punch. The other was impressed enough to step back warily, his cheeks fiery from the slaps.

'What's it about?' Walt asked, with Hughie and the others crowding through behind him. Dabbing a cut lip Blackie said the tall youth had wanted to cut in: '…but your judy didn't want to dance wi' him, so I told him and he let fly at me.'

The tall youth was glaring belligerently as he realized how much bigger he was than anyone opposing him. He half raised his fists as Walt said brusquely:

'There's more of us than there is of you. Drop it and clear off.'

'Who're you to give orders?'

'He's the one as fought Jack Ford afore he went pro,' Blackie said with relish. 'Held him six rounds and all.'

'Is she your girl?' The other lowered his hands a little. When Walt nodded he said, 'Why'nt you look after her, then?' and moved away, his friends following him.

'Let's do 'em, Walt,' someone urged behind him. 'You could take him easy!' With Bryan out he was their champion, it seemed. And he felt a champion, a lion rampant, with his drunken energies boiling as he looked around at the bigger ones who should be better ones but knew his reputation, as Elaine clasped his arm, shaking her head, as he thought with the same satiety and coming of temporary ease that had followed his fight with Jack Ford: *They look up to me. Bigger, and they look up to me*…

'What did he do to you earlier?' he asked her, with the audience still waiting in a ring. 'Nothing, Walt, honestly. I just didn't like the way he talked and looked at me. Please don't fight over me, Walt. I'd hate it.' She looked distraught.

He didn't want to fight. He had had his triumph. Slipping an arm around her waist, he guided her through the dispersing crowd with the disappointed gang following. Brenda looked at him over a shoulder, an eyebrow raised and the corners of her mouth turned down. The band began playing again.

'It's a horrible place,' Elaine said, as they reached Bryan. 'I was quite enjoying it until that happened.'

He sat down and pulled her on to his knees, while the others moved away to find partners.

'I shouldn't have brought you,' he said. She was docile and let him pull her against him, her head on his chest. 'Not all the dance halls are like this, Elaine. It's us that pick the rough dumps.'

'But if you hadn't publicly disowned me, they'd have left me to dance with you.'

'I didn't ...' Explaining was too much trouble. Instead he told her: 'I didn't want to spoil your fun—you wanted to talk to others, didn't you?'

'You didn't want to spoil your own fun!' She raised her head to look at him. 'With Brenda.' Lowering it again, she murmured. 'Perhaps you've got an Oedipus complex.' She was too upset to argue with, he thought. Trying to sound disdainful, but glad enough to remain curled on his knee and ignore the dancing. She was watching Bryan as he kissed Myra, nibbling her ear and caressing her.

'Hey-up,' Walt said. 'Can't you wait till you get home?' Bryan winked, a lid slowly drooping over a lustful eye, and Walt said to Elaine: 'Come on, never mind the party. Let's go.'

'Why?'

'Because I've a good idea about what kind of party it's going to be by the time this lot's finished collecting last-waltz pick-ups.'

'You're so fiercely moral about some things!' She sat up straight to study him. 'Why do you disapprove of a party like that?'

'Why? I just...' He wriggled his shoulders during an inarticulate moment of embarrassed shyness as she looked, puzzled, at his eyes '...I don't like that sort of stuff. It's not decent—some things should be kept private.'

They stood up, and as Elaine put on her short jacket she said: 'You know, under everything else you're just dying to be good —you're afraid to admit it for some reason. I think all of you are pretending to yourselves a bit—you all stop being wolves when you're dancing with a girl and she talks—except his kind,' and she nodded across the hall at the tall youth. 'But you especially, Walt.'

'What do *you* know?' he growled, gruff because her docility had soon gone. 'Let's go...'

In spite of Bryan's protests and the gang's appeals, they left the hall. It was growing dark and the cooler air made the girl shiver for a moment, rubbing her arms and shaking her head dazedly.

'I don't feel awfully well,' she said, taking his arm, with her bag in the other hand. They saw a taxi cruising in the main road and Walt hailed it, saying grandly as he helped her in: 'Might as well finish how we started...'

It was dark, the street lights flashing past and a breeze whipping their faces. Elaine leaned back and quickly sat up again, saying she daren't close her eyes: '...It's nothing for you to laugh at, getting a girl in this condition.'

Dreaming dance music came from the crackling radio in the front. He sat by the window looking at the flashing silhouettes of people and traffic.

'How long are you going to keep that kind of life up, Walt?' she asked.

'I don't know.' He added defensively: 'Till I find something I like better—it's no worse than drooling about politics in cafes.'

'Don't keep throwing Atwell's at me,' she said mildly. 'After all, I'm not a regular there—you know that. Besides, there's less harm in drinking coffee and talking politics than—all that fighting. The people there are harmless.'

'They've got Bill where he is. Mason didn't do him much good.'

'Poor old Andrew can't do himself much good—don't pick on him. Lots of people hold his past against him.'

'Being a Red? Walt turned. She was sitting up very straight, holding on to the strap and trying to talk naturally, though she looked a little anxious. Her handbag was on the floor. 'He said they'd forgiven him that.'

'No, not just that—even the Reds would probably have kicked him out when the scandal started. They couldn't afford to...'

'What scandal?'

'You didn't know—about his affair? I thought you'd have guessed, anyway. It was Judith who told me... They say he's changed now, but...'

'Mason had an affair?' Walt grinned, shaking his head. The horsy teeth and bald head! He slapped his knee. 'Didn't think he had it in him.'

'Well, it wasn't funny when it came out.' She looked surprised at him. 'He was lucky to keep his job—only nothing was definitely proved, of course. But they say it was a boy at the college...'

'Boy?' It was a moment before he could say: 'He's a queer? Mason's a queer?'

'Why are you so horrified?' Elaine asked. 'You didn't guess? I don't say he is now—his private life's a secret, if he has one but he's a terribly lonely, unhappy man. Didn't Bill know?' As he continued to stare, she said: 'Oh, Walt, don't look so thunderstruck. You're terribly naïve sometimes!'

'Is that so?' he muttered, only partly attending to her. 'You take it pretty casually...' He could not understand her. Queers were horrors who painted their faces and simpered; untouchables you saw in pubs and avoided with loathing if you were alone; jeered at contemptuously, perhaps, if you were with the gang. Hideous, mincing horrors, evoking both the disgust of present youth and the crawling fear of childhood warnings about strange men. To have been friendly with one, been touched by one, and not to have known what he was, shocked him and made him feel unclean.

'Well, he can't help what he is,' Elaine reasonably pointed out. 'Doesn't it occur to you how rotten life can be for him?'

'I don't like freaks,' he said coldly, turning his face to the window again.

'Oh, Walt—you're a puritanical wolf!'

'I don't like queers and freaks of any sort,' he said. 'I don't like that dreamy, talky crowd at all. You lot make me sick at times. Spouting about *me*!...'

'We lot, I suppose, being anyone not in your personal group of friends.'

'You know what I mean.'

She was taut and angry and he was sulky and angry, keeping his face to the glass in disgusted silence while the taxi hummed along with its tyres slapping the concrete and clattering over manholes. He felt the tension of this silent, angry nearness growing unbearable until a stifled hiccough sounded, followed by a giggle. As he turned stiffly, she hiccoughed again and laughed with her hand over her mouth. With sudden huge relief he began laughing too, and when she hiccoughed again they bent towards each other laughing helplessly.

'I can't keep my dignity,' she complained. She tried holding her breath, and Walt pounded her back, but the spasms persisted until the taxi stopped at Elaine's home.

'Pay him off,' she said, red-faced with laughter and effort. 'You can get another.' She had trouble unlocking the door, fumbling with the key and giggling until Walt took it from her.

'Keep quiet,' she whispered. 'They'll be in bed—I said I'd be late.' But when she switched on the light and saw a tray holding milk and biscuits on a table by the settee, she began laughing again.

'Milk!' she hissed, and doubled up. The idea of milk following all she had drunk seemed uproariously funny as she bent over with curls tossing, pulling faces at him.

'Milk, though!' she said, pointing, and they were both convulsed, staggering across the room and crumpling on the settee, laughing every time one looked at the other.

'Do stop it, Walt,' she pleaded, while he protested it was her. They had to look away from each other until the last exhausted shudder passed, and they lay back holding their stomachs. With a long deep sigh, Elaine removed her coat, then put her head back, spreading out her arms.

'I feel better, but I daren't close my eyes,' she said. 'It was fun, anyway, apart from that nasty ending.'

Walt lay quiet, enjoying the warmth and peace of the room. As she sat forward with her legs crossed and hands together, looking at him, he glanced uneasily at her bare shoulders and at her face, still glowing after their laughter.

'How strong is this love of violence, Walt?' she asked, abruptly serious.

'I don't know,' he said after a moment, frowning at her.

She studied him. 'You don't know? Well, why are you so violent?'

'I'm not.' He sat up. The questions and her intent look bothered him. He lit a cigarette. 'I'm not like that all the time. Just sometimes—when...' He shrugged, spinning the match over the top of the dead electric fire into a spotless hearth. 'When something gets me feeling like that.'

'You've got some deep-rooted complex,' she began sagely explaining, but he cut her off with: 'Oh, for Pete's sake, Elaine!'

'All right, then.' She made a slight acquiescent move of her shoulders. 'If you won't listen... But you can't go on like this. There's more to your future than these rowdy weekends, and if you're going to be a manager some day...'

'I'm not going to be a manager,' he said. He had not realized he felt so definite about it. 'I'm not cut out for it.'

'Well, whatever you're going to be—you'll have to start living your weekends a little differently some time.'

'You don't understand what I've put into being just what I am right now.' As she made to answer, he added: 'I'm sticking to it—it's my life.'

'But of course it's your life.' She smiled gently, talking in an adult way that irked him. 'But you'll change gradually, won't you? You'll want more than hectic weekends.' The sage, advisory attitude would have been more becoming, he thought, if she had not kept gently swaying now and again, and if her face were not flushed and hair disarranged. 'You read too much and you're quiet too often—you think too much, Walt—not to know there's more than that.'

'Getting married and that'll come in its own time,' he said irritably, restless because she had touched his discontent and he did not like to admit it. He did not know what he wanted. But he knew what he did not want. 'If you're thinking of politics and the Atwell's stuff—I told Mason what I reckon about that.'

She smiled: 'But you don't still believe in that diatribe about lions?'

'Yes, I do. It's as good as Bill's holy-Joe stuff and Mason's talk. It's no worse than you with your Socialist sister and well-off father. Honest, if you only realized what a queer bunch you were—you keep telling *me* what I've got to do!' He stood up, dragging on his cigarette and wishing she would leave him alone.

'Bill and his party!' he growled contemptuously. 'You lot and your "working class this" and "working class that"! You've got no bloody idea ...'

'Well, don't get all snobbish,' she complained, looking resignedly up at him. 'I didn't say politics.' She leaned back and said thoughtfully: 'You're just full of resentment. You rant at politics for some reason of your own —and someone you're down on, I suppose. You're awful for this, Walt— you blame me as though it's my fault Daddy doesn't push a barrow or something... You blame poor Andrew Mason for not being normal. You blame everyone for things they can't help!'

'Daddy!' he said contemptuously. 'If you're on your sister's side against your old man why don't you earn yourself a living instead of letting him keep you? That's what I can't stand.' He threw the cigarette in the hearth and looked down at her, jerking a hand fiercely. 'That gets me! If I'm against my old man or anybody else, I'm against them and I stick to it. But if you take from people you owe 'em loyalty. You're keeping in with *your* father and going against and all. It's two-faced...'

'I'm doing nothing of the sort!' She jumped up and tilted back her head to return his scowl, her face under his. 'There you go again! It's nothing to do with me what Judith is. You just resent what my father is!'

'You agree with her!'

'I'm not fierce about it... Besides, what would you want me to do? Wave a flag or something?—or go round punching people on the nose?'

'Don't get catty,' he said, the first to turn away.

'Don't you be childish, then. You've spoiled the whole night with all this. We could have had lots of fun.'

'You did all right...' He dropped on to the settee again. 'You were the belle of the ball, with all the men after you. I knew you'd love that. I only had to fish you out of trouble.'

She stood looking at him. She frowned and rumpled her hair with a few quick rubs as though trying to adjust to the change in subject.

'I wish you'd make up your mind,' she said slowly. 'Now you're jealous.'

'Me?' He grinned and waved an airy hand. 'Cut it out.'

'Yes you are,' she insisted, as she sat down, turned towards him.

'I am not!' he snapped, and sat glaring while she put her head to one side and looked thoughtful for a while. She folded her hands together. Walt looked away.

'Did you sleep with Brenda?' she asked, and he jerked round.

'No.'

'But you made love to her? That's what I mean.'

He blushed, and this made him defiant. He mumbled: 'Yeah, I did. And she was the first, if you want to know everything.'

'Did she seduce you, Walt?' She sounded greatly interested.

He hunched his body, red-faced, and blinked at her, but she continued to watch with her head cocked on one side, eyes twinkling.

'I didn't need much seducing,' he admitted. 'I was pretty keen.'

She nodded, and thought for a while. Then she said seriously, judiciously: 'I wouldn't mind being seduced, only I'd like to feel it was really worth while—well, romantic even; there's nothing wrong in wanting it to be romantic. I think it should be—well, it should all feel—good— you know.'

He sat staring at her gesturing hands.

'Why don't you act more romantically with me?' she demanded impatiently. The blood rampaged in his face and neck again. He felt like a schoolboy watching a woman undress. 'Plenty of others have tried to seduce me— and you've seduced other girls. But you never try with me.' It was a complaint: peevish.

'I don't *want* to seduce you!' He was on his feet again, so acutely self-conscious that he felt nothing could cause him to go near her now. Her shoulders lifted and she sighed.

'I didn't say you had to—I just want to understand. You say one thing one minute... I'm sure you don't want me for a steady girl because you want to go chasing after—Walt, do stop blushing, it's so childish!' She looked annoyed, and to his surprise his cheeks began to cool. After a moment she went on: 'Just be serious. You know, it's this decency and indecency idea of yours, I think. You don't mind with girls you don't care about. Oh, Walt...' She rounded her eyes reproachfully, shaking her head. '...And the way you rant at me about hypocrisy.'

'No, wait a minute,' he protested. He began scratching the back of his neck, trying to answer her seriously, and seeing nothing ludicrous about their solving between them the riddle of why she wasn't being seduced. 'I'm too soppy at times when it comes to girls. There was Brenda tonight and me feeling...' He thrust his hands in his pockets and explained, frowning: 'Look—I don't know what makes me like I am or I'd do something. But I'm like this and I feel all this, that's all. Look—I just know when I'm doing something that won't work. I knew with Brenda... I keep kidding myself—but underneath... in the end... I know, all right.'

'How do you know?' She rose and faced him as his voice tailed off. He said distractedly: 'I just *feel* it!'

'Well, you must try to think it out. I'm not going to come every time you whistle...' She stood against him with her head back. 'How can you tell?'

He brought his hands out as she lifted her arms to his shoulders. He wanted to break away because he was half frightened. He felt he almost understood what was wrong. But he wanted the girl and wanted to keep her. The light above them shone on her shoulders, her elfin upturned face; on her deep, lustrous eyes which looked at him, yet were concerned with something else, something private. Their mouths touched and her hands clasped his neck, the dark stalking urge in him springing up voracious. Yet there was no loss of clear thought this time; he was too conscious of them both, desperately straining together. Her eyes were closed tight. As his hand touched the zip at the back of her dress her face pressed harder against his, her eyes screwing more tightly closed, and he thought: What the hell's going on in her head? What's she trying to force herself to feel?

She moved her head back.

'We could get engaged,' she whispered. 'Then it would be all right.' Her eyes were too hazily ecstatic, too empty, as though she had evicted her personality for the sake of sheer impression. He had never seen a girl so intense.

'You engaged to a miner? Married to a miner?' he asked, smiling.

'A long engagement.' She dreamily returned the smile. 'You're so much at odds with yourself you'll have to change. I can help you.' As he began shaking his head, she freed her arms, seized his coat lapels and vigorously shook them. 'You idiot, a girl is exactly what you need—and the kind of girl you get will make all the difference. Look, I know something's been tearing at you —I can help you.'

'I don't need any help,' he said, moving back a little.

'Of course you do.' She shook him again, urgently. 'What about that night in the pub—when you were hurt? Didn't you need me then? You haven't got over all the things that were making you so upset. They'll keep coming back. Oh, Walt, I helped you then, didn't I? You were glad I was there!'

'Sure I was. Sure I was. But once we get engaged'—he removed his arms—'can't you see us rowing about everything under the sun? We wouldn't hit it off. We're different sorts.'

'Then why have we kept seeing each other? Why on earth do you think I went to that fight and all those other places? Walt, I want to have someone I can help—and we *do* hit it off.'

He certainly needed her. As she put her face close and they kissed again, with her lips parting and widening, he caught her head and pressed her against him. His eyes closed. But if he needed her, why hate the fact? Why fight against knowing it? Why the antagonism and the wish to hurt? ...Because my old man hated what *she* came from, he thought... and she never stopped rubbing his nose in her family—and it was him that went into me, not her...

As he broke away, seeing her eyes full of expectancy and nothing else, she smiled, not to him but herself. Her weight tugged downwards, and she said: 'You know I'm right. Come on, Walt.'

'No.' No intense ritual to leave him bound to her. He would not be mastered by her—a potential Charles with Elaine a potential Joan—perhaps to turn out like his parents. He said doggedly: 'I can't pack up the other lads yet. We're too young and...'

'Them?' Her dress flared as she whirled away and dropped on to the settee. She stared up incredulously: 'You're lying, Walt. You know very well you're not like them.' Which was exactly what Brenda might have said, he thought, and showed you they were all alike in some ways.

'I'm not like your sort, either. I can't help it. You can't help where you come from and what's put into you.' His hands sought his pockets. He stared miserably at her bent head, thrusting his own hates into himself.

'It's nothing to do with where people come from,' she said in a low voice.

'You think I don't want to make love to you...' his words blurted out, 'but I do. A lot. I'm not having you despising me, though.'

'But why should I?' She clenched her hands, her eyes huge as she stared.

'Well, because you build it up too much—there's something about you and me...' He was finding more to it than his sources. 'You'd expect it to be everything, slap-bang first time—and it's not like that. It's never been like that with me and I got pretty disappointed. But you? You'll despise the first man that makes love to you when it's over. I just know it...' He remembered the couch and maternal murmurs, and other furtive whispers and kisses and fumbling in dark corners, and that he had never lost or rediscovered himself or shared more than wet-lipped fleshy embraces. He had never found the long-anticipated ecstasy.

'It isn't like that,' he concluded uncertainly. 'I don't know... You're just never going to blame me—I couldn't take it. I couldn't stand you looking down on me or—me feeling I'd, oh, done bad.'

'Well, I look down on you now,' she said flatly. 'For being a coward—if I just knew why it's me!' They were silent and then she said: 'You might as well go. She let him go to the door alone. He looked over his shoulder, but she was sitting with her back to him and her head lowered, the glossy curls springing from her brown neck.

'Look.'

'And don't call me again,' she said. 'I don't want you to. Don't…'

'All right.' He almost went back to her. He knew this would be much worse than the break with Brenda, and his shame was already corrosively spreading and seeping, but if he went back shame would still come later. She belonged in the light and he was a long way off.

'You can't help what's in you…' he said. 'You don't always know till the time comes…'

There was no answer and he went out, quietly closing the front door behind him. He walked down the path with his hands in his pockets. At the gate he swung his fist down on the wooden post, knuckles striking first, and flinched as the skin was broken and thin blood smeared his fingers.

Oh, that's great, he thought, with consummate self-disgust. As if they don't take enough knocks in the pit. As if they'd ever let you down…

He walked on with his knuckles to his mouth, looking for a taxi.

Couchant

I

'I took thee for a lad o' some sense,' the undermanager growled. 'Tha's stuck it one year; why the hell chuck it up now?'

'If I pass all the exams going I don't want t' job.'

A naked bulb burned above the big desk to compensate for the meagreness of September sunlight filtering through dusty panes. In the yellow light the beefy, perspiring man was knitting his shaggy brows in an attempt to intimidate Walt, who scowled back, lounging black-faced, with a thumb hooked in his belt and empty water-bottle dangling.

'You'd think it were for my good...' Tired of argument, Anderson rubbed his hand over his glistening jowl. He was fresh from his shower and his skin glowed. He asked more gently: 'What's up, son? I had hopes o' thee. Tell me right, what set your mind against it?'

'I don't want that kind of life, that's all,' Walt answered, and the stick clattered on the desk as Anderson bellowed:

'And you won't give yourself a chance to change your mind! Burnin' your boats at—what are you? Eighteen?'

'Nineteen.'

'T' coal-face soon changed thee. Stubborn young tyke, aren't you? All right...' A fat hand motioned disgustedly. 'It's a pity to see a good future chucked away, that's all. But if you want to end up wi' nowt only a pick an' shovel to live by ...'

'It'll do me,' Walt said, and he left the office. As he crossed the pit yard, nodding to afternoon-shift men on their way to the shaft, he was thinking that Anderson was as bad as the old lady with his mixture of 'you' and 'thee'. He was not thinking of his refusal to attend classes, because that had been decided months ago. He still knew the things he did not want to be.

That night he went out alone, as he had grown accustomed to doing in the past three months. Bryan, who had been going around with the red-headed Myra for several weeks, had expected Walt to return to the gang when he did. But Walt was tired of hectic amusements and even tired of company. To his work-mates he now appeared a laconic youth, churlish at times in the pit, who sometimes visited their clubs and sat drinking quietly with them. Some had given him gruff, good-natured advice: 'Get thisen a nice lass. This stuff's too old and steady for a lad thy age...'

Alone, as on other nights, he prowled the stone-flanked pavements moping over Elaine and at odds with himself. He had visited the jazz club occasionally before summer ended and Elaine returned; he had listened appreciatively when they played slow blues, feeling that he understood why the music had to sound weary of illusions about love and life. But if he acted the untouchable he did not want to feel an outcast, and he had grown very fond of the steel and concrete surrounding him, thinking it gave him comfort. He felt an affinity between him and everyone else who lived and worked and slowly aged in the stone embrace, and the sources of their affinity, the points where all ends gathered, were the towering grimy walls, and the lamp-lit streets on which traffic wheeled and hurried.

His guilt and shame over Elaine were yielding place, however, to his old restlessness; the feeling there was something he wanted. He was thinking more frequently of girls again and told himself that a steady girl was what he needed, as his mates had advised. Yet he wanted no repetitions of his other two affairs, and he was not positive that a girl was what he needed, so that his blind restless urges, his questions, the rump of his shame, all milled and tumbled around in him uncontrolled and only half recognized.

He liked to walk to the blitz sites around the city centre and lean on wire ropes to look at the ruins; tall solitary walls looming above piled rubble, at night resembling dead gods looking down on shattered altars and desolation. They called to his own dark solitude; they were also the city's wounds, he thought, as he had thought before, testifying to its courage and ability to endure. On afternoon shift he liked to go to a place from where he could see the bowl of the city, watching the changing patterns of light and darkness as flames sprouted and were cut off against the black sky, as headlamps flashed and as other lights arranged themselves in intricate rows, with the hills looming up around like protective shadows. There was no doubt that he belonged here now; he and the night-crouching city understood each other. He was sure, in fact, that he knew the city better than most people.

On the Tuesday following his argument with Anderson he went to the infirmary after work with a mate who had injured his hand. Returning alone he was passing the college at four o'clock and saw the students coming out. He ducked into a doorway until Elaine appeared, wondering how she looked and if she had got over the unhappiness he had caused her. He saw her red coat in a group at the gates, saw the books under her arm and her laughing mouth as she chattered to another girl and a young man, then turned his head to the window as they passed on the opposite side.

How could she still talk and laugh so easily when he had been so lonely and unhappy? He wondered, watching them go down the street. He felt indignant; cruelly wronged. She should have been at least as wretched as he had made himself.

That week-end, therefore, with his old ebullition, he was out with the gang and being feted like a returned warrior. He went with them to the club on Sunday, and so he met Susan.

Bryan was asked outside and returned with four girls, taking them to a table across the floor from where the gang sat watching curiously, buying them drinks before rejoining his friends. As people began dancing, Hughie Sawford said: 'That's Margaret Howard and them, isn't it? What you doin' with them, Bry?'

'I only signed 'em in,' Bryan said defensively, looking at the faces watching all around the long oak table, some of them frowning. 'Well, they wanted to come!' He explained to Walt, who was puzzled, that two of the girls lived on the Clifton estate and that he had told them to come some time.

'They're all right to dance wi',' he said. 'But nowt else, tha knows…' Walt blinked at his gruff firmness. 'I mean I've known 'em since they was kids and they're not our sort. We don't want 'em at our table—they're *nice* lasses…'

'I never guessed you knew any,' Walt grinned, but though Bryan grinned back and kept up the joke for a while, he finally repeated: 'I've known 'em right since they was kids, Margaret and Susan. They're not our sort…'

Three of the girls were talking volubly as they looked around the hall and sipped from glasses of beer, but the fourth sat very quiet and almost unmoving. She was the kind of girl at whom one can look time and again without registering either attraction or dislike, merely passing and forgetting. She was of medium height, but slender, her figure scarcely yet developed. Her face was heart-shaped and her features well proportioned, but the way her brown hair was swept on to the crown of her head pinned up by combs, did not suit her, although the hair-style suited her friend, a small, cheerful attractive blonde who was doing most of the talking.

'Them two…' Walt grunted. 'You can tell they're mates—copying each other's hair-styles and clothes.' They were both wearing dark dresses with white cuffs and collars, and it was again the blonde who compared best. 'The blonde is Margaret,' Bryan said, grudging the information. 'The other one is Susan Holmes. They're not your type, Walt.'

'How the hell do you know?' he demanded, deciding to ask the blonde for the next dance. 'Bry—this mother-hen act don't become you. I won't rush 'em all of a sudden!'

'No—sure—it's just—well, you know what you are, Walt…'

Walt choked on his beer, and then sat grinning at Bryan's anxious face. The large hall was filling up, but there was always room to dance properly in the club, the tables being lined two deep close to the walls and the floor kept clear, except for a small congregation around the bar. Its only faults were that the distempered walls and ceiling needed cleaning and the stage microphone had a tendency to break down, so that at one moment music was blaring at you, at the next you were dancing to the shuffle of feet and drone of voices.

'Hey-up, they keep lookin' over here,' Tich Edwards told Bryan. 'Maybe they're expectin' us to buy their ale.' As everyone looked across the girls turned away, except for the solemn brunette, who appeared not to have been looking in the first place.

'We ought to dance wi' 'em,' someone else said. Since there were eight of them and only four girls, the argument over who should dance with them first lasted until that dance was over. Hughie Sawford, who never danced, Walt, who abruptly decided it wasn't worth arguing over, and two others finally volunteered to remain at the table, and the next dance saw a charge of the other four across the floor, Bryan winning and claiming the blonde, Tich, smallest of the gang, losing and being left with Susan. Walt grinned again when he saw the girl trying to hide her consternation at finding Tich several inches shorter than she was. He nudged Hughie gleefully as Tich guided her towards them in a straight, stiff-stepping line.

'She can't dance any better than Tich,' he said. But as they passed he saw her reddened face, her mouth compressed and an agonized embarrassment in her eyes as though she dare not raise her head. It was painful to look at her. She was worse than he had been at his first dance, he thought, remembering that ordeal and how Brenda had helped him.

Bryan passed, with the blonde urgently telling him something. He called to Walt: 'Get Susan away from Tich. Tha knows he can't dance!' This was said severely, as though Bryan had not dreamed of Tich joining the cavalcade to the girls' table, and as though his own dancing were not confined to one forward step, one turn and a few improvisations after plenty of beer. Calling back resignedly that there was only him who *could* blooming dance, Walt stood up. It was all right for Bryan, he thought, making a big impression on the only good-looking one... As Tich passed again Walt cut in, with the small youth looking as relieved as the girl did. She could follow his steps, he found, but hesitantly and stiffly, and she would not look up. He remarked that it must be tough being a girl: '... You can't pick your partners, love, can you?'

The girl shook her head; he understood how difficult it was for her to talk. Her cheeks were still pink, so looking over her shoulder he chatted casually until she relaxed a little. In the next set she glanced up twice and in the third he won a brief smile. She answered a few questions. She worked at one of the big factories in the city. 'We do the handles for table knives,' she told him, in a slightly husky voice which he thought pleasant but did not remark on in case it were simply due to a cold. He was half enjoying the difficulties of soothing her and making her act more naturally. She wasn't so bad-looking really, he thought, ignoring the hair-style and looking at the bone structure of her face.

'You're not a bad dancer, you know,' he assured her when the last set was finished. He was rewarded with another careful smile. When he returned to the table, Bryan said: 'You're a good mate, Walt. I'm glad tha's back wi' us.' Then he glowered indignantly at the apologetic, sheepish Tich. Walt accompanied him when he went to the blonde again. He asked Susan to dance.

She rose without answering and gave him her hand, dancing awkwardly at first. She kept glancing at the seated people and lowering her eyes and his right hand could feel the tenseness of her body.

'You're all tightened up,' he said. 'Take it easy. Don't you go dancing much?'

'Only classes since I was seventeen and a half—this is the first right dance I've been to.' She looked up. Her eyes were brown; not the dark, deep brown of Elaine's, but a light hazel. She glanced round again, a little flushed.

'You think everybody's watching you, don't you?' he said. 'Why should they be?'

'Margaret says it's wi' me bein' tallish. Folk look at tall girls.' She kept her head down.

'Because tall girls are attractive, that's why. They're not looking at you, kid—they're all too busy thinking about themselves and how they look—all on 'em.' As she glanced up, he nodded and explained: 'Everybody's like that—it's their egos. I'm not kidding you, that's honest psychology.' She did not look convinced, and since he could think of no more psychology to offer, he told her of how shy he had been: 'I was terrible, honest.'

'But you're not shy now, are you?' she commented, and he sensed significance in her tone. She was suspicious of him, he thought. A moment later she said: 'You don't have to dance wi' me just 'cause Bryan's your mate, you know...' As he looked hurt, she added: 'Well, there's plenty other lasses here as can dance better, I mean.'

'No, there's not—you're as good as any on 'em,' he insisted, and received another small, uncertain smile. He understood part of the reason for her suspicions when he and Bryan bought gin and orange for the four girls and stood talking at their table.

'Try a proper drink,' Bryan advised them grandly as he set down the tray. 'Girls shouldn't drink beer.' He fussed over them: '…It's nice to see lasses from our way in here. Decent lasses…' He promised protection from the less trustworthy types who were unfortunately to be found in any dance hall: '…But if you have trouble wi' any on 'em, just whistle me and old Walt here. Old Walt's my mate, tha knows. You know me, don't you?'

They assured him that they, did, then the pert-faced blonde looked at Walt and said: 'You're Walt Morris, aren't you?'

He nodded.

'Used to fight for the Clifton Club, didn't you? You fought Jack Ford…'

'That's right.' Walt's chest expanded and he smiled. 'Went to the Memo, didn't you? Used to go wi' Brenda Carter.'

His smile went awry and his chest slowly shrank. They all looked interested except Susan, who was experimenting with the gin and orange and frowning as she sipped.

'A long time ago,' he said. When he returned with Bryan to their own table he demanded how the blonde could know so much about him.

'…I've never seen her before,' he exclaimed.

'Ah, you know how it is, Walt. She comes off the Clifton, don't she? And Susan don't live far off your street.' Bryan shrugged as he sat down and lifted a glass from out of a foaming cluster of them. 'T' women talk in t' shops and t' lasses talk at work and hear their brothers—they's nowt happens one end o' t' Clifton as don't reach t' other afore a week's gone.'

Some other young men got the girls up for the next dance, with the gang watchful at their table as they drank. Walt felt gratified to see Susan dancing very stiffly and without talking to her partner. These shy girls were prickly if handled wrongly, he told himself. It took a man of some experience to know how to make them relax… As she passed she glanced at him, but immediately looked away when he smiled.

During the interval, when every light was switched on and the hall was filled by talk and cries and laughter, the stage deserted except for neglected-looking instruments, the gang quietly drank their beer in a fashion which astonished Walt. It seemed they were all following Bryan's sober, dignified example. When Tich remarked that Bryan and Walt must have made a hit because Margaret and her mate kept looking at them and talking, Bryan answered sternly: 'Margaret's a nice lass. We're just lookin' after 'em—they're only kids.' A moment's reflection, and he added: 'Except Margaret. She's nineteen.' He began talking of something else, while Walt sat wondering how long this new attachment would last, thinking it at least a novelty. He looked over as the little blonde said something which made the other three laugh. As Susan threw her head back gaily, he glanced at the others to see if anyone else had noticed her, then turned to watch her again as she smiled at her friend. She was different with the wide, merry smile, he thought; she had beauty for a moment. He sat trying to imagine what clothes would best suit her and what hair-style might best frame her face, feeling excitedly that he had discovered something the others had missed.

After that he asked her for every dance. He enjoyed the feeling that all he said affected the girl's personality, talking a great deal so that she forgot the watchers and relaxed a little, flattering her enough to make her pleased but not suspicious, and making many jokes at his own expense. When she laughed once he felt surprising pleasure in seeing her look happier. With his knowledge of Bryan's taste, and his own observations of the forceful chattering blonde, he could guess Margaret's effects on Susan. He remarked that she should always walk behind Margaret rather than beside her: '...You see, you're tallish and—more graceful, you know—Margaret's so short she looks dumpy and funny beside you.' So he went on, trying to give her confidence and making her feel he admired her, and in spite of puzzlement in her eyes at times he was sure he had succeeded when he saw her walk off the floor with her head higher and movements more graceful.

'I never reckoned you'd go for the mousy type,' Hughie Sawford murmured once. Walt turned an enigmatic face to his beer as he answered: 'She's not so mousy, kid...'

The gang went home with the girls; Walt on one side of Susan and Margaret as they walked to the bus stop and Bryan on the other. On the bus he sat beside her with the others beginning to tease them. He saw her blushing and called over his shoulder: 'Shut up, you lot. You're jealous because me and Bryan always get the best-looking pair.'

This brought a burst of laughter from the other two girls, with a natural suggestion of scorn for his judgment in it, but Bryan turned to admonish them and the high-spirited youths.

'Just knock it off, now,' he instructed them. 'Me and Walt knows how to act with decent lasses!' He leaned over from his seat beside Margaret to assure Susan: 'You're all right wi' Walt, love. Me and him knows how to act...' Walt felt there was a hint of warning for himself in this, but merely grinned, though both he and Bryan looked uncomfortable, the girls glancing doubtfully across at one another, when one of the other girls cried in a screech of laughter that this wasn't what *she'd* heard. Half-way up the long hill these two girls left the bus, and when it had rumbled for some way across the estate where the houses were crowded in peaceful darkness, Susan rose and pushed past his knees, muttering: 'My stop. Good night.' They all called good night to her as she hurried downstairs.

Suddenly Walt jumped up and followed, leaping off the platform as the bus began jerking forward again with the conductor shouting did he want to break his neck. She turned and looked back, with Walt amiably grinning while she regarded him as though he were a frightening dog who kept following and might attack if ordered off.

'I only live down this road,' she said, moving her head to watch the red light disappear around a corner and then to look anxiously down a street where lonely gas-lights were separated by long stretches of darkness. Slits of light from curtained windows streaked the gardens but failed to penetrate the privet hedges.

'What Bryan said was right,' he told her, still standing several yards away as he fetched out a packet of cigarettes. A standard lamp over the bus stop cloaked both of them in its glare. 'I don't know what you've heard—but I'm harmless, honest. I can behave.'

'What do you want to go home wi' me for?' It sounded as though this had been bothering her for some time. 'They was plenty of nice-looking lasses in t' club.'

'Who says you're not nice-looking?' He lit the cigarette and stood with one hand in his pocket. She said grudgingly:

'Nobody, only—I know what kind you and Bryan Foster reckon to...' She shrugged and went on: 'Margaret was asking why you kept fussin' over me and never bothered over her.'

'Her kind's ten a penny! Come on—I'll walk you to your gate, huh?'

'I suppose you can...' she muttered, unsure of him.

They went down the dark street, the girl's heels tapping, Walt silent on thick crêpe soles. With one hand kept in his pocket and the other holding his cigarette, he thought his harmlessness manifest, and the girl walked close, looking more nervous of sudden gateways and black patches than of him. She was very nervous, he thought. Even her walk was stiff and jerky. At a lamp near her gate they stopped, standing on the shadowy edge of its yellow cone, and Walt raised his hands, grinning at her.

'See? No harm done. One scream now and your old man will come flying out and chase me up the street with the poker.'

'Not my dad,' she said, laughing at him for a moment as he stood with his hands up to shoulder height. 'My mam, happen.'

'She's a dragon, is she?'

The girl dug her hands into the pockets of her grey tweed coat.

'Well... You know...'

'My landlady's one,' he assured her. 'I know how it is.'

As they stood smiling, the sight of her good, even teeth and attractive eyes made him say bluntly: 'Don't mind me telling you something—a bit personal.'

'What?' She looked immediately wary—ready to be frightened, he thought. He spoke very gently, smiling all the time to reassure her. 'You shouldn't wear your hair like that... You're nice-looking, you know—you should wear it...' He made vague motions as she touched her piled-up hair. '...Sort of fluffy—all round your face.'

'Margaret said it suited me,' she slowly answered. 'I never bothered till I started dancin'—just put a ribbon round it.' She smiled again, as though this meant she was confiding in him. 'I didn't fancy it that much either.' Then she looked down, embarrassed, hiding her hands again.

'You wear it your own way,' he said firmly. Deciding he might as well go on, he asked: 'Who picked the frock?'

'My mam—I put the trimming on...'

'Does she buy all your clothes?' He could not tell her it was no good while she looked down like that.

'Not now I'm eighteen. I started gettin' my own now. I've got a nice new costume—' she looked up animatedly as she said this, her eyes bright —'only it's not for dances. Aren't we daft talking like this?'

'You didn't mind, did you?' he asked, still gentle.

'No.' Her pocketed hands lifted her coat outwards a few times as she swayed a little, looking down again. Her head jerked up and she said in a spate: 'You're a funny lad—you're not a bit what they made out you was. I thought you were all for fighting and trouble—and leery...'

'Everybody says I'm a funny lad!' He shrugged, spinning the cigarette in a red curve over a hedge. 'Well...' Not for a long time had the opening gambit been so hesitant or difficult. 'I'll see you again, eh?'

'We'll be at the club next week.'

'Yeah...' They stood, half turned to leave one another. He was suddenly disgusted with the old routine of playing girls along... not being too eager... making them wait...

'Never mind the club,' he said. 'Let's go out tomorrow—I'll have a shift off.'

'I can't.' As he shrugged and turned away, she said: 'I could Wednesday, if you like.'

'Okay,' he agreed. 'I'll have Wednesday off I'm on afternoons, see?'

'You must do all right if you can afford to take shifts off just like that,' she commented, both of them lingering yet keeping fairly well apart.

'Oh, I wouldn't do it for just *any* lass,' he said. He left her and walked home, feeling some pride in his tact and understanding and good behaviour... You have to understand girls, he mused. Not just any bloke can help a lass like her... He decided he could begin to like himself a little again.

Next morning the old lady informed him that Bill was leaving at the weekend.

'It's nowt as I've said,' she assured him. 'He's just gi'ed notice, that's all.' Bill explained to him that night that he was going to live with another family: '...They're all comrades,' he said. 'We're interested in the same things, and I'll have—more freedom.'

'You're getting in awful deep,' Walt said thoughtfully. When Bill looked irritable, he mollified him: 'I'll miss you—it'll seem funny without you.'

'I'll miss you, boy,' Bill answered. 'I'll be seeing you around.'

The truth which both of them recognized underneath was that they had little in common now. Both had almost ceased reading novels and had gone on developing those ideas over which they differed most. There was no real sympathy between them any longer, and Walt felt that Bill had changed much more than he had. He had no time for friendships outside his political life; it had become his entire life.

When he met Susan on Wednesday he felt again that he had seen in her what the others had missed. She was wearing a tight-jacketed brown costume with a shell-pink blouse and had obviously taken much trouble over her appearance. Her hair was set in large waves above her broad brow and hung in thick curls around her face. When he showed his admiration, she looked shyly pleased with herself.

'I tried it like this afore,' she told him. 'Only me mam said it didn't suit me...'

'It's your hair,' he said heartily. 'You wear it your way, love.'

It was a quiet evening, because she rarely spoke unless he asked a question. She seemed to lack completely any talent for casual conversation. On the Saturday he persuaded her to go to a dance with him instead of with Margaret. On Sunday she and the other girls shared the gang's table, with Bryan looking at them all like a protective uncle in between sessions of whispering in Margaret's ear with his arm on the back of her chair. That night, he found that once the barrier of inarticulate shyness was pierced Susan could talk. She described her work and her friends while they danced, chattering on and on, relating trivial details with words streaming out as though she were afraid to stop, or as though she did not know how to stop. She finally became conscious of how much she was talking and went abruptly quiet.

'Gosh, I don't reckon to natter like that,' she said guiltily while they were sitting at the table. She looked easier, her eyes much livelier, and he said: 'It's the gin, love. You talk all you want—I like hearing you.'

He said good night as usual to her at the gate, keeping his distance in spite of the companionship that had been strong between them all evening. During the next week they went out together several times and she asked occasional questions about his home life, carefully casual as though wary of offending him. He told her about his family and why he had left home, and when she asked why he had chosen to become a miner said simply: 'I wanted to.' She frowned, and he asked: 'You don't see owt wrong in being a miner, do you?'

' 'Course not. But your brother's well off and that...' She was obviously much puzzled. He explained how home and family had nothing to do with what he did with his life, but she seemed rather troubled by all this.

'Look,' he said. 'Some folk like one life and some another. The thing is to be what you want and not let other folk make you what they want. You just think about that...'

'I'd sooner have a man as worked wi' his hands,' she said thoughtfully. 'I reckon you can't really call the other sort *really* men at all.'

He was delighted. A girl after his own heart! He was more delighted when she agreed that a woman should be prouder of a hard-working husband than of one with an easy job and that a plain ordinary life was better than any fancy, stuck-up kind.

'I couldn't be owt else but plain and ordinary,' she said. 'I don't know enough to be owt else.'

'That's not it!' he protested, but he still highly approved of her. Besides, he felt that she was truly lacking in duplicity. What she liked made her happy and show her pleasure; anything not appealing to her was met with a blank, solemn face and bored eyes. He had seen how she could smile when she had cause and how the smile changed her. He felt that only her acute shyness, the nervousness which occasionally showed in a twitching arm, a jerky movement or spate of speech, prevented her from being much more outspoken. But he was sure she was allowing others to shape her, and this was why he kept stressing his own independence.

On the next Sunday when he took her home from the club again he was leaving her at the gate with the customary polite good night, but she asked: 'If you really want to go wi' me and that, why do you never kiss me?'

He turned back. Her face was dim in the merging of gaslight and darkness. This had been bothering him, too. Once he kissed her it was going to be different; no more claiming his only idea was to do a good turn...

'I thought you were still a bit scared of me. I didn't think you wanted me to.'

'I don't mind,' she answered, with her hands still in her pockets. 'Not now.'

He took her shoulders and gently kissed her. She was passive, with her eyes open, watching his face. He kissed her again and felt a tentative return of pressure.

'You haven't been with many lads, have you?'

'I haven't been wi' none,' she said, fetching out her hands and putting her arms around his waist. For ten minutes they stood clasped together, talking and exchanging kisses. He felt she was enjoying this experiment; carefully storing her sensations so that later she could examine them properly and come to some conclusion about kissing, perhaps about love.

'You've had a lot o' girls, though,' she said quietly, and then asked him, as she had in one way or another on almost every evening spent together, why he wanted to go out with her. And he repeated, slowly stroking her hair against his shoulder, that she was far more attractive than she realized.

'If you followed your own ideas about clothes and everything,' he urged her, 'you'd make Margaret and most of the rest look silly.'

She thought this over quietly for a while and decided at last: 'I think I'll get a perm. I've got money saved up.'

'That's the idea,' he said, grinning to himself. This encouragement, with Walt sometimes talking like an indulgent father wishing to be proud of his little girl, was the basis of their continued courtship.

Soon after Bill left home the news was announced that Russia was manufacturing atom bombs, and Walt wondered wryly what jibes he might have made about it. No more ultimate peace of mind in thinking: Well, we've always got the bomb... Bill's 'awful mess' seemed on everyone's mind for a while at the pit, but the world after all had grown accustomed to years of perpetual crises and Walt was more concerned with the progress of his new courtship. He had deserted the gang again, and when Bryan suggested they join up with Margaret and him Walt resolutely refused. Susan was happier and more at ease in his company alone, he felt, than in that of their friends. She depended on him in many ways; for his approval of dress and books, for help in learning to mix with people and for protection when rowdiness broke out in some dance hall. He took her to working men's clubs and protected her from their rough, good-natured teasing by answering for her, while helping her to acquire a taste for gin and orange. He wanted to take her to a boxing match, but she refused to go.

'I'm frightened of fighting,' she said, and he could see how true this was in the way her lip tugged at the word. 'I mean—a man should stick up for himself and that, but I'm terrified when they start shoutin' or rowin'. I could run a mile. You won't get into any fights, will you?'

'Who, me?' he asked, completely sincere. 'I don't want to fight, love.'

Because of her incognizant nervousness, he never spoke angrily or roughly to her. He told himself often that he wanted to help her and be good to her, that at last there was a girl to whom he could bring happiness instead of hurt, feeling pride over, and not shame over, his actions. Susan approved of all that he did and was not interested in his being ambitious or changing or looking for something else. There were times, in the bedroom he now had to himself, when he lay awake with a hunger for the deep eyes and teasing voice, the black curls under the red hood; there were times when restlessness shifted and heaved and it was himself who asked: Is this all? Is this all there's ever going to be?

But Elaine belonged with the light and he and Susan shared the same sources; Susan could appreciate the dark side of his living. And work and courtship kept restlessness mainly quiescent.

December brought cold dreary weather with wet streets and sullen clouds. He was invited to Christmas dinner with Susan's family. Her father was a tall, hunched man, thin-faced through thirty years of suffering from a stomach burned out by mustard gas in the first world war. Susan had explained: 'He's got pipes and all sorts of stuff in his belly.' He was a watchmaker, working at a small firm, but since his illness often prevented him from working the family was fairly poor and their furniture was old. Mrs. Holmes did part-time work in a factory but also had to stay at home sometimes to nurse her husband. She was of medium height, her body shapeless though not fat, and her face hard and almost fleshless; a hustler in worn-down heels, thick wrinkled stockings and untidy, greasy pinafore. Her grey hair straggled, and it was soon obvious that she domineered the whole family.

She looked surprised when Walt offered his hand and released it after one doubtful jerk. He sat on an old sofa under the windows with its wooden back covered by a bright cloth, frills demurely hiding its wooden legs. Susan helped with the dinner while he talked to her fourteen-year-old brother Joe and twelve-year-old sister Sally. Susan's older brother was married with a home of his own. Joe belonged to the youth club and knew all about Walt.

'I were tellin' t' kids at school you was courtin' our lass,' he said, eagerly pushing his sister along the sofa so that he could sit beside Walt. He was small, with a thin face and body like his father's and frank hazel eyes like Susan's under a brown fringe of tousled hair. Sally, to whom Walt took an instant dislike, was a fat girl with green eyes like her mother and long fair hair bound by a babyish huge pink ribbon. As Joe squirmed a way in, she drove an elbow into his ribs, crying in a nasal whine: 'Will tha gi'e o'er, thee? Tha'rt allus there, thee.' He found that both the nasal tone and expressions were endowments of her mother's, when Mrs. Holmes kept looking up from laying the table to order them to stop fighting or shouting or pestering Walt, ending each reprimand with: 'Tha'rt allus there, thee!' He flinched twice as she advanced on the sofa with a swinging hand, but it was Joe who received the slap, though Sally went unpunished. The boy grew quiet, glowering at his mother, but as soon as she went into the kitchen he burst out: 'Hey-up, Dad. This is one on our old lads, this. Fought for Clifton, he did.'

'Oh aye,' his father said, but he was obviously suffering some pain. Mrs. Holmes explained to Walt that he had drunk several glasses of beer on Christmas Eve: '...He would go out... He's only got what he deserved, I told him...'

Her husband sat by the fire without answering, leaning forward in his worn-armed easy chair with his face drawn and hands pressed above his navel. He ate no dinner with them.

It was a long, dreary afternoon. Wind and rain ricocheted off the windows as they sat around the fire, the man hunched in pain, the mother continually nagging at Joe, who grew more sulky, then gossiping about some neighbours to Susan, who listened with manifest boredom and smiled at Walt as though pleading with him to be patient. He winked back cheerfully. At one point, Sally, who Walt was sure must weigh at least eight stone, plumped herself on his knees like a confiding little girl to show him a book she had received for Christmas, only moving when her mother went out to the kitchen and Susan rose menacingly with whispered threats.

After tea they went to the club and sat with the gang, although Bryan's period of respectable courtship was over and Margaret was at another table with her friends. Bryan was his old self again, and though he was effusively friendly towards Susan and bought her several drinks, Walt felt that they should not be here. The gang wanted to discuss girls freely and to get drunk, as was only proper at Christmas, but they were trying to behave discreetly out of courtesy towards Susan and deference to Walt's new role as one of the hooked unfortunates.

While they were dancing Susan mentioned his visit for the first time, saying abruptly: 'Well, she kept pestering me to bring you home so she could see you, and we've done it now, haven't we?'

'She didn't ask me much,' he commented.

'Oh, she'll get all her information from quizzing me. Only talking she can do is quizzing or nagging or gossiping!'

He squeezed her to him.

'Never mind,' he said with sympathy. 'It's over now.'

In the changing rainbow of a spotlight weaving over the moving heads he saw her smile. He had been right in thinking she could be pretty, he told himself proudly. Her hair was waved and curled and she wore a turquoise frock with, around her throat, a string of pearls he had bought for her Christmas present. Her face was happy, although her eyes still held shyness, and he thought her more attractive than most girls there. Her figure was slowly developing; she was the kind of girl who passes deceptively slowly through that change to a mature-bodied woman which other girls emerge from with startling quickness.

'She don't know what to make on it, you know, now I've started standing up to her. She don't like it—she's allus on at me. I don't care.'

He imagined that she did care; that she must often suffer her mother's nagging for fear of the scene that might result from resistance. He had watched the sullenness in Joe's expression growing more cowed as the nagging went on before a visitor he must have wanted to impress. He wished he could offer Susan even more protection, and with the light flickering over their faces told her encouragingly: 'Wait till we're married —you won't have to stand up for yourself then. I'll look after you.'

'Married?' She pulled her head back, staring uncertainly at him. He was half astonished himself. '...Walt, honest? We're not even engaged or anything!'

'We'll get engaged, then,' he said. What better could he do than look after her? 'I'm twenty in the summer. We'll get engaged then.'

Her body against his was softer than ever before, her face was soft against his jaw.

'You *can* relax,' he said. 'You see.'

She smiled; he felt her lips moving.

'You should've said you love me. You haven't yet.'

'Well, of course I do,' he said. Suddenly he was the shy one, but he managed to say: 'I love you—how's that? Now I've said it.'

'Tell me after. You've got to keep telling me now—every night.'

He frowned, thinking it wasn't a thing you could go around saying as easy as all that. It took effort. But when she was under the lamp near her gate, looking bright-eyed and attractive, she acted so sure of herself, even becoming coquettish, experimenting on whether she could tease him by smilingly refusing kisses, he was so pleased with her that he repeated he loved her several times, and repeated his promise that they would become engaged in the summer.

'And when we've saved up enough,' he told her, 'we'll get married and live on our own, eh?'

'That's what I want,' she said. 'My own place...' She began smiling off into the darkness as she went on quietly, to herself, he thought, instead of to him: 'I want a nice house. I'd keep it all clean and no shouting and t' kids could have a room to bring their pals to play in... It'd all be bright... Bright and new and clean—and right happy. They'd never have to be scared of me.'

'Me neither.' He wanted her to know he was still there.

'Oh, I'd love it.' She returned to him, looking up and fiercely, hungrily, hugging his waist. 'I'd be ever so happy. Gettin' things and building it all up. We wouldn't be like other couples, eh? We'd never get fed up wi' each other and have rows or that would we?'

'Oh, no, never,' Walt said, satisfied now that he had been included in her dream.

She finally whispered that she loved him, kissed him hard several times, and he went home happy. The next morning the old lady remarked:

'I reckon it's that Holmes lass you're courtin'!' He admitted it. This was what Bryan had meant about news travelling around the estate.

'I was going to tell you,' he said. 'But it wasn't that serious till lately.'

'Aye; well, don't get too serious! But they's a bit o' sense goin' wi' a decent lass like that—only watch her mother 'cause she's a bad bitch—another Watson!'

A week later she was demanding to know if he was soft in the head or something: 'Gettin' married at your age to a bit of a bairn like yon?'

'Married?' He was pulling on his raincoat preparing to go to work, but he stopped and explained the position to her.

'Well, you'd best tell her mother you're only gettin' engaged, then,' the old lady snapped. ' 'Cause she's getting it about as you're talking her lass into gettin' wed soon—and scandal soon starts over a thing like that...' Her suspicious-eyed look made him highly indignant.

'So help me,' he exclaimed. 'If I've made one wrong move or said one wrong word...' He stopped in disgust, and thought that being suspected wouldn't be quite so bad if you had the satisfaction of being guilty. 'Honest, I haven't.'

'Well, I shall gi'e that meddlesome rattle-gob a piece o' my mind an' I see her,' the old lady said, looking fierce.

It was at the pit he became truly annoyed. Bryan wanted to know what was all this about getting married, and when the colliers heard this spicy piece of news they hurried in to the face, so that Walt was among the last to reach it, greeted by 'Here comes the bride...' from every man as he crawled past him to his stint. He crouched there, brushing off coal-dust which had been showered on him in lieu of confetti, muttering angrily as a score of pick handles beat on shovel blades with their owners chorusing: 'How will she go on at nights wi' the Marquis by her side?'

When they were trooping towards the shaft with the face cleared, someone remembered his proper name and he almost groaned as a shrill falsetto pleaded: 'Walter, Walter... lead me to the altar...'

His imminent marriage, in spite of frantic denials, was the favourite topic of the week; the largest applause each day was awarded to whoever thought up the most ludicrous or obscene words to sing about him and his betrothed. They lectured him on sex in marriage, and when he lost his temper and shouted he wasn't damn well getting married they lectured him on the penalties for breach of promise, adding a list of the probable crimes he had committed concerning the girl's virtue.

On the Saturday evening he met Susan outside the Luxor cinema and immediately began storming at her:

'What the hell's the idea?' he demanded. 'What did you have to go bunging your old girl up with stuff about us getting married for?'

'I didn't,' she protested. 'I only said we was getting engaged in t' summer.' She glanced at passing people and at those waiting outside the cinema. He saw the quick suffusion of her face and the old embarrassed agony in her eyes before they filled, glistening. 'She always does something like this—I had to tell her, the way she kept quizzin' me.'

'You'd better put her right, then,' he said, but he was finding that he had trained himself too well in sharing her feelings and understanding her pain to keep up anger against her. He was already putting out a hand to her arm, when she burst out furiously: 'I will! I'll make her keep her rotten great mouth shut!' Her jaw jerked out and the pain in her eyes changed to proud fury, reminding him startlingly of Brenda.

'No, love.' He squeezed her arm and they began walking. 'Don't start rowing with her over this. You know...' he smiled and pulled a face at the same time. 'I'm just mardy 'cause the lads at t' pit were having me on—can't take it. But let 'em talk. We haven't done anything.'

'All right,' she said. 'But I won't half tell her when we do get wed.' He grinned at her again. Later that night she told him: 'I don't know what I'd do wi'out you, Walt. We'll never fall out, will we?' He assured her again that they never would. She was good for him, he thought. Without her, how would he have learned to control himself so well? How could he have cured his old violence which never overcame him now?

A week later they went to the annual dance at the factory where she worked. The huge white-walled canteen had been festooned with decorations, a stage erected for the band and a counter equipped as a bar. Hundreds of dancers circled under the spotlights and there was an atmosphere of mass companionship with everyone knowing almost everyone else. Since Susan had come here when she left school, she had many friends among the young people grouped by the walls, and a succession of youths came to ask her to dance. Her success pleased him at first. She was wearing her turquoise frock and the pearls, her face framed in soft waves. Realizing that she was suddenly popular, she smiled more, laughed more and talked to her partners almost vivaciously. Pleasure with herself gave a delightful radiance to her eyes and expression and even Walt felt he had never seen her look like this before. He watched her from the bar and heard two youths, both having danced with Susan, discussing her while they drank bottled beer.

'She hasn't half come on in the past few months... She's turned out not a bad piece, eh?'

'I've been fittin' in their shop for a year now,' the other said ruefully. 'I never looked at her twice till lately. They reckon she's courting strong, mind you...'

'You know what that does for 'em!' They both grinned. 'She might court a few more before she's finished—she's all right, mate.'

It was this remark which burst in his face his distended pride. He contemplated for a moment descending in wrath on the gossips, but he was more worried about Susan and turned to look for her, wondering: What's to stop her making the most of it now she knows what she's got?

He was very jealous. She was his girl; he had made her like this, he told himself. As the evening passed he became convinced that Susan was making the most of her attraction. She was asked out for every dance and excused several times on the floor. Having been cut out twice while dancing with her, Walt took his resentment to the bar, where he encouraged it to blossom into indignation, drinking one bottle after another of gassy bottled beer. Susan came several times to sip at the drink he had bought her and ask if he were enjoying himself, but when he airily told her to go ahead and have fun with her friends she spent a lot of time among groups on the edge of the floor between dances. This seemed to him downright desertion.

In a rational moment he argued that she had a right to this; it was like a debut. Suddenly she had realized she was attractive and desirable, talking easily and gaily to people—and she wasn't used to it. She needed time to become used to it.

Only what happens when she does get used to it? he wondered, and reached for his beer again, scowling at people who presumed to smile politely to him.

What if she started trying out her powers on him, becoming as demanding as the others? His encouragement, his admiration and vows of love had taken her to this stage where she was no longer afraid to be looked at, to display her attractions—and it was he who might suffer for it. Everybody knew he had promised to marry her—she had a hold over him if she wanted to be that way.

With such vague, undefined and undefinable imaginings he goaded himself into a brooding, surly mood, turning with his elbows supported on the counter, glass in one hand, bottle in the other, to watch a young man smiling as he talked to Susan with a hand on her shoulder in a chattering group. When the bar closed at half past ten she came and found him, took his arm, smiling and talking about her friends, and led him to a seat. He moved, returning the smile, with an old lightness of balance and an old dark turbulence of energies within. When she reproached him for having drunk all night and scarcely dancing with her, he said: 'Well, now, I haven't had much chance, duck, have I?'

She seemed only then to realize that the smile was faulty and to understand the sulkiness in his eyes. As they sat down together she put an arm through his and asked:

'You don't really mind, do you? It's t' first time I've been to one o' these. I never knew they were like this.' She looked happily over the dance floor and he leaned to look solemnly at her eyes.

'Know you're a good-looking lass now, don't you, though? Don't you?'

'I must be,' she said, without looking round. 'Else an old wolf like you'd never have bothered...'

He grunted.

'I'm not the wolf!' He waved at the whole hall. 'That lot are.'

'We'll dance together all t' time now,' she promised as music began. A young man immediately approached and asked her to dance; the same one, Walt observed sourly, who had been standing with a hand on her shoulder.

'She's not dancing,' he said, and the youth looked at him.

'I didn't ask you—I asked Susan.' He was peevish but not pugnacious.

Walt regarded him with mild surprise for a moment, then slowly rose, removing the hand which tugged at his arm. Taller than the other, he frowned down and said: 'I've told you, haven't I? Go on, take off!'

The youth stepped back a pace.

'I know your sort—but I've got pals in here, you know.' Some people turned to look as Walt laughed.

'Sit down, Walt. Please.' Susan tugged at his coat. Walt rose and fell on toes and heels, smiling, full of concentrated malignant lust for a fight.

'You'll need 'em,' he remarked. 'I've got more pals than you've got, and I know where to come. Now you hop it.'

The youth looked at Susan and began saying: 'I didn't think a nice lass like you would...' but Walt moved on him, and he backed away, watching Walt's hands, then turned and went over to a group who were looking on and talking among themselves. Walt stood a few feet in front of his chair, aggressively returning all the stares until the heads turned away again, closing in to murmur and nod or shake. He returned to his chair, found that Susan was gone, and hurried out into the corridor to find her.

She was emerging from the cloakrooms pulling on her grey coat, a scarf over her head as he came towards her.

'Where you going?' he demanded, as she pushed past him.

'Home—you showed me up in front of everybody.'

He followed her, then had to run back for his raincoat, and by the time he caught up with her again they were half-way to the bus station. The streets were cold and gloomy, the sky low with coming snow and he raised his collar around his ears. She was hurrying, her hands in her pockets, head down and scarf fluttering with each jerking step, her dance shoes tucked under one arm in a paper bag. He walked alongside in silence.

'All right,' he burst out at last. 'I showed you up. But I didn't take you to parade about for their benefit—you're my girl!'

'Don't shout at me,' she said. 'I never thought you'd start a bother like that—I know you used to. You was going to fight.'

'Well, he—' He stopped talking, digging his own hands into his pockets. They hurried along like strangers going the same way, two hunched, head-bent figures, curiously alike. They were silent in the streets and silent in the bus, silent as they approached her gate. She reached to push it open, but he caught her arm and roughly jerked her back.

'Hold on,' he said. 'You've learned to stick up for yourself and I'm the first you turn on, eh? I'm the best bloody friend you've got, you stupid...'

'I'm not turning on you!' She tried to tug his hand away. 'I never thought I'd get mixed up in a row—I told you I hated it! I thought you'd stopped being leery and big-headed.'

He bellowed: 'But I saw him ...'

'Don't shout at me,' she cried. Her hands covered her face and he heard her sobbing. As her shoulders began to jerk he reached out to touch them.

'Don't cry, then,' he said. 'Please don't cry—I'm sorry, honest.'

'I didn't think you was like that. I don't want a bully. I don't want somebody that's cruel.'

'I'm not cruel, honest. I don't really like to hurt people...'

He rocked her gently against his chest, as tender and soothing as though she were a frightened child. This was what he wanted to do; this was how he felt towards Susan. 'I was jealous, that's all. I lost the place and got mad for a bit. It won't happen again...'

'You don't trust me.'

'Sure I do.'

'No you don't. You always get between me and other folk. You're always answering before I get a chance to...'

His jaw tightened as he pushed her back to look at her wet face. She sniffed, closing her eyes and raising a handkerchief. He thought: She really has learned to stick up for herself... Then he thought: But it's true. It's true... Because I've been trying to shape her too...

'I'll never do that again, either,' he promised. 'Unless I know you need me.'

'I only want you,' she said, drying her eyes. 'You don't have to worry!'

Looking at her, thinking of her sudden fear at one shout, her unhappiness, and uncertainty, he realized that he did not yet understand the girl. Nor would he for a long time, because she did not yet understand herself. She knew only the sudden violence of reactions she could not stop nor cope with, making her feel in danger, and so she was like him; and so they shared the same wish to be ordinary, to repudiate any kind of life more complex than that they now lived.

'We're the same sort,' he said. 'We've got to stick together and help each other.'

She nodded, but would not look at him.

'We'll talk about it tomorrow—at the club.'

She nodded again.

He kissed her gently and left her. On the next evening he waited outside the club for her until eight o'clock, then went in alone and drank until it closed down. She never came and he went home wondering what to do.

II

He was on afternoon shift the following week. At nights he lay wondering whether to go to Susan's house or wait outside the gates where she worked on Saturday morning, or whether he should admit that he was simply hopeless with girls and return to the gang. Thoughts of his breach with Susan evoked thoughts of his breach with Elaine, until his tangled problems revolved in his mind like a bundle of clothes in a washing machine.

I'm just not cut out for girls, he decided—there's never any peace when you're mixed up with one... How do they manage to stay friendly long enough and keep together long enough to get married?

His misery was increased because the idea of getting engaged and eventually getting married had given him a sense of increased status among his workmates, as though it were the necessary final step in becoming their equal. He had begun feeling quite superior towards Bryan and other unattached young men, and now he was relegated to being one of them again.

On Wednesday morning he forgot these troubles for a while. A letter arrived from Charles informing him that their father was now critically ill. Charles would spend the weekend in a village near the hospital and wanted Walt to meet him there. He wrote:

'...It seems likely that he won't live much longer. We are his sons, after all, and since he lost the one he most cared for, we must try to do what's necessary. We have our different reasons. Perhaps you're still gaining satisfaction from hating him—but even barbarian peoples who also find good and evil obvious, as well as we civilized ones who find it less simple, believe in respect for the dead. Come and help me bury our dead...' It was a long, thoughtful and unhappy letter, but the tone Charles employed each time he referred to Walt's feelings annoyed him. At a post office near the pit he scribbled on a telegraph form: 'Your dead. Mine already buried.' But he tore the form up as he was about to hand it over the counter, and left without sending any message. In the pit he thought constantly of his father and of Charles, realizing that Charles loved the man, and next day he wired that he would come. On Friday he drew his wages and went straight to the railway station and that evening he reached the village and found Charles waiting for him in the private bar of its only hotel. He had booked a double room and said they could visit the hospital next day. Charles chatted casually about their mother and the boys, but he was reticent about Joan, which seemed natural to Walt after what had happened.

They sat in the small, carpeted room, drinking before a large gas fire. With his plump neat features, his spectacles and short schoolboy's hair, Charles reminded Walt of more serious students at the college; except, he thought, for the silver sheen at the temples.

'When do you get this new post?' he asked, and Charles said:

'Soon.' He looked through his whisky at the light. '...Sooner the better... Well—how goes it with your life? How's your revolutionary friend?'

Walt talked for some time, asking himself how much had changed since he had last seen Charles. There had been Elaine and Susan—he had been buried—all the work and all the nights with the gang... But how much had changed? How much had he changed? About Bill, he said: 'Now that bloke's *really* changed. He's a real go-getter now—knows books of stuff by heart—I don't know if he's grown up or what...'

'The lucky chap has found his framework,' Charles said. 'His be-all and end-all—removing the need for anything else. Nice if you can accept it.'

It was like one of Andrew Mason's self-mocking yet pained statements, Walt thought with some repugnance. He said quietly:

'You had your chance if you'd wanted it. You could have joined them.'

'Oh, certainly,' Charles agreed. 'But their framework isn't the one I want. This Bill of yours—however well up his type may be on their own people's troubles, like industrial disputes and political ends and so forth, their only point of view is the advancement of one brand of Socialism—and I would call it Sovietism.'

'Yeah...' Walt grunted vaguely. 'Anyway, Bill's okay—and he's pretty sure he's right.'

'Maybe he is,' Charles said, shrugging. 'But if your Bill insists *his* beliefs should be forced on humanity—by whatever means he considers historically necessary—if he claims that force can be justified by the ends—that's when I'll fight him.'

'Well, so would I,' Walt protested. 'Nobody's forcing me! But Bill isn't like that!'

'Good,' Charles said cheerfully. 'Let's hope not. God knows...' he looked at his glass: Walt imagined his sudden trouble must come from thought of their father '...there must be some touchstone for all humanity. All humanity keeps seeking it.'

'It's just that they say he'll get hurt.' Walt repeated Mason's prophecies about Bill. He said finally: 'I just wouldn't want to see old Bill get hurt bad like that.'

'It's the risk you have to take in building a good solid framework...' Charles reached for his pipe—to hide the little frown, Walt thought, wondering what was wrong; to prevent the fine-edged lips from betraying some inner preoccupation. 'You build too solid, Walt, and find there's no breaking it down again. You just have to live inside it however much it hurts.' He doubted Walt's ability to understand, it seemed, as he looked at him thoughtfully, loading the pipe. The idea of pain under self-disparagement, the resemblance to Mason, made Walt move and shuffle in his large easy chair as though his body itched. 'I wonder if you appreciate that men only survive by their ability to change and develop? I wonder if you know how great a gift that is? Truer today than ever, perhaps...' He struck a match, nodding at Walt over his pipe. 'That's why too strong a framework is so bad. That's why your own ideas stink.'

'What?' Walt sat forward. 'What's it to do wi' me? What have I done?'

'This good-lion stuff,' Charles answered, steadily watching him. 'The more I think of it the more it offends me. It's such an insult... A family like ours shouldn't have a good lion in it.' He smiled to win Walt's good humour, but Walt stood up huffily, carrying his glass to the hatchway as he said: 'He's not *much* in the family, so don't get worried. You're a bit too intellectual for me tonight—I'm going to bed.' This time no one was going to send him back home upset and unhappy, he thought.

'These cracks about intellectuals,' Charles remarked as Walt went to the door. '...You take me back years.' When Walt turned, he explained with a head-shaking smile: 'I remember how we sometimes talked in that tone of voice—after spending half the night thrashing politics to pieces and arguing in the abstract. It's funny, really...' As Walt opened the door, he added: 'It was a catch-phrase of your father's too—once he was on the down-grade and sliding fast... Just something to say, I suppose.'

'I know what I mean when I say it,' Walt told him. He went upstairs to their room, which contained two single beds, a wash basin and a chair. It was cold; a dismal room with dull brown wallpaper like melted chocolate. He hurried into bed but was still awake an hour later, thinking about Susan and the morrow's visit, when Charles entered.

Charles undressed in silence after glancing at Walt. When the light was out and they lay still, he remarked: 'You don't have much time for people different from your own kind, do you, Walt? You're full of resentments.'

'I'm sorry I was rude,' he said, a pricked-out memory of Elaine uncoiling unhappily in his mind. 'I'm a bit worried.'

'I sort of goaded you without meaning to. Families seem to be able to do this... I'm worried too and I have a knack of picking on people in rather roundabout ways at times. Tell me what's wrong, if you want to.'

Walt talked about Susan and his quarrel, reaching out to light a cigarette, the spurting match showing Charles's closed eyes and a disturbing smile. When he had finished Charles asked what he meant to do and Walt answered: 'I don't know yet. Girls are—oh, well...'

The cigarette-tip flared. Charles laughed softly, and Walt demanded: 'What the hell's so funny?'

'Nothing. I'm sorry. But such a fine conventional ending to your flouting of conventions—such eager acquiescence.' Charles chuckled again and Walt drew angrily on his cigarette, slightly confused. '...After sowing your wild oats you settle down with the girl of good repute. Such a good lion, Walt. Such a very good lion—I should have realized...'

Walt sat up for a moment, crushing out his cigarette on a matchbox. 'Just forget it,' he growled. 'It's no use telling you things...' He pulled the bed-clothes over his head, but he could hear Charles saying soberly:

'Look, remember what I said about frameworks. In spite of all your leonine proclamations you could be erecting a pretty strong little structure around yourself. For God's sake, don't you...'

'I'd bust it down if I wanted to.'

'Sure?'

He flexed his arms under the bed-clothes, rubbing a hand over the knots and cords and tightened strength.

'I did it at seventeen and I could do it any time. And I am a good lion and I'll stay a good lion—and I don't see why you should be against it!'

'Because it's a denial of humanity—that's why.'

'Don't talk tripe.'

'Haven't you heard of evolution? Don't you know that when men emulate lions it's a retrograde step?'

'They did it, not me,' he protested.

'Who? Look, Walt, does the lion really have the collective survival potential that man has? If that's what you're after...'

'What about destructive potential? Lions won't blow themselves to bits, will they?'

'No,' Charles murmured after a moment. 'I see your point.'

By the time he had thought this argument over, Walt was asleep.

As they set out for the hospital the next afternoon a few snowflakes fluttered in their faces and settled on their coats. Hoar frost covered the paths through the grounds and had turned each separate blade of grass into a brittle silver spike, naked branches into pale cold arms. Grey clouds rose out of the earth only fifty yards away on every side, pressing down over the hospital in plumed and whorled ripe heaviness. They followed an attendant through long, cold corridors and were met outside a door by a Sister.

'You understand he's only semi-conscious?' Her pale face was severe, as though to show she had no wish to be involved in any sorrow that was rightfully only theirs. 'He may not recognize you—if he does it may not be for long...' She opened the door for them. As she walked away, her stiff clothes rustling, Walt said: 'You go in first. Talk to him—tell him I'm here.'

'He may not even understand,' Charles said, his face half hidden by his upturned brown collar, and his hand on the door-knob. 'You heard her...'

'You see him first.'

Charles nodded. As the door closed, Walt turned with his hands in his pockets to look down out of a window at the white grounds. He had always been able to think of his father as a strong man, in spite of his missing leg. He did not want to see him helpless. His eyes were heavy, half closed, as he looked at the slowly spinning white flakes and the clouds massing, isolating the place in grey twilight as screens isolate the dying; and a chill, a cloud as grey as those outside, filled him and made his mind dull, almost blank.

The door opened.

'Well, he knows you're here.'

He turned and slowly walked past Charles into the small white ward. There was an iron bed and locker, a chair on either side of the bed, a white cocoon of blankets and a black smooth bush of hair on the pillow.

Just the same, he thought with relief, seeing the glistening hair. He approached the bed and looked down. The broad brow, thick black eyebrows and heavy jaw also remained the same; but as landmarks by which to recognize a ravaged scene. The bones were steep hillocks with bleak hollows in between, and the full lips, the now sharp and prominent nose, were blue-tinted, emphasizing the whiteness and near transparency of the skin. Veins showed all over the ruined face like cracks in a fallen mirror. Walt sat down as rutted eyes slid sideways and saw him. He nodded.

'Hello,' his father said, rumbling deep. Charles came to sit on the other chair.

'You should see your grandsons,' he said cheerfully. He talked about them and their resemblance to the Morris line, while the hollowed eyes remained still, staring at Walt, as though because moving away would need too much effort.

'You've grown up,' he said, when Charles finished.

'Yeah...' Walt answered, and Charles said he was the biggest in the family now. As his cheerful voice halted again he looked appealing at Walt, who was returning his father's stare. The grey cloud in his mind had thickened; he could only think that his father looked very ill and that he hated hospitals. He cleared his throat and asked: 'Are you getting any better?' and the swollen mouth twitched; a tiny smile.

'Sure. I take some killing off.' Slowly the eyes rolled to look at Charles. They had no colour now, Walt thought. They were dark and tired, yet intensely lit by the sickness. 'Just like him...'

'I told you he was,' Charles nodded, smiling and touching the bed-clothes.

'Changed like that... in two years...'

'He was always like him a bit, probably. We just couldn't see it so plainly.'

'He were like me...' The way the forces in him struggled, the eyes moving more frequently, the breathing speeded and the voice losing some of the weary blurring, made Walt lean forward unconsciously, projecting his own force into the prone body as though watching the struggling loser of a gruelling boxing contest. '...You know he looked like me? I was just the same at that age... I was a bit bigger, though... stronger...I was a fighter...'

From Walt the eyes rolled towards the ceiling. '...I tried to show him that. He was a pacifist at fifteen... only eighteen when he went. But he only looked like me... He wasn't really.' It went on, the bones jerking as the lips moved, disconnected half sentences croaking in the twilit room. '...His mother's side. Said I couldn't go back on my arguments... So I had to let him...'

Walt sat back. The indistinct mumbling went on and on, as though the man's thoughts were pouring out haphazard, as though his most intense life were escaping; as though blood gushed from a wound. Charles leaned over, his face above the twitching mouth; he seemed to think it a last message which must be caught and understood.

It's not, Walt thought. In spite of the outpouring, he sensed, he knew that his father was fighting not to die alone in this bleak isolation. Then the glazed eyes cleared, recognized Charles, who patiently smiled once more, and the voice became distinct:

'I've done a lot of wrong, Charles. You know I have, don't you?'

'It's the past.'

'No, no. I've done you wrong too. You were just out of school when I started...' Full of strength, lucid, clear, confession of sins began as Walt pushed back his chair and rose, walking to the window.

He's got no right... he thought bitterly, watching flakes slowly descend to lie twinkling and thickening on the window-sill... No right to pass it on to us. He should die with it still locked in so nobody else has to suffer. That's not the way a man should live or die... We've got enough with our own pasts...

'But I understand,' he heard Charles say softly. 'I know.'

So Charles knew...

He glanced over his shoulder. The brown hump of his brother's back hid the face. Twilight was darkening in the room, snow was endlessly fluttering down outside, slowly curtaining the window, and cold greyness was shrouding his mind.

Charles knew... just as he knew that the good-lion idea was retrograde and stank. While Walt knew only what he had learned and was right now learning for himself. He knew that each man's past was enough for him; that when your past had much that was bad in it you might as well not have lived, for there was no pleasure in remembering, and a life forgotten was like no life at all. You tried to gloss over the bad bits, but that left ugly, disturbing gaps. Even if your father was bad your childhood was lost, because recalling it would mean recalling him and how he had failed, and that was like a personal failure. There was no need for death-bed confessions or passing on of guilt to make a son feel that the failure was a personal one.

The window became a white screen, making their isolation complete. When you were young it was bad enough, he thought, but at least you had the present and the future and much to do. But when you were old—or dying like the man droning on in the shadow-wrapped bed with his son hunched over, listening and accepting? When there was little future left and little place in the present and the past buried because it had bad in it?

...You'd have to quit thinking, he thought. Or be real good at lying to yourself...

'He wants to talk to us both,' Charles said over his shoulder. 'Can't you spare him just a little of your time?'

He walked back slowly, his eyes unfocused as though the white screen were still before him. He sat down and saw his father's eyes still moving, though the voice was quieter, but he heard enough to know that sins were still being tallied, and sat withdrawn as though he himself were now isolated by the gathering darkness.

He was full of sadness. His self-communion, his effort to understand had made him aware momentarily of the dark forces of all history and of the living world; as though he were a focal point for all mankind and felt all its sorrows, its lack of learning from its past, its suffering of oppression, its disregard of its own principles and its ancient starved need to understand itself and what was true for it. All his books, his own experience and introspection; all he had unconsciously garnered from idly read newspapers, inattentive conversations and unthinking observance; all this worked in him as he gazed vacantly down at the gaunt, vein-streaked face with the voice croaking its guilt. There was a greater truth than any glib, docketed honesty constantly sapped and shamed in wordy orgasms; there was the knowledge that some day he would look back as his father was looking back; knowing each betrayal of his urgent forces, knowing each unspoken self-destroying lie, knowing the difference between the sources and the achievement. Heaven and hell were both there, bundled up and tossed in your lap with your life to sort them out in. That went for his father, for him, for everyone else; for the whole world.

'...I haven't been so damned honest myself, he thought, and saw Charles making urgent gestures to him.

'Lean closer!' Because of the delicate twist to the lips and the creased brow, he bent his head towards his father. But he jerked it back on hearing exhortations to live a better life than their father had, never giving in to weakness, selfishness or wickedness. The sunken eyes were watching Charles, who nodded understanding and promises, patting the bed-clothes as reassurance.

'He's got no right,' Walt whispered fiercely. 'I don't care how sick he is. It's just too late to make us his sons again and tell us how to live. He should have done that...'

'Be quiet,' Charles ordered, clipped and hard, without looking up.

'He never cared a damn for me. He was never my father in his—'

'Walt!' He looked at Charles's face and sat back. His father was mumbling unintelligibly, but after a while his head struggled round on the pillow and he looked at Walt.

'Me all over again. Only ...' The words faded, but his father stared, raising his head a fraction for a moment. Charles said: 'Lean over.'

Walt sat erect, his father's eyes watching him.

'You hard young swine,' Charles said. 'He doesn't really know who you are or I am or what he's saying. He's just got to get it over with. You don't hate *him*—not him!'

Walt leaned over slowly, turning his head to listen, his hands on the white covers.

'You're not the kind... I was in the last war... I was never in a fight yet I didn't win... That's how you've got to be to come back. You be like that...' At last the eyes closed and Charles said:

'We'd better go now.' Yet he sat without moving, his hands in his pockets, looking at the sleeping man.

'Too late,' Walt said, straightening up. 'His William got killed. I would've come back.' He looked up as Charles rose. 'The one he wanted came along twelve years after.' He was angry, with grief swelling in his chest and throat and choking his voice. 'I'd've done it.'

'Come on,' Charles said, walking around the bed. At the door he said again: 'Come on.'

'I'm more like him that you could ever guess. But I'd hate myself if I'd done all he's done.'

'I know,' Charles said, opening the door and then standing aside as Walt rose and walked past him with his head hunched into his collar. As they walked down the corridor, Charles said: 'It's for your own sake you should forgive him. I imagine it doesn't much matter to him now.'

They descended stone stairs and emerged into the darkened, snow-flurried grounds, with the snow already whitening them before they had walked fifty yards, softly yielding under their feet. 'It's no use waiting till you've made so many mistakes you have to forgive him,' Charles said, the snow whirling between them as he turned his head with a hand protecting his spectacles. 'You'll have tortured yourself silly. You have to give him a chance—a lot of chances. Everybody has to be given them.'

'He had plenty of chances. He had a union job once—he got that money of my mother's—he flunked all his chances. And then talks about fighting.'

'He was dogged by bad luck—he was victimized long after the big strike. Cripples shouldn't stick up for themselves if they want to work...'

In the obliquely falling snow they were shouting and waving their arms. 'And he just wasn't a business-man.'

'All right!' Walt caught at his brother's arm. 'All right, then. What are you going to blame?'

'I don't know. Blame the war that crippled him—blame the way things were then—blame alcohol if you like. And him too—he's guilty. But I'd like my sons not to judge me too harshly.'

'Will you confess to them too?' Walt shouted, releasing the damp sleeve. 'And ease your conscience?' He dug his hand back in his pocket.

'He wasn't cut out as a husband and father,' Charles said and Walt laughed. He shook his head, disgusted.

'He had five bloody good tries! Knock it off, Charles…'

They walked in silence the rest of the way. They spent that evening in the private bar again, listening to noise and voices from other rooms. Charles drank several whiskies, but Walt scarcely touched his pint of beer. He sat thinking of the cold ward and the lonely man fighting to live; fighting on reflex as though he had truly been a fighter all his life and not a failure. Fighting, perhaps, because he still retained a little of the sources of his youth.

'Maybe I don't hate him,' he said at last. 'You can't hate them when they're like that.'

'The next step,' Charles said, 'is to forgive him.'

'That's different—it's bothered me a long time, you know.'

'Yes, I know.' Charles finished his drink and walked over to the serving hatch. He returned with a fresh pint of beer for Walt as well as his own drink. When he sat down again, he said: 'I could have gone to university if he'd stuck by the home. Instead I had to work for nine shillings a week. Sometimes I hated him—but not now. I've forgiven all that, and you've got to.'

'Was William the forgiving sort?'

'Not about that. He was like you in that too, I suppose.'

'I wish he'd really been like me,' Walt said sadly, finishing his first drink and then going on: 'You said and my father said he wasn't cut out as a fighter. I don't know what he had to go to Spain for and get killed—I wish he was still here.'

Charles nodded thoughtfully a few times, lying back in the chair, his chin almost on his breast. 'For you he's a better brother dead. You can make him anything you like with no disillusionments.'

'I wish he hadn't gone.' With this cynical yet forgiving brother confusing him, he longed for William to be alive, so that he could not only be loved and respected but could give something back. 'I just wish he hadn't gone…'

'You'd have gone in those days,' Charles said. He cocked his head to look at Walt and then nod. 'Yes, you'd definitely have gone. Spain would have been your testing-ground too—never mind good lions. And if your Spain comes I don't doubt you'll go…' He sighed. 'I must be old—I can't see how it's going to shape. There's more conflict and enmity than ever, but no new Spain yet for our young men—unless we just can't see it. Or perhaps the dream is missing—good lions don't believe in anything outside themselves, do they?'

'In the truth,' Walt said.

'You know the truth?' Charles beamed at him but with obvious sarcasm. 'In this world? In this alliance of capitalism and Socialism against Socialism? In the "free" West against the "free" East? You can see the truth, Walt, in this growing chaos of mass-produced frantic entertainment and escape? Wonderful! I often wonder what's real!'

Walt shrugged. He could not have explained his feelings to Charles. As for reality—that was the sweating nakedness of the dark coal-face—that was where you knew reality. You knew there what men were, and in spite of obscenity and buffoonery and lack of subtler thought you gained a kind of wisdom from that place. Or was it merely endurance? But perhaps those two were part of the same thing.

'Its always difficult to see what's true during an interregnum,' Charles mused. 'I suppose in a way that's what this is. We're between two ages. The good-lion theme jars on me because I keep praying that man is adaptable enough to come through all this—he'll only go on if each half of the world learns to live with the other, and that's a tall order. Good lions just won't do.'

'You'd better tell the ones that are running things, then,' Walt said. 'Don't tell me—I'm just adapting my way through.'

Charles sighed, then he smiled at Walt.

'You're young, I suppose.'

'Yeah...'

'That laconic "yeah" of yours with all its ambiguous implications—it expresses so many things. And you don't forgive him?'

'No, I don't think so.' He decided Charles must have drunk too much whisky with his vague talk and vague expression. There was little authority about him now.

'I see. You know...' In the bar the landlord was shouting for last orders and Walt drank some beer. 'We're always saying age is too hard on youth and always expect youth to be hard on age. And while youth is so busy indicting the past it never seems to realize that in the future it might stand itself indicted. Youth can get hurt if it keeps on being tough on age too long, Walt.'

They finished their drinks and walked to the door. As Walt opened it Charles touched his shoulder and said when he glanced round: 'We'll keep on fencing till you hate my guts, I suppose, and I didn't really want that. But you see too many things in black and white.'

'Oh, I wouldn't ever hate your guts,' Walt answered him gravely. 'I don't really hate such a lot of folk.'

They went to bed and Walt turned the lights out after a final cigarette. He was thinking of the hospital and of his father's ruined face, when Charles said: 'I'm going to tell you this—though I'm probably a fool. But it might do you good.'

'What?' he asked, turning on to his back and clasping his hands under his head.

'Joan is having an affair,' Charles said evenly, and went on in the same calm way to tell Walt about it. One of their neighbours was a man whose wife had been in hospital for many months. Since he lived alone they had invited him to dinner frequently. '...Joan obviously took to him. He's a fairly attractive bloke—intelligent and with a nice private income so that he needn't work. To her, that's one kind of success. It seems she's been visiting his house pretty frequently while I was at work. And—there are other signs...'

The calm manner shocked Walt as much as the revelation about Joan.

'You're not just standing for it, are you?'

'Yes, I am, actually,' Charles said. 'She might walk out on me otherwise—I couldn't stand that.'

'Jesus!' Walt gasped. He was revolted. At the thought of such a thing being done to him his pride had blazed, his hands clenching and jaw stiff. The simple statement had smothered his sympathy for Charles.

'Don't think I can't imagine how you feel, Walt. You'll look down on me now as much as on your father, I suppose. But I have a moral to all this...'

All that Walt could answer was a stiff: 'I'm sorry.'

'Oh no. Don't be. This is merely retribution. Let me really finish you off.' Charles was trying to sound light and ironic. To Walt it was as though he could see the puckered forehead and pinched smile. 'When I first went abroad—a not too-long-married man, mind you—I was alone and got involved with a lonely female. Don't ask me why. Perhaps I was so intensely in love with Joan that I had to prove I could win another woman if she left me. You see, I loved her so that it made me feel weak and utterly dependent on her returning my love. Anyway, I took it all less seriously than the woman did—but she, unfortunately, made sure that when Joan joined me she got to know everything...'

Walt waited, quiet. Some of the greyness of that afternoon seemed to be still wreathed in him; he felt very tired.

'She didn't leave me, at least. After a while, when I'd explained a thousand times, she said she understood. We set about the fashionable business of rejoining broken threads, making our marriage work and so on... Only, you see, she didn't really understand, any more than you would, I suppose, in her place. And she didn't forgive me and things never did come right again. I just kept on paying every time we talked or quarrelled or made love—because I knew she hadn't forgiven me and couldn't forgive myself. And I love her very much...'

After a long time Walt sighed. He asked:

'So what happens?'

'I don't know. I hope she won't leave me and we can some-how work this out. If she just doesn't leave me for him or someone else. She feels she has a right, you see...'

'My God...' Walt grunted, and Charles said: 'Yes,' adding after another pause: 'Perhaps you can see what I'm driving at now. You know your father was that kind who can't forgive either. He smashed his life in pieces on his own resentments and malignities... Don't ever get like that, Walt.'

'How do people mess up their lives like this?' The question broke out as a low cry.

'You'd be surprised how easily it can all happen,' Charles said.

'Let's go to sleep.' Walt was pleading rather than making a suggestion. He pulled the clothes over his head, but it was a long time before he did sleep and when he woke next morning he still carried the weight of a tiredness which dulled his ability to think or feel. He said nothing to Charles about their talk. At the hospital they were told that their father was too ill to receive visitors. Walt asked the doctor who met them at the reception desk if his father were going to die.

'Not necessarily—he's a tough character and could pull through all right. But he'll never be completely well, you understand...'

As they walked back, Walt was thinking: He won't die. It'll go on and on. But no more hospitals or death-beds for me...

'I'm going straight home,' he told Charles, who silently nodded. At the hotel Walt checked the time of his train, ran upstairs for his case and came down to find Charles in the bar, a glass of whisky in his hand.

'Couldn't you cut down on that a bit?' Walt asked him.

'I think this weekend could be regarded as an occasion.'

Charles smiled at him. 'You're not starting to concern yourself with others, now, are you, Walt?'

As they shook hands, Walt said awkwardly: 'I hope—you work it out.'

'So do I,' Charles said. 'No message for your mother?'

'Oh yeah...' He had completely forgotten her in his eagerness to return to the city. Only there would he shake off this clouded tiredness. 'Give her my love.' He imagined his mother's grief when she heard of how ill his father was, and turned back to say: 'Tell her—you know—not to worry, eh?'

'I'll give her your love,' Charles said. 'Leave the rest to me.'

Although it was six o'clock when Walt reached home he was ready to go out again by seven. His offhand answers to the old lady's inquiries seemed to satisfy her. She merely said: 'So he's real bad, eh?'

'Yeah,' Walt said. They seldom talked now, anyway, although they often sat together in front of the fire. It was not that they had so little in common, Walt would have said, as that they had no need to talk most of the time.

'Tha had a visitor,' she remarked while he was having his tea.

'Who? Bryan?'

'Nay. That Holmes lass—strollin' past as if she never dreamed you lived here and watchin' t' windows all t' time...'

'When?' he demanded eagerly.

'Today. You two been rowin'?'

'Just a tiff,' he said, jumping up. 'But we'll be back together next week.'

Later, when he was combing his hair, bending at the knees so his face was opposite the least distorting segment of mirror, she remarked:

'She's gettin' a big lass, yon.' She sounded thoughtful. A piece of sacking for a newly begun rug was spread across her knees.

'You said she was only a bairn,' he reminded her.

'Aye?' She sniffed. 'Pair on you's big enough for any kind o' trouble, I reckon.'

'I know what you mean,' he said hotly. 'But she's not like that.'

'They're all like that once they get courtin' strong.'

'You're a bad-minded...' He turned away and put on his coat. As he went out, she said: 'Are you bringin' her home to let us have a look at her when you get engaged, then?'

'Well, of course I am,' he answered. As if young men didn't always take their girls home when they were engaged, he thought.

On the way to the club a tired succession of images kept circling in his mind: of his father's sick, finished face with the sunken eyes moving with such effort, as though their own great weight had hollowed out the deep sockets, of the snow that had fallen outside the isolation ward and of his brother's self-demeaning smile and creased brow... Words and phrases repeated themselves so that, in this stupor of repugnant memories, his only personal thought was: I don't have to be like them or get like them...

He ran up the steps and entered the club, and Susan rose from Margaret's table, meeting him among the couples on the floor with both of them beginning automatically to dance.

'I knew you'd be here,' she said. 'I was just frightened, Walt. I didn't know what to do. So I stayed at home.'

'You're not frightened now, are you?'

'No. I just can't think or owt when I am—like I used to be in t' blitz.

Every time there was a raid I got a terrible pain here,' she touched her flat belly, 'and I just couldn't think or owt.'

'Listen,' he said. 'I'll never hurt you. Never be scared of me. We won't ever row again.'

'You're the only one I can talk to. You're the only one as understands things.'

'I told you last week,' he said. 'We're the same kind. Just us on our own and we've got to stick together. We don't need anybody else...'

III

On his twentieth birthday they became engaged and Susan visited for tea like any other girl meeting her prospective in-laws. The old lady, a stranger in a new bright pinafore instead of her green overall, informed her that Walt was a muddle-head without much sense but at least you could leave your money around and know that he'd never touch it.

'He's not bad-hearted...' Susan sat facing her, honoured guest in Walt's easy chair, trying to hide her anxiety at the way it sighed and sank each time she moved. Walt sat at the table scowling fiercely at the old lady, who ignored him. '...Many's the little gift he's bought me...' Walt felt slightly guilty. '...Thinks he can get away wi' owt if he buys thee summat...' Walt became abruptly interested in his cup of tea. '...But it's common sense he lacks most and it'll take a fair lass to keep him right...'

'I'll keep him right,' Susan said, and he blinked at her confidence.

In spite of their vows Walt and Susan had quarrelled at times and there had been periods of doubt followed by remorse and reabsorption. He felt that this was an inevitable cycle for any man and woman; at least it did not probe deeply, or tear or claw at the most precious feelings in him. He had returned from his visit to his father with his passions and force half exhausted. He had chosen peace. He wanted love without too much conflict or pain or goaded conscience, and needed a girl like her who would accept him, let him be ordinary, without constantly probing at quiescent troubles. Although, there were times when old urges heaved, and he would he awake wondering and worrying. It was better for some parts of yourself to be smothered than to let them drive you into that cul-de-sac where two people's agony waited at the end. By a metamorphosis of mind and heart the lion was emulating the patient ox, working and living with eyes lowered and shoulders forward, using all his strength in earning a contented if not exciting leisure.

Susan was full of plans for the kind of home they were going to have, buying something every week which was shown to Walt before being carefully stowed in her bottom drawer. She was less concerned with her wedding trousseau than with what they would need afterwards, and could describe in detail the kind of furniture they were going to have in each room as well as the number and sex of their children. He knew her future happiness completely depended on him and was glad of this knowledge. She was a happier, busier, different girl from the one he had first met in the club, as though the changes in her corresponded to those in himself.

They went for walks in the long summer evenings, saving all their money, and gang life was finished. He tended to shake his head nowadays over the way in which Bryan and the others still drank too much and spent their weekends in riotous pleasures. Bryan, he felt, had a long way to go, but he would make a good husband some day; he had all the strength and willingness to work that a good husband needed.

In letters from his mother he learned that his father was slowly recovering but would never leave hospital. He wrote to him once, promising to visit again, but his father was too ill to reply and Walt never went back. A letter from Charles in the spring had said:

'...at least she's given up my rival. We never talk about it. The details are all too painfully involved for you to want to know but I have hopes we'll work it all out somehow. No certainty—only hopes and wishes...'

Walt made no reference to this when he replied. Prospects of marriage seemed to have freed him from his family at last.

A week after becoming engaged they went to the city's housing office and having been duly enrolled were informed that, with luck, they would have a house in eight to ten years.

'How long?' Walt asked in dismay. The . talked about housing shortage, restrictions and allocations in building, of a long, long waiting list. The information was given in a matter-of-fact, offhand manner which testified to thousands of repetitions and thousands of couples.

'But we'll be thirty afore we've got our own house!' Susan said The clerk pointed out that it was going to take a long time to get over the war. 'So many things are short—there's so much building to do—there's an awful lot in the same boat. The cost of war, you know...'

In the sunny street they looked woefully at one another, then Walt squeezed her hand and said they would find something: '...We can always get rooms somewhere.'

'But it's not t' same,' Susan said. 'It's not t' same as starting off on your own.'

He told the old lady. As he was preparing to go out that night she said: 'You could allus stop here.'

'You mean it?' he demanded eagerly. 'Most sensible thing, isn't it? If you can't get your own place? And she'll be goin' out to work, won't she?'

'We haven't thought about that.'

'Nor owt else past t' first night, I suppose. You can come here—but if owt happens to me you're not forced to get t' house wi' thee not bein' proper kin.'

'What could happen to you for another twenty years?' He grinned with relief. 'We'll make the kids call you Grandma.'

'You can keep them for your own house,' she called, as he went out in a hurry to tell Susan. Every Sunday after that they had tea with the old lady and she promised them a pegged rug for a wedding present.

'She must like you a lot,' Susan said one night. 'She's good to you.'

'Yeah…' They were strolling through quiet streets, the day's heat gently rising and fading in the dusk. 'Only she still thinks I'm a kid. She'll never see me as a man.'

'I reckon you are.' He smiled and said: 'That's all as matters, isn't it?' Yet he felt that if the old lady ever once said it, then at last he would know it was true. He had been trying for a long time now, it seemed, struggling towards this achievement; something you felt rather than were called he was sure. Yet if she said it he would believe it and be proud; and now that the lion was dormant it would have been a token to hold on to.

'Wait till we've a little lad runnin' round.' Susan squeezed his arm with both hands, leaning against him. 'She'll have to admit it then. And when she gets *real* old, she'll have to depend on you.'

'She'll never get real old,' he answered. 'If she did, she'd boss us from her arm-chair and we'd have to give in just because she was old. Her sort's never dependent.'

A week later he arrived home from the pit at dinner-time and was met at the front gate by an agitated Mrs. Watson. She had been breathlessly chattering for five minutes before he understood that the old lady was in the infirmary. She had fallen and injured her head while out shopping.

'Just comin' past t' cinema she were and suddenly fell off t' pavement into t' street. Like a black-out, they reckon—a stroke or summat.'

He hurried down the street. On his way there he kept thinking: It couldn't have been a stroke. She's too tough for strokes she doesn't have them… God Almighty, a hospital again…

When he inquired at the reception desk a doctor came to meet him; a sandy-haired young man in a white overall who looked at Walt, at the cap pushed back, the snap-tin bulging in his pocket, the dust streaked in the faint lines of his face and flecked in his eyes, and said: 'Yes, I'm afraid it's very bad. Are you the son?'

'Not exactly.' The doctor was sympathetic as he led the way, but Walt was afraid they might not let him see her if he admitted he was not a relative. He said: 'I'm all she's got around here.'

'If she has any relations you should contact them right away. But I doubt if...'

You had to die some time, he told himself. But this was a personal loss, this death. This was a part of his life; a whole segment of his present, not his past...

She was in the casualty ward, closed off by white screens at the end of a long line of beds in which heads turned as he passed with his heavy boots ringing. She was conscious, looking up with her head swathed in a white skull-cap.

Closed off to die decently, he thought, as the screens were replaced by the doctor, who waited outside. To die alone, no one allowed to watch her defeat.

'I came straight from work,' he said, sitting down and bending over her.

'Watson could've gi'ed thee some dinner, the fool...' Even her eyes remained still, except for the long moments when they closed and he sat tensely, smiling when they opened again. While they were still closed, she muttered: 'She'll gi'e an eye to thee while tha gets a fresh place—God knows how tha'll go on wi'out me...'

However weak her voice and faded her eyes, he dare not insist that she wasn't dying in case she grew fretted. Nor dared he show his feelings.

'I'll wire your lads right away,' he said, as she opened her eyes.

'Nay, I'll not last while they get here. I can't see a damn thing...'

When the wrinkled lids lowered again he leaned right over her face. He thought her, too still to be breathing, but she muttered after a moment: 'I had a good man and I reared three good lads. Made men on 'em, I did.'

'Four,' he said urgently, his face near hers. 'What about me? Four men you made...'

Her eyes opened and she tried to look for him, closing again as she whispered: 'Tha'rt no man yet—no sense yet. Happen tha'll make one...'

He heard the scrape and rustle of the screens behind him but sat for a moment longer, studying her face. He could not remember having seen her eyes closed before.

'What is her Christian name?' the doctor asked. 'The initial's M,' he said. 'I don't know the rest.'

She no longer looked stern. She looked very old. Her cheek, when he touched it, heedless of the watching doctor, felt wrinkled and yet smooth, like leather mellowed by great age. But the touch seemed a breach of their relationship, so he looked at her again and then stood up.

'I'll come again later,' he said, and that evening Susan came with him to the infirmary. When he stood staring at the doctor after being told she was dead, Susan took his arm. They walked away together and she said: 'There's still you and me, Walt. I'll look after you.'

'She never changed, do you know?' He smiled down at her, nodding. 'She never took back one damned thing, Susan, good or bad...'

One of the colliers at the pit offered him lodgings and he moved in a day later. A week after that he returned to Mainby Road with an empty suitcase for the last of his things. The sky was cloudless and heat rippled over the pavements ahead; the houses and gardens looked exactly the same; but they were so lacking in individuality that he already felt a stranger here as Mrs. Watson met him on the path and chattered while she unlocked the front door. The windows were naked and the house was only a shell; he turned away to watch two boys playing a concentrated game of marbles in the gutter.

'Last time you'll be seeing this, eh?' The bird-like bespectacled little face peeped up as he entered. 'Eh, she were a fine old lady. A fine old lady she were...' Everything was prepared for removal; the chairs mated one on the other, the linoleum rolled, the cushions stripped and the china cabinet bare. As they stepped on the wooden floor it sounded hollow, and the room looked larger than he had expected. It looked dismal too, as though lifelessness were emanating from the cold, glittering fireplace.

He answered Mrs. Watson's questions about his new lodgings while she stood clasping the front-door key in her pinafore pocket with a custodian's pride. When she offered that, of course, he'd be getting wed soon, anyway, he merely grunted.

'Tell her nowt,' the old lady had always said. He went upstairs with the bare wood clattering underfoot and had reached the landing when she smoothly inquired: 'We thought you'd have been at t' funeral, though?'

'They're not in my line.' She was peering up at him, her head cocked. 'They're family business.'

'Well, you were all but family—I mean, you were good to her, now weren't you?' He knew the old lady would never have told her what money he paid or anything else so he made no answer. After a moment she went on: 'It were a lovely funeral, anyroad. T' street bought a wreath. And their Joe came back from cemetery t' other day and said they was a lovely one from you there. From Walt, it said, and...' She waited.

'Susan... It was personal.'

'Aye... Next door a whistling began, rising quickly to a shriek, and she cried: 'Oh, the kettle! I'll make some tea...' She hurried out and he turned to the bedroom door. The door of the old lady's room was open and after a moment he entered. The bed was dismantled, but the old truncheon was still hanging on its nail and he walked over to take it down and stand looking at it. He had liked her sons: each of them tall and stalwart and smartly dressed. When he found that Joe, the youngest, was forty, he had realized how old she had been; realized how young he must have been to her.

He went into his own room and slipped the truncheon into his case; it would never be missed. Then he collected his belongings, snapped the case shut and sat on the chair in the middle of the room, lighting a cigarette, with sunlight streaming around him.

The two beds were propped against a wall, reminding him of how many times he had lain talking with Bill. A few weeks ago he had seen Bill in the city centre on Saturday afternoon, walking in a column of marchers who carried placards which Walt, standing on the other side of the busy street, had not been able to read. A few men and youths had been following the column, jeering and calling their own slogans, but the marchers ignored them. Walt had recalled Bill's talk of past political struggles and street fights in Germany and the rest of Europe, and he had thought: I suppose it's still going on over there. Even here it is—even if it's not so violent and they don't show so openly how much they really hate each other. Just like it was when William went off... He remembered Charles saying: 'You'd have gone...'

Why haven't we had a Spain then? he wondered. 'Why haven't we had a chance to fight for a real something? I'd have liked to fight for something great—a testing-ground is what I wanted... But not Bill's kind...

Still—Bill had looked quite happy, marching along with his placard stuck up, looking straight in front of him. A strange, an awfully strange way to be happy, though. Blotting out everything about yourself except what fitted with dedication.

His own plans were better, he thought. He was eager to be married and settled, and they were looking for rooms. He remembered how Charles had called this the conventional ending, but he shrugged, blue smoke coiling and waving away as he disturbed it. He was doing what he wanted just as he had at seventeen; he could handle what came later as it came. No one, after all, had given him much in the way of reasons for being different from what he wanted to be—only arguments.

Everybody had wanted him to be something else—that was the worst of being young. They saw in you what they wanted to see and if they couldn't force you to be how they saw you, they just kept on wishing. His mother, Brenda, Thorpe, Elaine, Bill, the old lady, and even Bryan—all had wanted to tell him what to do and what to be. All sorry when he refused. He knew there would be times when he would think about Elaine, wonder, and that it would hurt a bit—but Susan was like himself;

she had spent a lot of time in the dark...

As for Charles and his frameworks—

...I can bust it down if I ever need to, he thought... Any kind there is...

He hoped that Susan would help him do it if that ever happened, whatever it might be. He could give her what she found she wanted out of life, and she could be his something else. And he would always be capable of bursting down any frameworks; he was sure of it. To hell with the rest of them.

He dropped his cigarette and crushed it on the boards under his foot. A sun-shot mist of blue smoke went wreathing and spreading through the room as he stood up and took a last look round. Nearly three years he had spent here; nights and nights and nights—of anguish, ambition and contentment, and the sound of the city still functioning while he slept. A young man's bedroom was his last retreat—something you didn't have when you were married. You weren't alone even in bed.

But the thought of the advantages made him grin, and he told himself: You take life too seriously, you know... you don't laugh at yourself enough...

He clattered down the stairs and out into the sunlight. Mrs. Watson came from her front door, but he refused her offer of a cup of tea. It would only mean a host of questions about Susan and himself anyway. She followed him to the gate, where he stopped to look back at the house. There was nothing left in there of his. A definite part of his life was over, he thought. Something new was begun. But he knew now that you couldn't just leave things behind.

'You'll miss her...' Mrs. Watson's spectacles glinted fierily. The grass was almost ready for cutting again. 'She thought world o' you and all didn't she? Allus bragging you off in t' pub, what you'd done and what you hadn't—happen it were wi' her man bein' a collier and all, eh?'

'She talked about me a lot?' He looked down at the starved little face.

'What?' With a thin screech of laughter she raised a hand. 'By, she's gone off about you. Called you a big school kid—nowt but a big school-kid, she'd sometimes say you were. And when you two's been rowing. I've heard her say: "He'd break my heart if I let him, but I'll break his cheeky neck first..." Oh aye, she's gone off, lad. But she thought world on you—I mean, you were just about all she'd got, eh? I think she wished you her own, so she could clip your ear for you at times.'

'I needed it clipping at times, I guess.' She must have thought of him often, he realized, when he was not considering her at all. His mother too, he supposed.

'Ah, but she were proud on you at times and all.'

He smiled at Mrs. Watson, lifting the case.

'I know you'll miss her,' she said.

'Yeah...' He said good-bye and began walking down the street. Women were funny, that was all. But they could give a man an awful lot of help—sometimes only a woman could do it... There ought to be some way of keeping them all in your life together.

Which would be pretty interesting, he realized, thinking of the girls he had known. But next year there would be a fresh wreath on her grave. You shouldn't forget people like her when they were lost from your life and became your past. You couldn't anyway—any more than you could forget all the other things that had mattered. In this kind of world you needed a few things to hang on to.

As he turned the corner with the suitcase briskly swinging, he looked up and saw brown and grey smoke coming drifting, over below the high polished blue. Tonight was Saturday; best night of the lot... He began cheerfully whistling as he walked along.